# Gold in the Red Desert

I dedicate
'Book One'
Of
'The Owl Hoot Trail'
To my baby girl,
Patricia Carol,
Who I loved so and miss dearly

# Gold in the Red Desert

## Book One

of

## T. H.Bear's Trilogy:

# The Owl Hoot Trail

The contents of this book regarding the accuracy of events, people, and places depicted; permissions to use all previously published materials; opinions expressed; all are the sole responsibility of the author, who assumes all liability for the contents of this book and indemnifies the publisher against any claims stemming from publication of this book.

Gold In The Red Desert
The Owl Hoot Trail Book One
First Edition by AuthorHouseTM
03-29-2006
Second Edition by BluewaterPress LLC.
2011

International Standard Book Number 13: 978-1-60452-047-7
International Standard Book Number 10: 1-60452-047-7

Library of Congress Control Number: 2011936185

BluewaterPress LLC
52 Tuscan Way Ste 202-309
Saint Augustine Florida 32092
http://bluewaterpress.com

This book may be purchased online at -
http://bluewaterpress.com/gold

# The Owl Hoot Trail

This trilogy, we call the *Owl Hoot Trail*, is the story of a man, not unlike many of this very day, who leave their home and everyone they love to serve their country in the time of war. This man was a soldier, like all good soldiers, who did not question the politicians or their motives, rather he devoted his all in serving to protect his nation from an invader, only to return and find almost everything he had loved had been swept away and his homeland in the hands of corrupt officials and an occupational army. How different were the feelings of the people of Belgium, France, and Poland between 1940 and 1945 from the people of Alabama, Florida, and Georgia between 1863 and 1873?

These books were named 'The Owl Hoot Trail' because in those times, a person who was considered a criminal fugitive was often referred to as an Owl Hoot and the roads they took to ply their trade and evade their pursuers was known as 'The Owl Hoot Trail.' It is upon this trail our returning soldier must travel until he can clear his name of an uncommitted crime.

**Book One:** *Gold in the Red Desert* tells us how, in a vain effort to protect his family, Clifford Brown, was unjustly accused of murder and thrust upon the owl hoot trail, and finding this trail leading him to the gold fields in and around South Pass City in the Territory of Wyoming. There he witnessed a murder and as a result became entangled in a struggle to right this wrong. There also he found the only woman he would ever love.

**Book Two:** *The Withlacoochee Renegades* reveals his return to his native state of Georgia during the infamous Reconstruction Period, and of his forming a band of brothers, who like vigilantes everywhere throughout time, were created only by desperate souls in desperate times when legal authority either failed or was too corrupt to protect the people.

**Book Three:** *The Long Trail* allows us to ride with Cliff Brown in pursuit of the almost mythical villain who was responsible for the murder of several members of his family. A pursuit that takes him more than six years, on a 3500 mile journey through seven states, where in every corner he must struggle with the evils of greedy people and the revenge burning fiercely within himself, each begging, often commanding an inner peace that would be denied him for over seventeen years.

# Acknowledgements

To say that this book is totally fiction would be an insult to most historians. Surely, all with a general knowledge of American History, especially the times of Mr. Lincoln's War and those twenty or so years after, when great immigrations occurred into what we now call 'The West', would know that there was indeed a Gold Rush in the Sweetwater Region of Wyoming, that indeed there was a General Nathan Bedford Forrest, a Judge Esther Morris, a Lieutenant Caspar Collins, a Wild Bill Hickman, and other true to life people who lived and contributed to the future of America, and some of these people offer a small contribution to this story. Regardless, I must make clear that this is a novel not a history book, and the main characters, and the people and events in this story that they become involved in and with, are totally from my imagination and not to be confused with any living or dead individual or occurrence.

# Appreciation

The illustrations contained in this book are either from my own family's collection of photographs, by courtesy of The State of Wyoming Department of State Parks and Cultural Resources, State of Wyoming Archives; or taken from the web site "Wyoming Tales & Trails". Were it not for the enormous labor and endless hours of devotion in preserving the pictorial history of The Great State of Wyoming by Geoff Dobson so much would not be available to the reader. It is to this site we give much credit and appreciation.

Thank you, Geoff.

# BOOK ONE
# Gold in the Red Desert

## Chapter One
## The Scogins Affair

Cliff Brown had stopped at the huge rock, there in the middle of nowhere, to look at the hundreds of names carved on it. He thought he might dismount and add his to the many western travelers, but a strong memory from deep in his past became painfully clear in his mind when he remembered the first week in February, in the year 1849. It had started as a special time for him; only the day before his mother had baked a cake as a present for his birthday. He surely felt special, for only once before in his life had she made a cake and that had been when his father had returned to Lowndes County after serving three long years in the service of the navy of those United States.

He remembered well, going to school that morning full of joy and energy. He, being so proud of that cake, had stolen a piece and brought it to share with and to brag about to Andy Bell and Jim Taylor, his two best friends. Unfortunately, the trio soon found themselves in mischief, and Miss Zimms, the teacher, caught them painting their names on the back side of the one room schoolhouse with her last pail of milk paint. Her fury had only been exceeded by his embarrassment when he was ordered to stand before the whole school and repeat one hundred times, "Fool's names and fool's faces are often seen in public places." He remembered well the face of Mary Annette as she giggled at him while he stood there reciting that phrase. And he wondered, *'Is she the one who told on us to Miss Zimms? It would be like her.'*

Now twenty-one years later, he decided against carving Clifford Brown, or even Reb, as he had become known, on the turtle shaped "Registry of the Desert." Instead, he gently touched his heel to the side of the big sorrel moving on to the promised river that was supposed to lay a short distance to the west.

Looking down at the narrow stream he laughed to himself, *'River'? Hell, I've seen ditches wider than that, back in Georgia.'*

**Independence Rock also known as 'The Registry of the Desert'**
**Looking across 'The Sweetwater River'**

Still it had been sixty or so miles of nothing but alkali desert covered by little more than scattered sage since he had left the remains of old Fort Caspar, and the coolness of the Sweetwater River did bid a friendly welcome. Cliff let Red enjoy a long drink as the sun began to settle behind the towering peaks some miles beyond. Then he took water for himself and gathered a few dead branches that had long since fallen from the three cottonwood trees on his side of the riverbed, the dead wood being more than enough to cook his supper.

After building the small fire, he sat a pot of Arbuckle's on to boil while he removed the saddle and hobbled Red close by. His next chore was to clean the alkali dust from his weapons. Slowly and carefully, he removed the cylinder from his revolver and wiped it clear of all signs of the white powder. With a small stick he had long ago whittled from the limb of a hickory tree, back where there were hickory trees, he pushed a portion of his red silk neckerchief through each chamber. Then using the neckerchief, her cleaned each of the six cartridges before reinserting them into the cylinder. Then, admiring his labor, he returned the cylinder into the frame of his old Colt.

Carefully with much tenderness, he caressed the revolver. It had saved his life many a time in the bitter days when he had been with Forrest in Tennessee.

Slowly his mind drifted from the brown plains of Wyoming Territory to the green fields of middle Tennessee. He had gone there in November of '62 where they met the enemy. It had been the Fourth Illinois who had been assigned by Sherman to hold the burg of Lebanon some twenty to thirty miles east of Nashville.

He had been issued a shotgun, being unable to afford his own musket, as were most of Forrest's mounted men at that time. These weapons were of little or no value except at very close range, and it was General Bragg's intention for Forrest and his men to get in that close amongst them. The shotgun did have the advantage, of having two shots before reloading, but that was the only advantage and no one, save a very few, looked at it with favor. Cliff had made up his mind he was going to trade it to the first Yankee he saw, and that was almost exactly what had happened.

Lebanon was centered around a square, as typical of most towns in the south, having once been a small fort where the town's people could enter to escape Indian attacks. The civilian buildings were built around the outsides of the fort, often using the walls of the fort itself as their backsides. After Jackson had driven all the redmen from their homes in middle Tennessee, the need for such forts had gone with them. What became of these forts, after their abandonment by the army? They simply became a town square. This little borough, however, held a special spot in Cliff's mind. It was here at Cumberland University that he had attended college, and he wanted desperately to keep the Federals from destroying his old school.

The square in Lebanon was also the intersection of the Knoxville-Nashville Pike and the north-south road that led from Murfreesboro into Kentucky. The men of the Fourth Illinois had barricaded the square, and Dickey had set up his headquarters in the newly constructed courthouse there.

It was dawn on a cold December morning when Cliff found

himself at full gallop westbound on the pike. He could hear the sounds of gunfire and knew Forrest had begun his attack from the south. When his squad arrived at the east barricade, they found it abandoned. All the defenders had run towards the center of the square to man the 12-pound Napoleon located there. Several blue uniformed men were just turning the big gun to ward off the attacking charge they could see was coming up the Murfreesboro Road, when Cliff's horse leaped the bales of hay and corn stalks that had been placed there as a road block. The square was already full of smoke from all the gunfire, and he knew that their flanking movement had been a total success. Not one Yank seemed to even know they were there before they opened up with their shotguns.

He had loaded the weapon with pistol ball, and the discharge of his right barrel caught an invader full in the chest, taking him off his feet and over the shiny barrel of the cannon.

Cliff's horse reared at the blast so near his right ear, before he began bucking. Finally when he could, with some sort of design on his own, he left the mount and hit the yellow clay with both feet. A man with bright yellow chevrons on his blue sleeve had just reached to the frog on his belt for the long skinny bayonet and was trying to attach it to his musket when he saw Cliff raise his shotgun. Frantically, he attempted to fix the long knife to the gun, but they both knew he had no chance. Again Cliff saw a man leave the earth for a short time when he was struck with the twelve .36 caliber balls full in the chest.

When the smoke of his shot cleared, he saw another man in blue standing there with a revolver in hand who looked first at his companion and then back at the man who had just snapped out his life. It seemed as if the world had suddenly begun some sort of half-time movement, or as some would say, everything went into slow motion in both of their minds. To this very, day Cliff remembered watching the man slowly cock the Colt and begin to raise it in his direction. Instinctively, he cocked the right hammer on his shotgun. His opponent saw the motion, turned his head and again looked at the lifeless mass of bloody wool and body parts that seconds before had been his leader. Immediately, fear mingled with good sense overtaking his courage. He raised his hands, letting the cocked revolver swing away, with his finger still in the trigger guard.

Cliff wasted no time in retrieving the pistol from Private John

Morris' hand along with his belt and cartridge pouch. Then without care he pitched the empty shotgun away, grabbed his prisoner and used him as a shield.

Before this minute was up, Forrest himself, who had led the frontal charge, was in the square firing his LeMat first to the right of his horse and then to the left. Very soon the remainder of Dickey's men were following their leader in a scattered and unorganized, though rapid, retreat towards Nashville. It was obvious that Morris had not taken the time to look at or perhaps could not see the spent percussion cap under the hammer of Cliff's right barrel. It mattered not either way, for the bluff had paid off, and Cliff now had a fine .44 caliber Colt. It was this same weapon that he now caressed on the bank of the Sweetwater River nearly eight years later.

The war had also brought him his rifle, although in an around about way. It was some two years after he had taken his prized Colt, that Cliff found himself again on a flanking movement pursuing the remains of a company of Union Cavalry who had tried to fire the home of Colonel Looney.

In November 1864, Forrest's men were in an advance circular maneuver ahead of Hoods Army, then marching north to retake Nashville.

In what was to become known as the Franklin-Nashville Campaign, the Union Army was preparing defensive positions ahead of the oncoming gray tide. Their line of defense extended from the Mooresville Pike to the Mt. Pleasant Pike. Major-General John M. Schofield's troops began their hasty withdrawal from Columbia, and a common defensive tactic often used by Union forces was to destroy important buildings along the line of retreat. Many of Maury County's majestic antebellum homes were selected to be torched that day.

Elm Springs was slated to be on the list, not because it had any important military value, but rather as an act of retribution because it was the historic home of Confederate Lieutenant Colonel Abraham M. Looney, whose often outspoken position for the southern cause almost resulted in the loss of his home.

Cliff was then a sergeant and leading thirteen men comprised of both mounted infantry and cavalry. They arrived just as three bluebellies were departing Elm Springs and two were shot and the third taken prisoner. His men were able to put out the fires started by these arsonists and soon were in pursuit of others. They had crossed the small stream that was surely a tributary of the Tennessee and were now awaiting the retreating union infantry that they could see some distance up the road. Cliff knew that Lieutenant Bob Willis had taken a detail of nearly twice his strength and was supposed to be on the opposite side of the road where their concerted crossfire should have been devastating to the fleeing troops. When the targets were at a point across from a small barn, which had been burned nearly to the ground, they were to open up and destroy or scatter the invaders.

Willis' men fired first, and almost immediately the Tenth Indiana, who was very close ahead of this company of arsonists, returned their fire with murderous results. Cliff knew of the repeating rifles some Yankee units were now being issued, but the Spencer did not have this rate of fire. '*The rapid firing from this unit is surely not from Spencers,*' Cliff thought. He had captured a Spencer once and decided against keeping it. Truly, it fired repeatedly seven rounds, but you had to manually cock it each time, and it was not as accurate as the Enfields his men were now carrying, so he had traded it on to another sergeant for a pound of real coffee, a commodity he had not had the pleasure of since March of '62.

What he saw being employed against Willis' men was much faster than the Spencer. He could see the men using them, and they were definitely not having to cock the hammer each time, besides, these rifles were bright and shiny in the morning sun.

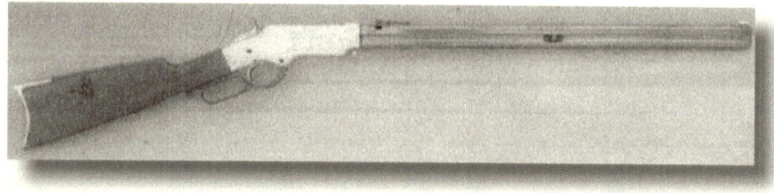

**The New Haven Arms Company's Repeating Rifle**
**Stamped B. Tyler Henry's Patent, Dated 'October 16, 1860'**

Sergeant Brown had his men hold their fire until he saw the Indiana men begin to reload, and then they opened up with their short rifles. This diversion gave Lt. Willis and his five remaining men an opportunity to escape. Before the union troops recovered from the counterfire, Cliff also had moved his men back beyond rifle range.

That had been his introduction to B. Tyler Henry's new self-contained cartridge and the gun that fired it, and he made himself a promise that he would one day have one. That day had never come, because he was captured near Nashville before the year was out.

On that fateful day, they were heavily outnumbered and doing the retreating themselves. Captain Bear had sent him and six men to try and find a weak point in the blue line that was advancing down Granny White Pike near their position. Cliff had just crossed a little stream called Otter Creek when a volley of mini balls came crashing through the leafless trees. Four of his men died before they hit the ground, and Cliff's horse reared and screamed before they both went down. Private Johnson immediately threw up his arms in an effort to stop them from shooting him also, and Cliff took advantage of this and crawled back into the cold water of the little creek. He moved as quickly as he could in a bent-over run until he was around a small bend in the stream. There he climbed the bank and slipped off into the timber. He had no chance to retrieve his carbine when his horse fell and was down to the rounds in his Colt. Finally, just as darkness swept into the hollow he found a small cave and into it he quickly rushed.

There he stayed for the remainder of that day, and when dawn broke he eased over to the entrance and peered out, only to find a squad of Federals with bayonets attached to their Springfields combing the hollow. He eased back and waited and hoped.

Then one of them said loudly, "Here are some tracks, Sarge."

Cliff knew his enemy was very close and that his capture or death was only minutes away. He determined to take as many of them with him as he could, but when he pulled the Colt he saw it was wet, and he knew it was doubtful if it would fire at all.

'Gosh, how I hate to give these bluebellies my Colt,' he thought as he looked out past the slight brush that hid the entrance to the little cave. Finally, he made a decision that would forever change his life. He took his neckerchief and wiped the revolver clean of all dampness, and then using the last of the whale oil in the little tin he always carried in the cartridge box on his belt, Cliff coated the gun well before removing his shell jacket and wrapping the revolver in it. He pushed this as far back in the cave as he could, among several rocks. Some of these he used to cover his cache before he moved forward towards the entrance. There he pulled some of the brush back and watched two soldiers, not twenty yards away, who were tracking him. Finally he called out, "Hey Yank, you got any coffee?"

The two men jumped as if they were shot and whirled around pointing their rifles at the sound.

"You come out a' there," one commanded.

"I'm a-coming," Cliff replied, and as soon as he could, he shoved both of his hands forward so they could see he was unarmed, and then he crawled out.

Immediately they searched him, and as soon they were satisfied he was unarmed, the taller boy asked, "How many more a' you in there?"

"Hell, that little dent in the ground ain't no bigger than a whiskey barrel. If'n it were, I'd still been in thar, and you'd been moving on past."

"We was tracking you. We'd a' found you soon enough," he replied and then looking at his shorter companion, he said, "Alvin, go check it out."

Cliff could see the smaller man didn't like being ordered by the other private, but he did go over, and using his bayonet he moved the brush back where he could look in. "He's telling the truth, too little fur mor'n one in thar."

The war finally came to an end for Clifford Brown in June of 1865 when he was released from Point Lookout Prison near Maryland's southern tip, some 750 miles from home, with no money and no shoes. He had a long and hard journey ahead of him, through a familiar land now in hostile hands, but he had survived the worst winter the country had known in many a year and done it in a tent. Fourteen thousand others at Point Lookout had not.

It took him seven days to make it to Richmond, but there he found a woman who fed him the first real meal he had in nine months. She also gave him a pair of shoes her husband had left behind when he marched away in '62. From there Cliff was able to get a pass to ride the next southbound train, and he took it no matter where it went. Later, he was not so sure that had been a wise choice when he saw the setting sun on the nose of the locomotive. Two days later he detrained at what was left of the 'L&N Station' in Nashville.

Having not eaten since the kindly woman fed him on his first day in Richmond, he was very weak and in need of nourishment, and soon. Eventually he found a can of peaches that some over-stocked Union soldier had dropped in a ditch, and he sat there and ate every slice and drank every drop. That night he slept in a partially burned barn on what was left of the old Lipscomb farm.

The next morning he was awakened by the sounds of two children talking. "You giv' me 'dat," one said, but his friend did not reply. "You don' giv' me 'dat I gwine a tel' Mam'."

Cliff peered out through the crack in the wall of the barn as the little darkies walked by. Finally he spoke, "Boys, you come here."

They both jumped, and the larger one ran, but the little one, who had been doing all the talking, just froze. Well not really, he was shaking too much to say he was frozen, but he could not find the words to tell his feet to move so he just stood there and shook all over. Cliff was amused by his actions. He seemed to be jumping up and down, but his feet never left the ground. Walking from the barn and up to him, Cliff nodded his head towards the dirt pike not far away and asked, "You know what road that is?"

The boy just nodded his head in return, but said nothing.

"Well, what is it?"

Again, he said nothing. Finally Cliff said, "If 'n you don't tell me, I'll go back in there and get that big ol' snake and throw it on you."

The boy then looked with bigger eyes than before, past the man into the dark old barn and finally said, "It be the road to Granny White's Tavern." And when he suddenly found his voice, he also found a way to talk to his feet, and before Cliff could ask him anything else, he was gone after his companion.

'Granny White Pike,' Cliff thought, 'Hell, then yonder a ways is Otter Creek.'

It took him most of the day to walk to the little stream and then another hour to locate his cave, but in the rotten gray coat was his prized Colt. There was some light color on its surface, but no pits, and the bluing was mostly the way he had left it. Of course, he knew the cylinder chambers would be ruined from laying there so long with gunpowder in them, but that would only be a small chore to replace, if he only had the money to do so.

Finding his revolver brought the first smile to his thin face in over a year, and he carefully concealed it in his trousers, at the small of his back, under his shirt.

The next day, he worked his way around Nashville and headed east on the Knoxville Pike towards the village where he had taken the gun in the first place. There he was able to find Captain Sowash, one of his professors of long ago, who was once again teaching science at the school. Most of the other buildings had been burned to the ground, but Cliff was proud to see the science building had, for the most part, survived, although there were several small holes in it here and there where mini balls and canister had punctured her walls.

Chuck Sowash did not recognize Cliff until he spoke, and then a huge smile crossed his face.

He stayed there for two days and was able to trade his shoes for a sway back mule from a farmer who had lost his land out near Tucker's Crossroads and was no longer able to feed the animal.

The next day Cliff headed for Georgia.

After a full day's travel on the old animal he stopped at a crossroads, near the village of Manchester to ask for a bite to eat, but all he got was arrested by the new government which fined him one mule for wearing a Confederate belt buckle. From there on, he walked. Even so, he was happy they had not located his Colt.

Arriving home one month later, he found his father's sawmill had been taken over by a former slave, who could neither read nor write, but was being kept well-supplied in shine by the new banker. Cliff learned there was now a law, that congress had just passed, allowing freedmen to be awarded businesses or other property owned by former Confederate sympathizers who could not pay their taxes in Federal currency or gold, which very few Southerners had in 1865.

He also was proud to find his mother had kept his second pair of brown cavalry boots which were as beautiful as any he had ever seen, especially after walking barefooted for hundreds of miles.

He took a job as a teamster hauling logs from the swamps to the same sawmill his family once owned and worked there for several months before he was arrested for spitting on a Negro. Actually, he had not spit on the man; rather he'd simply spit to the side of the wagon. It was, unfortunately, the very time Isaac Washington was walking up beside the load of cypress logs, and the tobacco juice spray hit him. This would not have been a big deal had not several of Cliff's co-workers suddenly begun laughing loudly, attracting the attention of a Lieutenant of the Occupational Government, a man who hated anything and anyone who was considered a secessionist. He had spent the last three months of the war in the prison at Camp Sumter,[1] only some hundred miles from where they now stood, and his feelings were obvious. Isaac, who had come to know Cliff and knew him to be a fair man, tried to stop the arrest, but it was a no-go with the Officer in blue. Cliff spent the next three months in the military stockade that had been constructed from the remains of the old Baker's Hotel on the north side of town.

When released, Cliff went straight to the old hollow tree near the little spring, in the big pasture that had once been home to several of his father's mules. There he retrieved his Colt. He had wrapped his prize in a large oilcloth and hid it the first day he was home. Carefully, he loaded it and then he started for the mill.

Just after sundown he saw John Tidwell, the new banker, drive up in his Studebaker surrey.

The door of the small slab building the new owner used as both office as well as sleeping quarters opened, and the glow from a coal oil lamp inside clearly silhouetted both Tidwell and the Darkey.

*'This is going to be easier than I thought.'*

Hiding behind the big saw, he waited until Tidwell had unloaded the three dark brown jugs and taken in trade a small black metal box from Booker-T Polk, the new owner of his father's business. It was then Cliff rose up and called out, "Reach for the heavens Yankee scum, I have a 44 revolver pointed at your thieving guts and would love to add another Yankee to the list I done already sent to hell."

"Who dat?" the Darkey yelled.

"Never you mind, Nigger. I'll send you along with him if 'n wus you to move either."

"Who are you, what do you want?" Tidwell asked anxiously.

"Who I am ain't important, just another wronged man far as you're concerned," Reb replied to the question, and then turning his attention to the matter at hand he said, "Alright, Nigger. Get that box, and bring it here."

"Yas, Suh," the colored man answered, and he reached for the box in Tidwell's hand.

---

[1] Camp Sumter was the prison located near Andersonville Georgia.

When he was ten feet from the big saw, Cliff stopped him. "That'll be far enough. Set it down there and back away."

"Yas Suh, Mistuh Brown," he replied and did as told, but in doing so stepped between Reb and Tidwell, who immediately grabbed a concealed Remington Rider revolver and fired it at the robber. Unfortunately for Polk, Tidwell was not the shot he thought he was, and the small ball struck the blackman just right of his spine. Polk dropped to his knees and hollered at the sudden pain.

Cliff returned fire and his round ball hit Tidwell in his right hand removing the bottom two fingers before it crashed into the walnut grip. Tidwell also screamed as the gun flew from his hand, and then he turned and ran around the slab building and out of sight into the darkness. Cliff could hear the splashing of his feet in the shallow swamp to the north, but pursuit was out of the question.

*'Someone from the camp surely heard the shots and will be soon coming to investigate.'* He also was sure Tidwell had heard Polk call out his name. That left just one thing to do, leave the country and be quick about it.

Returning to Polk, he saw there was little that could be done for the wounded man. The flow of bubbly blood was steadily foaming from his mouth. Cliff stuffed a handkerchief in the hole in the man's back and then retrieved the box and removed its contents before heading for the surrey. Three miles south he unhitched the horse from the carriage, mounted his back, and turned towards home. Before sunup he was southbound enroute to Florida.

Sixty-three dollars was what his first crime since painting his name on the school house wall, had netted him, but in a time and place where a Southerner could work all year and expect to earn maybe four Yankee dollars, it was quite a fortune.

A week after the death of Booker-T Polk the following was published in the *South Georgia Times*.

### A Proclamation:

By Rufus B. Bullock
Governor of this State,
Commander in Chief of the Army
and Navy and the State Militia

Whereas I have received official information

that a murder was committed on one Booker-T
Polk, (a Freedman) in the county of Lowndes in this
state on the 12ᵗʰ day of April 1866 by one Clifford
(Reb) Brown resident of same county and it being
represented to me that said Brown has fled from
justice, I have thought it proper to issue this, My
Proclamation, hereby offering a reward of $100
for the apprehension and delivery to the Sheriff or
Jailor of said county, the body of said Brown, and
I do moreover charge and require all Officers both
Civil and Military, to be vigilant in every endeavor
to apprehend and bring to trial the said fugitive in
order that he may undergo a trial for the offense
with which he is charged, or otherwise be brought
to justice.

Rufus B. Bullock.

On the very day this was published in Valdosta, one hundred miles away in Jacksonville, Cliff hired on a sailing ship captained by a man who not only had a seaman's accent, but spoke it with a drawl. He explained his troubles to Captain Sheldon, and by the time the proclamation of him, "Wanted For Murder," had reached the Sheriff of the Saint Johns region, Cliff was off-loading in New Orleans.

There he stayed nearly three years and there he found and bought his yellow Winchester. It was not the Henry he had promised himself, but rather a newer version with Mr. King's patented loading gate. It, too, used Tyler Henry's self-contained cartridges, and he was more than satisfied. The first thing he had done, when he learned it was possible, was to send his beloved Colt back to Hartford and for the unheard of sum of $3.00 had the Richard's Conversion done. His cylinder's bores were badly pitted from the many months it had remained loaded in the cave in Tennessee, and this conversion would replace that. Also by specifying the conversion be done in 44 Henry Rim-Fire, it allowed the old cap & ball to use the same loaded round that his Winchester fired. Cliff felt his weaponry was finally complete.

Now, here he was some two thousand or more miles from Valdosta in the middle of nowhere cleaning this same Colt. When he had finished with the revolver he began removing the dust from the rifle.

Cliff had been warned that it was unwise for a man to travel alone in this country, but he had seen no Indian sign since he had left the old fort. Nonetheless, when he had made his fire he had placed it near the largest tree so the leaves and branches above would break up the smoke.

Reaching for the pot, he quickly sat it back down on the fire and shook the burn from his fingers. Taking his neckerchief, he again lifted the pot and poured himself a cup of the dark liquid. Setting the pot back just off the flames he added a number 8 frying pan over the fire and dropped in a slice of salted pork.

For several years the only thing that resembled coffee in the Confederate camps was a terrible excuse made from boiling crushed goober[2] hulls, and now that the real bean was again available, Cliff had developed an addiction to the smell and taste of it.

After he had finished with the bacon, he cleaned his pan with sand and washed out the coffee pot. Then he placed both in his saddlebags, always ready for a quick departure should it become necessary. Leaning back against his saddle he took out his makin's, rolled a smoke, and began reflecting on his new adventure.

His fire had been out for some time, and there was only a faint glow from the embers when he was awakened by Red, the big sorrel, blowing at something he didn't like out there in the darkness. Cliff had bought the clay red horse with the beautiful flaxen mane and tail from a widow in St. Martin Parish, Louisiana not long after he fled Georgia. She had been very reluctant to sell her dead husband's pride and joy, but she had been served with a new federal tax and simply had no more cash to cover it and was looking sadly at losing her home. The stud had been well trained by its former owner, and even though it took some getting to know one another, before too long Red and Cliff came to an understanding. Thereafter, Cliff never failed to have total confidence in the big animal.

Quickly and silently Cliff removed his Winchester and then eased over to where Red was hobbled. The horse was staring into the blackness of the starry night. Try as he might, Cliff could see nothing. Regardless, Red was most concerned, and he decided to saddle up and move away as soon as possible.

Just as he was pulling the cinch tight, he heard the unmistakable sound of several horses moving fast in his direction. Suddenly some one hundred and fifty yards to the east, there was a bright flash of light followed by the report of a revolver; almost at the same

---

[2] Goobers: A southern expression meaning peanuts.

moment, he heard a loud groan. One horse continued on, but the others pulled up.

The voices were faint, but in the stillness of the desert night they could be clearly understood.

"Where is he, Chip?"

"I don't know, but I sure as hell hit him. I heard him yell out."

"Yeah, I heard it too," another added.

"Look around, we need to make sure of him."

Holding his left hand over Red's nose, Cliff slid the carbine into its scabbard and then he lifted his Colt from his holster. *'If there is to be a running fight on horseback, I had rather be holding a revolver; in fact I wish I had two.'*

The war years had given him much experience in such a fray, and Cliff figured he was better at it than they. Still there were at least three of them and maybe more, not the kind of odds he liked, and too, he was not sure which side was the right side.

*'Could be this is a law posse after some killer,'* he thought. *'Or it could be this killer is the same kind a' murderer I myself am considered to be, back in Georgia.'*

He never saw any of the riders or their horses, but finally their conversation became too faint to understand, and then all was silent again.

Cliff waited another twenty minutes and then decided he would cross the river and ride north, the opposite direction from where he had last heard the men moving. Just then there was a splash in the water only a few yards from him, then another. He quickly recognized the sounds as a man walking in the knee-deep river.

When this man made it to his position, Cliff spoke lowly. "Hold it or I'll drop a hammer on you."

There was a gasp from the man, and then he fell forward into the river. Even without a moon Cliff could see he was face down and would soon drown.

Holstering his revolver he waded out and lifted him above the deadly flow.

The man's shirt was completely wet, still the dark stain on his back showed the evidence of where the pistol ball had entered.

The next hour was spent doctoring and loading the dead weight on his saddle. Cliff tied the man's legs to the stirrups and his hands to the horn, and then he lead Red on his predetermined route to the west and away from any company.

Sunrise found them west of Devil's Gate halfway to the split rock. He had stopped to rest himself and Red in a little washout that led north from the river. This draw would be a raging stream during the spring thaws, but by early July, this part of Wyoming was just plain hot and dry.

The man had awakened once, an hour before, but quickly passed out again. Now as he rested, lying on his side, he moaned from time to time, but little more. The bleeding had started again, and that, along with their fatigue, had been the cause for this rest period.

Cliff bandaged his wound once more, but he knew if the lead didn't come out soon, the man would surely die. He never considered himself a doctor, but with three years of the kind of war he had fought, taking care of bullet wounds was not new to him. Also, watching the field surgeons had been nearly an everyday affair by late '62.

While searching the man's clothing he found a folded paper in his vest pocket, but the writing on it had been by lead pencil, and the water from the river made it impossible to read.

Just as he built a small fire to heat the knife, the man suddenly jerked a time or two and then sat up looking around strangely, totally unaware of his location.

"What ___? Where ___ am I? Who are you?"

"I'm the man who's gon 'a take that slug out a' your back."

"What?"

The man suddenly seemed to lose most of his strength, and he fell backward. Finally, he asked again, "Who are you?"

"Most people call me Reb." Cliff answered. "Who are you?"

"Ah, my name's Rob Scogins."

"Why were those men after you Rob?"

"Ah, my mine. My mine, over to Monia," he gasped.

"Well, I got 'a take that bullet out or you'll die fur sure," Cliff said.

"Yes. Yes, I guess so."

"Do you know who it was that shot you?"

"Some of Ed Sholtz' boys, I reckon."

"You and this Ed Sholtz don't get along, I take it."

"We use ta, but we had a fight, and I went off on my own. Then when I got to making the riffle, he came after me."

"Wants your diggings, eh?" Cliff asked, more out of conversation to keep the man's mind off the steel that was now nearing white-hot.

"Yeah, he does, but won't do him no good. I done filed on it, sent a letter to Snow and all, and I gat relatives in Missouri. He kills me and my diggings go to my brother and sister."

"Well, we've talked long enough," Cliff said and started towards him with the knife. "Wish I had some whiskey fur ya, but I don't. I'll do my best though. You won't feel much after this here iron touches you."

"Wait, wait a minute mister. You got 'a promise me something first," he gasped. "I might not wake up!"

"Oh, you'll wake up, maybe tomorrow though. I never lost a patient yet."

"Still you got 'a promise me___."

"Alright, what do you want?"

"If I don't pull through this," he stopped and wet his lips before continuing, "You'll see my kin gets word of my diggings."

"Sure I will. Where are they living?"

"Higginsville, at the Ashley Farm, I have a brother there." It was the last thing he said.

It was near noon the next day before Cliff had him properly covered. He had lasted through the night and was looking better come morning, but about three hours after sunup Rob Scogins sat upright and gave out a loud sigh, then fell back dead as a door nail. It surprised the hell out of Cliff Brown when he did.

Cliff and Red were back on the Oregon Trail five miles from the dead man's grave when he heard the riders coming. Pulling up, he turned to watch their approach.

There were five of them. Three dressed in chaps of the kind he had seen in Texas, the other two were more casually attired. When they were on him, he gently laid his hand on the butt of his revolver and smiled. "Howdy."

"Howdy yourself," the young man with blond hair that hung from the back of his derby replied. "New here 'bouts?"

"That I am," Cliff answered keeping an eye on one of 'the chaps' that seemed to be slowly working his pony around behind Red.

"What ya doing in these parts?" the other chap-less man, asked.

"Minding my own business," Cliff calmly replied.

"You kind a' a smart ass, ain't cha'?" the same man snapped at Cliff's answer.

"Kind a' good with this here six-gun too, as that short horn there is fixin' to find out if'n he don't quit trying to sneak around behind me," Cliff warned, looking straight at the man on the dark brown cayuse.

"Hey, there's no call fur that kind a' talk," 'Mr. Derby' said. "We just wondering if you might a' seen an outlaw we trailed this way last night."

"Didn't see nobody last night, too damn dark," Cliff answered.

"Well, we almost had him, but he give us the slip back a' ways. We cut your trail and figured you might a' been him."

"I guess you see, I ain't."

"Yeah, you ain't."

"Ain't seen nobody, eh?" the other chap-less man said.

"As I said, too dark last night, and I ain't seen a living soul today," Cliff answered thinking, '*Well, that's almost the truth.*'

"Alright, sorry we bothered you," 'Mister Derby' said then added, "By the way what did you say your name wus?"

"I didn't, but most folks call me Reb."

"You a Johnny Reb?" the younger man spat at him.

"Wus," Cliff replied stout and proud. "Now days I'm just a drifter headed for South Pass City. If it's any a' your business, Sonny."

Cliff could see that his description of the young man had hit a nerve. He was still shy of thirty, himself, but still he guessed that was thirty percent older than 'The slicker,' and it was obvious the man was quite sensitive about his age.

"Come on Phil, he's just hacking on you," 'Mr. Derby' said.

"No, Chip, I ain't got 'a put up with that kind a' crap from no saddle tramp."

"Phil, I got the feeling he knows how to use that shooter he's got his hand resting on, now I ain't planning to explain to your Pa how I let you get yourself shot. So drop it and let's go. He ain't Scogins, and it is obvious he ain't hiding him."

The young rider moved back closer to his friends never taking his eyes from Cliff. The hate building there was plain and Cliff knew that sometime he would have to deal with this one.

The leader touched his hand to the brim of his derby and turning his gray dapple horse, started back the way they had come. The others followed with Phil last in line. Just before he was too far away for it to have mattered one way or the other, the shave tail turned around in his saddle for one last defiant look.

Cliff simply nudged Red around and again headed down the trail. The man operating the ferry barge at the Platte River Crossing had told him to follow the Sweetwater River to Split Rock; once there, if he was to then line up the split, as if it were the rear sight on a rifle, his eyes would be shooting straight at South Pass City. Of course, it would be some forty miles away. Now he was here, and the sight of the big mound of huge rocks certainly looked strange enough, as they did have a split in them. Taking aim he started on, in hopes that the old Mormon didn't have a bad taste in his craw for Gentiles. "Sure don't want to be a-leaving this fine river for more desert if it ain't the right direction, now do we Red?" he remarked as they moved out.

**Split Rock Wyoming**

This night he made his supper stop just after sundown. Shortly after chewing on a couple pieces of jerky, and drinking his fill of good black coffee, he made sure there was a nice bed of rocks around his small fire and no kindling close by, then left it to slowly burn itself out, before moving off about half a mile where he bedded down. It had been a good move, for some three hours later Red began to again blow at something off in the night, and Cliff could see movement back where his camp had been. He couldn't really see anyone, but there was something, and it appeared two or more somethings crossed between him and the dull glow of what was left of his fire. He stayed awake for a long time, but Red didn't seem disturbed again after the activity at his earlier camp quieted down.

# Chapter Two
## The Sisters

The next day Cliff came over a small rise and there in a little rolling plain was a town. It was quite a good sized one, too, being considerably larger than the gathering of buildings back at Platte River Crossing. He could see it was more or less laid out with three main streets running east to west and a few smaller ones between. Sizing it up, he judged it to support some 2000 inhabitants.

"Well, Red, the lights of this here South Pass City could a' been seen a considerable distance last night, had it not been over this little rise."

His horse made no move to give anyone the impression he even knew he was being addressed, had there been anyone about that might have cared to look at a horse's expression.

They entered town on the centermost street from the east and soon came to 'The Idaho House,' a fine hotel with a saloon next door. Tying Red to the hitching post in front, he entered through the double doors. The interior was tastefully done in quality drapes, and there was a large oriental rug on the floor.

Lightly tapping the bell on the counter, he waited. In time, a tall thin man appeared from behind a wall and looking at the dusty cowboy asked his business.

"I need a room."

"Very well, sir, and a bath I presume."

"Yeah, sure."

"That will be four dollars for the room and another for the bath," he said to Cliff. Then he added, "In gold."

"Hellfire, Mister, I just wanted to rent the room not buy it," Cliff replied quite taken aback by the announced prices.

"But, sir, this is 'The Idaho House.' Mr. Robert Todd Lincoln himself, along with his whole party, stays here when he's in the area."

"Is he here now?"

"Well, no, he only has been here once," the man said, pausing then added, "That is once this year."

"Well, hold that four-dollar room for him, and give me one of the dollar ones."

"There are no dollar rooms at this establishment, sir."

"Well then, you need to build yourself some," Cliff said swinging his saddlebags back over his shoulder.

"Perhaps you might find something more to your class down on Eddy Avenue."

"Where's this Eddy Avenue?"

"Just follow South Pass Avenue to Dakota Street, and turn north, it's a little past Black & Gallagher's Law Offices."

"Yeah, I guess I am in the wrong class place at that," Cliff said sarcastically. He returned to the boardwalk, but instead of following the clerk's directions, he entered the saloon next door only to find a drink of rye cost a whole dollar. Cliff was beginning to think he was sure in the wrong part of the country and was just about to leave, when a more than attractive girl came up and smiled at him.

"Hi, cowboy," she said.

Her hair was as black as a crow's wing in the Georgia sun, and her skin almost as white as new snow. He immediately surmised her flesh saw little or perhaps no sunshine. Her dress was a long affair made of white cotton with yellow paisleys. It was the type a church going lady would have buttoned to the neck, but it now was split down to where a body could have seen her navel, had it not been laced up some with a matching yellow ribbon. Still the valley between her breasts was very visible, and her mounds moved independent of one another when she moved.

Her smile revealed straight white teeth and a small dimple on her cheek. He figured her to be four or five years older than he, but carrying it well.

"Hello, Purty Thing," he replied.

"Well now, a Southerner, you must be a Texican?"

"No Ma'am, Georgia."

**South Pass City 1869**

"Alright, Georgia, buy me a drink?" she asked, letting another large smile cross her face.

"One," Cliff said moving over to a table and pulling out the chair for her to sit, "but I got 'a tell ya, if you're as over priced as everything else around here, I can't afford you."

"You're new here," she said as she sat down.

"Been here maybe twenty minutes."

"Well, this is gold mining country, everything here is high," she informed him.

"Mee'be I'm here at the wrong time. I barely got fifty dollars to my name, and that's got 'a last me a while," Cliff admitted, taking a long sip of his whiskey.

He then blew from deep in his lungs and took a small gasp for fresh air. "Boy, that stuff must be nigh on a week old."

She smiled again at him and then said, "I like you Georgia, it's refreshing to hear your drawl, and it's too early for my trade anyway. Let me buy you a drink," she told him holding up her hand with two extended fingers to the barkeep.

When the man with red garters on both sleeves looked her way, she called out to him "Klu, bring two of my Marshals."

The large round man looked strangely at her as if he thought she was wasting her time on this one, but he did as she had asked.

"These are on me," she said when he sat them down on the hardwood table.

"You sure, Miss Tipper?"

"Yeah, Klu, I'm sure. You have no idea how long it's been since a man has pulled out a chair for me or called me Ma'am," she said, looking up at the barkeep and then back at Cliff. "I'm paying for this round."

"Alright," he said turning and walking away shaking his head, "but Mr. Morris ain't gon'a like it none."

"Try this one," she said, handing Cliff a new glass with a much darker liquid in it.

He sipped it, being well warned by his first drink, but this one was something else.

"Gosh, I don't think I've had anything that went down as smooth as this since before the war."

"It's Marshal's Old Kentucky Bourbon. A friend of mine who made a good strike here a year or so ago sent it to me from back in the States. There's not much left, I'm afraid," she said sorrowfully.

"Tipper, is that your name?"

"Miss Tipper, at least that's what they call me here," she said, again smiling.

"Well, Miss Tipper, I thank you."

"And what do they call you, Georgia?"

"Well, now that you put it that way, they call me Reb.'"

"Alright, Reb, that's good enough for me. You planning on mining these hills?"

"Thought about it, but I may not have enough to get the supplies I need."

"Yeah, that will cost you some all right, and most of the good earth has already been holed around here; you probably can get a job at the Carissa. I could put in a word with Tommy Ryan if you want."

"There's another town somewhere around here that I heard about," Cliff said. "I think it's called Monia."

"There is a mine called Monia, over east of here some ten miles, but the nearest town to it is Hamilton."

"Oh, I saw a man back at the ferry crossing that told me he had hit a good strike there," Cliff lied.

"I haven't heard nothing of a new strike around there, that is of any size, except 'The Monia' herself."

"I'm sure he said it was near Monia, he was headed back east to get the rest of his family and bring them out here."

"Really?" she said taking interest in what he was saying. "What was his name?"

"Oh, I'm not sure Stoggens or Scallins or something like that."

"Rob Scogins?" she asked surprised.

"Yeah, that could have been it," he said wondering at her interest.

"You said he has gone back east?"

"Yeah, to get the rest of his family. Why?"

"Well, it's just that Chip Roper and some of the Sholtz bunch was in here a few days ago looking for him, and I was feeling bad for ol' Rob," she said showing some relief.

"You know him then?" Cliff asked.

"Sort a', he came to see me a couple times when he had found a little color ___, but he was always nice and gentle, not like most a' these bums," she said. "I kind a' liked him. I worried a little when I heard that bunch was looking for him."

"Who is this Chip fellow?"

"He's a no good son-of-a-bitch who does Ed Sholtz' dirty work."

"And then who's Ed Sholtz?"

"He owns 'The Monia Mine', richest hole in the Wyoming plains they say," she replied downing her bourbon. "And he's a low down coyote, too."

"Sounds like you don't like the man too much."

"Let's just say I know him too well," she replied.

Just then, a stern, well-kept woman called out to her from the back of the room. "Miss Tipper. May I speak to you?" The statement was more of a command than a question.

"Be right there, Mrs. Morris," she said and started to get up.

"The boss lady?" he asked.

"Well, sort a'. Her husband owns the place, and she sure as hell is his boss, but no, not directly; she's the local judge."

"A woman judge?"

"Yep, only in Wyoming," Miss Tipper said.

"I'll be damned," Cliff replied shaking his head.

"Look Reb, you might try over at Teachman's on Colfax Street. Tell him I said to be kind to you."

"Sounds frightening," he replied.

"He'll treat you right," she said.

"How do I find Colfax?" he asked sincerely.

She smiled, allowing a dimple to reappear in her right cheek that only added to her remarkable beauty. "Here, I'll draw you a map of the BIG CITY." Standing, she went over to the long bar and had the barkeep produce a scrap of paper and a lead pencil.

Returning, she again sat at the table, only this time she chose the chair next to him and began a simple sketch. When finished, she turned it so he could see what she had done and began, "This of course isn't all the streets or all the buildings here, but it is likely the ones you need to know, the main ones," she added and then nodded her head agreeing with her statement. "And it will get you by until you are here a spell. You are going to stay a spell aren't you?"

"If everybody is as nice as you I'll be here until I die."

"You southerners, you always are the charmers," she replied and slapped his wrist gently before she began explaining her drawing. "Here we are on South Pass Avenue, it's more or less the main pike in town, runs east to west, and then over here is Dakota Street, it runs north to south. Here are a couple of restaurants and a few of the saloons, most everything else just happens to be located where there was a vacant lot at the time someone wanted to build."

After going over her map, she took her bottle in hand. "I reckon I had better get on back while I still have a job; come back and see me, Georgia," she said in a soft voice, and then standing, she turned and started for the backdoor, but she stopped half way across the room, looked around at him for a moment, then turned again and was soon through the door.

Cliff finished the drink she had bought him and then with great courage, downed what was left of the one he had bought. After catching his breath, he stood up and left the building.

Colfax Street ran up the hill towards a large wooden cistern that would hold hundreds of gallons of rainwater, should it ever rain in this part of Wyoming. Thankfully, Willow Creek flowed most of the year, so the water tank was not the only source of drinking water.

Cliff was pleased to see the only buildings north of the intersection of Colfax and Custer were a store and tall barn. The two story clapboard store had a shingle hanging out on which was painted 'Teachman's Goods.'

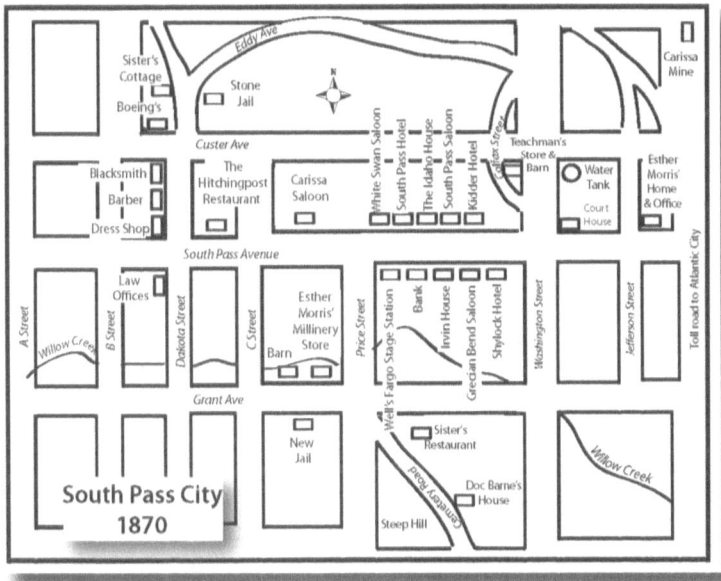

Entering, Cliff saw that the main business here was that of a dry goods store with a few other items of general merchandise scattered about.

The man, working behind a small desk, stood as he came in. Ernie Teachman was in his late thirties with a wife but no children. He stood some 6 feet tall, but weighted no more than 145 lb. His dark brown hair had just started to take on a few strands of gray. When he spoke, Cliff detected an accent from western Kentucky or southern Indiana. "May I help you, sir?"

"Hi, I'm new in this burg, and the only person I know told me to come here, that you would treat me right."

"That's very kind of them, just who was that?"

"A lady over at the saloon next to 'The Idaho House', Miss Tipper," Cliff replied.

A sudden look of panic shot to Ernie's face, and he quickly turned to see if anyone else had heard what Cliff had said.

"Yes, well, I appreciate her kindness, but I wouldn't want Mrs. Teachman to hear that I even know of her."

"I see, then let's just say we have a mutual friend," Cliff suggested.

"Let's just say you happened in here on your own, and let it go at that."

"You got it, Mr. Teachman."

"Yes, well what can I do for you?"

"As I said, I just got into town and wanted a place to put up my horse and get a room for a couple nights," Cliff replied, "after that, I'll see what happens."

"Well, I can help you with your needs if you aren't too particular."

"What I am is almost broke, and I find everything here too expensive for my purse strings."

"That's what we service," Teachman remarked, "Come with me." He turned and led the way out the backdoor. There, Cliff saw a corral and a barn that could house half a dozen animals.

"You can use one of the stalls for your horse, there's grain in that bin over there, don't use the good stuff. This time of year we haven't gotten our hay in yet, so I rent out space upstairs for drifters to sleep in," he said, pointing to the loft. "I know it's no soft bed, but it's dry, and there is little chance a screaming savage will lift your hair up there," he said, and then added, "As has happened to more than one fellow trying to sleep out on the prairie."

Cliff was not so sure he liked the idea. It was obvious that others were also sleeping there. He wasn't sure if his chances of being happened upon by a roaming Cheyenne was as great as being stuck between the ribs with an Arkansas Toothpick by a fellow roommate.

"A dollar a day for you and another dollar for your horse, two bits more for the horse's grain," Teachman said as he turned to go back into the front building. "Take it or leave it."

Cliff thought a long moment then replied, "Alright, I'll take it for a couple nights," reasoning *'It will be good for Red to get the grain for a change.'*

Returning to the store he looked around and selected a few tools, among them a pick, a shovel, a good tin pan, and a two-pound beater. He then turned to Teachman and asked "Do you have any cartridges?"

"Some, I have .50-70 Springfield and the Spencer round, good powder, and excellent lead balls I make myself," he said proudly.

"No, I need the Henry," Cliff said.

"Oh, well yes. I do have one box, but I was planning on keeping them for myself, I have a down payment on a Henry over to Doc Barnes."

"The Doctor sells guns?"

"Well, not normally, but he took this rifle in on account 'cause his patient couldn't pay his bill any other way, and it was all he had of real value."

"I don't think much of a sawbones that would take away a man's gun in Indian country," Cliff offered disgustedly.

"Oh, I guess I didn't make myself clear. The reason he could pay no other way was because he was dead," Teachman chuckled.

"Some sawbones," Cliff said, raising his eyebrows.

"No, you're wrong for thinking that way. Doc Barnes is a good doctor, leastwise for this country, we got three doctors here, and Doc Irwin is over to Atlantic City, but Doc Barnes is the best of the lot. The man had been shot twice in the back and had lost a lot of blood before the Doc saw him," Teachman added.

"Seems like a lot of men get themselves shot in the back around here," Cliff said.

"It's a tuff time, in a tuff and hostile country."

"This here place is tall cotton compared to what happened in Georgia after the war," Cliff came back quickly.

"Well, sure, Georgia is home to those of the rebellion. What else could you expect?"

"I expected the government to live up to what they said they would do. Why, I don't know?" Cliff retorted.

"I suspect you were one of the Secessionists. Probably a rebel soldier, too."

"You suspect right, two times. I suspect you were one of those I shot at."

"No, I was neither, I was working for the Union Pacific Railroad during the rebellion and would still be had not they give them damn Chinaman so much of the work."

*'Damn conscription dodger,'* Cliff thought but said instead, "Put this stuff aside for me and I'll settle up with you before I go."

"It's a come first, get first world we live in, sir. I can't promise you anything."

"I'll remember that," Cliff said returning his Stetson to his head and walking out.

First, he took Red around to the barn and put him in a clean stall, then combed and rubbed him down. Lastly, he gave him a large portion of grain before he left.

He walked back to the main street. Stopping near a young Mexican boy who was sweeping off the boardwalk with a straw broom, he asked, "You speak American?"

"Si' Señor, a lee'dal."

"I need some grub, where is there a place to eat?"

The boy stopped his sweeping, removed his large straw hat, and scratched his head, giving the impression that this was a really hard question. Finally he replied, "Very good grub at the Cantina. Most Gringo's no like though. Some go to de' Si'essters."

"The sister's house?" Cliff questioned. "Where is that?"

"There by the graveyard, up de' hill."

"Gracias," Cliff said and started off in the direction the boy had pointed.

Finally, after walking south through the next intersection, Cliff saw a small building and beyond was the cemetery. Several feet past the boneyard was a single structure. *'I kind a' wonder if that is where he was talking about.'* Cliff thought.

Taking a deep breath he started walking up the hill, but realizing the building before the bone orchard was what he was looking for, he entered.

The small two-room slab board affair was bright inside having had the walls white-washed sometime in the not too distant past. A lady a few years his junior was clearing one of the five tables of wooden dishes. Her face lit up with a large smile when she saw him.

"Good morning, sir. We're happy you came in."

"Ma'am," Cliff replied touching the brim of his hat just before he removed it.

"We have a good stew made from an elk brisket that should be hot by now."

"Stew, Yas Ma'am, that will be right good."

"Carol, we have another customer. Is the stew ready?"

"I'll check, but if not, we don't have no more hen eggs, that last gent et 'em all," came the reply from the backroom.

"I told him stew, Carol."

Cliff let his mind ponder on his situation while he waited. *'I gave that dead man my word, I would get the news to his family back in*

*Missouri, and now here I am in a gold miners' town with almost no money and no way of getting any. I done made some enemies from the very people that I had wanted to get a job with, and now here I am going to have to sleep in a loft with a bunch of others who surely are also down on their luck. Hell, my horse has it better 'n me these days.'*

When the stew was ready Cliff knew why this had been called the sisters' place, for the woman who brought him his bowl was a copy of the other one, only perhaps a year or two older and a few pounds heavier.

"Here you are, sir. I hope you like it. We put in some boiled potatoes and a big carrot this morning."

"Thank you, Ma'am. It surely smells wonderful."

"Well," she said touching the round bun at the back of her golden hair, "we try, Mister____?"

"Brown," Cliff said, "but my friends call me 'Reb'."

"Well, Mr. Brown, I hope we see enough of you that calling you 'Reb' will seem natural," she replied before turning and walking back through the door.

Cliff could hear her faintly saying, "Connie, you didn't tell me he was so handsome."

"Well, Carol, you never asked," her sister replied, then they both giggled.

*'I think I might like this place after all,'* he thought. *'The men ain't so friendly, but the women I've seen in this town are a heap better 'n most.*

Finishing, he asked for another cup of coffee and was pleased to see both women come out and make some excuse for being there with him.

"You certainly are way out on the end of town."

"Yes," Carol replied, "we didn't want this building, but it was all we could afford and figured with enough good food and pleasant atmosphere we could bring the business out to us."

"Well, you sure have plenty of both. I'll bet the town will grow to you."

"No," Connie said, "nobody wants to be beyond the cemetery."

"Well, there's someone already there," Cliff said nodding toward the log building at the very end of town.

"Oh, that's Doc Barnes' hospital," Connie told him.

"Yeah," Carol added, "you either get well there or they lay ya out next door."

"Doc Barnes, eh?"

"Yes, sir. He's your last chance to stay alive in South Pass City," Carol remarked.

Although uphill, the walk to Barnes' house was not as far as he had thought. Stepping inside, he called out.

"Be right with you," the voice from the other side of a quilt that was hanging as a door between two rooms said.

"Now young man, what's ailing you?"

"I understand you have a rifle for sale," Cliff replied.

"Well, I sort a' do, but Ernie Teachman has asked me to hold it fur him."

"Yeah, he's the one that told me it was for sale," Cliff replied.

"That's just like Ernie. Ask you to hold something fur him, then welsh out on the deal."

"What's the price?"

"I told Ernie he could have it fur $10.00," the Doctor said.

"I'd like to see it, if I could."

"I reckon it'll be alright, if Ernie sent you up here."

The man brought out the long barreled rifle and handed it to Cliff. "It's got four loading tubes that go with it as well," he said, laying the brass tubes on the table. Cliff lifted them and could tell they were all fully loaded.

'A full box of shells here,' he thought, and then turning his attention to the rifle he saw it had "US" stamped on the right side of the frame above the lever screw. 'One of those damn Yankee rifles.' Cliff thought, 'Wonder if this one killed any of our boys in gray?' He turned it over and looked at the open magazine tube and saw there were at least another ten or twelve shells in there. 'I would think dirt could get in there mighty easy and jam it up.' Otherwise, he had to admit it looked almost as good as his '66.

"I'll give you nine cash, right now. If you don't mind giving back the down payment Mr. Teachman put on it."

"Hellfire, Ernie never put nothing down. He just asked me to hold it fur him," the Doctor said rubbing his chin. "You say cash?"

"Yankee greenbacks."

"Well, around here most pay in gold, but I'll take it."

Cliff laid the yellow frame on his shoulder as he walked back towards Teachman's hoping the man would see him, but he apparently did not. In the barn he wrapped the rifle and loading tubes in his duster and left it all under his saddle in Red's stall, then he headed for the backdoor of the store.

"I sure would like you to sell me that box of Henry cartridges you've got," he said to Teachman who again was sitting at his desk.

"Not a chance. I done paid five dollars on that Henry at Doc's, and I aim to keep them shells," Teachman lied.

"Well, I give you the chance to sell them to me twice; I may not give you another."

"Won't need another chance. Soon as you pay me what you owe I'll go get my rifle."

"Suit yourself," Cliff said smiling in his mind.

That night he turned in early so he could see anyone else who would be coming in. He had put everything he owned in the front of the stall with Red except his Colt and a blanket, knowing Red would raise a ruckus should anyone try to get at his poke. Then he moved over by the front wall near the top door and bedded down. Seven more men came in during the night and all made some comment about the big sorrel that was new there, but no one bothered him or his stuff.

Come morning, he knew he had to find some place to take a bath before he went back to see any of his new friends.

The bath came easier than he had expected. The water trough at the back of Teachman's barn was full, and he found a small cake of soap on the back porch of the store where Marlene Teachman had left it after doing her wash. After taking leave with her soap and the water trough and with the clean shirt he had folded in his saddlebags and a good brooming of his Levi-Strauss' he was ready to go back and see the sisters.

He saw there were many men in the little building this morning, and he found no table unused. Standing just inside the door, he waited. Finally Carol came out with an armfull of wooden platters and saw him.

"Mr. Brown, do come in," she said looking around the room, finally she noticed two men sitting at the table nearest the kitchen door. "Bill, how about sharing your table with a friend of mine?"

"Sure, Miss Carol, if you want," the dirty-faced man replied.

"Come on over here," she said, waving to Cliff.

Reluctantly he made his way over to where she stood smiling at him.

"This here is Bill Thomson. He works night shift at the Carissa. Bill, make Reb feel welcome while I rustle up some more coffee."

"Sure, Miss Carol," the miner replied, feeling sort of special that she had remembered his name.

"'Reb she said?" Bill questioned.

"That's what most call me," Cliff replied.

"Well, good to meet ya Reb. This here is Tucson. He hails from down south in Arizoniea," Bill said between gulps of coffee.

"Howdy," Tucson said as Cliff sat down.

The next time Carol came through the door, she again had three platters on her left arm and one in her right hand, which she sat down in front of Cliff without saying a word. She then quickly moved over to another table and sat down the other three before saying to a big man with a full face of red beard, "I'll bring yours out in just a minute, Sandy."

"Gee, Miss Carol must surely like you," Tucson remarked. "I ain't never seen her favor nobody a' for."

For the second time since he came in he felt a little shy, but the sight of the two big eggs looking up at him atop a sizable beef steak overtook his embarrassment. "She's a nice lady," was all he said in response before pulling the small knife from the stovepipe of his left boot and digging in.

"That's a handsome cutter you got there," Bill said. "I always been an admirer a' good steel."

The knife had a six-inch blade that followed the style of Colonel Bowie, and it was topped with a straight piece of bone fashioned from the antler of a big Texas whitetail. The pommel and guard were of silver, making the handle too heavy to be used for throwing, but perfect for his needs as a tool.

"I like it," Cliff said as he used the knife to cut his steak.

"Get it here 'bout's____? Looks almost new."

"Naw, a fellow down to Denton, Texas, made it for me, some years back," Cliff answered, wishing he had not had to sit with these two. It wasn't that he wanted to be unfriendly; rather he wasn't accustomed to having to explain himself so much to strangers.

"Oh, well I admire it. Should you find the need to part with it I'd be interested," Bill said and then added, "Should the price be right, that is."

"I'll keep that in mind."

His two companions left soon, and before he had finished a second cup of coffee the place took a lull in business.

It was then Connie came out from the kitchen. Obviously, she had been doing the cooking as she was wet with sweat and showing streaks of wood smoke smeared here and there on her apron and face.

She moved past his table and refilled the cups of the other two customers that were still there. Before she had finished her chat with the men, Carol came out and looked around and then suddenly sat down at Cliff's table.

"How was your night, Reb?"

"Proud to see we're past that Mr. Brown stuff," he replied. "Oh, it was peaceable enough for a barn's loft."

"Barn's loft? Where are you staying?"

"At Teachman's with my horse."

"That sneak," she said with disgust.

"Do I detect a moment of bitterness toward Mr. Teachman?"

"When Connie and I first arrived, that louse offered us the use of his little building on Dakota Street, where the barber is now. Then when he came to pick up his rent he wanted more than money for the use of his property. I saw him as a rat right off, but Connie kind a' fell for him. He even had Connie believing she might have found her a man until Mrs. Teachman came in one day and retrieved a set of real silver spoons he had given her ___, given Connie that is. The next day we found this place and moved up here. It was slow at first, being so far from downtown, but our loyal customers make the walk, and we get more everyday. Just like you."

"So Connie is looking for a man," he said.

"Every woman is looking for a man, if she is over twelve years old, Reb," she replied, with a knowing look. "It's the sad truth, but few things frighten a woman more than thinking she will have to support herself after her youth fails."

"Well, I doubt anyone as attractive as you two will have to worry long," he reassured her.

"Oh sure, we could get ourselves a man, but the kind a woman wants doesn't walk in here every day," she said looking back at him.

"What kind is that?" Cliff asked not really liking the direction this conversation was going.

"Someone strong and loyal. Someone who treats you kindly and appreciates what you do for him, and someone honest," she added as a last thought.

"Never met such a man," he said in jest. "Doubt he even exists."

"Sometimes I think you may be right," she agreed with a big smile as she stood. "You be coming back for your dinner, Reb?"

"I 'spect so," he said smiling back, "Probably be supper, though. I don't usually do dinner, ain't much for food in the middle of the day."

"Alright, I'll be looking for you," she said as she turned and went back into the kitchen just as another crew of men came rushing in the front door.

"Come in boys, come in. I'll get back to the stove and start frying some beef," Connie said over her shoulder as she passed Cliff, and went back with her sister.

Cliff recognized two of the men that had come in as being the chap-less riders of Sholtz' bunch he had met on the Sweetwater.

Retrieving his Stetson from the peg on the wall, he dropped two bits on the table and started out, his gun hand close to his stock.

One of the men started to get up as Cliff passed, but his friend placed a hand on his forearm and shook his head. Cliff walked on by and went out the door.

Around four, he entered Morris' saloon and ordered a beer, being shy of the rye he had gotten the day before. Surprisingly, it was nice and cool. Sitting down at a table with his back to a wall where he could see the doors and floor at the same time, he sipped on his schooner and watched.

In a few minutes, a man of about forty came out from the backroom. He was wearing a clean boiled shirt and striped trousers. His hair was combed neatly, and he looked quite confident in himself. There was just a touch of something about him that stirred a memory in Cliff, but he couldn't put his finger on it.

The barkeep came over to where Cliff sat after about twenty minutes and asked, "You ready for another?"

"Not quite through with this one," Cliff answered.

"Well, this here ain't no resting place in the shade. You sit in here, you buy something to drink," the man said sternly.

"I'll do the buying," a voice from across the room said. A voice that was soft and alluring and each looked towards it. Then both watched Miss Tipper stroll their direction, each with a different thought. She placed one hand on the shoulders of a man who was sitting at the far table. "Don't lose all your money Jack; I'm going to be hot tonight."

"You bet, Miss Tipper," the man said, and then he took ten dollars from the small stack, folded them and put them in his vest pocket.

"Hello, Reb," she said as she arrived at his table.

Cliff stood and pulled out a chair for her, and she smiled and sat down.

"Ernie was in last night. Said he took good care a' you."

"Can't say I got all that much of a liking for your friend," Cliff replied.

"Oh," she said looking down at the table. "I guess he didn't treat you so good after all."

"Not bad, just not so good."

"Well, sorry about that. He's not really a friend, more of a steady customer. Comes in here at least twice a week. When I said he would take care of you I meant he had the cheapest place in town to stay."

"I'm not here to complain, I came in to be refreshed by your purty face."

"Oh, you dog. You know just what to say to make me feel good," she replied enjoying the compliment.

"Where do you hail from, Miss Tipper?"

"I grew up in Clay County Missouri. Not much left there now, the war ruined it. I was off to Kansas City by '63, all of sixteen and naive as they come, but it didn't take Colonel Schofield's staff long to work that out of me," she said with bitterness showing in her memories.

*'Gee, that would make her only twenty-two or twenty three years old, I had her pegged for several years older than that,'* he thought before asking, "What brought you here?"

"A husband," she replied once again, losing herself in sorrowful memories.

"A husband? Where?" he asked looking around knowing full well there was none at this time. She had the look of a grass widow[3].

"Oh, he's not around anymore, got himself shot dead two winters back."

"I'm sorry, I should have minded my own business," he said, now also feeling her gloom.

"No, it's all right. I've mostly gotten over it. It's just that he was such a special man. I don't mean special in what most women would call special. He wasn't tall or even handsome, but he knew I was

---

[3] Grass Widow: A divorced woman

a whore, and he married me anyway and forgave me of my past. I never let him down either, till after he was gone, and what little money we had was gone too," she sighed. "I know a woman will never find two men in this world that could live with a past like that. So, here I am. For as long as my looks hold out," she paused then added, "after that who knows?"

"What is your name?"

"Nadine Tipper. He was Brady Tipper," she said. "But don't tell anybody. I don't want anybody in here to call me Nadine. It was the last word Brady ever uttered."

"I understand," he said.

After a long awkward minute of silence he asked, "Do you ever get a day off around here?"

"Sundays. Mrs. Morris won't allow us to work on 'The Lords Day' as she calls it."

"Well, that's tomorrow. What say you and I go for a ride tomorrow morning bright and early?"

"Early?" she said, "Hell, I don't get done with Saturday night until the sun comes up."

"There's no time of the day as purty as first light," he said.

"That's true, that's the time a day when I get to go to sleep," she said looking around the room and seeing Mr. Morris looking at them. With a sigh she added, "No, Reb, I better stay in my place and get some much needed rest. Thanks anyway."

Cliff just nodded his head understanding.

She stood up, and before she walked away she said, "I hope you come in again soon. Sometimes at night I sing, if we can get a piano player."

"I'll do that."

She walked towards her boss and then stopped and bit her bottom lip for a second before turning around, and nodding her head she said, "Georgia, Sunday morning, sunrise," then she quickly whirled and walked back to the bar.

"Who is that man?" John Morris asked.

"Just a drifter. He seems to like me."

"All men like you Miss Tipper, even me."

"Well, I like my job here, and I don't want to get the judge on my case, so just you forget it."

The well-dressed man looked back at Cliff and stared hard.

Finally, Klu seeing Morris' expression ask, "You want me to run him out a' here Boss?"

"No, no it's just something about him."

By the time he arrived at *The Sisters'* for supper he had learned that Rob Scogins had some diggings south of town several miles. Cliff also had learned any real smithing and sales of guns and powder was mostly done at the E.I. DuPont de Nemours Sporting Goods Store on South Pass Avenue which was run by the Freund Brothers; there he was able to buy two boxes of Henry cartridges. It was Freund who told him that he could find Scogins' diggings near where the Lander/Rawlins Stage Road crossed the 'Ol' Oregon Trail'. This was confusing to Cliff for he remembered distinctly Scogins had definitely said it was at Monia, which he now knew was out near Hamilton or Atlantic City, both a far piece from the crossroads.

Carol brought him a platter of beef liver smothered in fried onions with a large potato on the side. "Eat this quietly," she said. "There ain't no more liver."

Cliff smiled not wanting to tell her he didn't like liver. In fact, there was no way he was going to let her know after it was obvious she had made it special just for him. Surprisingly though, for the first time in his life he found the rich meat tasty, and he was glad he didn't have to lie when she ask how he liked it.

"You know I normally don't like liver, but this was good."

"That's because I did it my special way," she said smiling as she sat down a slice of peach pie.

"Well, it was the best I ever had."

"I have something else that might be the best you ever had," she said just as she walked away towards another table without looking back.

When most of the other customers had left and Cliff was finished and about to go himself, Connie came out and stopped at his table. "Another cup of coffee, Mr. Brown?"

"Oh no, I couldn't hold another drop," he said and then added, "I really had better be going."

"Oh, please wait, I thought Carol had asked you. We want to talk to you" she paused, "Alone."

"Well, alright. Maybe I had better have one more cup of coffee," he said a little unsure of himself.

In another twenty minutes the sisters had closed and bolted

the front door, and they came together to where he sat. Connie was removing her apron while Carol touched the bun on her head.

"Mr. Brown," Carol started, "we would like to ask you a question."

'So it's back to Mr. Brown.' he thought. "Alright, shoot," he answered.

"Well, this may seem a little forward____," Carol started but Connie interrupted her, "Will you come live with us?" Connie blurted out.

"Both of you?" Cliff questioned.

"Oh, Connie, you have given him the wrong idea," Carol said. "We are not so desperate that we have to ask a man to be our lover Mr. Brown, we just have been having problems lately with some of our customers dropping by after they have spent a couple hours in one of the local drinking establishments and feeling frisky."

"Oh," Cliff responded.

"We have two bedrooms in our house and a nice sitting room where you could smoke if you wanted to," she said.

"See, Carol and I have been sleeping in the same bed ever since this has been going on anyway," Connie added.

"I see."

"There is one small matter though," Carol said.

"Yes?"

"It's the matter of money," she stumbled on. "We are business women and feel that there should be a charge of some sort."

"Yes, that's right," Connie agreed.

"I understand," he said "Just what do you have in mind?"

"Well, we have no barn, but there is a stable just down the way from our house, and you could keep your horse there," Carol said.

"Yes, Mr. Boeing's stables," Connie added.

"Well, Mr. Brown," again Carol paused, "Would a dollar be reasonable?"

He laughed to himself as he thought, *'I am paying Teachman that for a barn loft and much less desirable company.'*

But before he could reply, Connie added, "That would include your breakfast every morning, too."

"Ladies, you have just rented out your spare bedroom."

"Oh, wonderful!" Carol said excitedly, while Connie jumped up and down three times.

"There is one thing I must stipulate," Cliff said.

Connie stopped jumping.

"I will stay there while I'm in town, and you can let everyone you want know that they will meet my 44 should they come visiting when not invited, but I have to go to work, and I won't be there every night."

"I see," Connie said slowly.

"No mind," Carol said, "they will never know when you are there and when you are not. Can you move in tonight?"

"I'll see if I can get my horse in Boeing's Stable this late."

"Oh, you can," Connie said. "We already asked him."

Carol looked scornfully at her for saying that.

Cliff made sure Red was settled in, and then he went to check out his new home.

The little cottage sat back behind another larger house that he later found belonged to Luther Boeing. It was tastefully built with a glass window in the front and one on each side.

There was no front or back porch, wood being too valuable for fuel in these mountains, but he decided they weren't really needed. All the windows were open because of the summer heat, but South Pass had so little water, save Willow Creek and it flowed steadily. There were few to no mosquitoes. However, there were those big black flies everywhere.

Just as he was about to undress for bed, there was a knock on his door.

"Yes?"

"Are you decent?"

"Always," he replied.

"I meant____," Carol said as she leaned her head and shoulders inside from behind the door. He had removed his shirt, and his broad shoulders and large chest muscles caused her to catch her breath for a moment. Normally, he would have lifted his shirt to cover himself, not wanting anyone to think him vulgar, but there was something in the hungry look in her eyes that kept him from it.

"I know what you meant," he said. "You can come in."

"No. I mustn't, but there is one thing that I wanted to ask you, kind of a favor."

"Sure, if I can."

"Well, when I was much younger I loved to fish in this big lake back in Shelby County. If you would escort us to church in the morning perhaps you would accompany us fishing afterward. We never open *The Sisters'* on the Sabbath, so we could take a picnic basket and go down to the beaver pond on Willow Creek and try and catch some trout. If we do we'll cook them for supper afterward."

"Shelby County?'

"Shelby County, Missouri," she said.

"My, my isn't that a coincidence."

"Really? You know someone from home?"

"No, not home, just I recently met someone else from Missouri."

"Oh, I see. Well what do you say?" she waited.

"Church is a little out of my line these days, and besides, I have already made arrangements to go someplace tomorrow," he paused not wanting to lie to her, but not wanting to tell her who he was planning on spending the day with either. "I promised a man the day I got in this country I would do something for him, and I am going to work on that promise tomorrow."

"Oh, I see, I am sorry for interfering. I should have thought____,"

He stopped her. "Carol, would next Sunday be all right? I'll make sure I have the day open just for you."

She smiled and then added, "Connie, too."

"Oh, too bad," he said which caused her to smile again before closing the door.

He removed his trousers, but not his long underwear before going to bed. Normally in the summer when inside he would have slept naked, but considering his landlords, he thought better of it.

Sometime after eleven, he heard a banging on the front door followed by the laughing and cursing of two men obviously roostered.

"Come on, Girls, let us in, we just want to talk a little while."

Cliff quietly slipped on his tall brown boots and reached for his revolver. Stepping out his window he slipped around to the front of the house. There he saw two miners that had been in the diner earlier in the day. He was sure they had so much to drink that neither could have accomplished what they came for, had the girls let them in.

'These are the perfect pair with which to accomplish my new job,' he thought as he was stepping around the corner.

Cliff slapped the nearest one on the side of the head with his Colt and then fired a shot in the face of the other. He made sure nothing but the burning powder hit him, but the noise of 26 grains of pistol powder exploding suddenly so close, and the muzzle flash combined with the powder burns scared the man straight. Almost immediately, Cliff knew his actions had done the trick as he began to smell the obvious fact that the man's bowels had failed him from fright.

"Now, get your friend, and get away from here. If I ever hear of you bothering my sisters again I'll not miss the next time," he shouted as he shoved the long barrel into the end of the man's nose causing one of his nostrils to be pushed up and become distorted in the moonlight.

"Oh, my God, Sur, we didn't mean no harm, we wus just wanting to talk to your sisters ____, ah, we didn't even know they wus ____ ah ____ is your sisters."

"Well, you know it now! Now git!" he said again applying more pressure on his revolver until blood began to run from the man's nose.

"Yas, Sur____we's going. Come on, Butch," he pleaded, helping the other man to his feet.

"What happened, Arkansas?"

"Nothing, Butch. We just made a big mistake that's all."

"And you can tell your compadres should they come bothering my sisters I won't be so friendly next time," Cliff said as the two half-ran and half-staggered away.

**A 44 Henry Rim Fire Round**

Cliff could hear giggling from behind the front door, and he knew the sisters had been there listening. He knocked gently on the door, and immediately they opened it and both jumped on him and began hugging him joyfully.

The thin cotton gowns they were wearing did little to keep the feel of their body parts from him, and he suddenly felt a stirring in his loins. Never before had he felt four firm breasts rubbing on his chest at the same time. He also felt one of their legs bump into his manhood through his long johns and then suddenly move away only to return a second or two later. Now he was really feeling a stirring. All the time both were laughing and giggling and thanking him for his performance.

Finally he said, "Girls, we had better close the door before we scare poor Mrs. Boeing."

At that point he saw Connie put her hand over her face in embarrassment, and one of them pushed the door closed behind them.

As quickly as he could, he got back into his room where for the next thirty minutes he could faintly hear giggling coming from the other bedroom.

He wasn't sure how long after, but sometime later, the faint sound of one of them using the pee pot crept into his ears, and then just as he was slipping off to sleep, his door opened.

There was just a sliver of moonlight coming in the window, and he watched her as she carefully moved over to his bed. Standing there for a moment she looked down at him then pulled the gown over her head. Dropping the cloth to the wood floor, she again stood there for a few seconds as he looked at the soft glow bathe her naked body, and then she slipped in beside him.

"I just couldn't resist after feeling you against my leg. It's been so long," was all she whispered.

He got in perhaps two hours sleep before he awoke at his usual five A.M. She had left him exhausted, and he could have made an exception of always being up before the sun this morning, but this was one morning that he could not let that happen.

He was tying Red to the hitching post as Klu was putting out the oil lamps in front of the saloon.

"We're closed," he said. "Come back tomorrow, after ten."

"Came to see Miss Tipper," Cliff said

"Come back tomorrow," the barkeep repeated.

"Just tell her I'm here."

"I don't like repeating myself," Klu said placing his hands on his hips.

Cliff looked at the man and decided that he could whip him, but it would not be worth it, and besides, he was too tired, so he just pulled his Colt and stuck it deep into Klu's waist. The man groaned loudly.

"I think you should tell her I'm here," Cliff said with a very determined look on his face.

"Alright, Mister, just take it easy with that shooter," Klu said turning and opening the door of the saloon. Just as he did she stepped out all decked out in a riding skirt and matching Gipson blouse.

"I'm ready, Reb," she said.

"And you look great," he replied, and then turning towards the barkeep, he added, "Don't she look great?"

Klu just nodded his head as he watched this man holstering his gun.

"I didn't know if you wanted a buggy or____?"

"No," she said. "I like to ride. I have a horse at Ernie's stable."

As she stepped from the boardwalk onto the dusty street she said, "I was planning on coming down and meeting you there, but I got tied up and couldn't get away as early as I wanted."

"It's better that you didn't."

"Oh?"

"I'll tell you about it later," he said taking her arm with one hand and leading Red with the other.

"Which one is yours?" he asked as they approached the barn.

"The little black and white paint," she replied. "I call her Treasure. My saddle and bridle should be in her stall."

Leading her pony out of the barn, he saw Teachman step from his backdoor.

"Brown, you have not paid me yet," he said with an obvious twinge of jealousy in his voice as he watched Cliff help her mount.

Without looking at him, Cliff walked around and mounted Red and then said, "I'll be back later and settle up with you," as they rode off.

Heading south on the stage road he couldn't help but smile as they passed The Sister's restaurant.

"Do you have someplace in mind?" she asked.

"I would like to go down to where this road meets the Oregon Trail, if it's alright with you."

"Sure, it's a long ride, but I'm game, if you want."

Arriving there over an hour later, he looked around but saw no sign of a mine.

Finally, she spoke. "If you were to tell me what you're looking for, I might be able to help."

"Well, you remember I told you I met Rob Scogins on the trail coming here?"

"Yeah," she said nodding her head, "I do."

"Well, he told me to watch over his diggings while he was gone and I was told it was near here."

"It was, a year ago, but he has been digging up near Hamilton somewhere lately," she said.

Nodding his head, "Near 'The Monia'?"

"Could be, I'm not sure. He just said something about Hamilton one night after we___ah ___."

"That's kind a' what I thought," he said. "Well, it's too late to go there today."

"Yes it is, but I'll show you a nice place to rest the horses not too far from here," she added, turning Treasure's head southward.

"That's the wrong way."

"Not to where I'm headed," she replied heeling her filly, which started off in a trot. Cliff followed and caught up with her soon.

The land here was quite rolling with many low hills and little shallow cuts. If one were to look at it from afar they would think it was flat, for surely in the over all perspective it was, but not up close. Up close, you could hide an army behind a hill and another could pass it right by. It was up one of those little hills she was headed, and when they topped it, he saw a wide spot in the Sweetwater River where there was a little island in the middle. Both banks were clothed in towering cottonwoods, and it seemed to be a small bit of paradise from where he sat gazing.

"Come on," she said giving Treasure a little free rein so the pony would head for the water.

No sooner than they had reached the green grassy banks than she was on the ground pulling at her boots. "Come on, help me."

Cliff walked around and bent over holding to her boot heel as she placed a foot on his backside and pushed. When she was free of them she immediately removed her skirt and blouse and jumped into the waist deep water wearing only her white camisole and knee length knickers. She swam around splashing water at him. "Come on in. The water is wonderfully cold."

"That's what I'm afraid of."

He too pealed to his long john pants and dove in beside her.

Her thin cotton under things, now wet, were darker than her snow white skin, but hid none of the near perfect body they held captive. Her breasts were beautiful and large, her darker areolas contrasted sharply with her pure white skin. He could not help but notice her dark triangle was visible and also added to the contrast.

For a few moments he thought he might poke two women the same day, but he never really grew hard, and he contributed it to the work-over Carol had given him earlier, rather than the temperature of the water.

After a while she tired of her play. crawled up on the bank and lay down in the soft grass. He followed her.

She laid there with her head cradled in the junction of his arm and shoulder and expected him to make an advance at her, but when he didn't, she suspected it was because she was a whore, and he didn't want to lower himself to that level. Tears formed in her eyes, but she fought them back so he would not see her weakness and finally she went to sleep, he soon also gave into to his fatigue and joined her, both having had a long busy night.

It was some time after noon when he awoke. Red had made some noise and he came up with a start. She jumped too when he did. "What is it?"

"I'm not sure," he said reaching for his carbine before adding, "Get dressed quietly."

He grabbed her horse's bridle and moved her back into the trees, then returned for Red who was now staring strongly up river. Looking at his point, Cliff spotted several riders approaching.

"Grab my clothes and come on quickly," he said to her as he pulled Red around and raced after Treasure.

"What is it?" she asked, as she was reaching for his gray pants and buckskin shirt.

"Indians."

"Oh God!" she gasp, and then followed with, "How many?"

"Not sure. Five I think, mee'be more."

"Oh, shit!" was what she said this time as she sat down and began pulling on her riding boots.

Cliff hurriedly slipped into his duds and then with rifle in hand kept close to Red's head.

"Maybe we should make a run for it," she suggested.

"No good. Their ponies will out run us, and besides there may be more over the hill that we don't know about."

"Oh shit!" she said again, obviously frightened.

Then just as they came into her view she whispered to him,

"Don't let them take me, Georgia."

"Don't worry."

"Don't worry, sure."

He held up his first and last finger to his mouth signing for her to keep quite and then he placed his left hand over Treasure's nose.

Looking up, she relieved him of that chore so he could have both hands free for the Winchester.

**A Winchester Model 1866 Saddle Ring Carbine**
**'The Yellowboy'**

# Chapter Three
# The Sky People

The Sky People[4] rode slowly into the little clearing where only a minute before, the couple was peacefully sleeping. They were talking to each other, and it appeared there might be a little argument taking place between them. The last in line, who was leading a riderless horse and was just far enough behind not to be part of the argument, reined up, suddenly looking at the bent over grass where the two had laid moments before. Cliff took careful aim at his face and slowly tightened his grip on the carbine. At the same time, he felt her free hand touching his stomach, and then the weight of the Colt was gone from his cross-draw holster.

The Indian's eyes never really focused on them, but he was looking straight into the barrel when the bright flash burst into view.

The other three, whose horses were suddenly jumping about, turned as best they could, trying to see where the shot had come from. One of the horses jumped into the river, and Cliff lost sight of its rider as he swung the barrel around and on to another's back. His firing, re-aiming, and third shot was almost as if his weapon had been automatically reloaded and fired. Both braves screamed in unison and fell from their mounts, but Cliff could not see the one who had ended up in the water.

"Did you get them all?" she asked.

He only shook his head and again held his fingers to his mouth for her to keep quiet.

---

[4] 'The Sky People' is the name the Arapaho call themselves.

It could not have been more than two minutes, but to them it seemed like two hours. Finally, she whispered, "I think he's gone."

That was all the warrior needed to pinpoint their location, and immediately he began his stealth movements.

Cliff had just taken a deep breath and let it out when he saw the flash of the man's shoulder. In the next instant his carbine was knocked from his grip by a stone club, and suddenly his hands were filled with 180 pounds of Arapahoe.

The Indian was obviously more experienced at wrestling than Cliff and soon began to get the upper hand. He knocked the white man off his feet with a body blow, and then he was on Cliff's back holding his head down in the grass with one hand while the other was trying to reach the club that he had dropped only a few feet away.

She had pulled the trigger several times before she realized the reason it was not firing was because she had not cocked it.

The dark-skinned man heard the distinctive sound of the sear sliding off the hammer notches as she finally cocked the big revolver, and he turned his head and was looking at her when she pulled the trigger. The 200-grain lead bullet struck him in the neck, and he was knocked off Cliff. With blood pouring from his wound he knew he had only seconds to live, and he used that time to grab the stone club and pull it back for a last fling at the woman that had caused his death.

Cliff, seeing this, plunged his short Bowie into the man's right arm just above the elbow causing his aim to be off. The club passed a yard to the right of her head with such a velocity, she knew had it hit her, she would have been dead.

She cocked the Colt and again shot the man, hitting him full in the chest this time, but he never felt it. She then dropped the big gun and simply fainted.

Cliff gathered his strength, retrieved his knife, then his rifle and finally looked at her, not realizing she had fallen.

"Nadine!" he yelled and jumped to her looking for a wound. Seeing none, he, too, collapsed with her in his lap.

In seconds she opened her eyes and looked up at him. "Did we get them all now?"

"Yes, I think so," he managed to get out.

Soon, gathering energy, he was up and moving about checking

the dead men. His first shot had hit the Indian just below the left eye and had taken off the back of his head. His second struck that man just under the left armpit, aft of his shoulder. It never came out. The third man was also hit in the body below the shoulder blade. Cliff was surprised as he remembered his sight picture had been behind his left ear when he pulled the trigger.

'His horse must have reared,' Cliff thought, never once entertaining the idea that he might have jerked the rifle when he pulled the trigger.

This one moaned at that moment, and opened his eyes. Cliff bent over and slit his throat immediately, and within seconds, the Indian's eyes rolled back, and he stared at the blue sky above.

"This is a bad piece of luck, running into this little bunch," he said to her.

"I think we are damn lucky," she contradicted.

"Well, we are damn lucky there were no more, but what are we going to do with them?"

"Leave them, and let's get the hell out a' here."

"Can't do that," he said looking about. "This looks too much like an ambush."

"Who cares, nobody is going to blame us for defending ourselves from a bunch of Indians."

"Their families might," he replied.

"Gee, I never thought of that."

"This is the kind of stuff wars get started over," he added.

"Then what are we going to do?" she asked again then added, "Why don't we bury them?"

"They'd find them. If they come looking for them, they will trail them right here and read this as an ambush."

"Well, I ain't going to carry them back to their loved ones."

The horse that had fallen into the river with his rider was gone, but the other four were still standing close by.

Finally, Cliff took each of the bodies and loosely tied them astride a horse. While doing this, he found on one horse a pommel bag, and in it were two good sized sacks of gold.

"Look here!" he said to her, showing her the dust.

"What would Indians do with gold dust?" she asked.

"I don't know," Cliff replied, thinking hard. "They might have stolen this horse and discarded the saddle, but found use for the pommel bags and kept them." Checking further, he found it had been shod and recently had the shoes removed, the nail holes were still clear in the hoofs. '*This one recently belonged to a white man,*' he surmised.

Cliff lead the four animals and their dead riders up over the little rise and set them on the run, hoping that each rider would fall somewhere separately and away from all signs of shod hoof prints. Then quickly they mounted and started back.

"Stay in the river. It can't be too far back to the stage road, we will leave less sign this way," he told her.

It was well past three o'clock when they rode back into South Pass City. "I wouldn't say anything about this to anyone. If there is Indian trouble, I would hate to try explaining how we started it."

She nodded her head in agreement.

Stopping at the saloon, she dismounted. "Will you put Treasure away for me," she asked. "I'm bushed, and I need a drink."

"Sure," he said and smiled.

She walked up to the front door and knocked. He waited until the door opened then pulled on the reins, but she turned and spoke before he moved. "I can say with much truth, going out with you, Reb, is a hell of a picnic."

Charlotte, the girl who had opened the door for her, quickly looked out to see who she had said that to. "Hell of a man to get a whore to say something like that about him," she said to Tipper as Cliff rode off.

"Yes, you're right. One hell of a man."

"Whew," Charlotte said, blowing air across her upper teeth in admiration. "I ain't never poked a man I liked. Not that much anyway," she added.

"I never have either," Nadine replied as she walked to the bar.

Cliff had taken Treasure back to Teachman's barn, there unsaddled her and fed her a large pail of grain. He was walking out when the man came out his backdoor.

"Alright, Brown," he said, "it's time you settled up. You said you would only be here for two days and you already have been here three and have paid nothing. You owe me six dollars and seventy-five cents for the rent and grain and another six dollars for the tools you had me set aside fur you."

"No, you have figured it wrong, Teachman," Cliff said dropping several coins into his out stretched hand. I owe you four dollars and fifty cents for the rent and grain. I only stayed here two nights,"

Cliff said back bumping the thin man with his wide shoulder as he walked passed him into the store to pick up his tools.

"Don't start that," Teachman said following him in. "I saw you leaving the barn this morning."

Cliff saw that Teachman's shouting had caused his wife to crack open the door that led to their residence, where she could now see and hear what was going on. Smiling to himself at such an opportunity, he said, "No, Teachman, what you saw was me getting Miss Tipper's horse for her, and what I saw was the jealously all over your face because she was going riding with me."

Teachman immediately turned and looked around to see if anyone else was in the store, then he said through gritted teeth, "I told you not to mention her name here."

"What's the matter, Teachman, you afraid the Mrs. will find out that you are keeping a woman over at 'The South Pass Saloon?"

"I'm not keeping her, I just, well; it's none of your business. Now skedaddle out of here."

"You got it," Cliff replied with a satisfied smile across his face as he walked out the backdoor.

Leaving his newly acquired tools in Boeing's corral with Red, he headed towards the little cottage.

The girls were in the sitting room and both looked up with surprise when he opened the door.

"Oh," Connie said with her hand up to her mouth, "I, I, it's you."

"Yes," he replied realizing that he had not announced his coming and had obviously startled them.

"It's just we are still new at having someone live with us," she answered.

Carol turned her face away from him not wanting to make eye contact, a gesture that did not go unnoticed by him.

"Well ladies, how was church?"

"To be truthful, Mr. Brown," again Connie spoke, "after all the excitement last night we both slept in." She paused and then added, "Especially Carol. I just couldn't get her to wake up." With that statement, her sister quickly left the room.

"Wonder what's the matter with her?" Connie said. "It's not like Carol to be the shy one."

"Mee'be she just enjoyed herself too much last night," he replied then added, "Watching those two gents trying to high tail it out of here."

"I don't know," her sister replied doubting the thought, then added, "But we went fishing anyway and caught a bunch, some trout, four big ol' ones, too. We had a great time. Too bad you missed out."

"Yes, fishing is fun at times," he agreed.

"Well, you will just have to wait on your fish until tomorrow or Tuesday and eat them at the restaurant."

"Alright, if you say so."

"I do. Carol said she was just too tired to cook tonight."

"My tough luck, I guess."

"Yes, it is," Connie said, and then she turned and also went into their bedroom.

Cliff then went to his room to get some much needed sleep of his own, but within an hour there was a knock on his door and then quickly afterwards came a head and shoulders. A much-changed Carol looked in at him disappointed to find he had lain down in his Levi's.

"Yes?" he asked of the beautiful intruder.

"Ah, we thought we might go over to 'The Hitching Post' for supper. Kind a' see what the competition is doing. Want to come along?"

He started to decline, but then realizing his stomach was in greater need than his rest at the moment, swinging his legs off the bed, he replied, "Sure."

"Good. Then we'll go," she answered giving the impression they would not have gone had he not come with them.

The looks of the other men they encountered pleasured him while he walked down Dakota Street with a lady at each side. "Tell me, what do you ladies do about food on Sundays normally?"

"Well, except when there is a dinner on the ground at church, we fast," Carol explained.

"Fast?" he questioned.

"Yes, fast," she confirmed.

"It helps us keep our girlish figures," Connie said then added, "and it's good for the soul."

'The Hitching Post' was located on South Pass Avenue at the intersection with C Street. It was a large place for the west, a one-story building with a low roof. There were ten tables and a long counter. *'That would have made a wonderful bar,'* he thought, *'In fact this place would make a wonderful saloon.'*

One could see through a large open window behind the counter that there was another room used for the kitchen, where at least two Chinese Cooks were working.

Most of the tables were full with three or four men sitting at each. Several of them were ones he recognized as having been in 'The Sisters'. They didn't fail to notice the trio's entrance, either. There was some murmuring as they passed, and he overheard someone whisper, "He's their brother; Bennie told me he's staying with them for a while."

Finally, after locating a table near the kitchen, Cliff held the chair for each lady to sit down, thereby making sure they left him the one that faced the room. After some time had passed and no one had approached them, Cliff noticed the procedure was for the cooks to place plates through the window, and then a small man would set them on the counter. If you wanted one you just went up there and got it. Excusing himself he went and got three.

"Well, we sure have better service than this," Connie said.

"Better food, too," Cliff added as he bit into a very tough piece of venison.

A few minutes later, one of the men that he had seen often in *The Sisters'* walked by and tipping his hat, spoke, "Good day, Miss Steele," he said looking at Connie. "Miss Steele," he repeated looking at Carol again touching his dirty old floppy hat, then with a smile still on his face, but without the hat salute he added, "Mr. Steele." They each nodded a return recognition fighting back the urge to laugh out loud.

The next day the same man was in their place apologizing for having been over at 'The Hitching Post'. "There's no need to apologize, Mr. Samuel," Carol replied, "We are not open on Sundays. A man must have his vitamins to work."

"Thank you kindly," he said back, and when she had moved away, he asked his companion, "Did you et any of them viadamonds over to 'The Hitching Post' yesterdee, Smithy?"

"Can't say that I did. Don't rightly remember 'em serving none yesterdee."

Just before noon, a wagon came up Price Street from the south with the driver yelling and causing quite a stir. "Indians! Indians!" he shouted. "Indians done kilt poor ol' Kirt Puckett."

Cliff was just leaving the South Pass Saloon when he heard the commotion. Several men had run out into the street and stopped the wagon. "What's happened?" someone asked the teamster.

"I just found him east of the stage road, on the trail about three miles. His horse was gone, and everything. Just him laying there with all them arrows in 'im."

Cliff walked over thinking the war he sparked had finally begun. It was then someone said, "He's been dead a day or two. God, he stinks."

"He do, he sure do," Jack Bean, the teamster, agreed.

There were two arrows in his chest and two more in each leg. Cliff guessed that there had been more in his back, as these looked as if they had been shot in him after he was lying down near death. There was very little bloodstain around each hole, and since an arrow kills by bleeding, this man had already been on his deathbed when he ended up on his back.

"They's cut up his arms and butchered his back," the teamster shouted for all to hear.

"Why'd 'dey have to go and do dat?" another questioned.

"To get the sinews fur their bow strings, back sinews make good bow strings," answered a man dressed in buckskin with a lot of fringe.

"I wonder where Kirt's horse and tools is?" someone commented in a matter of fact sort of way.

"And his dust, he surely had dust on him or he wouldn't a' been a coming to town," another suggested.

Cliff turned and walked towards the boardwalk where several people had come out from the Saloon to see what was going on, among them was Miss Tipper. Taking her by the elbow, he turned her around and started back inside. "You don't want to see that awful sight, Purty Thing. Let me buy you a beer."

Looking surprised at him, but not questioning, she replied, "Alright, cowboy."

Inside they were alone, and he quickly led her back away from the front door before saying anything.

"You remember that last Indian was leading a horse yesterday?" he asked her and continued before she could answer. "And I showed you where it had had shoes recently?"

She nodded her head slowly.

"Well, that gent they just brought in, must a' been killed by them bastards," he said to her. "And I'd bet not long before. He ain't been dead more than a day. Not in this sun, he ain't."

"Should we tell anyone we killed them, that done him in?"

"No, don't say anything about our fight to anybody," he again told her.

She nodded her head at him.

He stood there a minute and then asked, "Did you know him?"

"I don't even know who it is."

"Some miner named Kirt or something like that."

"No, I don't think so," she replied.

"Well, it's bound to be the talk of the town tonight. Try to find out if he's got family and anything else you can about him."

"Sure, but why?"

"Just do it, for me. I want to know."

Suddenly she remembered something. "You know you're right about him. I remember seeing something long and gray on one of the Indian's horses," she said. "Now I know what it was, a scalp!"

"I don't remember seeing that, but this fellow did lose his hair."

"Yes, I'm sure. It was tied to the lead on the first horse."

"The one that got away," he added.

People started coming back in, and even though no one noticed them, he spoke softly to her "Don't forget, find out as much as you can," and then he moved away.

Almost nothing was spoken that night that did not have something to do with Kirt Puckett.

By the time Cliff was having supper at 'The Sisters', the conversation there was of the Indian uprising. "We got to get some army here," one of the men said loudly.

"Hell, they's clear to old Fort Bridger," his friend answered. "You won't see them out this far. Not fur one dead miner. I sure do wish they'd build 'dat fort here lik' they said da' would." On and on the talk of the Indians continued until closing time.

Cliff was glad to be in his room and in bed, so he didn't have to hear anymore about it.

Just before he went to sleep, there was a knock on his door. "Yes?" he said pulling the cotton sheet over himself. Both girls looked in and asked almost in unison. "Do you think the Indians will come into town?"

"Not tonight," he assured them.

Cliff was up a little before dawn, as was his usual practice. Surprisingly, he found the girls were already up and dressed when he came out of his room.

"Good morning," Carol said to him with a warm smile.

"Morning," he replied back thinking, *'She seems to have lost the embarrassment she had yesterday.'*

"Oh good morning, Mr. Brown," Connie said as she came out from their bedroom. *'She always seems to have half again as much energy as her sister,'* he thought as she moved quickly about doing first one small chore then another.

"Girls," he stopped them, "if we are to make anyone, other than a couple a' drunks, believe we are family, you must stop calling me Mr. Brown. Especially, since everyone knows you as the Steele Sisters."

"Oh," Connie said. "I never thought of that."

"We could say, if anyone asked, that our mother was married to a Mr. Brown, who died, and then to Daddy, a Mr. Steele," Carol suggested.

"Oh, that's brilliant, Carol," her little sister said. "Don't you agree Mr. Brown?"

"It's the Mr. Brown that will cause them to not believe you," he said again.

"Oh, yes. I must stop that."

"But we only know you as Reb Brown," Carol injected, "Calling you a name that you obviously took on in the last eight or so years will also raise suspicion. Will it not?"

*'I don't like too many people knowing me as Cliff Brown. There are Murder warrants out for a Cliff Brown from Georgia,'* he thought before he replied, "I been known as Reb since I was knee high to a grasshopper. So please just call me Reb unless you are cornered on it. Which I doubt will happen. It's just an old nickname and I've had it a long time."

"Why don't you want people to know your real name?" Connie asked.

"A man's past is his own business," Carol said to her sister.

"Oh!" Connie said realizing that she might be asking something she should not. "Alright, Reb," then she said, "I'll just say you are very proud of the service you gave to your state."

"You would not be lying," Cliff said back to her.

His first duty every morning, was to take Red out for a short ride to keep him exercised and his bowels working properly. The eight o'clock hour that morning, found them atop a steep hill over looking Atlantic City.

**Atlantic City Wyoming**

It, too, was a boomtown that had been brought to birth by the finding of gold in these hills, but it was perhaps half as large as South Pass City. He had been told it only had seven saloons.

He watched a light-colored coyote run after a jack for two minutes before the rabbit got away, and then just as he started to turn Red's head away, a cow moose stepped from the thick growth of alder and walked casually past the outskirts of town and up the slope into an aspen thicket not far from where he sat. *Very brave of her,* he thought.

Returning to South Pass City he was anxious to hear what Nadine had learned, but it was both too late and too early to do that. He was surprised to see Ernie Teachman coming out of a small house and walking towards his store so early.

"Morning," he said not looking at Teachman as he rode past.

"You son-of-a-bitch," Teachman yelled at him, "you stole my rifle."

Cliff didn't even look back nor would anyone have guessed he even had heard the man's shout, that is unless they were close enough to see the devilish smile slip across Cliff's face. "I might poke your wife, too, before I leave town, 'conscription dodger'," he said just above a whisper with only Red close enough to hear.

His breakfast at *The Sisters'* was good, as always, but he noticed the other men had taken on a new look at him. In reality, he realized that now they simply were looking at him, all knowing him as the ladies' brother. Before, no one had really paid him any mind.

He was pleased when, during a lull, Carol came over and sat down with him. He enjoyed her company. She seemed warm and friendly, and he ingested her good looks as she talked. "It seems there is trouble in paradise," she said.

He could sense she had gossip she wanted to tell, so he replied, "Oh?"

"Yes, Mr. Coones said this morning that Marlene Teachman kicked her husband out."

"Really, I wonder why?"

"Well, I understand it was over some scarlet woman he's been keeping company with."

"Really?"

"Yes, it's true. He is now sleeping in the little house where we used to stay."

"It'll happen every time," Cliff replied not giving the slightest hint that he had any knowledge of what she was talking about. "Just can't trust those Scarlet Women."

"Amen to that," she agreed, causing him to chuckle under his breath.

After finishing his breakfast, he left and started back towards the center of town. *I'm not usually the vindictive type, but there was just something about that draft dodger that brings out a mean streak that lives deep within the Brown clan.* He knew better than to go there, but still he let his direction point straight towards Teachman's Store.

The front door was open, and everyone within fifty yards could hear her, "Go tell it to your hussy or go tell it to your horse or go tell it on the mountain, but just go, or so help me, I'll put a ball through your miserable skinny frame, as sure as I am a Yates."

"You ain't a Yates, no more. You're a Teachman."

"Not fur long, or if I am I'll be known as the widow Teachman."

Ernie stepped out onto the boardwalk and shouted back. "You don't know nothing about running a dry goods store. You'll have us broke inside a month."

"Get," she screamed as Cliff stepped in where Ernie had just left. Teachman seeing this, yelled at him, "I thought I told you to stay away from here."

"Came to see if Mrs. Teachman, or is it Miss Yates? Well I came to do some business with the proprietor," he said to Ernie, as she lowered the old Springfield musket.

"Yes," she said, "I am the proprietor of this establishment. What may I show you, sir?"

"Well, I'm a little low on cartridges," he answered. "Would you happen to have a box of .44 Henry?"

Though faint as it was, both could hear the word, "Shit!" come from outside.

"I don't know, sir, but I will be pleased to look."

"Thank you, Madam. I think they may be over here," he said pointing toward the small beige box with green writing on it.

"Oh, yes, you are right Mister ___?" she said smiling at him.

"Brown, Reb Brown," he replied.

"Well, Mr. Brown, it's nice to finally meet you. Is there anything else I might have that you are interested in?" she asked back, loud enough for someone outside to hear. Her effort, however was in vain, Ernie had already headed for 'The South Pass Saloon'.

"As a matter of fact," Cliff replied. "You aren't a seamstress by any chance?"

"I did do some of that for the war effort, before I made the mistake of marrying."

"Great, I saw this shirt over to Cheyenne last summer and admired it aplenty," he said. "Been sore at myself ever since for not getting it when I had the chance."

"Can you describe it, Mr. Brown?"

"I think so, you wouldn't happen to have a lead pencil and paper would you?"

"Somewhere, sure. Please excuse me a moment while I find where that no good dropped it last."

Cliff didn't really need a new shirt, but it seemed like a good excuse to come in the store, and he wanted to make Teachman think he had a relationship going with his wife. In fact, looking at her as she zipped about the room caused him to enjoy the thought.

She was perhaps five years older than he, but she had taken good care of herself. She was tall for a woman, perhaps five foot eight inches, he guessed, and one could not look at her without having his attention jerked to her hair. It was the color of a flaxen mane on a fine palomino horse, and it showed no signs of gray. Carol and Connie were also blondes, but a totally different color. Mrs. Teachman's hair was much lighter and seemed to shine when the light struck it just right. Her waist was small, and her face, although not pretty, was pleasant to look at. Her nose was somewhat wrong. Not too large or too thin. It was not too short or too flat. It certainly was not crooked. In fact, were one to judge it in and of itself, the conclusion certainly would be that it was a perfect nose, but it was a nose that belonged on a different face. This however, once the critic had examined it and made a conclusion, was simply accepted and did not distract from her otherwise good looks. It was impossible to get a good judgment of her true figure, in the 'proper dress' that she wore, but there was no cavity in the bosom area, and her hips seemed to be full, before being lost in the skirt. *I wonder how long it's been since she had her toes curled?* he thought, then finished it, *If she ever has?*

When she returned with a pencil and a piece of brown wrapping paper, she asked, "See if you can draw it for me on this."

Cliff suddenly realized that he had no particular shirt in mind and really didn't know where to start. His mind began racing around trying to remember a shirt of a different design. Finally he began to draw a pull over with a split in the front. He added lacing to the split and then a collar. "I, I would like a collar so I can turn it up in the back to keep the summer sun from burning my neck, and this here loose front, where I can open it or not, depending on the heat."

She looked at his work and smiled at the simple drawing. "I think I will be able to take care of your needs, Mr. Brown. Do you have a preference as to the material?"

"Oh, no, not particularly. Something light-colored for summer. Mee'be some stripes," he said spying a roll of such fabric on a far counter.

"I think I have just what you are looking for," she said. Bringing it out, she unrolled a yard or so and held it across her chest. "Something like this?"

"Yes, that's it exactly," he said smiling. "When can I pick it up?"

"Oh, it will only take me a couple days to make it, but I'm afraid I'm completely out of any material to make a decent collar. I'll order some from Granger," she said. "I'll get right on it as soon as it comes in. I have so much to do here, now that that beast is gone, but I'll squeeze you in, Mr. Brown. It will be fun to do some creative sewing again."

"That will be fine," he answered tipping his hat before he turned to leave.

"Mr. Brown."

"Please, call me Reb," he said.

"Well, I'm not sure, I, I really think Mr. Brown is best."

"Alright," he replied then waited.

Finally she realized she had stopped him, "Oh, your box of cartridges."

He let out a short laugh. "Mrs. Teachman, you distracted me so, I plum forgot what I came in here for," he said, dropping two bits in her hand and taking the Henrys. Even in the darkness of the store he saw the redness cross her face. Not wanting to cause further embarrassment, he turned quickly and left.

High noon found him walking into Morris' Saloon. Nadine was standing next to the piano watching the new player work on *Sweet Betsy from Pike,* and she didn't see him come in. He walked up to the bar where Klu was wiping a shot glass. "You again."

"Now be nice or I'll tell Mrs. Morris what I have found out about you."

"Huh!" Klu replied suddenly, "What yaw' mean?"

"I'll have a beer," Cliff replied knowing he had found a soft spot in this tough old man.

"Here," Klu said placing a schooner on the counter, waiting, still expecting an answer.

Cliff ignored him, moving where he could watch her in the mirror as she worked with the pianist. '*She is the loveliest woman in this town,*' he thought as he relished her beauty.

Finally she looked up, and seeing him she said, "Wally, I think I'll take a break."

"Sure, Miss Tipper," he replied as he continued with the keys.

Cliff turned toward her as she approached, "Hello, Purty Thing," he said.

"Reb," she answered back. "Buy me a beer?"

"Klu, a beer for the lady," he said not looking at the barkeep.

When the mug was sat down in front of her, he reached for it and said, "Come on let's get a table."

She followed as he moved where their backs were to the wall and held out her chair.

"That's what I like about you, Reb. You never forget to be nice."

"I'm from Georgia, remember."

"I'll never forget."

Sitting down, he asked her, "What have you found out about Kirt Puckett?"

"Well, it seems he's been here for a long time. He had a claim near Hamilton somewhere. He panned Spring Gulch there rather than dig. No relatives that anybody knew of, at least not anybody that was in here last night. Pretty much a loner. Didn't seem to have any enemies."

Cliff digested what she said and nodded his head in approval.

"Why did you want to know?"

He reached down to his revolver belt and tugged on the string, pulling out a bag that had been hidden there. "Then this is yours," he said dropping it in her hand.

"What?"

"It's half of the dust we recovered on the Indian's horse."

"You are sharing it with me?" she asked unbelievingly.

"You earned it. Saved my hide when you shot that Buck off me."

"You are something else Georgia, this feels like near a thousand dollars," she said moving the bag up and down with her arm.

"That's about what I figured, mee'be a little more," he agreed. "Don't let no one see you with this. There's some that would slit your purty throat for a third a' it."

"Less, I would suspect," she agreed.

"I aim to go to Green River in a few days. If you want, I'll have it converted to paper notes for you."

"Yeah, that would be better. Do you think it wise going all that way with the Indian trouble?"

"I don't think there is much Indian trouble," he said. "Not really. That bunch we ran into weren't wearing no paint. My guess is, they wus just out hunting and happened onto Puckett, and they got into a scrap. Hell, Puckett might have shot at them first. I wouldn't doubt such from some a' the ones I've seen around here."

She nodded her agreement.

"And," he continued, "we just happened to be asleep in their path. Had that brave not seen where we had been lying they would have rode right on by," he paused and then added, "War party would not have been that lax."

"I see what you mean," she said. "You could exchange this here. J.W. Illif's Bank is always taking in gold."

"No, someone might wonder where I got it. Me not having a claim."

"Yes, you're right," she agreed then said, "Here take this with you and exchange it for me."

"Will do," he agreed.

"You want 'a come upstairs?" she asked. "Be my pleasure."

He shook his head. "Mee'be later. Got things I got 'a do now."

She concealed the hurt and replied. "Alright, then see you later. I got to get back to my practicing."

"Take care, Purty Thing," he said as he got up and headed out.

When she was walking back to the piano, Klu called to her. "Did he say anything about me?"

"Just said you were his favorite barkeep," she replied as she passed him by without looking his direction.

# Chapter Four
# The Hanging

Cliff returned to his room to hide the gold dust behind the little chest where he had stored the other bag. When satisfied of their concealment, he headed back into the little sitting room. It was there he heard a noise outside between the girls' house and that of the Boeing's. Looking out, he saw a man that he recognized to be one of the men he had seen with Chip Roper. The man was looking inside the rear window of the Boeing's house. Cliff had removed his gun belt when he had come in and was now unarmed. Slowly he slipped back into his room. There in one corner was the Henry and in the other was his Yellowboy. He looked at the Henry, but reached for the shorter carbine and then stepped out the window. Moving slowly around the house he could now see this man was not alone. A second, who he did not know, had brought a crate from around the side of the house where the Boeings had some wood stored in it. The first man used it to step on giving him easy access into the house.

"Hurry up, Concho," the man said into the window.

Cliff was lucky in that his attention was locked onto the goings on inside, and he never turned away from the dark window. When the round barrel touched his neck he wilted almost to the point of falling as his strength swept from him. Cliff relieved him of the Remington Army Model from his old cut-down union belt holster and then tapped it across his neck hard enough to drop him. He moaned, but not loud enough to be heard inside.

Cliff then turned the box right side up and stepped back. Pretty soon a leg came out of the window and then another.

"Yuel, hold zee box steady," he said as he slipped out belly down. Suddenly his right boot slipped off the topside and into the open box followed by his left boot.

"Ah chihuahua, chinggado!" Concho yelled as the box turned over spilling him on his backside. When he hit the ground he was looking up, and suddenly his mind was trying to decide just where the big barrel, which was pointed at his face, came from.

"Oh shiiit!" he said, followed by, "Señor', I can explain. You will ease off the hammer on that thing, no?"

"We'll let Mr. Boeing decide if you can explain," Cliff replied and then motioned for him to get up. When he had accomplished this, Cliff said, "Now drop that shooter in the dirt there, and pick up your friend."

Concho lifted the Colt Navy from its resting place. Then for a moment considered trying Cliff, but wisely thought better of it and dropped the revolver.

Luther Boeing, in addition to owning a stable also was the silent partner of one Ruby Barclay who ran, and everyone thought owned, 'The Grecian Bend Saloon'. But Luther spent most of his day sitting at the barbershop that was next door to his wife's business 'The Pass Dress Shop' on Dakota Street. It was there Cliff had seen him a few minutes before and to there he marched the two burglars. More than one man noticed the men being followed by *The Sisters'* brother who held a Winchester to their backs.

Entering the barbershop they found Boeing telling a story about his leadership in the Forty Second Ohio Volunteers.

"What's going on here?" Peacock, the barber demanded.

"Major Boeing, I just caught these jaspers breaking into your house."

"Breaking into my house?"

"Yeah, unless you told them to climb in your back window."

"We never did no such thing," Concho yelled back, "des' hombre, he ees loco en la cabeza."

"Open your shirt," Cliff said poking the barrel of his rifle into the man's stomach.

Concho hesitated, and Cliff reached over and ripped the old horn buttons away and the shirt sprang open revealing several pieces of jewelry that had been stuffed there, along with a gold watch.

"That watch is mine!" exclaimed Boeing. "He has been in my house."

"I told you that," Cliff said insulted for his having to prove what he had said was true.

There was quite a small crowd gathering in and outside the barbershop by now, and finally, Mrs. Boeing came to investigate.

"What's happened here, Luther?" she asked, pushing in past several men.

"Mr. Brown here caught these two breaking into our house. Look," he said to her, holding the loot.

"Oh my goodness! My jewels!" she exclaimed reaching for them and then she turned to Yuel and slapped him hard across the face almost knocking the man down.

"Where's the Sheriff?" Cliff asked.

"Went to Fort Bridger, about the Indian uprising," Boeing responded.

"Well, where is the jail then?"

"Up on Eddy Avenue, a stone one that's pretty old," Peacock answered. "Though there is talk of building a new stronger one."

"Well, what do we do with these two?"

"We can lock them in the jail, if we can trust that old door bolt."

Harley Snell added, "Put a padlock on the door, and I'll stay there to make sure they don't break out, fur five dollars."

"By God, I'll pay that," Boeing agreed.

"Now, this is no excuse to go using profanity, Luther," his wife scolded.

"Come on, you two," he ordered, ignoring her.

Just as they started with the men towards the jail, Phil Sholtz rode by and saw the commotion.

"What's going on here?" he asked one of the men standing across the street.

"Found them two breaking into some house, I think," the man replied, then looking at who he was talking to added, "Say, they's part of your Pa's outfit ain't they?"

"Used to be," Phil wisely said. "Pa fired them last week, caught 'um stealing."

"That figures," the man said back nodding his head.

By the time the supper hour arrived, the story of how their brother had caught the thieves was all over town, as well as all over 'The Sisters'.' When he came in, both Carol and Connie were all over him, demanding him to tell them all about it.

Cliff looked around at the other anxious faces and just couldn't talk about it. "I'll tell you when we get home," he said, and quickly added, "I forgot to get something."

He suddenly turned and left. Returning to the scene, he found where Concho had dropped the Colt, and he retrieved it and then took it into the house and into his room. Suddenly, he worried about the gold.

Robbing men for gold was not that uncommon out on the road. Sticking a blade in their ribs at night right here in town was not so uncommon an occurrence either, but entering a woman's home in broad daylight was new, even in a boomtown like South Pass City. *'I think I will go to Green River tomorrow.'*

Not wanting to talk about what he had done to strangers he stayed at the house and took a nap. An hour past full dark he heard the girls approaching. He had been out in the sitting room cleaning the dust from the Navy Colt, and he quickly gathered up the stuff and started for his bedroom, but he was not fast enough. He was still in the sitting room when the front door opened, and they saw him.

"Mr. Reb Brown, you just march yourself back in here, and tell us all about what happened," Carol ordered.

Turning slowly, he knew he had his foot in the jaws of a bear trap.

"Yes, Mr. Brown, and besides we brought you some supper since you cowardly took French leave on all of us earlier," Connie added sitting a cloth covered dish on the table. "Now you just sit right here, and eat this while you talk."

When he unfolded the towel there was a thick piece of sourdough with a nice slice of baked elk shoulder, and he had to admit it looked delicious.

"Gee, this is great. I just wish I had a cold beer to wash it down."

"Sorry, no beer," Connie apologized.

"No, no beer, but we do have a jar of peach brandy we keep for fevers and such," Carol offered reaching down into a small chest that they had a quilt lying over.

"Peach brandy, gosh I haven't had peach brandy since before the war," Cliff said.

"Now sit down here and eat, and tell us all about you catching those bandits," Connie demanded.

He told them what had happened, and when he finished Connie said, "Our hero!"

He also told them that he planned to go to Green River City the next day, and Carol asked if he would drive her in the wagon so she could pick up much needed supplies at nearby Granger. Reluctantly, he agreed.

An hour later the mason jar was nearly empty, and the three of them were quite tipsy.

"You know this stuff will slip up on you," he said when he got up to go ring out his rag and found his head spinning. "I think we had better call it a night or you girls will not be able to open up in the morning."

"Who cares?" Connie said and then giggled. When she looked at Carol, her sister also began giggling, and Cliff knew it was time for them to call it a night. As soon as he returned from out back he headed for his bedroom, but before he fell asleep he could hear one of the girls snoring loudly. '*Boy, that brandy was something else,*' he thought.

Very soon after, he heard his door open followed by the sound of a cloth garment falling to the floor.

He had drunk enough that he was glad she had come in, and from the sound of the snoring, he didn't try to keep it quiet.

An hour later Carol waved to him as she left the room, dragging her cotton nightshirt behind her.

The next morning he was awake at five, as always, but his head felt like it was going to explode. "Damn brandy," he complained aloud.

Normally, while he was getting dressed, he would hear the girls moving about too. Their alarm, the rooster two doors down was on time daily, and they had always been disciplined to jump up and get ready for the breakfast rush. Not so this morning. Finally, he knocked on their door. No response. He knocked again and a third time much louder. After that he heard stirring inside or groaning he wasn't sure which. Finally, ten minutes later Carol came out looking like she had been run over by a six-up team.

"Connie is sick," she said. "I can't go to Granger with you. I'll have to work the place by myself. Oh God! Give me strength not to throw up at the first sight of an egg."

"Come on, I'll help you," he reluctantly suggested.

An hour later there were nine men eating there as she carried out the food while he cooked it. Suddenly, a miner they knew simply as "Catfish" came rushing in yelling, "You fellows come quick, they done hung ol' Harley Snell."

"Who hung 'im?" someone asked.

"I guess it was Concho and Yuel or maybe somebody who come and helped bust them out."

"What happened?" Cliff asked.

"They's gone. Sure as shooting, both gone and Harley was a swinging there in front of the jail door. Abe Kelly saw him when he come to open up his Tin Shop."

"Just you wait 'til Sheriff Boyd gets back. He'll be a-trailing them with a posse, by golly," Catfish said.

Carol had followed him out from the back when she heard the shouting and now just stood there biting her bottom lip.

When the commotion settled down, she came up to Cliff. "Reb, will you go back home and check on Connie. I'm suddenly fearful for her."

"Sure. You think you can handle it here for a while?"

"Of course," she said bravely.

In his walk back to the little cottage he scolded himself for not spotting the dead man when they came out that morning. Of course he knew it was still dark, and it would have been very unlikely for either of them to have seen the lynched body, but still, they had passed so near it and he missed it, and that bothered him.

When he reached their home he could only get a response of moaning through the door, and finally he opened it. Connie was lying across the bed on her stomach with her head off the side. She had vomited everywhere, on the bed, on the floor, all over herself, and she now had the dry heaves. He couldn't say she was conscious, but she was not out either. Looking about he saw their bathtub and filled it with cold water and pulled her soaked gown over her head. Lifting her he carried her over to the tin tub and as gently as he could; set her down into the cold water.

"Ohhh-ohhhh," she screamed and then let her head fall forward.

Cliff took a towel from a small shelf and began washing her with it.

"Just let me die____just let me die!" she kept repeating.

Finally, having her as clean as he guessed he could get her, he returned to the bed and began stripping it down. He then wiped up the floor, as best as he could with the sheets.

When he returned behind the screen that hid the tub, she was laying with her head tilted all the way back. "Come on young lady you have to get back in the bed."

"No, I just want to stay here," she protested.

"Not a chance. I have to go back to help your sister, and if I leave you here you may drown."

"No, I won't. Just leave me."

"Come on," helping her to stand in the water.

"You are always helping my sister. You never help me," she complained.

"Come on now, you know that's not true."

"I know it is," she said as she collapsed in his arms and passed out.

He laid her down on the floor and dried her front side first and then turned her over and did her backside. Satisfied she would not catch pneumonia he picked her up and carried her back to the bed and there he laid her out. Finding a light blanket, he brought it over to cover her, but first he had to take just one lustful look at her nakedness. She was almost a copy of Carol only 7/8 scale. Her light bush of very fine hair was already dry, and he almost touched her there, but he controlled himself and covered her instead.

When he returned to the restaurant Carol looked worriedly at him. "Is everything all right? You were gone so long."

"She had thrown up everywhere. I had to clean it up."

"Oh, really," she replied not sure just what his clean up included.

"There was a man in here a little while ago looking for you," she said.

"Looking for me?"

"Yes, I think the sheriff wants to talk to you."

"What about?"

"I don't know, the hanging I guess."

South Pass City had been the County Seat of Carter County when all of this was part of the Dakota Territory. In 1868, Wyoming Territory was cut from Dakota, and South Pass City remained the county seat of what was now Sweetwater County, Wyoming. It was at this time Mrs. Esther Morris became the first woman judge in the nation, at the same time John Boyd had been appointed Sheriff by Governor Campbell himself. Boyd was not one to let things like a hanging, in town, of one of its citizen's fly by with the ever present wind. There would be no vigilante work here and no murders in town, either. After all, this was not Cheyenne.

When Cliff asked about the sheriff, he had been directed to

the judge's office which was in the rear of Morris' home. Entering through the backdoor he asked, "You wanted to talk to me, Sheriff?"

Sizing up the man who was standing beside the very properly dressed Judge Morris, he reasoned the Sheriff to be near six foot, only an inch or so shorter than Cliff himself and weighed perhaps one hundred sixty pounds. His face was shaven clean, save a long, hairy mustache, and he wore a flat top, large brimmed hat. His tan shirt was of the double-breasted style that Cliff had seen firemen wear back in St. Louis. Leather suspenders held up the dark-striped trousers that would obviously fall to his knees had he not buttoned them securely. *'Tall and lean, with a look of mean,'* Cliff surmised.

"Maybe, who are you?" Boyd shot back.

"Brown, Reb Brown," Cliff replied just as sternly.

"Reb Brown, eh? I don't recall wanting to see no Reb," he said. "You got another name?"

"Not in Wyoming Territory," Cliff replied just before he turned and started to walk away.

"Wait a minute," Boyd demanded. "I ain't through questioning you."

"You're through questioning me in that tone," Cliff said back.

"Tuff one, eh?"

"Oh come off it, Jack," the judge said. "He's just giving you back the same as you're giving him."

"Well, I got a right."

"Well, I got rights, too," Cliff shot back at the man, "and one of them is not being treated like some jasper on the Owl Hoot Trail."

"I ain't so sure you ain't, going by some name like Reb Brown."

"Jack!" she said.

"Alright," the sheriff replied taking a deep breath. "They tell me you wus the one what caught them two busting into the Boeings' store."

"No." Cliff said back.

"No! I heard it from three or four good men. Luther Boeing told me he'self. To hear him tell it you should be a wearing this here star."

"Now, I understand," remarked the judge.

"Well, you heard it all wrong," Cliff said and turned around as if he was leaving.

"Wait a minute, Mr. Brown," she said. "Suppose you tell us just what did happen."

"Sure, Ma'am. I'll be proud to do that. First off, let's get our facts straight. I caught them entering the rear window of Mrs. Boeing's bedroom, not the store." When he had finished telling his story in detail he stopped and just stood there.

Satisfied and with less of a bulldozing attitude, Sheriff Boyd responded, "That was a good report. Now, do you have any idea where these two hang out?"

"I never seen Yuel before, but the one they called Concho I did see riding into town with a man I understand is known as Chip Roper."

"Chip Roper! Why he's one of Mr. Sholtz' top hands. Mr. Sholtz is the biggest man in this part of the country."

"You asked me, and I told you. There be anything else you want to ask me?"

"Naw, I guess not, unless you want to ride on the posse?"

"I think I would just get under your skin, Sheriff."

"I have a question," the judge said.

"Ma'am."

"Are you dead sure you saw this man with Roper?"

"More than once."

"Thank you, Mr. Brown," she replied. "I appreciate you coming over and also for what you did yesterday."

"Ma'am," Cliff said back as he touched the brim of his Stetson. Then he turned to leave, but as he did Mr. Morris came in from their living quarters, and they bumped shoulders.

"Pardon," Cliff said just before he left.

"Who was that man?" he asked his wife.

"A Mr. Brown. He's the one who kept the town safe while the Sheriff was away."

"Now Esther, don't you start too," Jack said.

John Morris looked in the direction Cliff had left and shook his head a couple times.

"What's wrong, John?" she asked.

"I know that man from somewhere. I just can't remember where."

"He ain't been here mor'n a couple weeks. I done found that out," Jack added.

"No, this was long ago."

"Maybe back in Peru," she suggested.

"Yeah, maybe," he said still trying to remember.

When Cliff returned to 'The Sisters', Carol had finished with the breakfast rush and was starting to prepare the elk roast for lunch. She had cooked it to the point of a crusted outside with a bloody middle. Now all she had to do was put it back in the hot oven and warm it up, and it would be ready to go with the potatoes she had boiling.

"Oh, Reb, I'm glad you're back. If you will stay here a little while, I want to go home and check on Connie."

He really wanted to get started to Green River, but she looked so pathetic, he couldn't turn her down. "Sure, you go ahead, but don't stay too long. I really need to get on my way."

"I do wish I could go with you. I really do need supplies."

"Can't you get them local?"

"Sure, but if I buy them from Mr. Curry's store, there is so little profit by the time we get them cooked. Of course, Mr. Houghton will freight them up for us, but that is only a little better. It would be so good if we could go and get them."

"I guess it would," he said back without showing his true feeling. The last thing he wanted was to drive a wagon at two miles an hour for some ninety miles, when he could cut across country on Red and make it in a long day.

Carol was gone for most of an hour, and he was beginning to worry that Connie had started throwing up again, when she finally came back. Immediately, he detected she had turned very cold, but before he could confront her, the dinner crew started coming in. This time of the day the customers were mostly some men from town as the miners stayed out at their diggings until near dark or those who worked at The Carissa until the shift changed. The talk was still on the hanging and the posse the sheriff was putting together to go after them.

"You going on the posse, Mr. Steele?" Rag Elder asked him.

"No, reckon not," replied Cliff. "And it's Brown, not Steele."

"That so?" Rag asked looking quite confused.

"The girls and I had different fathers," Cliff told him to keep the suspicions down.

"Oh," Rag responded still looking like he didn't understand.

Carol had overheard him, and when he came back to the kitchen, she asked, "Why aren't you going? You could identify them, and then that would give you something to do for a couple days while Connie gets back on her feet." He could tell she was still mad about something, although what, he couldn't figure out, and he was in no mood for it.

"He don't need me to identify them. There are a dozen men who helped lock them up that can do that. Besides, he don't plan on catching them anyway."

"I don't understand, I have always heard Sheriff Boyd was a bull of a man," she quickly responded.

"Bully of a man is more like it. Hell, they could be in Colorado by now, and he's still bumming around town talking about getting up a posse. A fellow would think he was afraid of them or on the man's payroll, one."

"What man's payroll?"

"I told him where he could find them, and he quickly let me know, I didn't know what I was talking about."

"Really, you know?"

"I got a blame good idea they will be on the land of the same bunch they been riding with."

"And just who is that, Mr. Know-it-all?" she questioned sarcastically.

"Oh, women," he said and removed his apron, threw it down and left by the backdoor.

First, he went to the house to get his saddlebags and a rifle. This time he decided to take the Henry, but before he could leave, Connie heard him and cracked the door to her room slightly and stuck her head out as he came from his own room. "Boy, Carol was really mad at me," she said.

"Yeah, she got her dander up about something all right," he agreed turning to look at her. When he did, she moved just a fraction, and suddenly there was one of her pointy breasts very visible.

Taking a deep breath he turned and started for the front door. "Glad to see you're feeling better."

"Thank you for what you did this morning."

He just lifted his free hand as a waving gesture.

"Hey, where are you going?"

"Green River City," he answered.

"Oh, please take the list Carol has made up. If you just give it to Mr. Houghton he will fill and deliver it."

"Where is it?" he asked, stopping and turning around.

"Over here," she said leaning out further from behind the door so she could point at the brown paper lying on the table, doing so she completely exposed her nakedness and then said, "Oh, goodness!" and quickly jumped back out of sight.

"Damn!" he said under his breath at the sight, and then he picked up the paper and shoved it into the inside pocket of his vest. *'That's just what I needed to finish out this wonderful day,'* he thought as he headed for Boeing's stables, *'trying to ride a stubborn sorrel with a hard on. It's not enough that Carol's got her back up about something, but now little sister has got to go and show her purty ass like that. This is going to be one hell of a trip.'*

Red appeared irritated at him also. He guessed it was for not getting to go out for their sunrise ride this morning, and he acted like he was going to bite him while Cliff was saddling him up.

He headed out of town as soon as he mounted without looking at anything or anybody. When he rode past Morris' Saloon, Miss Tipper was standing on the front boardwalk, and she raised her hand to wave, but he never saw her.

"Hmm," she said to herself.

# Chapter Five
# Salzburg

Herman Schultheiss in the company of his wife, Hilda, their two sons, and his brother Eli, had fled Salzburg, Austria, in the summer of 1829, only hours ahead of a mighty determined lynch mob led by no less than the village mayor. The Schultheiss brothers had been seen leaving the cobblestone street where the victim Ernst Gorman lived only moments before Ernst's body had been found. It, too, was well known that these brothers were a most greedy and unscrupulous pair.

In other issues of this nature, the mayor would simply have had the Schultheiss brothers arrested and held on the charges of murder and theft, but in this case the victim, who turned up with a rather large dagger implanted beneath his fifth rib and the contents of his strongbox missing, was the Mayor's personal secretary. To complicate matters it seems that Mr. Gorman's wife was known throughout the village of Reinarburg as the most beautiful woman of the region. Also, it was generally accepted that she had an unusual friendship with Mayor Swift. As a result of the friendship, some embarrassment could have resulted had a public trial been brought forth.

The chase continued for two days, but finally the town's people returned to Reinarburg, and the matter was mostly forgotten by all, except the mayor's wife.

It was May of the following year when the family of five boarded the 'Barque Sterling', at the port of Bristol England, bound for Buenos Aires. During the third week at sea, the captain's quarters were found to have been entered and the purser's strongbox opened with several hundred pounds of Sterling missing.

There was no true evidence to point directly at a suspect; however Titus Schultheiss was found playing with a sixpence that appeared uncirculated and his parents failed to give any explanation for where the lad of five had gotten it. A search was made first of their luggage and then person, save Mrs. Schultheiss herself, with no result. Still, the family was put ashore at the nearest British port.

On Tortola Island, two days after the departure of the 'Barque Sterling', Eli Schultheiss under the name of Sholtz, purchased a small sugar cane farm with British Sterling coin.

Eli's brother, Herman, agreed that the name change, although not a great change, perhaps would ward off some unpleasant family history and so they were from that day onward known.

At first, there was just he, his brother, and three black slaves to work the fields.

By 1833, the name Sholtz was well known in the area as having some three thousand acres in cane and some eighty slaves. However, this happened to be the year Parliament issued the emancipation law on all British Colonies and waters. By 1835, with no labor force willing to work the sugar industry, the economy of the Virgin Islands collapsed.

With barely enough money to secure passage, the month of May 1836 found, once again, the Sholtz family on a sailing ship. This time aboard 'The Governor Fenner' bound for New York harbor.

By this time, the brothers had learned to speak reasonably well and to a smaller extent, read and write the English language. Hilda had no need.

Both Jonah and Titus were being schooled by a friend of Herman's, one Miss Vashti Jude, who also taught English to new immigrants arriving from Europe. She was a pleasant girl to look at, and Jonah, who was now fourteen, had an enormous crush on her. In the fall of 1839, Herman and Eli joined a train bound for Minnesota; Titus' brother stayed behind.

Locating in the village of Becker near the banks of the Mississippi River, the Sholtz brothers set up shop as a farm implement supplier, and young Titus was soon seen on the family's delivery wagon handling a team of four mules. James and Jimmy were the leaders, followed by Bill and Buck. James was by far the largest of the four. At the time, he was what was called a Missouri mule and quite valuable.

However, it was this chore that would lead to Titus losing both family and fortune. The month he had turned twenty-two he had a load of plow blades that were to be delivered to the Growen's Farm across the river in Wright County.

Titus was moving along slowly, not so much for the benefit of the mules, rather he didn't want to get home before dark. Coming around a curve in the road, he saw a wagon ahead drawn by a single horse. It was stopped along side the road, and as he neared it, he could see that it had lost a wheel. Looking around he saw no one anywhere. There was a path of broken wheat where it appeared someone had taken out across the field on foot. He was just about to go on when he spotted the beautiful Pennsylvania flintlock lying on the spring-seat. Immediately, Titus pulled up the mules. Again he looked all around, but saw no one anywhere. Larceny ran deep in the Schultheiss bloodline, and Titus was no different than his father or uncle. Setting the brake, he got down and walked over to the disabled wagon. Still there was no one anywhere to be seen as he reached for the rifle. At that moment, a huge forearm shot out from beneath the canvas cover lying in the wagon bed, and a mighty hand locked onto his wrist. His shouts of fright only served to signal the two men who were hidden off the road behind him. In seconds, they were on his back and the struggle only lasted a minute or so before he was semi-conscious, and lying with his face in the dirt. A hard kick to his temple and Titus lost consciousness altogether. He was not out for long, however, but he did not have the energy to move. It was at that time he overheard the men talking.

"That thar' Remington gats 'um e'ra time, huh Kyle?"

"It do Bobo, it do at that."

It was the last he heard before he passed out again. When he awoke, there was no sign of the other wagon. He had been beaten badly, and his shirt and coat were gone as was the money he had saved to buy some candy when he got to a town. Only his wagon and mules were left untouched, save the money he had in his boot for the vegetables.

*'Them implements are too blame heavy fur 'em to off-load,'* he thought to himself, *'but I wonder why they didn't steal the mules.'*

As soon as he could muster the strength, he was on the wagon and yelling out at the team. On and on he drove the mules as fast as they would go.

Finally as he topped a little rise, he saw the river some two miles ahead. He also noticed a surrey had just turned onto the road, about half a mile in front of him, from a dim trail. It was also headed towards the ferry crossing. Between the surrey and the river was plainly seen the same wagon, again in the same disabled condition.

Titus now began slapping the long reins against the backs of the mules, and they picked up speed as the weight of the load began pushing them onward down the grade.

Titus could see, as he approached the scene, a man in a black frock coat was driving the surrey, and sitting beside him was a woman wearing a blue bonnet.

To the left of the disabled wagon was a tall patch of berry bushes, the only place where anyone could hide. It was at those bushes Titus had his eyes fixed.

Just as the man in the black coat pulled up near the other wagon they heard Titus coming on in a mighty thunder of hooves pounding and wheels squealing, and they turned to look back. At the last second, Titus yanked with all his might on the left rein, and the lead mules turned that direction, off the road.

The Reverend and Mrs. McNeil heard him yell "Die, you sons-a-bitches!" as he approached them.

A second later his voice was drowned out by the screams of first panic, then pain, as the four mules and heavily laden wagon crashed through the bushes that hid the Mullier brothers.

Kyle was stomped down by James first and then Bill, a split second before the iron rim of the wagon wheel cut into his throat. His head bounced onto the dusty road and rolled on down the hill after Titus for a few yards.

Bobo was not exposed to such an elaborate death as his older brother; he was simply stomped by the team and crushed by the subsequent wagon.

It took quite some distance for Titus to get the mules stopped, and when he did, he saw the large man standing in the middle of the road looking at the mangled bodies of his sons.

The Reverend was getting down from the surrey while his wife was leaning over the side losing the lunch that Mrs. Smith had recently spread for them.

Hans Mullier looked up at Titus, who was now walking back, and suddenly he reached for the flintlock. "You murdering bastard! You deliberately ran 'em over," he screamed.

Titus could see he was in a bad spot being unarmed, and he turned again for his mules.

Reverend McNeil tried to stop Mullier from shooting Titus, but the huge man simple shoved him aside as if he were a small child.

Titus heard the whistle of the ball fly past his left ear a split second before the explosive report reached him. However before Mullier had time to reload he was too far down the road for the next shot to reach him.

John Snell opened the gate for Titus to drive the wagon onto the ferry barge, but being too far away to have heard all the commotion, refused to carry the one wagon across as he could see the others up the grade and knew there sat his profit.

Finally Titus found a cut piece of hickory and slapped Snell hard on his right ear knocking him to his knees with a blurred mind and vision.

Titus then launched the craft and began pulling on the rope with all his might. He had almost reached mid-stream when the next ball came slipping over his head. Ducking behind the team he pulled on.

The next ball clipped Buck's ear, and the brown mule almost dumped the whole outfit into the water.

Titus could see the fix he was in and reluctantly cut the rope, and soon the barge was turning slowly around as it drifted down river.

He heard another report from the Remington, but there was no sign of anything hitting nearby. However, after floating a mile further, he realized it would be nearly impossible for him to beach the huge raft that now was slowly rotating counterclockwise. Finally with great reluctance, he cut the team loose and climbing on James' back heeled the mule until it jumped into the cold water.

He did have his Pa's money and a good Missouri mule that would take him home as soon as he found a way to get back across the Mississippi, but little else. He admitted to himself, things were not rosy, but he was alive, and that was more than he thought he would be half an hour before.

He remembered Joseph Adams saying there was a new ferry built at Monticello and that was only a few miles south. *'I'll go there and get back across and find Pa,'* Titus thought, *'Pa will know what to do.'*

Arriving on the outskirts of the village, he heard someone call out, "Look yonder, here comes a boy on a mule. I'll bet that's the one what destroyed Snell's Ferry."

"You betch 'um, Crocker. Go get the law."

"No need fur no law," another man said, "We'll hang the murdering son-a'-bitch ourselves."

'Murderer?' Titus thought, 'I ain't done no murder.'

"Quick, grab him."

Before he could get his mule turned around, there were three men riding fast horses in his direction, and suddenly a rope was around his chest pulling him from James' back.

Titus fought as hard as he could, but he was overwhelmed quickly, and a coarse horsehair noose was slipped around his neck.

"I didn't do no murder!" he yelled, but no one paid him any attention.

Jerking his head about, he was thankful to see no trees nearby and it was obvious they would have to take him into the town to accomplish their dirty deed. 'There, I might have a chance. I wonder how they were onto this news so fast?' he asked himself.

Soon after, they reached a large barn displaying a shingle painted red with the name "Rub's Livery." He saw the extended pole where the hay was hauled up on a block pulley, and knew his fate would soon be sealed.

Suddenly, there was a blast that took everyone by surprise. Turning, Titus saw a small man in a striped suit standing in the middle of the dirt street. In his hands was a double-barreled shotgun.

"Men, there'll be no lynching in Monticello. Not while I'm Town Marshal there won't."

"Come on, Josephus, he's the one. We seen him atop that thar mule yonder," the tall man said, pointing towards James.

"I don't care what he done. He'll be hung legal, and that will be after Judge Karn says so. Now take that rope from around his haid."

"I says, no," the man who had first given out the alarm yelled. "Hans Mullier done said he would pay fifty dollars fur 'im dead, the day he wus hung, and I caught him and don't aim fur no judge to let him go."

"He won't be a-let go if'ns he's the one."

"I says, hang him."

"And I says, this here scattergun don't know you, Reni Cobb, from Judas Iscariot. If'n you don't take that rope from his head, I will cut you and some of your accomplices to bloody ribbons."

"You's just bluffing, Josephus," the man said, looking around for support, only to find everyone had moved clear of the pattern of the scattergun. "Well, all right, but I get the reward," he finally said.

"Come on, boy," the Marshal said, removing the rope from Titus' neck, "I got a good safe place fur ya' till Judge Karn orders your hanging."

"But I didn't do no murder. Them boys done up and robbed me and beat me and wus' about to do it again to an old man and his wife. I just tried to stop 'em."

"Yep. The fellow I hung last month said near the same thing."

"You mean thar' was another man who told you about them thieving' boys?"

"No, he neered' said nutton' 'bout no thieving but he did say he hint' done no murder'n', we hung him anyway. Legal too."

Titus was locked up in a small smoke house that had been made of heavy hewed logs to keep marauding bears away from the meat while it cured. He soon realized there would be little hope for escape.

The sun was almost down when the heavy door opened and a sheet of light came rushing in.

"That the boy?" he heard Marshal Paul's voice say.

"That be him all right," a deep and ruff voice replied, "he done murdered my two sons fur no reason at all 'cept' they had a little money to buy some tobaccee' on um'."

"We found four dollars worth a coin in his boot," the Marshal said.

"Yep. It were four dollars in coin all right, my boy Bobo had on 'im."

"Well, then I guess this belongs to you."

"No," Titus yelled. "That's my Pa's money. He give it to me to buy vegetables over to the Growner's Farm."

The door was slammed shut and he heard the men walk away. "Wait! Come back. He was one of them what was doing the thieving."

No one seemed to hear him. Neither did anyone come to the smoke house the next day. He found a small piece of hog skin that had fallen from the last animal that had been hung in there and he chewed on it but this only made his thirst increase ten fold.

Finally, on the third morning, the door again opened. This time the light was so strong it blinded him, and he could only see dark figures standing there.

"Yes sir. That's the boy all right. The Misses and me were stopping to help the disabled wagon when he came riding like hellfire was after him, and he wus yelling for them to die," the voice paused, "It was awful. Caused Mrs. McNiel to lose her lunch, it did."

"Thank you, Reverend. I shor' do thank ya fur coming all this way. You gon'a stay and watch him be hurled into eternity? It will be as quick as the twinkling of a' eye."

"I thought we might stay if'n it ain't too long in a-coming."

"Tomorrow or the next; Judge Karn wus in Minneapolis when we got word to him about us capturing the killer."

"I ain't no killer!" Titus yelled just before the door again slammed shut. "Water! I need water!"

The next time the door opened, his mouth had swollen so he could not speak, but he recognized the voice.

"Yeah, that's my son all right. Why can't he speak?"

"Well, I suppose we forgot to bring him water this morning," a strange voice said.

"Well, get him some," Herman Sholtz demanded. "I need to talk to 'im."

Some minutes after Titus had drank the water he looked up at his father and painfully spoke, "Pa."

"What you done with my mules and wagon?"

Slowly Titus began to explain what had happened. The longer he talked the more he noticed that the Marshal seemed to be taking an interest in his story. Finishing, he said "And that's the truth, Pa."

"You mean you lost my mules and all 'em implements in the river?"

"Pa, I had to or they would a' got hung-up and drowned."

"And whar's the money I give you fur the vegetables?"

"The Marshal here done give it to one of the thieves," he said nodding his head at the small man.

Standing a head taller than the Marshal, Sholtz turned and looked down at the lawman. "You mean you done up and give away my money, a whole four dollars in gold coin?"

"Well, Mr. Mullier said that was what your boy had stole from him," Marshal Paul replied a little defensively.

"I'll tell you right here and now, I have a respectable family over to Becker and it happens to be my farm what the Governor stays at when he's in these here parts, and I aim to see he gets a full report on you arresting the wrong people and giving away honest folks' monies to known thieves."

"Now here, sir, I didn't knowed he was your son or I'd never give away your money, or arrested him in the first place. I was just trying to keep him from being lynched."

"Come this time next month, you will be lucky if'n you still have that thar badge, and you better be a-finding me four dollars, too, just as soon as you let my boy out a' thar."

An hour later Titus still was fighting off the headache his eyes were causing, when he suddenly said to the big man seated next to him on the wagon, "Gee, Pa, I didn't know you wus friends with the Governor."

"Shut up, you damn fool kid. You ain't got no more brains than that stupid Marshal."

Herman knew it would only be a matter of time before Marshal Josephus Paul figured out he had been bumfuzzeled so immediately upon returning, he began making preparations to see his youngest son was eastbound on the rails to rejoin Jonah in New York, far beyond the hands of Minnesota law.

# Chapter Six
# The Sweetwater Mining Country

Cliff had come to know the land around South Pass City mostly by listening to the talk of others and a little by moving about himself. Of course, his picnic with Nadine had been a help in that direction, but the Sky Warriors had hurried their return to town before he had made the search he wanted. Still, it was plain to see how this area was both growing and dying. The first good lode found became 'The Carissa Mine,' and half a mile below it on Willow Creek, South Pass City was soon to be born which, in December of '67, was selected as the County Seat of Carter County in the Dakota Territory. Three or four months later on Rock Creek, some four miles north, the township of Atlantic City was laid out after 'The Caribou Mine' became a success. Then on Spring Gulch, some four or so miles east of Atlantic City, 'The Miners Delight' became a huge strike, and the town of Hamilton sprang up. Now 'The Monia' was the newest big happening and he wondered just how long it would be before a town would be laid out there.

As is usually the case with golden cities, the easy pickings that cause the flood and the boom are quickly scooped up. After that, only those with enough capital to go deep would stay and make a profit. The pure fact that South Pass City had once held several thousand inhabitants was evident everywhere, but now there were only a few who did not work for others and of course, those who profited from them. Hamilton still had some pickings, but the dreams of placer mining never panned out anywhere in the Sweetwater Area.

'The Carissa Mine'

'The Monia' was running around the clock. Crews and many more were finding work over there where a tent city had been born. Even some of the men who had left to go to work on the Union Pacific Railroad were returning to the tent city as the lure of color and nuggets had never quite been washed from their dreams.

Some ten miles due south was the Sweetwater River. West along this ribbon of clear cool water around five miles, it crossed the stage road that pretty much followed the Oregon Trail, cutting down through Big Sandy Creek and on to the railroad just east of Granger 140 miles distance, more or less. A trip of eleven or twelve days in the winter, if one made it at all alive, which many who tried it did not, and some three days by freight wagon in the summer. If the hail and thunderstorms didn't hit him, a man on a good horse could be there in two days, maybe one if he really pushed hard. Cliff wanted to try.

He was all too aware he had made a promise to let Rob Scogins' family know of his strike, and everyday he put it off was just that much more of a chance something might keep him from doing the obligation he had to the dead man. The close call they had with the Arapahoe had brought this realization out vividly in his mind.

Cliff looked out at the desolate, flat prairie before him; he knew the first telegraph wire in the region had been run in by the 'Carissa Mine'. *'Now that the army finally started construction on Camp Stambaugh, they surely would have a telegrapher, but there was always the chance that somehow Ed Sholtz would find out if I sent a wire to Scogins' brother from a nearby location, and that would surely put me on a death list as well as any Scogins family member that might be headed this way. No, I must go to either Green River City or Granger, and I am sure glad I ain't going in no wagon. Carol is a great piece of ass, but sitting there for several days beside her on a spring-seat might just be too close for comfort. Red is more my kind of traveling companion, and besides, if there were Indian trouble, with Carol along there would be no chance at all. Carol is no Nadine; by myself I might just out run them,'* he thought, knowing full well there would be little chance of that.

Sundown caught him just as he was approaching Big Sandy Creek a few miles east of the stage road, it looked to be a good place to make camp, but just before dismounting he stopped sharply. His forehead immediately drew tight in a hard frown; he thought he heard something, and turning his good ear towards where he thought the sound had come from he listened, but he heard nothing. Eventually he realized what had alerted him was not a sound, rather a smell. *'Smoke!'*

A few yards west of the trail was an anthill-looking bulge on the prairie, only perhaps twelve feet high and some hundred or more feet around. Quietly, he moved Red around so it was between him and the riverbed, there he waited with every sense he had at attention. Finally he caught another whiff, only this time the smell was unmistakable. *'Arbuckle's.'*

That pretty much ruled out Indians. It wasn't that Indians didn't like coffee, but they seldom had enough to carry along on a hunt. Coffee was as precious to the Indian women as was a good cooking pot, and it was highly unlikely they would have given it to a brave for his nightly camps. No this was almost surely whitemen, but here in gold country they could be just as deadly as the redman.

'The Frontier Index'[5] had some story in almost every edition of some poor miner losing his diggings or his life to bushwhackers here in the Sweetwater Region, and surely he himself had seen this very thing the night before he arrived.

---

[5] The Frontier Index was a newspaper printed in Green River City but distributed throughout the region.

An hour after dark, just as the quarter moon was rising, he saw a dull glow up river maybe a mile to the west. As quietly as he could, he led Red to within a couple hundred yards of the glow on the prairie and there drop-reined him behind a small bush near the creek. Red would wait; he was that kind of horse. Even though a drink of that cool water was surely on his mind, he would wait.

It took Cliff another ten minutes to cover the distance. First he saw the horses on the opposite side of the creek, but they were busy chomping at the long green grass that grew there near the river, and none looked up as he slipped past their view to a good size boulder almost directly across from the campfire. Waiting there out of sight, he caught his breath. It was then he heard a man call out the name.

"Hey Chip, you sure he's coming tonight?"

Then the familiar voice replied "He's coming, I saw him head out myself."

"Hell, he no take de road me'bee, eef he cuts cross country he will get away clean, no?"

"Concho, don't show your ignorance. He's new to this country. He will take the road," Roper said.

"And it's getting about dark enough for us to see his campfire," Phil added.

"And for him to see ours, douse that fire, and let's start getting ready," the blond man said back to them.

Cliff never saw any of them, not really, just shadows occasionally between him and the campfire, but he had heard enough, and when he heard the hissing of water being poured on the fire he knew he was close enough for them to see him if he showed himself out there in the open with the moon rising behind him.

He crawled back for a long ways before he stood and ran to were Red was waiting. He was given a gruff look when the big horse realized he was not going to get a drink, but he also realized that there was something wrong by his master's movements, and the look was the only protest.

Cliff now moved towards the road and crossed it before heading along the south side of the creek for a couple of miles, then he let Red stop and drink. Finally they turned south walking slowly for two miles or more before they stopped and made a cold camp.

Sitting there leaning against his saddle he thought of what he had heard. *I'm sure they were talking about dry-gulching me,* he thought.

*'But why? They don't know about me having any gold, and I haven't let on to anyone I knew about Scogins. Mee'be it's because I caught Concho and his buddy breaking into Boeing's place. I wonder.'*

An hour before sunup he was again moving south well away from the road. Late that afternoon he cut the Green River, and there they made a camp before sundown. After a slab of bacon, two cups of coffee, and a makin's, he doused the fire and scattered the ashes so that only an Indian would notice that a campfire had been there, and then they moved on another hour and made another dry camp for the night.

The sun was high in the sky when he saw the tops of some buildings and knew he had followed the right river.

Green River City was nothing more than a railroad town, but there was a stockpile of track and ties as well as a repair station there, and it was obvious that this whistle stop in the middle of nowhere was growing. It had, after all, six saloons, even though two of them were only large tents stretched over a wooden frame behind a false front. There were several other wooden structures on the west side of the river, as well as a few older adobe ones mostly used as living quarters for 'the down-on-their-luck' at Old Town on the east side.

As soon as he found a livery to house Red for a couple days, he headed out for the telegraph office, which he located in the ticket depot of the Union Pacific.

Green River City Depot

"Please send this," he said to the telegrapher, reaching into his vest pocket for some coins.

The man counted the words before setting the price. Upon receipt he then read the note, satisfied, he turned and made a couple of identifying clicks on the wire and then began tapping away sending the message far away to someone Cliff had never met, in a place he had never been.

```
Deliver To Mr Scogins
At the Ashley Farm Higginsville
Mo


Folks it is my sad duty to inform you
of the loss of your brother Rob
                STOP
He succumbed to wounds received
in an attack by claim jumpers d12
ultimo[6]
                STOP
His last words were to request me to
inform you of a rich strike he had made
in the Sweetwater Mining Region
                STOP
Please send back reply no later than
day after tomorrow as to when you will
be coming to claim his property
                END
        Signed His Partner C Brown
```

Cliff waited for the telegrapher to finish tapping out the message before he turned to leave. Stopping for a moment he then asked, "What times do you operate?"

"Daylight mostly, of course, at any other time the railroad wants me to. I sleep in back."

"Can you recommend a good hotel?"

"There ain't no good hotel, but there is 'The Blade.'"

---

[6] Ultimo - Last Month

"'The Blade'? Sounds like you need a knife to get out of it," Cliff answered.

**Street Scene Green River City 1870**

"Oh, no. No, it's really 'The Green River Blade,' but we locals just call it 'The Blade'. The U.P. owns it, and it's whar' our people, er ____ high-falutin' people, stay when they are in town."

"Sounds good and a bank?"

"'The Great Divide' is also owned by the U.P., but 'The Green River Bank' has my thirty-eight dollars."

"Thanks."

"Of course, if you like knife-fighting you could go to 'The Bridger'," the man added with a snicker.

"'The Bridger'?"

"Yeah, you don't need a knife to get out of thar', you need one to get in," he said back, now really snickering.

"Guess I'll stick to 'The Blade'," Cliff answered as he again turned for the door.

As Cliff stepped outside he heard the telegrapher say to himself, "Ain't much of a knife fighter I guess."

He left the Henry with his saddle at the livery and was now armed with his 44, plus he had concealed under his vest, in the small of his back, the 36 Navy he had retrieved from the back of Boeing's house.

When he walked into 'The Green River Bank' there were already three customers in line at the single teller's window. Looking about he spotted a well-dressed man sitting at a desk behind a half-wall. Approaching this desk he stood waiting for the man to look up.

Finally he did so, and inquired, "May I help you, sir?"

"Want to open an account," Cliff said.

"Very good, sir, I'm Isaac Harris and I can handle that for you. How much do you wish to deposit?"

Cliff removed one of the bags of dust from his belt and sat it on the table. "This," he replied.

"I see, this will take a minute," the banker said as he hefted the bag. "How much do you think you have here?"

"I don't think, I know," Cliff lied. "I just want to see how honest this here bank is before I leave it with you."

"Testing me, eh?"

Cliff smiled and raised the palms of his hands in a gesture.

"Alright, that's good business," Harris added before he lifted his heavy frame from the squeaky wooden chair and headed for a large walnut cabinet at the rear of the room.

It was at that moment they all heard the yell, "Everybody, hands in the air," followed by the unmistakable sound of a gun being cocked.

Cliff turned around to see two men standing in the middle of the floor. One had a long barreled shotgun and the other a handgun. Cliff noticed the absence of a recoil shield and immediately identified it as a 36 caliber Dance Brothers revolver. The man with this pointed it at Cliff and said, "Alright you two, get over here with the others."

As they walked past the man with the shotgun he lifted the Colt from Cliff's holster and stuck it into his trouser front without saying a word.

Cliff recognized the other man as one of those who had been in line when he came in and wondered whom else in that line might be in on the heist.

"You," the man with the revolver said suddenly pointing his gun at Harris, "you own this bank?"

"I do."

"Well, get over here and open your safe."

Harris slowly and reluctantly moved towards the big black strong box.

"Hurry up," the talker said and poked Harris hard in the kidney with the barrel of his revolver.

Harris almost went to his knees gasping at the pain.

"Come on, get a wiggle on."

After he twice misdialed the combination, it became obvious Harris was stalling, and the man cocked the Dance Brothers and placed its long gray barrel just behind Harris' ear, at that moment the front door opened and in stepped a lady perhaps fifty years of age. Before she realized what was happening, 'the shotgun' stepped in behind her and slipped one of his arms under her left arm, and clasping his palm over her mouth, he easily lifted her up where all could see her black button shoes dancing wildly a foot off the hardwood floor, and her purse fell, spilling much of its contents.

She tried to scream, but it was muffled by the gloved hand covering her mouth, and no distinguishable sound was heard.

The robber with Harris saw the opportunity and grasped it. "You miss that lock again and my friend over there will cut off one of the lady's ears," he said loudly motioning at the man holding the woman.

When Harris turned to look at them the man leaned his single barrel against the front wall and pulling a knife from his belt with a long curved blade, brought it up to her right ear and ever so gently drew blood from just below the lobe. It was not a large cut, but a strong run of red liquid began down her quivering neck. Again, everyone knew she had screamed, but none heard it.

Harris nodded his head and turned his attention back to the combination. Both bandits were now watching him.

Cliff looked slowly at each of the other men in the bank and simply couldn't decide if any were involved. Finally, with his back to the wall, he suddenly whipped out the Navy Colt and put a ball into the temple of the man who had cut the woman. Before the body fell and while her first scream was heard, he had turned back and was bringing up the round barrel for a shot at the other man with Harris, who yelled, "What the hell?"

Suddenly one of the men in line went to his knees, and Cliff whirled aiming the Colt at the new suspect, but this man merely began praying, and when Cliff brought his eyes back up he saw the Dance Brothers revolver coming his way.

It was a quick shot, and he never liked to take quick shots. He had learned years before, during the war, that it was most likely the man who took his time who survived a shoot-out but this time he fired before he had a good point of aim and it showed.

The ball hit the counter between them and ricocheted forward, striking the man in the left wrist cuff. Luckily his return fire was also quick, and his ball took a small bite from the brim of Cliff's Stetson.

Cliff's next shot was not hastily done, and the hombre dropped his gun and grabbed his chest just left of center. The expression of disbelief swept across his face, and then his knees slowly drifted inward, and he fell forward.

The room was now almost a cloud of blue-white smoke, and the smell of burnt sulfur was gagging.

Just then two more guns were heard going off outside, and Cliff raced for the door. He reached down and retrieved his 44 as he passed the dead man lying beside the fainted woman, and headed out. There he saw two mounted men riding up and down the street shooting off their revolvers chasing everyone back inside the stores.

Cliff recognized one of them as Concho, the other he did not know. Taking aim he dispatched the closest one from his horse. A moment later he took a hit in his leg from his old enemy.

Concho immediately turned and sliding off on the left side of his horse, riding with only his one foot in the stirrup and a hand on the horn, he fled northward into the red desert, presenting no target save the beautiful black horse.

In less than a minute others began to refill the street, and shortly a man with a star came running towards the scene.

By now Cliff had returned his Colts to their proper places and was trying to tie his neckerchief around his leg.

The lawman approached him with drawn gun and yelled for him to freeze.

Cliff simply looked up at him with a disgusted expression and continued tying the silk rag.

Very soon others were coming from the bank, and all could hear a woman's hysterical sobbing emerging from inside.

Harris grabbed Cliff's hand and began shaking it over and over again as he explained Cliff's involvement to the Marshal.

As soon as he could, Cliff told the City Marshal that he had recognized Concho as the one who had shot him, and the bandit was wanted in South Pass City for murder and burglary.

"I'll send a wire to Sheriff Boyd about the attempted holdup and will get out some wanted posters as soon as I can," he said back.

"You ain't going after him?"

"I'm a City Marshal. My jurisdiction ends at the town limits. It will be up to Sheriff Boyd to go after him now that he's in the county."

"Son-of-a-bitch," Cliff said, slapping his hat against his good leg.

"No need to be vulgar," Marshal Teag said. "There is an ordinance against cussing in the presence of womenfolk."

"Well shit, then I guess you better arrest me. You got to do something to earn your pay today."

Teag took off his hat and threw it on the ground. "I can't help it. I have no jurisdiction," he shouted at Cliff. "I wish I could, but Boyd won't deputize me."

Harris then asked, "Sir, do you need help getting over to the doctor's office? I'm afraid he is not coming here."

"No, I'll make it. It ain't that bad," Cliff said then looking up added, "Besides me and you still got business inside."

"I guess we do at that," Harris said suddenly remembering why this man was there to begin with.

The first bag of dust totaled $1,113 and the second $978.

"Do I dare leave my money in here after what I saw today?" Cliff teased Harris.

"Sir, after what you did today if you ever lose a cent in my bank I will repay you from my personal funds."

"Hell, that will be gone too if 'n they rob you."

"No it won't," Harris said quietly, and realizing his meaning, they both laughed.

"Alright, Mr. Harris, I trust you. Make out the $1,100 plus account in the name of Nadine Tipper, South Pass City, and the other", he paused "I'll deposit $900 and take the $78 in folding money. Make that one to me, Reb Brown, also from South Pass," he said.

"That can be arranged immediately Mr. Brown. I just wish you were staying here with us," the banker said. "We could use a man of your caliber around here."

"Got a promise to keep before I take on any more responsibilities," Cliff replied, "but I take the request as a kind compliment."

Just then a man came in, along with the Marshal, with a pencil and note pad in hand.

When Teag pointed towards him, Cliff knew he was a new target.

"Mr. Harris, if you really want to thank me, take this here reporter off my hands."

"I think I can do that," he said and patted Cliff on the back.

"Mister, I need to talk to you about the robbery," the young man said approaching Cliff.

"Come on in, Jimmy," Harris said opening the gate for him as Cliff moved out past him.

"But, I need to____"

"Come on in here Jimmy and I will give you all the skinny. Mr. Brown must go over to Doc Hembold's Office to have his leg tended to. You don't want your star witness to bleed to death do you; you can talk to him later."

"But Mr.____"

"I know what Mr. Collins told you, but I assure you 'The Frontier Index' will get the news out before any other paper in the district even finds out about this trouble," he promised turning the young man around and walking him over to the big desk.

Cliff spent the next day in the depot building waiting for the telegrapher to tell him that one of the many messages that were coming in hourly was for him. Just before sundown the skinny man motioned for him. He hobbled over to the counter where the yellow piece of folded paper laid.

```
Deliver to Mr. C Brown Esquire Green River
City Wyoming


Sir thank you for your message of d2
instant⁷
          STOP
You have no idea how it cuts the heart to
know one has lost both siblings the same
month
          STOP
Due to responsibilities beyond my control
can not arrive before October one
          STOP
Please take necessary steps to secure my
brother's portion of the mine until I arrive
          END
             Signed Ash Scogins
```

---

[7] Instant: This month. d2 instant is two days ago.

Cliff read it twice and then said aloud, "Damn!" *'I never should have said I was his partner,'* he thought as he walked out of the door. *'Now I'm right back in the middle of just where I wanted out of.'*

His leg was giving him plenty of discomfort, and he was not sure he could sit a saddle for the long hours necessary to make the ride back to South Pass City. Pondering on this he started towards where he had left Red.

Hobbling along in much pain and having only a few buildings to go before reaching the livery, he stopped short, reading the sign painted on the side of a bat and board building, 'Houghton & Cotter, Mine Supplies.' That caused him to remember the list Carol had written, and he ran his fingers into his vest pocket retrieving the paper.

Walking stiff-legged into the store he saw a man, several inches shorter than he and ten years older, looking at a long iron box and scratching his head. The man seemed in deep thought, and Cliff hated to disturb him. Finally, after two or three minutes without having his presence acknowledged, he cleared his throat, and then the man looked up.

"Sir, my name is Brown, Reb Brown, and I have this here list of supplies that the Steele sisters up to South Pass City asked me to bring to you."

Reaching for the list the man studied Cliff for a moment before reading the paper.

"I thought you were out of Granger," Cliff said.

"We do have a shop in Granger. My pard runs that one. Just opened this one here. It be mine to manage," he answered as he read the list.

Finally he laid the note down and looked around, "Well, I got this here stamp mill battery that needs to go to Hamilton as soon as I can get it there. Don't see why I can't take this to the ladies at the same time."

"Good, I know they will be real pleased."

"But can't do it right away."

Confused, Cliff looked at him as if he hadn't heard all of this correctly.

"Mr. Brown, you say?"

"Yes, sir," Cliff answered, "but most just call me 'Reb.'"

"You wouldn't happen to be the 'Reb Brown' that cleaned out that bunch of bank robbers, now would ya?"

"I guess I am, but I didn't clean them out. One got away."

"The way this here paper tells it, you must be a one-man army."

Cliff was now about ready to turn and leave, and he started to do that very thing then he remembered Carol's supplies. Finally he answered, "Well, Sur, you know how newspeople blow everything up, to sell them papers."

"What I'm asking ya is, you as good with that there shooter as it says here, or not?"

"Well, I learned to shoot as a boy."

"I see'd you a-limping when you come in," Houghton said.

This surprised Cliff as he thought the man had not noticed him at all.

"That there leg good enough to set in a saddle?"

"I'm afraid not just yet," Cliff admitted.

"Good," Houghton replied.

"Huh?"

"I don't make the run to the Sweetwater alone no more, Injuns, just too scary. I seen what them red niggers done to Bill Rose back in '68. Helped bury him and Hayes too____a terrible sight. My bullwhacker took off the other day and went to work fur the darn Union Pacific and left me alone. Cotter, my partner is up to the Sweetwater now so I can't go nowhere unless I was to come up with a teamster or a good man with a long gun," he said; rubbing his chin he added, "Know where such could be found?"

"I may not be able to handle a team with this leg, but I can shoot the left eye out of a jack at thirty paces," Cliff answered back smiling.

"I was hoping you'd say that. Art's my name Arthur Langford Houghton, but call me Art," he said extending his hand.

Cliff extended his left hand accepting the shake as he replied, "Please call me Reb."

"Tell ya what, Reb. I can get the darkey out back to help me get this battery loaded if you will take this list yonder to Josey Baldwin, she runs a store over to the river bank, and tell her to send Popo back with the groceries when it's filled."

"Baldwin's store on the river bank," Cliff repeated his instructions making sure he had them right.

"And be here, come first light to morning, so we can make some time 'afor dark."

"I'll be here."

"Oh, you got a long gun?"

"I do."

"Figured you would," Art said turning without any more needing to be said.

Cliff found the Baldwin's store and paid her with some of the Colorado bank notes he had saved out from his deposit at the bank.

Then he went to the gunsmith's where he had left the Navy. Entering, he looked at the man who wore thick-lens spectacles working on a Sharps carbine behind the crude counter.

"Ah, Mr. Brown," he said removing the glasses.

"I'm leaving early in the morning. Is my gun ready?"

"It is, at that. Finished it yesterday," the smithy said reaching under the counter and retrieving the 1861 Colt now sporting a three and a half inch barrel.

"I cut it here," he said pointing to the barrel. "Any shorter and you couldn't work the ramming arm at all. Didn't install a front sight neither, didn't figure you would need one on this short a' barrel."

"You're right; it'll just be a back up," Cliff said reaching for the gun. After handling it some he slipped it into the small of his back under his vest and turned around.

"Can't see a thing," Chamblin said.

"Good, how much I owe you?"

After settling up with Baker at the livery for Red's board he headed back to 'The Blade' to take the load off his leg.

Resting there, he reflected on his good luck. *'This ride will give me another break, I doubt Roper and his boys will try anything against a Houghton freight wagon, so many people being aware of his travels and the fact that I was the one who identified Concho in the hold up. If we were to turn up dead without arrows stuck plum through us, a fury would come down on them.'*

And at that very moment on the Owl Hoot Trail near Samson's Hollow around a small campfire gathered seven men. Phillip Sholtz, the only son of Ed Sholtz, who felt he had to prove to his father he was just as mean as his genealogy; a half-breed Comanche they called Squatty Devil; a vaquero who hailed from the same village as Concho known as Mad Dog Carlos; Bones Harvey who had learned his trade riding with the Kansas Jay Hawkers during the rebellion;

Yuel who had been a cook in the Sixth Cavalry at Ft. Caspar, who, in a drunken brawl, cut a man so badly that the poor devil lost his arm and Yuel was then bob-tailed out of the Army; and lastly Chip Roper, the ramrod of Sholtz' goon squad.

Roper was thirty-one years old and sported an accent that the well-learned would have called New England. Little is known of him before he arrived on The Sweetwater scene in '68. The first day he was there, so the story goes, he happened upon a sharpshooter hid in the brush on Rock Creek who had a rifle aimed at Ed Sholtz as the older man headed out of Atlantic City. Roper shot the man dead with one round from his revolver, and Sholtz hired him on the spot.

It was Concho who was talking to the others, "I tell you, *dis* man Brown, he ees the cause of too many problemas. He shoot Lefty in the head while he ees riding like lightning. *Dis* man we must *keel*, and be pronto, too."

"Concho is right," Bones agreed, "he is dangerous. I saw him come out with a hid-a-way and put a ball in Ol' Griz' head in the blink of my eye. I went for my boot gun, but he was on me before I got my pants leg up. I had no chance to help them without exposing myself to his fire so I just acted like I bent down there to pray, it wus the only thing what saved me. Then before I could do anything more, he was blasting away at Latigo."

Phil spit tobacco juice onto the burning cotton wood limb and added his mind, "I don't see no cause to make this hombre into some kind a' God. Hell, I seen 'im and I know I can take 'im. Just let me get another chance."

The tall blond who had stayed back and listened to Concho's and Bones' explanation of how the job had gone bad, placed a boot on the rock Yuel was leaning against before he spoke. "Well, one thing is fur sure; the boss ain't gon'a like it that we botched this one. He had placed twenty thousand in that penny ante bank and expected us to take it back. This is going to set back his plans a few weeks, and I'm the one that's got 'a tell him."

"How'd we miss Brown last week?" Yuel questioned.

"My guess he just went straight south to Rock Point and then took the train west," Chip answered.

"Well, what if he does that again?"

"I'm not sure if this is the right time to take him out," he paused then added, "You're right about that Copperhead[8] though. He is getting in the way of business."

"What you say? We no keel heem?" Concho questioned.

"Everyone in the county now knows he is the sole witness against you two in the Boeing caper, and now he is the only one who can identify Concho in the bank job."

"Si, dat's why we must keel heem."

"I don't think so. Should he turn up dead right now, they will be after you, Concho, like flies on a turd."

"You're right," Phil agreed. "I should take him in a fair fight, in front of everybody, as soon as he gets back to South Pass City."

"Don't kid yourself, Phil. He is a shooter. Haven't you been listening to what Concho and Bones just said?"

"I can take him," the boy said before turning and walking back away from the light.

"Ah loco, muchacho, you would be deed' dis' quick," Concho said to Phil as he snapped his fingers.

"What we do, boss?" Mad Dog asked.

"We'll talk to 'The Boss', that's what we are going to do," Chip answered back.

Red had been tied to the back of the long wagon the first few miles, but the dust there was so bad he began to raise a ruckus, finally Cliff just turned him loose, and he moved along at his leisure mostly beside the wagon, but sometimes in front of the team of six matched bays, looking back at times at the draft horses with what Cliff was sure was a smirk on his face.

The weather was good but hot, with temperatures closing in on the three-digit mark before a thunderstorm passed by a mile or so

---

[8] Copperhead: Before there was a nation of the Confederate States of America, before the War Between the United States and the Confederate States, before any symbols of the Confederate nation had been adopted, those who were loyal to the cause of secession made a lapel pin from the penny by removing the words United States from the rim of the coin indicating a withdrawal from the United States. This coin at that time was the copper Indian Head penny and the lapel pin then consisted only of that Indian Head made of copper. Thus those who supported secession were called Copperheads by their enemies.

to their left. Not a drop had fallen on them, but the road ahead was drenched and cakey.

Approaching the burned out remains of the old stage station at Simpson's Hollow, Art pulled up and said, "We'll let the boys rest here twenty minutes or so. Good place for them to water."

Cliff climbed down and began to move about stiff-legged. "How long ago was this burned down?" he asked.

"Oh, I reckon it was back ten years or so. It was when the Overland Stage Company ran this route. I wus living up in Montana then, getting my start in this here gold business."

"You were a miner?"

"Shore wus. Just as dumb as most what gets bit by the fever. Went to Alters Gulch in '63 to strike it rich and saw nearly everybody that did hit color end up making fertilizer fur the mountain flowers."

"How's that?"

"There ain't one in a hundred, hell a thousand, what heads into a field that makes it big digging. Most that did got themselves shot fur their troubles. I seen right off that the money in a gold field was in supplying those who did, with what they need most. Since I don't sit on no pus, as some do, I decided to haul freight. Hell, even the robbers need supplies and would be a-cutting off their own arms to wipe out the supply trains," he said as he rubbed down his horses with some long grass he had pulled from the creek bed.

Cliff thought long on what his newly acquired friend had said and determined he was right. *'Even the money I used to pay for these supplies was dug by someone else.'*

"That's the same with this place, right here whar we're a standing," Art continued interrupting his thoughts. "This here was the place Captain Simpson was camped with a load of supplies he wus a taking for the Army yonder to Ft. Bridger," the man said, pointing at the far away mountains. "Camped here to rest his mules before the climb when the Avenging Angel swept down upon him and wiped 'em out."

"Avenging Angel?"

"Yep, Wild Bill Hickman he-self, leader of the Mormon Army what declared war on those United States. Back in '57, it wus."

"The Mormons declared war on the United States?"

"Yep, shore did, it were the first American Civil War, unless you count the one's we had ag'in the Crown," he said, and looking about, he added, "This is the only real battlefield though. They destroyed the supply train here and then shot some arrows around to make it look like Indians dun it, but somebody up and lost a *Book of Mormon* in the ruckus, and the truth came out. From then on they just retreated and burned everything behind them until Joe Johnson and his troops nigh on starved to death. This was hostile country back in them thar days. Not civilized like it are here today."

"I didn't feel like it was so civilized the other day when that Mex put a ball in my thigh."

"Yeah, still better than it wus," Art argued. "Hell, they will be building churches out here 'afor a body gets a chance to kick up a ruckus and poke a whore or two. You just watch my words, first come the churches, then 'aire be schools, and then the whole damn place will be run by them know-it-all women. Whole damn place will be up and gone to hell," Art complained as he climbed back on the spring-seat. "We need to make the next crossing at Big Sandy 'afor full night sets in. I got caught out here on a bad stormy night a few years back and lost the road and damn near ran off into a draw that would'a done me in fur sure," Art continued as he slapped the leather ribbons gently on the backs of what were obviously his prize horses.

The sun had slipped behind the western mountains when they stopped to make camp.

Art was tending to his team when a sign caught Cliff's attention, and he looked seriously over the ground before speaking to his new friend. "Looks like a recent camp has been made here. Last night, I would guess," Cliff said. "Mee'be seven or eight riders."

"Shod?" Art replied not taking his attention from his chore.

"Yeah."

"This here road gets its fair share a' travelers nowadays. Wouldn't mind the sign a' shod horses none. It's them what ain't, that a body needs to worry about," Art said.

Cliff made a strong pot of coffee, and they each ate from a cut of elk rump that Houghton brought with him, before turning in. Still, as soon as Cliff heard the steady rumble that assured him his companion was fast asleep, he led Red off a hundred yards from the little camp, and the two spent the night in the darkness. Cliff, being up before the sun, Art never realized the absence of his rider.

Pulling into South Pass City, two hours before dark the following day, Art drove right up to 'The Sisters'.' There were three miners eating when the big wagon arrived, and all pitched in and helped unload the groceries.

"You don't know how much we appreciate this Mr. Houghton," Carol said when the job was finished.

"No trouble little lady. I'll be proud to do it," the freighter replied smiling while at the same time checking out her figure.

"If you could give us an invoice, I will have your money for you tomorrow."

"Oh, if I were just ten years younger I would have a really good invoice fur ya, but I'm past ma' prime so I'll just bid you a warm farewell; I must be in Hamilton before dark," he said.

"But wait what do we owe you?"

"Owe him," Art said back.

"What, who?"

"Him, the Reb."

"What?" she asked surprised at his statement as she looked over at the Georgian who was still carrying in a large wooden crate from which the leaves of carrot tops were protruding.

Turning back she questioned, "I don't understand. Your freight, how much do we owe you for your freight, and the groceries?"

"Nary a dime, Sweet Thing, that thar one-man-army you have yonder earned this trip riding as my shotgun."

"Oh, my gosh! I never expected," she said wiping her hands on her apron several times before unconsciously touching the bun of hair on the back of her head. "But the cost of the groceries?"

"Paid in full by your handsome young prince, too, I'm afraid," he said as he climbed up on his wagon. Seating himself he looked back at the fair pair and said, "If I can find where my no-good partner is holed up, I suspect we'll be back fur breakfast though."

"Oh bless, you Mr. Houghton. I'll have the biggest two steaks I can find waiting for you," Carol said as she waved to him.

After watching him drive off she turned to Cliff and in a scornful tone demanded, "What's this about you getting yourself involved in a bank robbery?"

"Now, Carol, I wasn't exactly involved. Hell, to hear you say it, I was one of the robbers."

"Well, you were the story on the first page of 'The Frontier Index' yesterday morning when we saw it!" Connie added.

"Look girls, I'll tell you all about it when I get in tonight. I have to go and put Red up."

"You had better," Carol said.

"And you had better not be too late either," her sister added.

"That's really some brother you girls have got," Ron Bridwell said as Cliff rode off.

"You just don't know," Carol replied.

*'Neither do I,'* Connie thought as she watched Cliff turn onto Grant Avenue.

He put Red in Boeing's barn, giving him a large bucket of grain before putting his saddle in the tack room.

Satisfied with this chore, he headed east on Custer Avenue with the Henry over his shoulder toward Teachman's Dry Goods.

Marlene was near the back with a lady customer when he came in. Their talk suddenly became whispers, and he was sure they were talking about him from the looks they each kept giving him for a split-second at a time before turning their eyes back away. Finally, the lady gathered her plunder and Marlene said, "Thank you so much, Mrs. Baxkin, it's support from people like you that will give me the strength to survive this ordeal."

"Why, Mrs. Teachman, you're worth every penny of it," the other woman said as she started out, stealing just one more glance at Cliff before she exited the door.

"I'm afraid I haven't the collar material for you shirt yet, Mr. Brown," she said approaching him.

"Well, that's why I came in, Ma'am. I was down to Green River City, and I happened upon this," he said handing her a small package wrapped in brown paper.

Opening it she saw two yards of white cotton material.

"Oh, Mr. Brown! This will be just perfect, but I'm afraid you have purchased much too much for a single collar."

"Well, Ma'am, I really didn't know about those things."

"Oh, you must stop referring to me as Ma'am. It makes me think you consider me an old woman."

"Not at all. You are anything but old," he replied, beginning to feel a little nervous as he realized that this was probably headed in the direction he had hoped. Still unsure of himself, he took a deep breath and ingested her womanhood and added, "But we must make a pact then."

"What sort of pact, Mr. Brown?"

"If I stop calling you Ma'am, you must stop calling me Mr. Brown. Deal?"

"I see," she said pausing for a moment. "My good friends call me Marlene____,in private," she finally said.

"And mine, 'Reb'," he said.

She looked into his steel gray eyes staring deeply as if trying to see into his soul, and finally, in a totally different tone of voice, she softly asked, "Where are you having supper tonight____Reb?"

"I was hoping here with you, Marlene," he replied also softly but firmly.

"I was, too," she said. "I close in an hour."

"I will be back in two," he replied calculating the hour of full dark.

Hurrying to the cottage he bathed, dressed in clean duds and was out of the house before the sisters arrived home.

From there he headed straight for Morris' Saloon to see Nadine. Upon entering he was surprised to see the place quite busy at this time of the day, with what looked to be a third of Sweetwater's crowd in there. She was wearing a red dress that was cut low in the front and allowed a generous glimpse of her breasts each time she leaned over a table to talk to someone. When she did, the whole table seemed to brighten up. Finally, she saw him standing at the bar, and looking around, she turned and said something to Dora and then walked over and out the side door. Cliff finished his beer and left by the front door. Coming around through the alley he found her smoking a cigarette.

"Good to see you, Georgia," she said as he approached.

"Purty Thing," he replied and touched the brim of his Stetson.

"I've been hearing good things about you."

"Where did you hear them?"

"Oh, Judge Morris read in the 'South Pass News' about you eventuating that robbery, down to Green River."

"I just happened to be there."

"She says, not so. She says, let me see, in her words 'That Reb Brown up and terminated that gang of ruffians alone'," Nadine replied taking a long pull on her makin's, "Them was her words."

"I had to do something," he countered. "They were about to steal all our dust."

"And they didn't?"

Reaching into his right boot top he retrieved a small hardback book and handed it to her.

"What's this?" she asked before opening it.

"I had a little trouble with Roper's boys on the way down there and I figured it best to open you an account rather than bring back cash, just in case they bushwhacked me on the way back."

After looking at the bank book several seconds she replied, "Sometimes you amaze me, Georgia."

Smiling, he tipped his hat again and started to turn away.

"Wait, I wish you would come upstairs with me. Not business, just us," she said almost in a plea.

"Not tonight, Purty Thing," he said. "I have obligations I must do. Things that were started into motion the day I arrived here."

"Those things wouldn't happen to be two sisters, would they?" she shot back feeling totally rejected.

"No, they aren't. It's a pay back I owe, little more," he said realizing he was only telling half a truth.

"Alright, sure, some other time," she snapped and threw down her Bull Durham.

Again he touched his brim before turning and walking away.

'Damn him anyway,' she thought. 'He's the only man I have ever asked up that wasn't business since Brady was killed. Damn you to hell, Reb Brown.'

Just short of a half moon was rising, bathing small strips of silver between the building in the rear alley and against the barn door that was fully closed, when he rounded the back of Teachman's store.

Cliff knocked softly on the backdoor and he saw a lamp light in the hallway.

"Yes?" she spoke just loud enough for him to hear.

"Marlene," he replied careful not to speak his name in case neighbors were listening.

The door opened and he stepped in and she quickly shut it behind him. Turning, she led the way through the first door on the left which opened into a kitchen. Her drapes were drawn tightly and he suddenly felt the way he imagined it would feel in a cave deep within the earth where no one could see you and you could see no one.

Setting the coal oil lamp on the counter she turned so the light would bath her before him.

Her very dark dress contrasted sharply with her blond hair and light skin. He was not sure if it was blue or black, but it really didn't matter. There in the lamplight, suddenly she was simply lovely in that dress, and he hungered for her. Boldly stepping forward, he took her in his arms and kissed her hard. At first, she seemed surprised with almost a push of rejection, but then she released her inhibitions and met his lust with her own.

After all, this was what she had secretly wanted since the first day she realized just how much Ernie hated him. Now, she wondered, how am I going to let the bastard know?

When they stopped for air she stepped back and with a little trouble said, "Well, Reb, you certainly know how to wake up a girl's feelings."

"The sight of you in that dress woke up mine," he replied.

"Thank you, that is certainly quite a compliment."

"You are quite a lady."

Smiling at him she turned towards the icebox and opened the door. Bending over so that the soft material hugged her backside tightly she reached for the bottle therein.

"I hope you like wine with your dinner," she said as she stood and turned handing him the dark bottle.

"I think tonight I would like most anything with my supper," he said.

"Good, because I didn't have time to fix very much."

"I don't want very much."

"Oh, I do hope that is not true," she said holding out a glass for him to pour the wine into.

The goblet was the largest he had ever seen. Even back before the war when his Aunt Ludy would entertain with fine china and real crystal, he had never seen anything so large.

"Marlene, I do believe that glass will hold this whole bottle."

"Yes, I believe it would, but let's not fill it. It's so much better to sip it cold, and I know I could never drink it fast enough before it would get too warm."

"I see your point," he said filling it with about a quarter of the bottle.

"Just one glass?" he questioned. "Don't I get any?"

"Oh. I'm sure you will get all you want," she said as a devilish smile crossed her lips. Then she added, "But it's so romantic to share the goblet. Don't you think?"

"Yes, it is," he answered, not finding any other thing to say.

She had prepared a small cut of beef sirloin she had baked earlier in the week and a salad of lettuce and tomatoes she had gotten off a granger from the Wind River Valley, some forty miles north, two days before and had been saving for a lunch she had planned with her neighbor Pam Gadsden. Luckily, she and Pam had not been able to get together. Cliff liked neither the salad or beef very much. The salad was too dry and the meat much too over-cooked, but he was sure supper was just a scene to be played out. He was right.

Immediately after eating, she blew out the candles that were on the table, and then she said in a matter-of-factlike manner, "Reb, will you bring the wine?" Picking up the oil lamp, she started for the other door in the kitchen.

He picked up the large glass and then opened the icebox door and reached for the now half-empty bottle of dark liquid. When he turned, she was gone, and the trail of light was fading as the door slowly closed. Rushing to catch it in time he almost dropped the bottle.

Entering the room she had disappeared into, he realized it was a bedroom, and he looked about for a place to set everything.

She leaned over the bed to light a small reading lamp, and the fabric of her dark dress clung to her backside as if it were wet. She then blew out the larger lamp she had been carrying and walked around in front of him, and this time she did the kissing. Her lips were warm and wet, and he immediately felt himself begin to grow.

After what seemed to him to be half an hour of strain intermingled with pleasure she backed off and stood there looking at him.

Cliff was completely caught off-guard with her forwardness. He had been sure he would get a poke at her, but he had not been sure how many nights of her cooking he would have to endure to receive the desired dessert.

Almost as if she had received some clue she began to undress, first came the long gown. Beneath was a white camisole and matching pantaloons. The camisole had hid two grapefruit size melons with taut nipples, surrounded by small pink areola.

Cliff immediately felt his manhood come to full attention.

When the pantaloons fell silently to the floor, she stepped forward one small step leaving nothing covering her nakedness, save two black high top shoes that neither she nor he had time or desire to mess with.

The hair of her triangle was so light he could barely see that it was there, and when he ran his fingers through it he thought of cornsilk.

There was no more need or time for words. Two adults were about to copulate in the rawest meaning of the word, and they both knew it.

She had been fast the first time, and he was proud he had been able to hold off his passion until she was ready again. Afterward, she lay there breathing heavily.

Clifford Brown was a disciplined man. His father had been a disciplined man, and he respected that. One might say discipline had been bred in him. It was one of the reasons he had gotten along so well in the army. He observed the discipline required by the army, and he demanded it of his men. Another trait bred in Clifford Brown was, being a gentleman was as important as being honest and truthful. He had many years before learned to be a gentleman at all times the situation allowed, and this was especially true around women and especially true when in bed with one. He had disciplined himself never to succumb to his passion until the lady had done so and usually twice. This hard rule in his life had made him very popular among his lovers, but had also, at times, been a thorn when he was with a whore.

The light of the lamp above the bed revealed her every detail, both flawed and flawless, and he ingested them all. The color of her hair was beautiful, but he disliked the way she parted it in the middle. Her skin was pale almost to a fault, but the sight of it stirred nerves in him he did not realize he had. Her nose was thin as he liked, but it had a peculiar roundness to its tip that distracted from her beauty. Her mouth was too small, but her lips were full and wet. Her shoulders were smooth and clean, but too narrow for her height. Her breasts far too small for his liking, but were firm with nipples that stood proud and straight as a chimney. Her waist was small, and her belly as flat as the top of a cherry table, but her navel was too large. Her hips were not as round as he liked, but still when she rolled over on her stomach he saw her cheeks were full and tight as if there were two miniature copies of independence rock under her skin and there on her left cheek, was a purple birthmark that looked strangely like a small heart. Her legs were long and smooth, and he could tell she had taken great pains having the hair shaved from them recently, but her calves were too lean, her feet were too small for her height, but her toes were long and straight.

For every fault he could find, she would show him a plus, and for every attribute he could find, a flaw, but she was one thing that too many women were not, and there was no fault in that. *'She is a passionate woman, who knows well that sex is to be enjoyed. Knowledge for the most part only whores have, and even they often forget this way too soon in their lives.'*

Marlene rose and went into the next room to use the pot in there, and he was glad for the intermission. When she returned, she blew out the light and opened the drapes of a window allowing the southwest breeze to fill the hot room. Returning to bed she lay naked there with the moon shining on her body, and Cliff felt his blood once again begin to stir. The smell of her pure white skin was intoxicating, and he knew she had used a rose scent toilet water in her bath.

Slowly he began to touch her with his tongue, ever so lightly, and she became as a ball with a thousand pins sticking into her every nerve ending. Looking down at her feet he was mesmerized by the straightness of them and slowly he began to move down toward them, finally he began taking each toe and slowly running his tongue around and around it until he could tell she was building her passion, and then he would place it in his mouth and suck on it until he thought she had a mini-climax. Satisfied with her reaction, he would move on to the next until after having sucked each, he moved quickly up and entered her again, and immediately she exploded into a massive fit, screaming and bucking like the wildest bronco he had ever ridden. On and on they rode each other and the longer they did, the louder she screamed.

Pam Gadsden had seen the figure of a tall man pass between their house and the Teachman's Store shortly after dark, but had said nothing. She had not been able to see his face in the dim light and had lost sight of him when he rounded the rear of Teachman's. She assumed he was one of those who Ernie had let sleep in the barn, even though Marlene had told her she was getting rid of her barn boarders. She now lay in the back of her house and listened to the screaming coming from her neighbor's bedroom window; many might have thought a murder was taking place, but Pam knew better. When all was quiet she felt her own wetness and turned to her sleeping husband, but he refused to be awakened. Finally, she cursed Marlene under her breath, and in a jealous fury she bit her lip until blood flowed from it, then in desperation she moved her hand down.

It was an hour before sunup when Cliff slipped out of the backdoor and headed for 'The South Pass Saloon'.

He knew there was going to be hell to pay when he saw the Steele sisters for not coming in at all his first night back in town, and he wanted someone to be able to say they had seen him out carousing the bars.

Walking in, he immediately spied a table full of miners that regularly frequented 'The Sisters'.' Walking up he said smiling, "Hello gents, got room for another?"

"You were right, Chip. To have killed him on the trail now would have been a sure fire way to bring the hue and cry of the citizens out from their hiding places. No, we must find another way to deal with Brown," Ed Sholtz said.

"I understand Houghton brought up a stamp mill for The Miner's Delight."

"I haven't heard."

"Well, he did. Last night," the old Austrian said turning and looking out of the small window of the shack that served as mine office. "Find him before he leaves. I want to talk to him."

"Boss," was Ropers only answer as he slipped off the wooden table he had been sitting on.

Three hours later in the same shack, two men who had little regard for each other continued a strained conversation.

"I tell ya straight, Ed, I don't know how long it will take to get another here. Frank McGovern sent all the way to Pittsburgh fur that one, and it took near two months fur it to get to Green River."

"Listen, Houghton, I don't want excuses, I want a ten stamp mill for 'The Monia'. I intend to make 'The Monia' the most profitable hole in this valley. Hell, in this territory.

"I also plan on something else too," he said turning and looking out the window at the two acres of flat ground three hundred yards away. Wetting his lips before he spoke he added, "Don't you plan on hauling for nobody else for a while, Houghton. I aim to keep you busy working for me."

"That ain't likely, Ed Sholtz. I got regular customers."

"They can wait. When you get back, there will be an order for you wired to your office. I want it here 'afore the week's out."

"I'll get to it when I can," Art said as he turned for the door.

Suddenly a heavy Bowie flew past his head and stuck two inches deep in the door planking.

"Jesus!" Art exclaimed.

"Get this straight, Houghton, until there's a better freight hauler in these parts, you will be hauling for me."

Art Houghton went straight to Sheriff Boyd, but was soon to hear from the top lawman, "As far as I see it, Ed Sholtz has committed no crimes. Unless you want to swear out a formal complaint against him, there is nothing I can do."

The next morning when he and Cotter headed back south, their two wagons were escorted by five of Sholtz' men as far as the south cut of Big Sandy Creek. "The boss just wanted to see that you had no problems with them marauding Indians," Chip Roper said just before they turned back for Monia.

Until the fall snows began to cause real problems along the route, The Houghton & Cotter Freight Lines made steady runs from the U.P. tracks to the Monia. With the exception of several pieces of machinery for a stamp mill, the majority of the loads were of fresh cut planks used in the construction of the new town of 'Monia,' being built on a flat piece of ground near the mine.

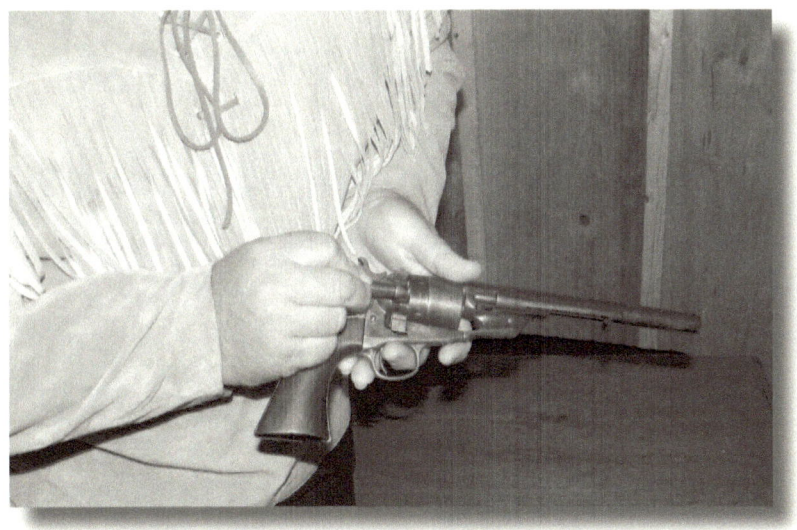

**Reb loading a Henry Round into his
Richards Conversion 1860 Army Colt**

# Chapter Seven
# Monia City

The first week in October, Esther Morris threw one of her tea parties at her cabin on the edge of town for several visiting politicians from Cheyenne. Miss Tipper and Lois Lovelle had been sent over to help with the guests. It was decided to move the party over to Morris' Saloon shortly after sunup as the snowstorm that had started around five that morning was intensifying, and the winds were picking up to gale force. They were running low on food and drink in the small house, and no one really was ready to stop the fun.

Nadine and Lois were left to clean up the place and then get some rest before they had to begin their shift later in the day.

This whole affair was very unusual, for Esther seldom allowed the girls to come to her home, let alone sleep there while she was away, but there had been some talk that the Governor was thinking about a woman as a running mate for the office of vice-governor next term, and she had chosen to stay close to the men from Cheyenne. Since Charlotte and Belle were still at the saloon and could pick up the party there, Nadine and Lois were allowed to rest up at the Morris home.

Around eight o'clock, John Morris made his way back to the house to pick up some of 'the judge's papers', he said, and told Lois she had better make it for the saloon before his path through the drifts was wiped out. By this time, the storm was so intense that one could not see the other buildings some fifty yards away.

At first Nadine was unsettled by this, but she did see the fury of the blizzard and he did go immediately to the judge's desk and began going through her papers. But within minutes when he was ready to leave, all signs of the path he had cut were gone and they seemed to be stuck there.

There was a partial cord for fuel, but none too much and he suggested a drink of whiskey to warm them up, bringing out a bottle of good eastern bourbon.

Half an hour later, he was all over her.

From the time Cliff had returned from his trip to Green River City, until late September had brought its chilling winds, he had enjoyed himself very little. His relationship with the sisters in general, and Carol in particular, had been going downhill. She was convinced he had spent the night of his return with another woman, and she had never forgiven him for it. Finally he had decided to find another place to stay, while he waited for the first of October to arrive, when he planned to be in Green River City for the arrival of Rob Scogins' brother.

Marlene Teachman had asked him into her shop on two occasions a week to check on how the shirt she was making fit. The project that was only going to take a couple days was now in its second month.

Pam Gadsden had made a point of stopping in the next morning after his first visit. "I am so glad you and Mr. Teachman are getting back together," she had said to Marlene.

"What on earth has given you that horrible idea?" Marlene exclaimed.

"Well, I was sure I saw him enter your backdoor last night."

"If he ever comes in my door again after dark, I assure you he will go out feet first," she said back and dropped the subject to Pam's dismay.

The very next day, when she saw Ernie on the boardwalk, Pam couldn't help saying, "I was so glad to see you going in the backdoor of your home a couple nights ago." Totally satisfied with the expression she received back from him she continued, "That is until Marlene told me it wasn't you at all, rather one of the miners who had come to pick up something he had ordered."

"If I catch any dirty miner slipping around there I'll kill him in his tracks," he screamed.

Marlene, who had come out her front door just in time to hear her friend spill the goods on her, replied to Ernie's statement. "I wouldn't be so sure that you could hold your own with a man, miner or other." Before she stepped back inside, she gave Pam a hateful look and then slammed the front door.

Ernie spent the next two nights hidden in the loft of the barn hoping to catch whoever she was entertaining, but the temperature dropped to just above freezing late on the second night, and he decided it wasn't worth it. He did notice the Copperhead's horse was once again in one of the stalls, eating the high-priced grain that he had ordered all the way from Salt Lake City especially for their better customers.

When this ad appeared in the 'South Pass Gazette' Cliff noticed it, and it seemed to be just what he needed at the time.

SOUTH PASS HOTEL !
THE ONLY FIRST CLASS HOTEL IN THIS CITY.
COMMODIOUS ROOMS,
NEATLY AND COMFORTABLY FITTED WITH
NEW FURNITURE !
TABLE CONSTANTLY SUPPLIED WITH
GAME AND ALL OTHER AVAILABLE LUXURIES.
STAGE COACHES
CONCLUDING THE LINE OF TRAVEL BETWEEN THE
U.P.R.R. AND SOUTH PASS CITY ARRIVE AND
DEPART FROM THIS HOUSE.

Janet Sherlock, who owned and managed the hotel when her husband Dick was not there, was a pleasant enough woman, but her strict overture was a sure deterrent to any thoughts beyond friendship he might have envisioned when he first saw her. He arranged for a room that had two beds: one for Ash Scogins and one for himself.

He also had found that indeed Rob Scogins had been digging somewhere in the area of the Monia, but as of the last week in September, he had not found anyone who could pinpoint the exact location. Charlie Lightburn claimed to have no record of Rob Scogins filling but one dig, and that was not near 'The Monia'.

He also learned a posted letter had been sent to the U.S. Assessor, E. P. Snow, in Cheyenne, but no answer had been received by the time he mounted Red for the ride to Green River City on the 28th. He was not sure of the identity or the importance of E. P. Snow, but he did realize that Rob Scogins had considered him important enough to make this contact, and he wanted to learn more of Mr. Snow.

A telegraph message was waiting for him upon his arrival.

```
Deliver To C Brown Green River City
Wyoming


Will arrive October two
                END
            Signed Ash Scogins
```

However, upon arriving at the depot on the second at the prescribed time, he found that the train was stuck dead in a drift on the snowy range west of Laramie. A relief crew had been sent from Cheyenne to try and dig it out, but no one knew for sure when the train would be moving again.

**Ol′ # 77 Stuck in a Drift**

On the fifth, after a dreadful wind had come up out of the southwest and blown all the snow somewhere to the northeast, and a barren but frozen prairie was visible once again Ol' Number 77 rolled in huffing, puffing, and belching black smoke.

Cliff watched the passengers detrain and saw no one who he judged to be Mr. Ashley Scogins. After waiting until the train moved on west, he reentered the depot and asked the telegrapher to send a wire back along the track, attempting to find Mr. Scogins.

It was then the small, thin young lady who was sitting very patiently on the hard bench next to the potbellied stove spoke. "I, sir, am Ashley Scogins." Clearing her throat she added, "I do hope you are Mr. Brown."

"Oh Lord!" Cliff muttered.

He let her have his room at 'The Blade', and spent the night in Mr. Houghton's warehouse, there being no other rooms available at either hotel.

Cliff had bought a horse for '*him*' to ride, which he then had to sell back, along with the tack, at a loss. He was able to secure her a seat with Art, who was attempting a load north on the seventh, since the weather had warmed so suddenly.

That evening after supper gave them time to get to know each other a little, and having gotten over his initial shock, they began to talk freely.

He learned that her brother Charles had been killed while working as a caretaker at the Confederate Cemetery in Higginsville, Missouri.

"It seems someone shot him from afar with a rifle, and no one knows anything more about it other than he was found dead," she explained, "Two days later I was presented with a bill for back taxes." She took a deep breath before continuing, "Charles told me they were paid almost a year ago." She stopped and shook her head before she removed the pins and took off her netted hat and laid it on the small table. "I have been unable to find a receipt, and if I cannot come up with sufficient funds by the first of the year, our family farm will be auctioned off, a piece of land that has been in the Scogins' family for more than 50 years."

"You see we have been labeled Secessionist because our father and older brother Rob both served with General Kirby Smith during the war, but Charles, who was only my senior by less that two years, was much too young to do any fighting during the war. Of course, he was a Democrat, as I myself am," she proudly added before looking out over the vast open whiteness, dotted here and there by dark sage and greasewood that was tall enough to show itself.

The small girl began to slowly shake her head as she continued her story, "He worked extra jobs as well as there at the farm," she paused, "to keep the place after Rob left for the gold fields almost two years ago. Father did not return from the fighting in Arkansas, and now it is only me," she ended with a heavy sigh.

Cliff had a hard time finding the words to tell her how he had come to know Rob. He also wanted to explain he was not really her brother's partner, and as a result, he did not know the location of the diggings. Somehow he needed to let her know Rob had told him of a rich strike, but at the moment he simply couldn't find the words, so he said no more on the subject; he just didn't think she could handle additional bad news at the moment.

It was near the ten o'clock hour when he left her to go to Houghton's warehouse, and he was sure she would cry herself to sleep that night.

Two days later when they finally arrived in South Pass City, Cliff rented another room at 'The South Pass Hotel' for Ash. He knew Carol would never understand, but their relationship had deteriorated to the point that he really didn't care. He would always have soft feelings and warm memories of Carol, but there were certain things that he simply could not tolerate and a fit of jealousy was one of them. He was not her husband; they had never talked of marriage. In fact, she wouldn't even admit their relationship to her sister, but she demanded he act the part of a husband, and that was not something he was willing to do. *'Too bad, other than these faults, she is a woman I really like.'*

Early the next afternoon he entered Morris' Saloon to find that Nadine no longer worked there. Klu did not know where she had gone or wouldn't tell him. Again, he felt a loss, a strange emptiness in his chest, not unlike the feeling he had experienced when he had to leave Georgia.

About that time Bodie Johnson walked up to the bar and stopped beside him. "I have information I understand you have been asking about."

Cliff didn't know him, but had seen him in the place before, so he asked, "What is that?"

"You buying?"

Cliff nodded to Klu, and the big man poured Bodie a drink as the coin was dropped on the bar.

"Understand you are looking fur the diggings Rob Scogins wus working."

"Could be."

"Is it worth $50?"

"It could be worth $20 if it is in the right place."

"Twenty, huh? That's all?"

"That's all from me. His kin might pay more."

"Kin?" the man jerked his head around and with a surprised expression said, "Hell, he never had no kin I ever heard of."

"Don't know as much as you think then, do you?"

"Let's see your twenty," Bodie said back with a nasty taste in his mouth.

Cliff reached into his vest pocket and removed a small roll of bank notes and pulled a twenty from it, then said, "If this ain't right, you'll wish you never bothered me."

"Oh, I won't wish that," Bodie replied looking at the roll Cliff was putting back into his pocket.

"Now, where?"

"Come on, I'll show you. It's east a' here."

Ten minutes later when he had returned with Red, Bodie was waiting in a chair on the boardwalk. He walked out into the muddy street and mounted a dirty brown mustang and led off towards the cemetery road.

After they had topped the hill, he turned and headed east in the general direction of Monia City, across country. For five miles he rode along at an easy pace while he blew on his mouth organ. The tunes varied from *Oh Susanna* to *Red River Valley* with others in between, but when he started *Marching Through Georgia* Cliff recognized trouble and slid from his horse, pulling his Colt as he did. It was none too fast a movement, for a bullet slammed into the saddlehorn the instant his boots were on the ground. Bodie turned in his saddle pulling his revolver and took a quick shot back at him, but he was in a bad position to do any aiming, and the ball missed Cliff by several feet. Cliff had already chosen his target before he knew danger was so close, and his bullet found its mark entering Bodie's right kidney and coming to rest against his left breast bone having passed through both lungs and cutting a large gash across the back side of his pumper. Bodie was dead within seconds of hitting the ground.

Rolling away from the little clearing, Cliff stopped behind a large rock and waited. There was no sign of the rifleman, and after twenty minutes he slowly moved out. Still no one could be seen. Satisfied the sharpshooter was gone, he brought Red back to the spot where he had been standing when the shot rang out and back-trailed the angle and path the bullet had to have taken. There, some sixty yards away, were three good size boulders.

Carefully walking over to them he found in the mud among fresh boot tracks, a spent rifle percussion cap. Following the tracks down a little deer trail, he came to where three horses had been recently.

Returning to the scene, he removed the $20 from Bodie's pocket before catching the brown mustang. He tied the body on it then led the cayuse back to South Pass City.

Sheriff Boyd was not in his little office, so he carried the body over to the blacksmith's shop where Jimmy Smith, who was also the Town Marshal, worked.

"This happened out in the county you say?"

"That's right, five or six miles east a' here."

"Well, that's out of my jurisdiction."

"I know that, but I got to tell it to somebody, and Boyd is gone again."

"Well, you've told it; now take that body somewhere else; I got nothing to do with it."

"Where do you suggest?"

"Try Doc Hubbell, he's the coroner."

Turning the body over to the doctor, Cliff went back to 'The South Pass Hotel' to inform Ash what had happened.

While there, Sheriff Boyd came in and placed him under arrest.

"For what?"

"Fur killing Bodie Johnson. That's what."

"Kilt him I did, but not until after he and his compadres had taken a couple shots at me."

"That's fur you to prove. I got a witness what says you told Bodie that if he didn't give you the information you wanted, he would wish he had never set eyes on you."

"That's close to being right."

"And he was supposed to have a new $20 bank note on him and I couldn't find no such on the body. Lets see if you got one."

"I tell you he shot at me first." Cliff yelled.

"That just don't add up with him being shot in the back." Boyd answered and reached over relieving Cliff of his Colt first, then his roll of bills. "Let's go."

Suddenly Cliff found himself locked in the same stone jail he had some months before helped lock Concho and Yuel in, only there was not going to be a gang to come and rescue him.

The next day he was brought before Judge Morris. Sheriff Boyd presented the evidence before the J. P. while a small crowd gathered around outside. There was some talk for a swift hanging, but most of it was that Reb Brown had done a lot for the town, and they didn't believe he was a back-shooter.

Cliff told his side of the story and then Boyd added that he had found spent cartridges at the scene that were the same as was used in Brown's pistol.

"May I ask the Sheriff a question?" Cliff inquired.

"Certainly," she replied.

"How did you know where to go and find them, you weren't at the shooting, were you Sheriff?"

"I certainly wus not. I got a tip on whar' it took place, and they wus right. I found these here spent cat'ra'gies and a blood spot on the ground, a big 'un too."

Cliff quickly rebutted with, "Then that means your tip must a' been there, or how else would he a' knowed about it?"

"He has a point, Sheriff," the judge said.

"I reckon he heard Brown bragging about it."

"I never said where it happened to no one, I only told Marshal Smith it were east of town. I want to see this here tip of yours; I got a right to question him."

"He is a good informer. His tips have panned out before; I trust him," Boyd said back in a rough voice.

"He's right Sheriff, if you want these spent cases introduced as evidence, you will have to produce the witness who told you where to go and find them."

"I can't, I can't identify him or I'd get no more out a' him."

"Then I will consider these as having no bearing on the shooting," she said and then added, "Let me see the revolver."

Boyd was mad and it showed, but he had to abide by her decision and he knew it, so he handed the Colt towards the judge.

It was right then her husband spoke, "May I see that gun?"

Esther was shocked; he had never uttered a word in any of her hearings before.

Slowly and questioningly, the sheriff turned and handed it to him.

The man looked at it for some time and then turned it over and looked at the serial numbers. Rubbing some dust from the stampings on the frame he slowly nodded his head, and a slight smile came on his face.

"What is it, John?" she asked.

"I'll wait until after you have made your decision, Your Honor," he said to his wife.

Again she looked queerly at him, but finally returned her attention to the matters at hand.

"I do not see sufficient evidence for a conviction of anything at this time, but this is not a trial, only a hearing; I do see sufficient cause for a trial, so I am binding you over until the Circuit Judge can get here," she said and then turned to the Sheriff and asked, "Do we have a place where he can be kept safely and securely?"

"Well, there's____"

"Now, I would like to say something," John Morris interrupted.

"What is it you are dying to tell us, John?"

"There's no need for a place to keep him locked up. I ask the court to place him in my custody, and I'll see to it he is here for the trial."

"John, have you lost your senses?"

"No Esther, I have not. You see this here Colt revolver," he began, holding out the gun almost with what one might call affection, "Well, it once belonged to me. This man took it from me back in Tennessee during the war, course it was a cap n' ball then. I know, see these serial numbers," he said holding the revolver for her to see before he handed it to the sheriff for his own inspection, "they are the same," he quickly added, and then he paused and thought a moment before he continued with his tale.

"He could have killed me. Been as easy as spiting, but he didn't.

He let me live, and I say such a man did not bushwhack nobody, and I'll help him prove it."

Cliff looked at the man with narrowed eyes, and then slowly he began to open them as his recollection of the incident returned to him. *'Well I'll be damned. Who'd a' ever guessed such?'*

Judge Morris raised her back to a straight position before saying, "This man known as Reb Brown is hereby bound over for trial as soon as Judge Kingman gets back from Platte River Crossing, and is entrusted to the custody of one John Morris known to all here." With that she stood, but before she moved further she added, "Sheriff Boyd, give Mr. Brown back his Colt or is it his?" she looked at her husband.

The small round man smiled and said, "It's his. He won it fair and square on the field of battle."

After everyone had left her office except Cliff and the Morris' her husband came around and stuck out his hand to Cliff. "You know the first time I saw you I said there wus something about you that wus itching at me."

"I do truly thank you, Sur. I never had no Yank do nothing good ta me before," Cliff spoke back to him.

"No, no, I want to thank you. I have so many times thought of you and wondered why you didn't kill me that day," the man said still shaking his hand. "It would have been so easy and the natural thing to do."

Cliff started to tell him about the empty shotgun, but thought better of it. "I'm glad you survived the war, Sur," he said instead.

"Oh, let me tell you. Being captured was the best thing that ever happened to me. They sent us down to Chattanooga to a camp, and I was traded about two months later. I had come down with the measles, and them Reb doctors wus glad to be rid a' me. When I got back to our lines I wus so sick, they sent me back to Peru, Illinois, and then, before I wus up and about, my enlistment wus up and I weren't no where nears crazy enough to go back fur a second run."

"Well, you shor' saved my bacon today," Cliff answered as he strapped on his Colt.

"Come on, I'm buying the drinks," John Morris said taking Cliff by the arm and leading him out of her office. "What brought you here, Mr. Brown? Gold, I suppose?"

"Yes, that was it," Cliff admitted.

"Well, let me tell you something. The only ones who really leave the gold fields with money are them what offers services to the diggers. I come here back in '68 and filed a couple claims, but only got a few thousand. That's when I come up with the idea to build my saloon here. Town with only three saloons is doomed, and that's all we had back then. Esther sold our store back in Peru and came out later and opened her millinery store here; we done well. 'Course she don't approve of the girls working upstairs," he said lifting his shoulder. "But they do bring in the men and the men bring in the gold, so she just keeps her distance, most of the time," he added.

As they walked into his saloon Cliff said, "Yes, you do have some nice girls here alright; by the way what happened to Miss Tipper?"

"Not so loud," John cautioned, turning and looking behind them making sure Esther was not near. Satisfied, he answered, "She left. And I hear she is working over to 'The Monia'."

"The mine?" questioned Cliff.

"No silly, the saloon Ed Sholtz has put up in his new city," Morris replied then added almost in disgust, "Won't last. Town won't last with only one saloon."

Morris had led him to the bar where he nodded for Klu to fill two glasses. "Here's to old times, may they never be relived."

"I'll drink to that," Cliff said lifting his whiskey in a salute.

They had two more before Cliff finally said, "Well Mr. Morris, I thank you again, but I got 'a be looking for some evidence to clear me."

"Naw, J.H. ain't gon'a let nobody get hung with no more evidence than they got on you."

"I do hope you are right, but just the same I think I had better do a little for myself."

"Well alright, now you just remember this is your watering hole from now on."

"Yes Sur, I'll remember," Cliff replied and turned to leave, but he stopped short seeing Chip and Phil just inside the doors. The expressions on their faces gave all the evidence one might need to believe they had come looking for him, or trouble, or both.

"Well, lookie here. If it ain't the back-shooter," Phil said as Cliff approached.

"Don't crowd me, boy. I ain't here looking for trouble, but I'm in no mood to eat any a' your shit."

"Oh, big man. Maybe you ain't so big with a body looking you in the eye."

Cliff walked on past the young man ignoring his comments. *'I been out a' trouble less than thirty minutes, and now this half-pint's got 'a start something,'* Cliff thought as he neared the bat wing doors. *'If I just keep on moving, he won't shoot with this many witnesses.'*

"Just like a yellow Copperhead. Won't stand up and face a man, got 'a shoot his victims in the back," Cliff heard him say fractions of a second before the unmistakable sound of hammer and sear slapping against one another thundered in his ears.

*'Mee'be I played this one wrong. I believe that crazy son-of-a-bitch is going to shoot me,'* he thought as his hand started for the Colt.

But the action was played out in a totally different manner.

Cliff whirled to meet his attacker just in time to see the huge arm come down. There was a loud thud, a sound not unlike what one hears when a squirrel takes a hit from a round ball in a Georgia swamp.

Chip jumped in surprise, as Phil slumped to the floor beside him. He, too, whirled into the assault, only to find the same barrel that had just laid a four-inch cut across his friend's head, now sticking into his ribs.

"What the____?"

"Just leave your hog leg rest and be a-helping your friend there. He don't seem to be able to keep to his feet," the big man said as he pointed to where the unconscious Sholtz lay.

"Mister, you done bought yourself a passel a' trouble. That's Ed Sholtz' boy you just buffaloed," Chip said in a low, but commanding voice.

"I know who he is, and I just saved him from the hangman's noose, seems to me."

"Hell, nobody's gon'a hang no Sholtz round here," Chip replied as he tried to move away a little from the hard steel that was still poking into his side. "Besides, you are siding up with a murdering back-shooter."

"Well, from where I stand, looked to me that kid there was about to do the back-shooting," the man replied and slowly removed his revolver and replaced it in a belt holster.

Chip bent over for a grip on Phil's shoulders, but as he did so the blond man looked up at Cliff, and at that moment he changed his mind and began moving one hand toward his holstered revolver.

At that moment, Esther Morris came from the backroom and saw what was happening.

"Now stop that, Mr. Roper. I'll have none of it in my place," she shouted.

When he didn't even look her way she added, "If I have to, I'll see to it your boss is served with a restraining order to keep you two out of this whole town."

Chip at that time reached back again, took a firm hold on Phil's shoulders and lifted the boy to his feet. "Let's go, Phil. We can catch up with these jaspers sometime when they ain't hiding behind skirts," he said loud enough so Cliff could hear but she could not, and then they turned and moved out.

"I find myself obliged to you, mister," Cliff said to the stranger that had perhaps just saved his life.

"Just never could stand by and watch that sort a' thing take place."

Cliff extended his left hand and introduced himself.

"Reb, huh?" The man replied. "I thought so from the drawl."

"That a problem?" Cliff said back defensively.

"Easy there, Reb. No, no problem. Leastwise nowadays. Maybe six or eight year ago," the man replied, "but now ____," he let the thought carry before he changed the subject. "Bruce Whittacur's the name."

Cliff took a measuring look at the man. He was at least two inches taller than Cliff's 6'2" height and a good hundred pounds heavier, a couple of which was the long coal-black beard, embedded with streaks of gray that hung from his face. He was wearing fringed buckskin trousers below a red and blue plaid shirt that contrasted sharply with his white suspenders.

While the man had been speaking, Cliff noticed his black belt was held together with a solid brass buckle carrying the crest of Oregon.

"You're one big Yank; I'll say that for you," Cliff replied. "What outfit?"

"First Oregon Voluntary Infantry," he said before adding, "I was with Phil Sheridan at Fort Yamhill Blockhouse."

"Forrest, Tennessee."

"Guess we never shot at one another then."

"Must not of, I don't see how I could have missed anything as big as you," Cliff replied and smiled.

"Many did, Reb. Many did," the man said placing a massive arm around Cliff's shoulders and turning him back to the bar. "We better have a snort or two and give them gents a chance to get dragged out a-hiding in the cold, just in case they's awaiting fur us."

Cliff looked at the lady who had just staved off the trouble. "Thank you, Ma'am."

"Trouble does seem to find you, Mr. Brown," the judge said.

"This one weren't none a' his doing," Bruce said back to her.

"He's right, I saw the whole affair," John agreed.

"I suppose not. Just the same, I want you here for the trial. My husband has placed us both in a precarious position," she said looking over at John Morris.

"Yes, Ma'am," Cliff agreed just before she turned and left the room.

An hour later Chip convinced Phil to leave the ambush location under the stairs of 'The White Swan Saloon', just up the street where they had spent the time cursing and shivering in the cold wind.

"Where you staying, Mr. Whittacur?"

"I wus over to Monia working at the mine, but since that fellow is who that fellow is, I guess I just whacked myself out of a job, and I don't answer to Mr. Whittacur. My friends call me Bruce, some Big Bruce."

"Alright, Bruce why don't we go over to my place. I have someone I need to check on."

"Alright."

Ash was all smiles and tears when Cliff told her of the happenings at the hearing that morning.

Bruce was all smiles at Ash.

"I sure thought I was going to be riding The Owl Hoot Trail in these parts for awhile. I just knew I was going to have to kill that kid, and that would a put me in bad with the local law again," Cliff said. "If Bruce hadn't stepped in when he did, it would a been me or him. I think I could have taken him, but not Chip too, for surely he'd a' entered it."

"I think the only trail you'd a' been riding would a' been to Boot Hill. Them boys had you braced," Bruce contradicted. "They wus ready. They wanted you to make a play."

"Well, they have been after me for some time. I just never figured they would try it in a place like that."

"Why are they after you?" Bruce asked.

Ash looked at him wondering if he was going to trust his new friend with the whole story or not.

"Come on and sit down, this might take a while," he said then added, "There's a couple of things Ash doesn't know about, and I guess it's high time to let her in on them."

Cliff had told her about finding her brother up near Independence Rock, but had not shared with her who his assassins were. Upon hearing this new information, she gasped and turned very pale and sat back on the bed as he continued.

"That's the story," he said to Bruce when finished.

"Yes, I see now why they want you out of the way," the big man said, "they believe you are a partner in this here mine, and they don't want nobody to find it; must be a good one."

"I don't know, her brother thought so," Cliff said. "Trouble is, we don't even know where it is."

"We will, when Mr. Snow answers Rob's letter," she said.

"I hope you are right."

"You better hope there is some load left by then," Bruce said. "My guess is they are hauling that stuff out a' there as fast as they can get to it."

"Yeah, probably concentrating on Rob's mine and letting theirs rest a spell," Cliff agreed.

"Then we need to move fast. If you are sure it was Sholtz' bunch that kilt him over it, I bet it is that new hole I been working on, south of the Monia's big shaft."

"How far south?"

"Well, the entrance is, oh say half a mile. It's over a hill and then some. But Captain Nickerson said that Sholtz was planning to run a connecting shaft from the Monia's south shaft through the hill over to the new dig so everything could be railed back to the stamp mill at the mouth of 'The Monia'. Never did make any sense to me. Why dig that fur underground when you could cut a wagon road in a fraction of the time."

Cliff sat up and began to take notice. "This new dig, it's producing good ore?"

"The best, Nickerson said as good as 'The Monia' did back in the beginning."

"Well, what if this new dig is really the Scogins' claim, and what if they want to keep it all connected to one mine so nobody would know it was really two?"

"Yeah, once they made the connection they could close off the old entrance," Bruce agreed.

"Not just close it off, but eliminate all traces of it. Then everything that was brought out a' there would be coming from 'The Monia'."

"Oh dear," she said in a despairing tone. "We are never going to get any of Rob's gold."

"Your gold, Ash, but don't worry we will work this out," Big Bruce said to her.

Ash Scogins placed her hands on her legs and looked down, "I don't see how," she said.

"Captain Nickerson is an honest man," Bruce said, then pausing he added, "I think.

If we can get this to court, he will tell the truth about what's come out so far. It's his job to keep such records fur Sholtz."

"How we gon'a do that?" she asked.

"With the word of Mr. E. P. Snow, that's how, as you know your brother sent word to him, and I think you should send another urging him of the importance of time in this matter," Cliff responded, standing and walking over to the window. Looking out as he spoke, he suddenly saw a man put something in the saddlebags of a big bay horse across the street and then look about suspiciously before hurrying away.

"Tell me, Bruce," he asked without looking back. "Do you ride a bay horse?"

"Matter a' fact I do. He's in front of Tom Curry's store."

"Well, some jasper just put something in the saddlebags of a big bay tied up there."

"What?"

"Come on let's go see."

Arriving at the horse, Bruce opened the unbuckled saddle bag and retrieved a small bag of dust. The bag was stamped **'Property of The Monia Mine'.**

"Well, will you look at this?" he said holding it up.

"Give it to me and hurry," Cliff said taking the bag. "You stay out here," he nodded to Bruce before hurrying into Curry's store. Once inside he quickly hid the bag behind a large box of canned peaches and then walked over to where Tom Curry was finishing with two women customers.

Cliff touched the brim of his Stetson as he approached the ladies and then turned to Curry when the man asked, "Can I help you, sir?"

"Need some 'Arbuckles Riosa', Cliff answered.

"I have some right here," the storekeeper replied before turning to a large stack containing several one-pound bags of coffee. "Will there be anything else?"

Cliff ignored the man, watching instead the approach of Sheriff Boyd.

"Big Bruce," the lawman called out as he stopped a few feet away from the man and horse.

"Yes, Sheriff?"

"Now, don't take this personally, but I got a tip that you wus fired from the Monia this morning and that someone saw you steal some dust from the mine before you left."

"That's a damn lie. Who told you that?" Whittacur shot back angrily.

Immediately Boyd pulled his revolver before replying, "Now Big Bruce, you just back away from that mount, and keep your hands where I can see them."

"I tell you it's all a lie. I never got fired, and I never stole nothing."

"Well, we'll just see," The Sheriff said going immediately to the right saddlebag. Running his hand in, finding only a small, birdseye coffee pot, he looked up with a queer expression on his face. Then, moved around the rear of the horse and unbuckled the other bag. There finding only a rolled-up union suit, he stepped back and holstered his revolver.

"I guess I got a bad tip."

"You damn right you did. Now who told you that lie?"

"I ain't telling on my informants, to you or nobody else, but I assure you I'll see to this one myself," the lawman said and then turned away without any further comment.

"Hey, you star-packer," Bruce yelled, "I got a' apology coming."

"I don't apologize fur' doing my job. This time I just got a bad tip. Next time it won't be," the Sheriff said back without turning around.

"That son-of-a-bitch!" Bruce said loud enough for Boyd to hear.

When the sheriff rounded the corner onto Price Street, Cliff stepped out on the boardwalk in front of Curry's Store with the bag of coffee in his hand. "Pull in your horns, Bruce, and put this in your bag with the pot. We might need it some cold night."

"Did you hear what that son-a-bitch said to me? Accused me a being a thief."

"Price you pay for helping me out today."

"Where is it?"

"Inside, I think I'll leave it there for now, just in case he comes back."

"No, get it, them jaspers planted it on my horse, it's mine now. 'Sides I'm out a' work it seems, and my outfit's back at the bunkhouse in Monia," he said, and then thinking for a moment he added, "I'll need that."

"Makes sense to me," Cliff said, and they walked back into the store.

While Bruce got a tin of powder and some # 9 caps, Cliff retrieved the small bag from behind the peaches.

"Six dollars?" Bruce questioned.

"It's the times," Tom Curry replied to him.

"Come on, I'll pay for them. You can pay me back later," Cliff said dropping the coins on the rough counter and then they left.

"I could a' paid for it with some a' my dust," Bruce said.

"I don't think that would be a good idea right now. Come on back to the room, and I'll exchange it for you."

Shortly after they arrived, Ash was knocking at Cliff's door.

"What happened?"

They told her of the incident.

"That was sure a streak of good luck that you happened to look out the window when you did," she said.

"It sure wus," agreed Bruce. "Otherwise I'd be locked up somewhars' now."

"That somewhere is over to the stone jail, and I tell ya, it gets plenty cold in there, come night."

"Feels like there's about a pound here," Cliff said bouncing the small bag in his hand. "Let's see, at 18 to 20 dollars an ounce that should be about three hundred dollars or so." He then counted out fifty dollars in bank notes and handed them to Bruce. "I'll have this weighed after I get it changed into a different bag and make up the difference."

"Not to worry, I did come by it rather easy," the big man said smiling at Ash.

She smiled back, almost in a snicker.

They all three went to *The Sisters'* for supper and were warmly greeted by Connie, but less so by her sibling. While there, Art Houghton came in with a load of supplies for the girls and stopped to have a cup of Arbuckles with the trio. "I got 'a tell ya, I'm sure glad Bill Slack opened up that sawmill and lumberyard. It has relieved me a' hauling all them cut boards up to Monia," he said sipping the hot brew. "Now I can get back to attending to my good customers."

"Like us huh, Mr. Houghton?" Connie added to their conversation. "Actually, Mr. Houghton never stopped helping us," she said looking now at the trio.

"You bet, child," he replied. "I always did seem to find room for a few staples for such a lovely couple as you two, didn't I?"

"That you did, Mr. Houghton, and it has helped us many a time."

"What did you bring this time?"

Coffee of the Frontier

"Oh, I got a load of steel bits fur the steam drills Sholtz is now running. I just don't understand how they can go through so many over there. Twice what is used at 'Miner's Delight' or even The Carissa."

"Sounds like they are drilling through a lot of granite," Cliff said.

"That they are," Bruce agreed.

"Art, are you going up there tonight with your load?"

"No, it's too late now. I don't want to be trying to unload all them heavy crates in the dark. I'll just wait until morning, if I can find a place to stay that is."

"That shouldn't be too hard," Connie said, "our business is way off now that Sholtz has built his own town. A lot of men have moved over there and left the 'Carissa,' there should be plenty of vacant rooms in town."

Cliff injected. "Well, what I was aiming at was, Bruce needs to go up there and get his poke from the Monia bunkhouse, and I think it would be better if he was to go with witnesses."

"I don't understand," Art said back.

Cliff told him of what had happened with Bodie and then with Chip Roper and Phil Sholtz. Bruce added what had happened to him after he had helped Cliff.

"I see you boys have got yourselves in a fix all right. I ain't got no love lost fur that Sholtz bunch either. 'Specially after they nearly took over my business, not that Sholtz ain't paid me good, but I don't like cutting ma' regular customers out a' ma' trade either. I 'specially don't like being ordered to do it."

"Then you will take us?" Bruce said.

"I reckon so."

"That's good," Cliff added. "We'll all three go."

"Maybe four," Connie said.

"Not you," Cliff said firmly.

"No, Mr. Smartly Britches," she said then turned and motioned to a man that was being served a large slice of elk shoulder by her sister, "Him."

"Him?" Cliff questioned.

"That's right, him. That happens to be Mr. Charles W. Howe, United States Marshal," she answered and then wrinkled up her nose at Cliff in defiance.

"That would be good," Ash said.

"Yes, Darling, it would," Bruce agreed.

After making arrangements with Howe to ride with them the next morning, they left and headed back to 'The South Pass Hotel.'

"Bring your horse with you," Cliff told Bruce. "I imagine there's room over at Teachman's barn."

It was a little past dark as the trio walked up to the backdoor of Teachman's store. Cliff knocked; the light of a lantern was soon seen followed by a soft voice. "Who is it?"

"It's me, Reb Brown. I have a customer for you, Mrs. Teachman."

The door opened, and a tall woman stepped into the light; the rising moon spilled onto the back porch.

Cliff introduced first Ash and then Bruce and explained his need for a stall in her barn.

"If you recommend him, Mr. Brown, I'm sure he will be a welcome customer," she replied. "Will you take care of him?"

"Sure," Cliff agreed.

Then she looked at the petite girl standing beside him and added "And Mr. Brown, when you have finished, please come back. I have your shirt almost finished and just need for you to try it on one more time."

Cliff nodded his head knowing full well she had finished that shirt a month before. "Yes Ma'am, I'll do that." he replied.

As they walked to the barn he nervously explained that the woman was making a shirt for him. "I really could have bought a store-made one, but after her husband left her, I thought I would give her some business."

"You don't have to explain," Bruce said trying hard not to snicker.

Getting the bay into a stall next to Red was no trouble and after giving both horses some grain, the two unlikely friends exited the barn.

"Will you see Ash back to the hotel?"

"Sure, you get fitted real good now," Bruce said as Cliff headed up Teachman's back steps.

Entering the hotel, Ash looked up at the tall man and said. "You know, I've been thinking, that sure is a nice thing Mr. Brown is doing for that poor lady."

"I do believe you are right," her escort agreed.

The midnight hour found Cliff walking along the boardwalk headed for 'The South Pass Hotel' when suddenly the fiddle music floated from the open doors of 'The White Swan Saloon'. It had been a long time since he had heard *The Wildwood Flower,* and it beckoned him.

Once inside, he walked up to the bar and ordered a beer. The brew was cool, and he enjoyed it as he let it flow smoothly down his dry throat.

The fiddler finished and then started in on *Good-bye Ol' Paint.* The man with the bow was good, and the mournful tune made a prefect ending to the task he had just finished. '*Too bad Marlene could not come in here with me. She probably could use a beer or two to soothe her strained vocal cords,'* he thought.

After the violinist finished, he took leave and approached the bar for a beer of his own. Stopping next to Cliff he began small talk. "You new around here, cowboy?"

"Not really, been here several months."

"Oh," the man said looking at Cliff. "I just got here yesterday. Wus headed fur Salt Lake, but ran out of necessities back at Platte River Crossing and had not the riches to get beyond this burg. Guess I'll work here fur a while."

"There's still plenty a' gold in these hills," Cliff said. "You just got 'a know how to get it from them what digs it."

"Now that's a guid thought," the man replied. "I wus planning to ceannach a pick and shovel with my earnings this week."

"Well, I doubt there's much left that can be found with them tools. Need placers or better still, a stamp mill. The surface color is mostly all gone," Cliff said, amazed at himself for talking so much to a stranger, especially on a subject he knew so little about.

"I see."

"I do want to tell you, I really enjoyed hearing *The Wildwood Flower*. I ain't heard that since I left Georgia."

"I rather perceive ye 'err a southerner. My name's Duncan, Jim Duncan."

Cliff took his hand and replied. "Yeah, I guess my drawl is a dead give-a-way in these parts."

The man smiled and replied. "Well, to tell you the truth, I wasn't sure. I took my lane some time back, but haven't been on these shores all that mairny years me-self."

"Yeah, I thought I detected a bit a Scotland in your own speech."

"Aye, that you did, lad," Jim replied now using the full strength of his native tongue. "Howp ye enjoy whit we hae tae offer?"

"I enjoyed it very much," Cliff replied, smiling. "You are quite good."

"I do try to speak American as much as I cann'. I got me citizenship twa year back," he proudly announced.

"That so?"

"'Tis so, it be."

At that time, a drunk at a card table began to talk loudly, almost shouting, and his slurred speech began to drown out their conversation.

"I ween I had better retour to me work," Duncan said finishing his beer. "Hope tae' see you e'gen, Reb Brown."

Cliff lifted his mug in a salute to the man as he walked back to the old piano where he had left his fiddle, but this time he sat and played the ivory keys.

It was then Cliff realized the rowdy drunk was Ernie Teachman. At the same moment, Ernie recognized him.

"Well, if it ain't the Copperhead," Teachman shouted loud enough for all to hear.

Cliff just turned around and ignored him. He would have left then, but he had just motioned for the barkeep to bring him another beer, so he stayed.

"Oh, look everyone; here is the Rebel that was arrested fur shooting poor ol' Bodie in the back, but he got away with it."

"You best let it lay, Ernie," Cliff said without turning towards him.

"Yeah, anyone else would a' been in jail, but not Reb Brown. The lady judge let him go. I guess he's got a way with the women," Ernie continued in a loud but slurred voice.

Several men were now looking at the two as they began squaring off with one another.

"Yeah, he's got a way with the women, especially old ones."

"Only those who have birthmarks," Cliff said back.

Suddenly with almost a sober mind Teachman stood up straight and questioned. "What did you say?"

"I said only with those with birthmarks on their ass, Ernie. Guess who I mean?" Cliff rubbed it in.

"What are you insinuating?"

John Maitland, who had been irritated with the drunk for more than an hour, suddenly caught on and asked, "Your wife got a birthmark on her ass, Ernie?" At that, most of the room started laughing.

"You son-of-a-bitch!" Ernie shouted as he took a swing at Cliff.

The Georgian sidestepped, and when Ernie lost his balance with his wild swing, Cliff gave him a swift punch to the gut.

Everyone near heard the wind blowing from his lungs as he went down gasping.

Cliff turned back to the bar and returned to the taste of his fresh beer.

After a minute or so, Cliff caught a movement out of the corner of his eye and turned and kicked the gun from Ernie's hand. "Good way to end up a long time dead, Ernie," Cliff said and then turned back to his drink.

Finally, as he was finishing his beer, the man next to him slowly pulled himself up on his hands and knees and shook his head. "You never, you never been with Marlene."

Cliff leaned over where only Ernie could hear and said. "Pretty purple, almost the shape of a heart, right there on her left cheek, and boy is she a screamer when she gets her cookies," Cliff paused then added, "Of course you probably never knew that, did you Ernie." Then he stepped around the drunk and walked out.

"Arrggghh," was the scream he heard as he left the bar, followed by the sound of *The Wildwood Flower* once again being struck, only this time it was on the ivory keys, almost as if in a tribute.

Walking back to his room, Cliff felt good for the first time since he had been arrested. He had waited a long time for the right opportunity to let the draft dodger know he was poking his wife, and this had been unbelievably good to not have been planned.

When he entered his room, he was so elated that he didn't even notice that it was Art sleeping in Bruce's bedroll instead of the big man. No one mentioned the next morning that everyone seemed to have done his own thing the night before.

They met the Marshal at Teachman's barn at nine, and the little caravan started out for Monia.

Less than two miles down the road however, the front wheel struck a good size rock causing it to roll away. When the rear wheel fell into the hole vacated by the rock, the axle broke. It was past four before they had a new one made and were moving again. The Marshal had gone back into South Pass City while they repaired it, but returned when sent for.

The hour it took to get from there to Monia was without further incident. This Cliff laid to the fact that the U. S. Marshal was riding with them. Even Ed Sholtz wasn't so big or so stupid as to take on the government.

All four towns in this ten-mile square were much the same, in that a rich strike had produced a strong mine, and then the town grew up around it. The first of course was South Pass City on Willow Creek and The Carissa Mine. Next came the Caribou, and Atlantic City was built there on Rock Creek. Then when Miner's Delight got into full swing and the few buildings that carried it's name increased, Hamilton was born in Spring Gulch; but with Monia, it was a little different. Ed Sholtz owned 'The Monia Mine' and all the land nearby or so he said. All the buildings there were on the small flat piece of land just south of the mine were also owned by him. All the businesses there rented their buildings from him. Although the town of Monia was not as large as South Pass or Atlantic City, it was near the size of Hamilton. Sholtz had laid it out in an H pattern. There was Lode Street on the west side and Riffle on the east, with Capital Avenue connecting the two in the middle. There were also plans to close the top and bottom with two more streets when needed, to form a perfect square.

The Houghton & Cotter wagon stopped in front of the newly painted building bearing a sign that read Monia Mine Headquarters. This was only three doors down from the long one-story log structure known as 'The Bunk House'. Miners could stay there for 10% of their earnings weekly. It was there that Whittacur had stayed and where he had left his poke. However, when he came to the bunk he had slept in ever since he had come to work at the Monia, he found another man in it.

"Hey, get out of my bunk," he shouted at the sleeping miner and slapped him hard on the back.

The man rose quickly and looked around not sure where he was or what was happening.

"It's not your bunk anymore," Chip said stepping from the dark corner, "You gave it up when you didn't show up for your shift."

"Fine, I'll just be taking my gear then," he said looking around for his knapsack.

"Gee, we didn't see any of your gear, Whittacur. You must a taken it with you."

"Don't give me that. All my stuff wus right here in my old union knapsack."

"I didn't see nothing like that, did you Buell?" he asked the new man, who shook his head.

"Well, I'll just take this fellows then," Bruce said reaching for the large white sack that lay at the side of the bedframe.

"I don't think so," he heard Chip say along with the cocking of a revolver. "Now get out of Monia, and stay out, if you know what's good for you, you dirty turncoat."

"I'll go, but it's you that had better know what's good fur him," Bruce said back in a very determined voice, as he stared down at the shorter man with the gun.

Reaching the light of the outside world, he turned just in time to catch a glimpse of Cliff as he walked in 'The Monia' Saloon'.

'*This is a big building,*' Cliff thought, '*bigger than anything in South Pass City.*' He stopped just inside to let his eyes adjust to the lamplight, and suddenly he recognized her voice.

*You can get a cold,*
*You can get the flu,*
*You may even get arthritis too,*
*But you'll never get to Monia by sleeping on the ground.*
*You got to keep a-moving if you're gon'a reach that town.*

It was the last chorus of the song she was singing, and several miners, now off shift, clapped loudly at the raven-haired beauty.

She gave them back a big smile and bowed deeply so her large breasts were displayed to an even greater degree for them. This was followed by shouts and whistles, but she said, "Come on boys, my throat is dry. That is the third song I've done fur you without stopping. I'll be back after I've had a beer."

She turned and started for the bar and then saw him. Her eyes immediately lit up, and a smile crossed her face.

"Hello, Purty Thing," he said when she arrived beside him.

"It's about time you looked me up."

"I didn't know you were here. I went to Morris' saloon, but you were gone, and no one seemed to know where."

"Yeah, I had to skedaddle out a' there before the judge killed me."

"What?"

"Oh, never mind. Come on over, and sit with me for a spell," she said, leading the way to a table near the door.

"Here, let's take this one," he said guiding her to one in the corner where he could see the whole room as well as the front door.

He held out the chair for her, and just as he was sitting down he saw Bruce enter. Obviously the big man was looking for someone, and he guessed it was him. When Bruce looked their way, Cliff motioned for him to come over.

"Come on, let's go," Bruce said harshly.

"Just wait a minute. Sit down, and meet this lady. She is a friend of mine," Cliff said to him.

Irritated at the idea, Bruce sat down anyway.

"This is Miss Tipper. She's an ol' Indian fighter I knew in another town," Cliff said smiling.

"Howdy, Ma'am," the big man replied as she slapped Cliff's hand for his statement.

"Now, what's got you in such a fuss?"

"Them bastards over to the bunkhouse stole my knapsack," he said slamming his huge hand on the table almost turning it over.

"Who?"

"That damn Chip Roper. He pulled a gun on me and run me out."

"I told you, you had bit off a passel a' trouble when you pitched in and helped me."

"I'll get that bastard."

"Reb, you are still in trouble with Chip?" she asked Cliff.

"Yeah, with him and the law, too."

"Now what?"

He told her about the Bodie shooting and how John Morris had stood up for him.

"Did you really save his life in the war?" she asked.

"Well, I don't remember it exactly the same as he does, but at the time, he was standing there talking on my behalf I didn't feel I should dispute him."

"Well, I'm glad he did something good for somebody. He never did for me," she said before taking a sip from her mug.

"Come on Reb, let's go back and take that Chip apart," Bruce angrily suggested.

"Not a good idea," she said. "Chip has three or four gun hawks close by all the time. They're sure to be watching fur you."

"She's right, Bruce," Cliff agreed. "Besides Marshal Howe came here at our request. We go gunning for some of Sholtz' men right here in his own town, and Howe may be the biggest witness against us."

"I guess you're right, but I don't like leaving without my poke. There's some personal stuff in that sack."

"I'll nose around and see if I can find out what they did with it after you're gone. Maybe I can find it for you."

"That would be real nice, Miss Tipper," Bruce said, for the first time looking at her as a person.

"While you are at it, see if you hear anything about who tried to bushwhack me. If I could get to him, I might have a chance a' clearing myself of that charge."

"I'll keep my ears open, but even if I do hear, I'll have a hard time getting word to you unless you come back in here."

"You can always get word to me by Mr. Houghton, the freighter," he said, and she immediately dropped the smile from her face and then stood.

"Well, I have to be getting back to work."

"It's great to see you, Purty Thing."

"Yeah, you take care of yourself, Georgia," she said coldly before turning and heading for the piano.

"That woman, she can be warm as soft butter one minute and cold as ice the next," Cliff said as she walked away.

"I think she is mad at you, Reb."

"But why?" Cliff questioned. "I didn't do nothing."

"That's right," his friend said as he stood.

It was well past full dark when they jumped from the wagon at the Teachman Barn.

# Chapter Eight
# The Ground Blizzard

I t was a little before noon when it began, just a little at first, small flakes widely spaced. Thirty minutes later, there was a shower so thick it was nearly impossible to locate a place in the air that was not occupied by the powder. Also the wind had picked up to gale force, and it was hard to see across the street. Cliff had just passed Doc Barnes' house when the wind set in, and he changed his mind on trying to get to the hotel, instead he urged Red on to 'The Sisters'.'

There were only two others inside, and he went back to the rear table as he almost always did. Carol came out shortly with her hands filled with two steaming bowls and headed for the occupied table.

"Here you go, boys," she said, "try this, and you'll be warm again in no time."

The miners replied some small talk that Cliff could not hear, and she turned with a big smile on her face. It suddenly left when she saw him there.

"Well, stranger, I guess you haven't forgotten where we are."

"Nice to see you, too, Carol."

"You want some soup or did you come in to see what else you might steal from me?"

"I never stole anything from you. As I remember, it was you that came calling, not the other way around."

"Well, I'll be calling no more, Reb Brown."

"I'll have some soup then," Cliff answered.

"You will, if you are lucky," she spat back as she hurriedly entered the kitchen.

The little restaurant was well made of hewn logs notched together with mortis and covered with muslin which in itself was covered with compo board and painted with a good coat of whitewash; the ceiling was made of beaded boards under cross poles and that covered with a rock and dirt roof several inches thick, all of which kept the wind at bay, but the temperature was falling steadily, and even inside, it was getting colder every minute. The only light came from four coal oil lamps with polished brass mirrors which were attached two abreast to the east and west walls, a glass window on either side of the front door, which were now totally frosted over, allowing very little light in, nonetheless it was cozy inside compared to what was going on outside.

**The Sisters' Restaurant**

The miners finished their lunch, and he overheard one say, "We better get going, leastwise we'll not make it to work on time." His companion stood nodding his head and turned toward the door. The first one then called out, "Miss Carol, you come, we pay."

She returned to the room with a bowl of lima bean soup and a slab of cornbread and sat it on Cliff's table without saying another word to him and walked over to the miners.

Cliff watched them lay coins in her hand and tip their dirty hats as they did. She was again smiling when she faced him and just as quickly it was replaced with a scornful look.

"I got 'a say you got some nerve coming around here, Mr. Brown."

"Why are you so mad at me, Carol?" he said back as she glared at him.

"Why, hell I know you took advantage of my sister when she was sick. And at the same time you were making me believe I was special to you," she screamed back as she threw her towel at his face.

Cliff stood and took her by the wrist, and she struggled to free herself from his grasp.

"Just calm down," he said strongly to her.

"Let go of me."

"I will, if you will stop and listen." Finally, she subsided struggling and stood still.

"First, I did nothing with Connie except clean her up where she had vomited all over herself, and the bed, and the floor, and everywhere else. I have never done anything with her but be a big brother, and that's the truth."

"I suppose you never did anything with Marlene Teachman either?" she shot back at him.

"Where did you hear that?"

"Hear it, hell; it's all over South Pass. Everyone who comes in here seems to be giggling about you poking Ernie's wife. Not that anyone cares about poor ol' Ernie; rather they all think it's a big joke."

"I never meant for it to become the town joke," Cliff replied releasing her wrist.

"Then you admit it?"

"I never talk about a lady's reputation," he replied searching for something to answer her question. Cliff didn't want her to rear up again, but neither did he want to lie to her. Especially on a subject that she already knew about and of course was the truth.

"I suppose you never talk about spending all those nights in my bed either?"

"I wasn't in your bed. You came to my bed, and no, I have never said a word to anyone about it."

"Really?" she questioned in a softer tone.

"Really."

With that she went back into the kitchen and left him standing there.

Cliff walked to the front door and opened it, but the snow was so bad he couldn't even see the hitching post a few feet away.

Turning, he walked back to the table and sat down. It was twenty minutes before she came out this time with a big coffee pot. She refilled his cup and then carried the pot over to the potbelly stove and sat it there.

"The boys will be needing this when the shift changes in a few minutes," she said in a voice so calm one could never have guessed a few minutes earlier she had thoughts of killing this man.

"I doubt anyone will make it here at shift change," he said.

"But why?"

"Haven't you looked out lately?"

"No. I know it's snowing, but ____?"

"Open the front door."

When she released the wooden latch, a gust of wind blew the door open bringing with it a cloud of snow.

"Oh, my God!" she exclaimed.

"See, no one in his right mind will try to walk around in this stuff."

"Oh, Cliff," she said turning to him with terror in her eyes.

"What's the matter?" he replied seeing her fright.

"Connie. Connie's out there."

"Where?"

"She took a delivery over to the King Solomon Mine. Mr. Carpenter sent us four turkeys one of his men had killed, and he asked us to cook them and bring them over with some pies for a celebration. They have been there one year today."

"She went in the wagon?

"No, in the Bob-Runner[9] Mr. Houghton loaned it to us. He said he wasn't using it and it, was just sitting there in his warehouse on South Pass Avenue. He said it would be safer than our wagon until spring comes.

"When did she leave?" he asked now standing.

"Three hours ago," she said with tears forming in her eyes. "It was just a few light flakes floating around then."

"Stay here, and keep the coffee hot," he said, "I'll go look for her."

"Oh, Cliff. She could freeze to death."

"I'll find her," he replied, doubting his promise.

Red was glad to see him emerge from the snow, but his

---

[9] Bob-Runner: a horse drawn sleigh used for business purposes, such as delivery and farm choring,

friendliness quickly vanished when they passed the street where Teachman's barn was located and headed out into the blizzard.

The toll road between South Pass City and Atlantic City was well traveled and quite familiar to him, but in the sheet of white he twice found himself off the road in a drift. He had to let Red have his head and hoped the stubborn stud would not turn back to the shelter of his barn stall.

They had been gone nearly an hour when he suddenly realized Red had stopped. Looking up he saw the dark form in front of him. At first he did not recognize what it was, but finally he realized it was the very top of a reasonably good size sleigh. Only the top of the railings and the double seats were above the snow. There was no sign of the horse that had pulled it here.

Cliff spurred Red on through the deep snow to the vehicle and called out, but his voice was lost in the howl of the wind.

He knew that had she left on foot, she would surely perish, if this fate had not already come her way. Looking about, he saw the light of the sun overhead through the swirling whiteness. '*Odd,*' he thought.

He searched around for her, but found no sign and soon was afraid of getting too far from the sleigh for fear of losing his way in the whiteout, finally he decided to dig down and make a shelter under the sleigh, hoping he might find enough room for him and Red if the big varmint would lie down.

Digging away he suddenly broke through from the side, and to his surprise he was staring at Connie.

She had come up with the same idea and had made a snow cave beneath the sleigh bed. Obviously frightened, but bundled in a heavy grizzly bear coat, she appeared unhurt.

"Oh, thank God," she said when she saw him and rushed forward to his arms.

Looking about, Cliff could see that there would not be room for the three of them under there, and he was not yet willing to let his faithful horse die if he could help it.

Remembering the sun, he reasoned that the storm was now subsiding. He took her and placed her on his saddle and began to lead Red up the side of the mountain.

They had gone perhaps a quarter of a mile, but no more than a couple hundred feet vertically when it began to become lighter. On he pressed and in little time they were standing in bright sunshine.

"Look!" he called out to her.

She raised her head and looked about. "I can't believe it!" she said back.

Below, the wind was still raging, and neither could see into the stream of flying snow, but they were above it. The snowstorm had passed on, but the tons of powder it had left in the valley below were being blown by the fierce wind.

"So, this is what they call a 'ground blizzard,' " he said, more to himself than to her.

The temperature was very low, and he was sure it would continue to drop.

"We have to get to shelter and fuel soon," he said and pulled on Red's reins.

"But the way back is that way," she said when she saw his direction.

"Bill Rhodes has a cabin up here on this ridge somewhere," he replied. "I've been there once, but that was last summer," he continued. "I think I might be able to find it." His last statement was truly more for himself than her.

Some thirty minutes later she saw through the thick timber, ice on a roof shining in the sunlight of late afternoon. The roof was all that could be seen as the snow had filled the sides, even though Bill built it in a place where it was well protected from the southwest wind. This time, the powder had fallen so much in such a short time, it had almost covered the one room cabin.

He dug down and finally found the door, and then with much digging and effort he was able to open it enough for the three of them to enter.

*'Bill certainly would not be noted as a tidy housekeeper,'* he thought looking around, *'But we are protected from the wind.'*

There was a cook stove in one corner where life-saving warmth could be ushered in. Along the wall near the stove was a considerable stack of cut poplar and shortly Reb had a fire roaring.

Connie found a jar of bullion that Rhodes had set on a shelf, and soon it had melted into a passable soup to fill their cold insides.

Red had nothing to eat, but was thankful for the shelter.

Not long after they had finished the last of Connie's soup, it became quite dark, and the only light was what escaped from the stove. He was sure the temperature inside was near freezing.

Finally he turned to her and said, "Take off your boots and let me have a look at your feet."

"Just my feet? I thought you liked more than that about me," she said coyly.

"I want to make sure you didn't get frost bit," he said back ignoring her obvious suggestion.

She removed her boots and lifted her long skirt so he could rub her feet and lower legs.

Finally he stopped and said, "You look pretty good. That was quite smart of you crawling under the sleigh like that."

"I was so scared. When the horse just stopped and fell over, I didn't know what to do, but I remembered Mr. Houghton saying that he had gotten lost once in a snowstorm and almost froze to death before he crawled under the wagon and used it for shelter."

"That was plenty good thinking for a girl your age," Cliff replied.

"My age!" she said placing her hands on her hips. "I'll have you to know, Mister Reb Brown; I'm twenty years old, next month!"

"And a pretty twenty year-old, too, but still, it took me sometime to think of it myself."

"Well, then I will take your statement as a compliment," she said, slowly pulling her skirt higher while he was reaching for more wood. Soon her entire legs below the knees were in clear view, and he could not help but notice.

"What are you trying to do?"

"My legs are cold. I just want to get them closer to the fire. That's all."

Cliff could not help remembering her naked body the day he had bathed her some months before, and immediately he felt a stirring in his groin.

"I'll see if I can find a lantern or something. Mee'be there is something else to eat in here," he said making an excuse to move away from her.

While he was moving around in the mostly dark room she saw a small candle above the pile of old skins that they both had surmised Bill used as a bed when he stayed here. Getting up, she walked over and picked it up. "Will this do?" she asked teasingly.

Turning he saw her standing there in front of the stove. The flames danced about the round air door behind her and lit her figure enticingly through the slip, she was now down to.

"Where's your skirt?"

"It was wet, and I wanted to let it dry before I went to sleep," she said back most positively.

Cliff lowered his head but kept his eyes looking straight at her, not believing a word of it. It was all too obvious that she intended to have him sample her delights, and he was not at all sure he would be able to resist. It had been several days since he had been with a woman, and this was not his nature. Usually when a willing woman was near, he needed sex at least once every three days, and it had been almost two weeks since he had seen Marlene. Still he thought he should resist her, she being only a child. '*Although, she did say she was twenty, well almost twenty,*' he thought.

He took the candle, lit it and moved away from her searching the room. Finally, he found a partially filled jug of whiskey, but nothing more. Returning with it he took a long pull before sitting down beside her. She had spread her bearskin coat near the fire and was laying on it on her side looking at him. "Can I have some?"

"No."

"Why Not?"

"Don't forget the last time I let you drink with me. I don't plan on cleaning up after a sick drunk up here in someone else's cabin with no ready water. Besides, it's going to be enough to keep your sister from having me strung up for just being here with you alone. I'm not about to have them find out I let you get liquored up."

"Come on, I don't want to get drunk. I never want to get drunk again," she said positively. "I just want a nip to warm up my insides."

"That was what the soup did," he said.

"Yes, and that was an hour ago, maybe two."

"No."

"I know who it was that dry-gulched you," she said letting a sneaky smile cross her lips.

"What are you talking about?" he suddenly became very interested.

"I overheard somebody talking about being with two others when Bodie Johnson was killed," she said coyly.

"Who? You got to tell me Connie, this is no joking matter," he said, sitting the jug down and walking over to her.

"Who's joking?" she replied.

"You really do know?"

"I really know," she said flatly.

"Who?"

"Trade you for a sip," she said back.

"Damn it, Connie."

"Only way you gon'a get me to talk."

Cliff took a short breath and walked back to where he had sat the jug. Slowly he reached down and retrieved it and just as slowly turned back. *'I got a bad feeling about this,'* he thought.

Once again, she was standing in front of the fire, and the flames exposed her inner thighs, and he thought he could even see the curly fuzz of her hair. This time he suddenly had a strong erection, and he was sure she would see it when he came closer. Not that he tried to hide such from women when he was this close to having them, but he was still reluctant to take her.

He stopped just far enough away so he was still mostly in the darkness and stretched forth his arm. She reached for the tan jug and took a swig from it. Immediately she began to cough.

"I told you, you were too young for such."

She looked up at him in defiance and then took another long pull from the jug. Again, she began coughing as soon as she stopped swallowing.

"Alright, that's enough. You've proved you can down whiskey. Now, who did you hear was there when I killed Johnson?" he asked as he again returned the jug to where he had found it.

"I'll tell you in the morning," she said with great difficulty.

"You'll tell me now," he demanded.

"Oh alright. He was bragging to a fellow called Mad Dog."

"Where did you hear this?"

"I was coming out of Mrs. Carter's shop, by way of the backdoor. It's closer to our house that way, and I heard them talking on the other side of the fence. They didn't know I was there, but when I heard him say how he should have not let the other fellow shoot at that Rebel, I guessed they were talking about you, so I stopped and listened.

"What did they say?"

"This fellow talking," she paused and then continued, "he said that this other fellow had asked to do the shooting, but he had missed, and then when Bodie turned, you shot him, and they ran away."

"Who else was there? Did you hear anymore names?"

"Someone he called Bones. I think it was him who was doing the talking," she replied, and then added, "Now have I earned another sip?"

"I guess so." He walked back into the darkness to where he had sat the jug. Reluctantly, he picked it up and turned around only to find her now standing there without a stitch of clothes on.

Cliff took a deep breath. The flickering flames exposed her perfect naked outline, and he knew he was defeated. The influence of the strong drink mixed with the glee he had from her news only added to the lust he felt for this beautiful nymph. Sitting the jug down, he took the few steps from it, to her.

The contrast of her pure white skin as he laid her down on the soft black fur of the robe was engulfing, and he was soon washed over with his passion.

Later laying there on his back with her hugging so close to him, he began to reflect on what had happened. He was sure glad she had not been a virgin. That would have been a wrong that probably would have sent him on a trip down the guilt river. He also was very relieved to finally find out who had been at the shooting, and too, he was relieved of his sexual tension. Now he only had to figure out something to tell her sister.

His thoughts were interrupted suddenly as she cooed, "Reb, you gon'a' make an honest woman out of me?"

Taking a deep breath he answered straight forward. "No."

"Why not?" she said sliding her hand gently over his chest. "You have now tasted my fruits, and I will not be fit for another man."

"Hell, Connie, save that for some teenage boy."

"Whatever do you mean?" she said back, still letting her fingers lightly move through the hair there.

"I've had enough women to know a virgin when I do one, and I didn't do one tonight."

She now slapped his chest before saying, "You could tell then?"

"I could tell."

"Are you going to ask Carol to marry you?"

"No."

"Good, because she would, you know," Connie again started moving her fingers around his hairy chest.

"I doubt that. She don't even like me anymore."

"Oh, yes she does," Connie argued. "Reb, was I better than Carol?"

"What makes you think I would know how good Carol is anyway?" he answered somewhat taken by her question.

"I've heard you two, lots of times when you thought I was asleep. I even watched you once through the door," she paused before adding, "I opened it just enough to see inside."

"Well, gentlemen don't talk about such things."

"I guess that's so," she agreed taking a deep breath before continuing. "And, you are a gentleman. A whoremonger, but still a thoroughbred gentleman."

Her statement caught him by surprise, and he almost gasped, but she started talking again before he could say anything in rebuttal. "I'm glad you aren't going to marry Carol. You are a lot prettier, but Mr. Houghton will be a better provider."

"Well, I'm damn glad to hear that," he spat at her. "Does Mr. Houghton know of your plans?"

"I see him looking at her when he comes in, and he always comes in when he's in town."

"I'll say a prayer for him the next time I'm in a church," Cliff said rolling his eyes in the dark.

"I'm also glad you are a gentleman," she said.

"Really?" he replied in less than a reassuring voice.

"Yes, I know with you, no one will ever know what went on here tonight," she said as she moved her hand from his chest down and encircled his limp manhood.

Cliff took a deep breath.

An hour later, just as she was about to fall off to sleep, she whispered, "Reb."

"Yes?"

"It was Ernie, Ernie Teachman who was talking to the man that shot at you." This was the last thing she said that night.

Cliff stared at the dimly lit ceiling as the wind howled outside.

The next morning the gale had stopped, and the sun was so bright on the new snow that it hurt his eyes. With great difficulty they worked their way through the deep snow and around the thick timber.

"How are you going to find our way out of here?" she asked. "This forest is so thick."

"Won't be long."

"What do you mean?"

"The rate this timber is being cut for fuel for the steam engines at the mines this will be all gone soon."

"Really?" she questioned as she looked around at the tall pine.

"Yep, my guess is even the stumps will be harvested, and this will all be as barren of trees as South Pass itself."

"That's hard to imagine," she replied, again looking all around.

They, with great difficulty, made their way back to the sleigh that was now covered completely in snow. It took him close to an hour to get it uncovered and the dead horse free. But he knew he needed to be moving away from the obvious trail in the deep drifts they had forged while making their way back to the road. It would be a sure signal to anyone wanting to follow and find where the two of them had really spent the night.

With much displeasure at the humiliation, Red pulled them until they were within sight of the Carissa Mine, and there he stopped, and right at that moment, a search party was seen coming up the hill from town.

Connie told them of her snow cave and that they had stayed there under the sleigh all night waiting for the storm to let up. Everyone thought it was a miracle that they had survived let alone not have been frostbitten. No one questioned where Red had weathered the storm.

Two weeks later, Cliff bought a new jug and took it back to Bill Rhodes' cabin. It was obvious no one had been there since the storm, so he straightened up around the place as much as he could, and then he left a note stuck in the thumb hole of the jug that read "Bill, needed to use your cabin recently. Be obliged were no one but the two of us to know that." He left it unsigned and felt reasonably sure Bill would not care who had used his hospitality or left his appreciation.

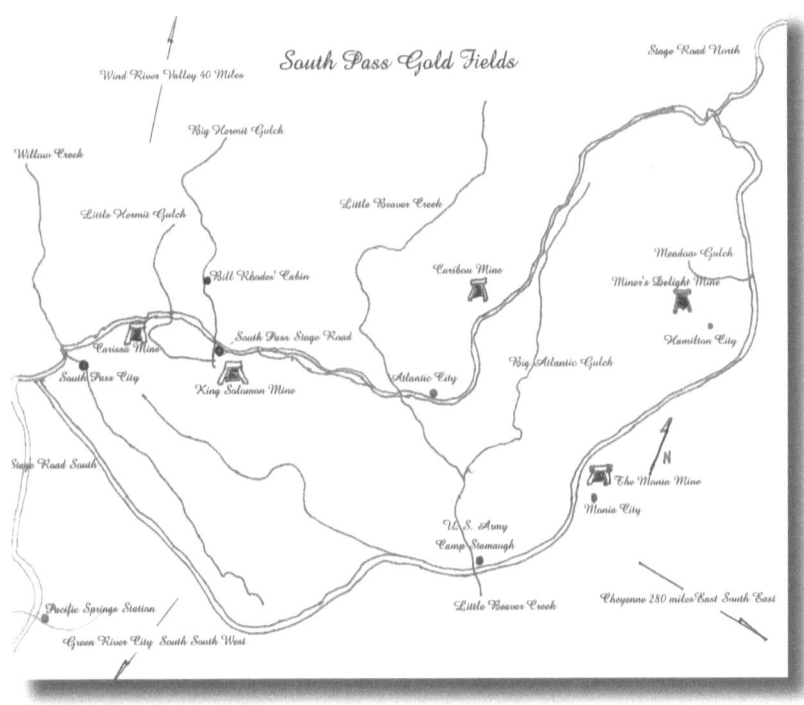

# Chapter Nine
# The Long Cold Winter

Cliff made sure that he was never again alone with Connie, not that she didn't flirt even more openly now than before, especially in front of her sister. She even made small attempts to arrange a chance rendezvous a couple of times, but he saw through them and was always able to be somewhere else or have something else pressing at the time. It was not that he had found Connie a poor bedmate, on the contrary, he had thought many times of the youthful fury she had displayed during their coupling, a passion not often found in such an inexperienced girl. *'At least I think she is inexperienced.'* His reasons of concern were more, he supposed, of the storm that would break should others find out about that night's affair, especially from Carol.

Of course, he also believed that such gossip would not go well with the court when he had to defend himself on the Johnson shooting. Now he really had time only to work towards that event.

Bruce Whittacur was devoting all his time to Ashley in her quest to find her brother's lost mine. They were sure when Mr. Snow arrived it would be cleared up. The problem was Mr. E. P. Snow had not returned from Cheyenne as expected. Instead, he had gone east to Kansas City, for a big meeting with several government officials.

So, on they waited while the snows began to fall almost on schedule. It seemed that every four days a strong storm would come rushing in from the northwest and dump several feet of fresh powder on them. Then the next day it would be very calm with nary a breath of a breeze, the sun shining bright in a sky so blue one would wonder where such a color came from. A day when the air was so clear that a body could see a hundred miles, a grand day, but also a day when the mercury thermometers would drop into their little ball and want to escape even further down, only to be trapped there. Then on the next day, the wind would come rushing in out of the southwest with such fury, that all the snow on the open plains would be blown to some point further eastward, where one only wonders as they look upon the brown grasses, that a day before were covered in a blanket of white. And then on the fourth day another storm would come and start the cycle all over again.

Cliff had known cold before. It was cold in the swamps of Georgia where the air was so damp, cotton spun garments would wring wet with what they captured from the air. Cold mornings, when it had been his chore to sit from before daybreak in the fork of a big sweet gum waiting for the elusive whitetail, the family's main source of meat when the smoked pork was all gone. Mornings, when the first rays of the sun would find their way down through the moss covered limbs. A time when he would move his foot ever so quietly, until it was in a location to capture some small degree of warmth offered there by the sun as it slowly rose, a time in the morning when this same ever so slight warmth would cause the stillness of night air to give up, and begin to move. All good southern hunters know that the coldest time of night is really just after sunup.

Cliff had also been cold in Tennessee and Maryland. They too were damp, and when the snows came to those rolling hills it came as a wet snow, a snow that would freeze bare feet.

In the winter of '64-'65, not one in five of the men he lived beside had shoes. He, along with a few others, had been fortunate enough to find boots that fit on the dead Federals who had fallen to confederate guns. It was suggested by one newspaper in Saint Louis that the rebels were at that time killing, not for the cause, rather for northern uniforms and boots. Cliff knew better. He killed because the blue army had invaded his homeland, his State, a place the Constitution said they had no right to be. At least that was what he thought he was killing for. Looking back, he was not sure; near the end perhaps he was killing just to stay alive. That winter of '64-'65 had been the coldest he had ever experienced, before coming to Wyoming Territory. Now he realized no one living at a lower elevation had any expectation of the fierceness of a winter spent a mile and a half above sea level, a place where drifts would be fifteen feet deep from October to May and in the mountains as deep as forty feet. A place where the wind would blow so hard, had it been in Georgia, they would have called it a hurricane; a place where the smallest exertion could rob you of your breath and then cause every gasp to be as painful as tearing of the skin, and a place where on the few good days it would warm up to five or ten degrees above zero. Such was the winter Cliff spent in South Pass City.

The powder had drifted so deep in the mountain range between Laramie and Cheyenne, no westbound trains were getting through. What little supplies they did receive had come by way of Salt Lake City.

Now, Mr. E. P. Snow was trapped by his namesake and had chosen to spend the winter in Cheyenne. Judge Kingman also stayed away. Esther Morris received word Kingman would be staying with Doctor and Mrs. Lathrop, at Platte River Crossing, until the weather broke. This was both good and bad news.

It was on the morning of December the fifth, shortly after the rising of the sun that Art Houghton, looking at the clear still air, decided to take a chance and make his run from Green River City to South Pass City. He had tried the week before, but had to turn back due to heavy drifts blocking the road. However, late in the afternoon of the fourth, a company of cavalry had pushed their way from Big Sandy Creek and Lieutenant Ewing told him the wind had mostly cleared the way, if more snow did not fall.

Cotter had urged him not to try the trip, but here as he stood in the cold morning air looking at the clear blue sky, he decided to go.

The wagon had been loaded with much needed supplies for the inhabitants there, and too, there was Mr. Stone who had paid a fair sum to be a passenger on his wagon, since the stage line had not moved north in three weeks.

Stone, a man in his late thirties, was tall and lean with a strong drawl, not unlike that of Mr. Brown; a distinctive accent on the western plains. Not that the southern drawl was unknown to the west, rather the contrary. After the war so many men had returned to find their homes burned or occupied and hundreds found all loved ones dead or gone, thus the migration to the frontier was often a beckoning call. Surely, a third of the workers on the U.P. were from the South, but the accent from deep in Dixie was different from most other drawls, and there was no mistaking the fact that Brown and Stone had their up-bringing close to one another. However, they would find it had been Stone who had first come to the region, not after the war, rather during it.

He had paid Art for his passage with new folding notes drawn on the National Bank of Austin, and he gave every appearance that there was more of the yellow-backs in his possession. They arrived on the little hill overlooking South Pass City an hour after dark, having had little trouble, save losing the road once for half an hour or so. The flickering lights of the saloons were a welcome sight to the nearly frozen men.

Houghton drove straight to Colfax Street, and there he unhitched his team and housed them in Teachman's barn for the night. Then, he and Stone headed, without further delay, to 'The Sisters'.'

The little wooden structure seemed a hundred degrees inside when they stepped in from the sub-zero outside, where in truth the small stove barely was able to keep it above forty. Still, the sudden change was both welcome and overwhelming at the same time.

Both sisters were moving about serving steaming bowls of elk stew, and each gave the freighter a warm smile when they saw who emerged from the frozen haired buffalo robe.

"Oh, thank Sweet Jesus, you've come!" Carol said looking at Houghton. "Did you bring our list?"

"Yours was the first I loaded," he said back.

"Oh, thank you so much. We are almost out of everything."

"Oh, Carol, stop talking about material stuff," her sister scolded. "We are mostly glad to see that no bad fortune came your way on that awful trip here."

"Of course we are," Carol agreed. "It's just we need the supplies to keep the place open."

"I know that, Miss Steele," he answered back, "That was one of the reasons I had to make the trip."

"Now, who is this you have with you, Mr. Houghton?" Connie asked looking at the stranger standing next to Art.

"Oh, I'm sorry. My manners," he added shaking his head. "This is Mr. Stone."

"Welcome, Mr. Stone," she said to the newcomer.

"Had I known there were a brace of beautiful women in this faraway place, I would have stayed here five years ago."

"Five years ago we were not here, Mr. Stone," Connie said, smiling at the tall man.

"I know," he replied.

"Another Southern Gentleman," Carol said in a cautioned tone.

"Is that bad, Ma'am?" Stone questioned as he removed his fox skin hat.

"No, it's just once burned, twice shy," she replied and then turned and walked back towards the kitchen.

"Come on and sit right over here," Connie said leading the way to a nearby table.

"Bill Sneed, this is Mr. Stone, and you know Mr. Houghton," she said to the seated man, "They will share your table, if that's all right?"

"You know, Miss Connie, if 'n you ask, it's all right with me," the miner replied.

She was just returning with two more bowls of stew when she overheard Sneed ask, "What brings you to the frozen plains, Mr. Stone?"

"Please call me Pebbles," the man replied. "I am in the textile business. I represent a large syndicate of mills in the south, and we are expanding westward now that the railroad is through, and the Indian trouble is over."

"Over?" exclaimed Sneed almost spilling his bowl. "It's hardly over in these parts. Hell, them thieving varmints butchered Kirt Puckett not six months ago right here nigh on in town."

"Really?" Stone questioned as he turned to Houghton with a concerned voice, but secretly smiling inside.

"I wonder why you would make such an exposed trip way up here, knowing that?" he said to Art.

"Well, to begin with, we seldom have Indian trouble, but a single man do need to be careful," Houghton admitted.

"I just can't believe you took my money and never warned me about the danger," Stone said showing great concern to Art, but at the same time he winked at Connie.

"No real danger."

He was cut off by Sneed's interruption, "Them Sioux put enough arrows in him to make a believer out a' Ol' Kirt."

"They were Arapaho arrows, not Sioux," Art corrected.

"I don't see what difference that makes," Stone added.

"Well, I guess it don't. I just like things to be right. Besides ain't no injuns gon'a be out in weather like this anyway. They got better sense than us whites," Art laughed.

"Well, I certainly don't think it is a laughing matter," Sneed added, "and neither did Kirt."

"I'm sure he didn't at the time," Art agreed.

"I thought these tribes had fought with each other until they were nearly all gone," Stone said.

"Well, some do but not around here. The Sioux, the Arapaho, and the Cheyenne for that matter, are allies," Art told him. "Now, they do have a fracas with the Crow and Shoshone from time to time, but it never costs them too many. It's more horse stealing than killing, anyway," Houghton said before he turned his attention back to his stew.

"I seen a Shoshone what got caught by the Sioux one time. They had done cut off his kahonnies," Sneed said.

"Jesus!" Stone exclaimed.

"Yeah, they don't much like the Shoshone," Art agreed. "I guess that's because of the treaty the Snakes made with the whites."

"Snakes?" Stone questioned giving all the impression he knew nothing about western Indians.

"Snakes, Shoshone, same thing."

"Well, that treaty might not keep, if 'n them Buffalo Soldiers don't stop a messing with their women," Sneed warned.

"Buffalo Soldiers?" Stone questioned still acting as if he knew nothing of the army or Wyoming.

"Freedmen that fought with the Union Army during the rebellion," Houghton explained. "There is a detachment of them at Fort Washakie over in the Wind River Valley."

"Trouble with them?"

"Yeah, the Indians have complained that they bother their squaws."

"Rape 'em and kill them, too, is what they do," Sneed added.

"Oh, we had similar trouble with them back in Florida," Stone said.

"Floridee!" Sneed said excitedly. "You hail from Floridee?"

"Yes, I lived there all my life, until the war."

"I always wanted to go to Floridee. I heard tell there is a spring there that the water is so good it plum makes a man young again."

"Yes, I've heard that, too," Stone agreed, and then he decided to have some fun with the miner. "It seems to work too. I will be ninety-two come April."

"No lie!"

"Can't you tell? Look closely at my eyes," Stone suggested.

Bill looked with great attention into the brown eyes of the stranger.

"My eyes were deep blue until I turned eighty, then they started getting darker each year. An old Spaniard told me to rub some of that water on them, but I just took a drink instead," Stone teased. "I fear this time next year they will be pure black."

"You don't say?" Sneed replied still staring into Stone's eyes. "Do it make other parts young, too?"

"Oh, that's the best part! I can't look at a female without my blood starting to pump. Why, when I came in here and saw those two beautiful women, I almost had to walk stiff-legged."

"No!" Sneed said. "And you being ninety-two!"

"It's true. Remember, I stood there by the door for a long time before I could walk."

"I do recall that."

"Had to let the thing soften up a bit before I dared move without embarrassment," Stone lied.

"Son-a'-bitch," Sneed said and then got up and walked towards the door.

Art could hardly keep from bursting out laughing. After Sneed had left he said "You have a mean streak, Stone. That poor jasper will freeze to death trying to ride shank's mare[10] all the way to Florida in the dead of winter."

"What are you two so amused about?" Carol asked as she came forward with the big coffee pot.

"Oh, just telling Mr. Houghton here about my home, that's all," Stone said back as he held up his tin cup.

It was December the twenty-third when a strange wind began blowing out of the southwest. Not that a southwest wind was strange in Wyoming Territory, but when a warm one blows in December, it's strange. At first it seemed a welcome blessing, but after two days the frozen streets were suddenly muddy and travel came to a standstill, as no wagon could move more than a few feet before bogging down to its hub in the mud. It was in just such a situation Art found himself as his team tried to pull the near empty wagon up the bank from the Sweetwater River some twenty miles south of South Pass City. Here,

---

[10] Ride shank's mare: Walk

the riverbanks were not steep, not like so many of them in the west; nonetheless, the sudden thaw had been too much for the traveler. He had worked from shortly before noon until near three, and still, there seemed no hope of moving farther until conditions changed. The thought of that was frightening as the only change most likely would be the return to below zero temperatures. Looking at the sun, now only an hour from sliding behind the western peaks, he shook his head slowly. His intention was to return to Green River City and meet the train that surely was taking advantage of the thaw to move through the passes.

His trips to The Sweetwater mining camps and towns were always fully loaded, but the returns were seldom more than a little ore or perhaps some broken machinery that was being sent away for repairs too great to be done on the spot. This time was different. The Caribou mine near Atlantic City had sent a fair size shipment of color to be locked in The National Bank in Green River City where they did most of their business. Had anyone known of the shipment, he would have been in a very perilous condition, but they had loaded under the cover of darkness, and it all fit in the false floor of the big freight wagon so anyone looking in would see no cargo at all. It was this weight that had caused his present dismay.

Art thought heavily on the matter. He could not leave the wagon for surely, when the roads again became passable someone would find and take it as abandoned property and then find the gold, some three hundred thousand dollars worth, at that. Still, he had little fuel to ward off the cold that would surely come in a day or so, perhaps at any moment. Also, he had only enough grain for his team of ten mules to last him for the trip, and that would be gone before morning. There, too, was always the possibility of Indians, but this seldom occurred in the dead of winter.

'*Indians have the good sense to stay put in December,*' he thought, now nodding his head in approval with his inner statement, then for no apparent reason he looked up, first behind him to the North and then ahead to the South before speaking aloud this time. "Also, there is the risk of road agents, who do not have so much sense."

It was then that he spotted the small dark spot on the road some four miles ahead. He watched it for almost a minute when it suddenly became longer than it was wide, and finally he realized it was a line of horses; mounted horses.

Subconsciously, he reached for his six-gun and moved the cylinder from the safe notch over slightly where the hammer would be resting on a percussion cap; next he reached for his shotgun and capped both barrels. As the line neared, it also became much longer, and he was now fully aware that the odds were he had witnessed his last sunrise on this earth, and he cursed himself for not speaking his feelings to the Steele woman.

Art looked about and wondered if there was enough cover in the thin brush along the river bank and decided there was not. Still, it would be as good a place as any to make his stand, and if it were his fate to die this day, the banks of The Sweetwater River were as good a place as any on this barren prairie and better than most.

Slipping around the wagon's tailgate he moved down into the muddy edge of the cold water and dropped behind the bare stalks of the small cottonwood and willows that grew there. It was there he prayed.

The sound of many hoofs beating on the muddy road was as foreign this time of year as the sudden Chinook winds that had come rushing north from the desert of Death Valley hundreds of miles away.

It seemed to him to be an hour or more as he waited there with only the top of his wagon to be seen from his hiding place, but he knew it could have been only a few minutes as the sun cast shadows very near where they had been when he slipped in there.

Finally the head of a horse was visible beside his wagon. No more, just the head, and through the willows, little of it could be seen. What he could see very well were the tracks he had left in the muddy bank when he had descended here. Eight inch-wide tracks that would surely also be visible from atop a horse.

The river had been frozen for months and still was in most places, where the two-day Chinook had not thawed it. Here and there the ice was quite slick and sharp. This made the river useless for an escape route, and it was plain he was in the thickest bunch of brush for a long ways in either direction so he stayed put.

Suddenly he heard a man speak. "See if there is anything in the bed, Kelly."

There was no reply.

*At least they are white,* Art thought.

Watching as the horse's head moved he then saw a buckskinned leg astride the pinto. He could not see the man's head, which was bent over and looking into the wagon.

"Nothing here," the man called back, before riding around the tail end of his conveyance. Now Art saw the man fully. He was clad in a red flannel shirt with a large black hat similar to the one worn by Cliff Brown, only the brim was larger and droopier. Tied across the back of his saddle was a buffalo robe. He carried in his right hand a yellow Henry rifle and in cross-draw fashion was a large bladed knife held there by a rawhide strap around the neck and shoulder, Indian style. The grip of the Bowie was made from the antler of an elk, and its scabbard was decorated heavily with small beads, mostly light blue in color, interrupted here and there with lines of pale yellow or red.

The man spit a heavy stream of tobacco juice into a deep footprint Art had left where he started down the bank.

"Looks like the teamster took to the river," he called out again turning his horse in that direction.

*'Well, here it is,'* Art thought.

"You see anything?" a new voice called out.

"Tracks in the mud," the rider replied then added, "fresh, too."

"How many?"

"Just one."

Suddenly the man's voice who had been carrying on the conversation with the buckskin rider spoke again, "Sergeant."

"Yo," was the rough answer that followed.

"Take four men and cover the banks up and down both sides of the road on this side. See if we can find what happened to the teamster."

"Yo," was the answer again followed by. "Jones, Smith, Counsell, and Braswell fall out."

*'Cavalry,'* Art thought as his breathing returned. Slowly he stood and called out, "Here. I'm over here."

The scout took a bead on him with the Henry, but Art raised his hands high, holding his weapon in a non-threatening manner before he began the slipping and sliding necessary to gain the road from the river's bed. Occasionally, he had to use the buttstock of his shotgun as an assisting cane, but he was sure by now they knew he was not going to shoot at them.

"Am I glad to see you," he said reaching the young Lieutenant still astride his bay horse.

"Lt. Turner, Sixth Cavalry. At your service, sir," the man said stretching forth a gauntlet-covered hand.

"Lord God above, am I glad to see you."

"Got yourself a little stuck I would say."

Art chuckled softly before replying, "A little, I'd say."

"Well, I think we can help you there," the Officer replied without looking at Art. Turning in his saddle he again addressed the non-com, "Sergeant, have a dozen men throw ropes over that tongue and have the rest of the men dismount and push. We must get this wagon out of here before we move on."

"Yo," was the reply again, but this time with less enthusiasm.

Soon, with the power of an additional twelve horses and eight men, the big wagon was again only a foot or so deep in the mud.

"Boy, that's one heavy wagon," one of the men said resting from his hard push.

"Yes, these Murphy wagons are sure that," Art agreed not wishing to tell of his hidden cargo.

"Well, Mr. Houghton, I can't recommend you continue south. The crossing at Big Sandy is worse than this."

"I see, well," Art thought a moment before asking, "In that case, if you will help me get turned around and up the other bank I will head back to South Pass City."

"We can do that, sir."

It was then Art became aware of a second civilian among the detail. A lean man some two or three inches shy of six feet approached from the rear of the detail. Art immediately realized the gent made no effort to assist in his escaping from the predicament his wagon had been in.

"Good day, sir," the man said extending his right hand. "I'm Morgan Crowe."

Art immediately recognized the accent of the Pennsylvania Dutch.

"Sir," Art replied taking the extended hand.

"I have been in Granger for several days awaiting the return of a wagon belonging to the firm of Houghton & Cotter. I see this one belongs to them."

"Yep," Art replied.

"Well, Mr. Cotter himself gave me passage, but since you failed to return as scheduled, I persuaded the Lieutenant to allow me to accompany them on their trip north," he explained, not looking at

Art as he spoke. "Now that we have found you, I will finish the trip on the spring-seat and bid that miserable animal adieu."

Art looked at the man with an inquiring eye before he turned away without replying.

The crossing of the frozen river was without incident and with the help of the extra horses pulling, he was able to climb the opposite bank without becoming bogged down. However, Art did feel a twinge of bitterness towards the Indians who had burned the bridge some years before.

The cavalry left them six miles south of South Pass City and headed east towards the new 'Camp Stambaugh.'

Morgan Crowe carried on conversation almost every mile as they rode along behind the ten mules before the splitting of trails, if conversation it could be called when one party dominates the talk. It was obvious to Art, Crowe considered himself his better, as every line of the conversation was in some way tainted with the air of one talking down to a subordinate. Never once did Art let on that he was the owner of the freight lines, or that his partner had only a 40 percent interest in the business.

When they came over the hill and saw the flickering lights of the village below, Art felt a warm glow fill his insides.

"Is this Monia?" Crowe asked.

"South Pass City."

"Well, I have passage to Monia. I must get there as soon as possible."

"You can get you a room here fur the night and maybe get someone to carry you over there come morning."

"I don't think you understand," Morgan said. "I paid Mr. Cotter in gold coin for safe delivery to Monia, and if you know what's good for you, you'll continue there without delay."

Art realized this Morgan Crowe was a man that was accustomed to getting his way; however, Art was not impressed and said nothing in reply to the order.

Pulling up in front of 'The Idaho House' he turned to his rider and said in very plain English. "This is maybe the best hotel in town. They have good clean rooms and a nice clean bar next door, with warm whores if you're so inclined. If you are nice to folks in there, maybe they will help you get over to Monia tomorrow. Now get off my wagon before I throw you off."

Crowe was obviously startled by the stern statements just spat in his face, and his hand shot inside his short coat, but he stopped with it resting on the pearl grips of his .31 caliber Colt. *'This is not the way I should enter this region,'* he thought, and looking into the face of Art Houghton, he let a nasty smile cross his lips before saying, "I'll be seeing you again."

Without replying aloud Art thought, *'Not if I can help it,'* just before the man stepped on the seven-foot tall wheel.

Little did Art know!

On Christmas morning, they all awoke to a foot of new snow.

Douglas Morgan Crowe, or Mo as he was known by most, had been born in Lancaster County, Pennsylvania, in the fall of 1844 to a shoe and leather repairman and his very overweight wife. Growing up there, life was somewhat strange to little Mo, as his was one of the few families that did not practice the faith of the brotherhood. There were few schools outside the colonies of the Amish and those were of a lesser standard than most in the state at the time. Mo's one fond memory of his hometown was that the very famous Thad Stevens lived there. He had spent many hours shining the congressman's shoes when they were left for repair at his father's shop. Mo always took special care to see they carried the very best luster that could be found anywhere. The congressman, too, had always praised Mo for his work. It was this alliance that had gotten him his first assignment as an adult.

When Mo was twenty, Mr. Stevens had let the Crowe family know of a special training corps that was soon to be conducted under the direction of several lawyers and businessmen who specialized in real estate and tax laws. Mo was accepted on the signature of the congressman himself and was a member of the first class of men who attended the training conducted in Philadelphia.

There, they learned the tax law system and the legal procedures of land confiscation. They also were well trained in the legal process of placing tax liens against personal property as well as real property. Upon completion of the training, Mo and his classmates fully understood it was their duty to use these tax laws to punish the Secessionists who had brought this great war upon the nation. They also knew should they find monies that could not be accounted for; no one within the Radical Republican Congress would allow any harm to come their way. After all, they were only doing their part in the conflict. No more, but as Congressman Stevens had said, certainly no less, than that of the foot soldier. Secretary of War Stratton also had assured them of that. While feeling this zealous pride, Morgan Crowe traveled to his first duty station.

Arriving at the depot in Jackson, Mississippi on the twelfth of May 1865, he was met by a Union Officer in a very old, dirty and torn uniform. "Mr. Crowe, I'm Lieutenant Glenn, sir," the man said wearily. "I am to show you to your office and quarters."

Not at all pleased with the appearance of his escort, Mo made it quite plain this man offended him.

Glenn recognized the attitude, but failed to understand Crowe's problem, and by that time in the war, he really didn't care.

Richard Glenn had been in the fighting for almost two years straight. He had been among those who had captured the state capital in late April of '63 and then pushed on to the river crossings that led to the fall of Vicksburg. After a short occupation there, he was again marching eastward into Alabama where he faced N. B. Forrest's cavalry unsuccessfully, and very nearly was captured. However, during the summer past, his Fifty-First Indiana Infantry had landed on Dauphin Island, which soon led to the capture of Mobile Harbor, and finally, he was sent back to Jackson. He had seen death and carnage of both blue and gray clad men and the near starvation of most of the civilian population and really didn't give a continental damn what this slick-dressed Pennsylvanian thought of him.

The first state to adopt the Button Law[11], as it became known, was Tennessee, but upon hearing of it, Mo immediately wrote the necessary language to have it also adopted in Mississippi. The Military commander in Jackson did not like it and so stated very loudly in Mo's presence one morning during his first month there.

"What in God's name is the government trying to do, start another war?" shouted the commanding Colonel upon reading the new order.

Morgan Crowe confronted the Officer, and a heated and loud argument between the two soon was overheard by many.

With the use of the now unbroken telegraph lines, within

---

[11] Button Law: No person may wear in any manner any uniform or part of a uniform that contains a symbol of any nation or military force that has drawn arms against the United States of America. Carrying a penalty of fine or imprisonment or both, as deemed necessary by the legal Occupational Forces assigned to ensure peace with in this land.

two days, Mo had the Colonel removed from his post by orders directly from the War Department and sent back to Indiana. After that, no one in the occupational army questioned the power of this young man.

Most all of the official uniforms of the Confederate Armies had either CS or state buttons made of brass. Those who still wore these rags that contained a button were fair game to any Union official, soldier or otherwise, who wanted to flex his muscle. The greatest offenders of this new law were very often those who had spent a long time in a prisoner of war camp, for the men who were still in the field generally were by this time without regular uniforms. These broken men who were now struggling to return to what was left of their homes, usually on foot, were quickly arrested and placed in a local jail or where there were none, in the military stockade. No one returning from the war had any money, but many had real property. Those were fined twenty-five dollars with a lien placed upon their property in that amount. Those who owned no property were sentenced to three months labor rebuilding Fort Gaines or the docks at Vicksburg.

The sum of twenty-five dollars often was elusive as a thousand to these vanquished warriors and in less than three months, Crowe had repossessed over ten thousand acres of land for the government. These lands were sold at public action, and many newly arriving businessmen soon found themselves holders of large tracts of what had been prime farmland before the war.

Mo had also been instrumental in developing an allotment system where freedmen could obtain government monies to bid on this tax-seized land. He had, with his own funds, opened a supply store where the freedmen could purchase needed goods with their allotment monies. By January of 1866, Morgan Crowe had more than twenty thousand dollars in the bank at Meridian and held title for, or in a few cases warranty deeds on, just over twelve thousand acres between there and Hattiesburg.

Morgan Crowe had also been accused of the rape and abduction of a woman from the former Walnut Hill Plantation some thirty miles south of Jackson, but the lady in question never came forth, and the only witness was a former slave who was obviously uneducated and whose statements were judged to be inaccurate due to her age and poor eyesight.

One year to the month from when he had arrived in Jackson, Mo and three of his fellow tax collectors were returning from a late evening's outing at the Natchez Tavern north of town when Mo halted and dismounted.

"What the hell are you doing?" Karns cried out as his horse reared at the sudden change in pace.

"Come on over here, and I'll let you aim it for me," Mo called back as he staggered off the trail behind a large white oak. His bladder was nearly empty when he heard the riders coming.

His first impulse was to step out into the road and halt them. *'Maybe they are former secessionist and I can somehow levy a fine upon them,'* he thought, but suddenly he felt a cold chill run the length of his spine, and the hair on the back of his neck stood on end. Instead of out, he stepped farther behind the great oak. A very wise move, for they were about to have a visit by a squad of men who had learned their trade riding under Forrest's command, but now wore white instead of gray.

The riders were ten or twelve in number, and two carried pine-lighter slabs that made bright torches in the still spring night. They came as in a charge and stopped in a semicircle around the three who were still in the road. As they came rushing in, Mo's chestnut mare bolted at the noise and flaming torches and ran back along the road in the direction he had come.

"Who are you?" John Buck called out.

"We're your button patrol," was the answer from one of the riders.

"What the hell do you mean?"

"There were four of them at the tavern," one of the men with a very deep drawl said.

"Whar's the other one?" a voice questioned.

Jason Bell wisely said, "His horse spooked when you came rushing on us, and he ran off back that way," pointing behind him and then building a moment of courage he challenged, "You had better move on. We represent the United States Government here."

"You damn right, you do!" the man on a dun horse said back. "That's why we want to talk to you. Now which one is Morgan Crowe?"

"It was him whose horse spooked," Bell answered.

"Damn," one of them said.

"What are we gon'a do now?" Crowe heard someone ask.

"Thomas, you and Josey go down the trail, and see if you can find Crowe," the man on the dun said, then turning back to look at the three men he added, "Now let's get on with these three."

At that moment, Bell, sensing the danger, went for his revolver and took a rapid shot, but the percussion cap failed to ignite the powder, and there was only a small snap and then a quick flash. This was shortly followed by three revolver shots and a shotgun blast from the white-cloaked riders.

Bell was literally blown from his mount. The horse also took hits in its head from the scattergun and reared before falling dead in front of Bell's body.

"Good God!" screamed Karnes. "You've killed him."

"I do believe you're right," was the calm reply from the leader of the riders before he turned to his right and directed his statement to the men there. "See if any more are armed, and then get the ropes on them."

"What do you mean to do with us?" Karnes asked in an almost terrified cry.

"Morgan Crowe raped Mrs. J. B. Ferrell on the supper table of her own home while her Mammy stood in the shadows and watched, and then he kidnapped her off into the night. She ain't been seen since he rode out with her." The man paused and wet his lips before he continued giving the men plenty of time to understand the reason they came calling. "Three weeks ago, your trumped-up court exonerated him. We don't cotton to womenfolk being treated poorly. You are part of his carpet-bagging thieves, and we are gon'a hang you."

"Oh, God!" Dirk said before he began to lose his stomach on the road.

"You better stop this. We are officials of the government," Karnes cried out seconds before he was pulled from his horse and stripped to his johns.

"He ain't got no guns, Captun'," one of the men said.

"This un' neither," another man said about Dirk Lealand.

"Alright, tie their hands, and put them back on their horses and lead them over here."

"What about him?" one of the men asked pointing to the lifeless body behind the dead horse.

"Put a noose on him, too. We'll drag him up."

Mo laid low on the damp leaves and watched as his companions begged and wept and then danced at the end of a rope until the life was strangled out of them.

Just then the two riders came back leading his horse.

"No Captun, didn't see hide nor hair of him. Just his horse about half-a-mile down the road."

"Well, we'll not find him in this darkness, but it ain't over. That's one Yankee I aim to see dangling from a tree, and by God, I will before I'm put in this yellow ground," the man riding the dun said, and then he pulled on his right reins and started north, with his companions following.

Mo stayed there for nearly an hour before he moved, and then he headed cross-country towards the railroad tracks to the east, some five miles.

Two days later, he was in Nashville. He could not get the sound his friends had made while they strangled to death, or the sight of their lifeless bodies slowly turning in the moonlight clad only in their johns, from his mind or his dreams. On his fourth day there, he sent his resignation to Washington by wire.

He thought hard on what he planned to do about the murder of his friends, but every idea that came was shadowed by that determined voice of the Captain on the dun horse. The words "That's one Yankee I aim to see dangling from a tree!" were ever-present in his mind. He had no idea who they were. Some former rebel soldiers obviously. One with the first name of Thomas another called Josey, maybe. One a former Captain, maybe. Perhaps they were relatives of that Ferrell bitch, 'No problem from her though,' he thought.

She had bit his left arm just above the elbow, and in his rage following that, he had slit her throat. There was a time there, when that stupid nigger had accused him, that did cause some trouble, but after the hearing Jim Karnes had seen she would talk no more; there really had not been any reason he couldn't just ride back into Jackson and continue business as before. He certainly could have had the military comb the countryside for the white-robed riders. He could have ordered a military escort for himself, but the sight of Karnes and Lealand kicking about as they strangled to death, in the eerie shadows cast by the pine torches, gave Mo a terrifying feeling. A feeling he had never experienced before.

Morgan Crowe had proudly signed up for a six month

enlistment with the Pennsylvania 61st Volunteer Infantry Regiment in Pittsburgh in '61 and trained for three months until his unit had been sent to Washington, where he spent the next several months on Capital Guard Duty. However, just before his unit moved out to stop the Confederate buildup near Bull Run Creek, Mo came down with a severe case of bronchitis and was hospitalized. Upon learning of the resounding defeat the Union forces took during this battle, Mo made no attempt to encourage his lungs into better condition. In September, as his Regiment again began to move towards the enemy, his enlistment ran out and so did he. He had seen the results of war from his hospital bed as the wounded were brought in after Bull Run and soon realized that this was not his idea of glory. Returning to Lancaster, he just let it be known that he had been hospitalized and no more. Most thought he had been wounded. The Tax Collector's training was right up his alley, and he was very grateful for Senator Stevens' help in securing the position for him. Now that he had resigned, he realized he might not be so welcome in Lancaster anymore; thus it was west to Memphis that the train took him.

The Mississippi River and the lifestyle that it brought was far more to Mo's liking, and with the monies he had collected while in office of the Government, he was well-suited for the river. No one could say he became an instant success as a professional gambler but with the cash he retrieved from the bank in Meridian, and with careful study by year's end, he began to win more than he lost. Soon he was known up and down the river as a gambler, and by every Captain that navigated the river. His reputation was not good, but even so, no one had ever found any proof he was a cheat. The largest objection most had to Morgan Crowe was his quickness with either the 6" bladed Arkansas Toothpick that he carried in his boot, or a Model 1855 Side Hammer Revolver that so often seemed to appear in his hand from nowhere. By the end of the year 1868, it was said he had been responsible for the deaths of seven gambling opponents.

New Year's Day 1869 had dawned with a dreary drizzle from daylight until dark, and everyone who ventured out soon became drenched and chilled. Shortly after eight, the rain turned to flurries, and two hours later there was a heavy wet snow covering the decks of the 'Gwendolyn Queen', half a foot deep. The wind that had been from the south all day was now on her eight o'clock, as she passed

Paducah bound for a stop at Cairo to take on wood. Captain Kibler had a frown on his forehead, and his little hacking cough, that was a sure sign he was concerned about something, had begun.

The docks at Cairo had been destroyed during the war and although rebuilt several times, were never repaired to the satisfaction of the riverboat captains. They were difficult to approach as one had to steer around old pilings from the previous docks and then slip into the new false bank that had been constructed by the Ninth Ohio during the occupation, a feat not easily done in good weather on a bright sunny day let alone on a night such as this.

Below in the large dining room, the dinner tables had been cleared and removed and now replaced with the smaller, round, felt-covered tables used for games of chance. It was at just such that Morgan Crowe was spending his evening.

These accommodated six comfortably and as many as eight at times. This New Year's night found Mo playing draw poker with six others. He had always preferred draw to other card games for it was here a man's expression most often gave away his hand.

No one, who doesn't cheat, wins all the time. A good cheat doesn't either. Mo had won six hands and lost four. It was the way to keep the game going. Tonight two of the players were businessmen from Owensboro, Netter Pharis and Franklin Faught.

Faught owned the largest mercantile store south of the Ohio River while Pharis had begun the first coal mine in western Kentucky. Both names were prominate in their communities, and both were frequent travelers on the river, especially between Evanston, Indiana, and Louisville, Kentucky.

Sitting to Netter's right, was a man in his early thirties who had boarded 'The Gwendolyn Queen' at Evansville. He played as though cards were a part of him, taking most of the pots not won by Mo. He had not given his name, and no one there apparently knew him.

Beside him was a stately gentleman who sported a Boston accent, and the cut of his suit gave no doubt to his wealth. George Bitterham had been in the banking business for over thirty years and now was the director of six such establishments, including the Massachusetts National Bank that his father had founded shortly after the removal of British troops from the Colonies. Next to him sat twin brothers, Ralph and Rodney.

The Kirkpatrick boys were from Saint Louis of late, but originally born in Marlborough, Massachusetts, and knew quite well who Bitterham was and why he traveled on 'The Queen'.

They had originally intended to disembark in Cairo and take the 'Delta Queen' north to Saint Louis after their work in Brookport had finished, but upon crossing paths with Bitterham, their plans had changed.

Bitterham had been instrumental in his bank's acquiring large tracts of land that had been some of the finest plantations north of Baton Rouge before the war, and now he had seen to it that they were once again bringing forth a profit in the cotton trade, not in the splendor of the Old South, but rather attuned to the acute mind of the prosperous New Englander. He also moved large sums of National Bank Notes from where they were worth a dollar in Massachusetts, to the deep south where a single bill was worth the sum of a man's wages per week. No one knew of this money movement, or so he thought.

Some few minutes before the midnight hour, as Captain Kibler was maneuvering the GQ from center stream towards the lights of Cairo, the stakes at Mo's table had suddenly become interesting. Laying there was over three thousand in cash and gold coin, and only Faught and Pharis had folded.

Mo had made up his mind this was going to be a hand he would win and was pleased but surprised when the Kirkpatrick brothers had stayed with the round. The nameless gambler raised the pot by two hundred, and they saw him, but it was Bitterham who came charging onward both seeing and raising another two hundred. Mo watched the expression on the faces of the brothers and knew their cash was nearly gone. He raised the pot another two hundred and so it went.

"Damn, Ralph," Rod whispered, "one of us had better take this. I've dropped all the money we got out of that Brookport job."

"Gentleman, if you will, please, talking at a table of chance is annoying but acceptable. Whispering between two players is simply not permitted," Bitterham said staring at the brothers.

To be chastised is always a bitter pill for a grown man to swallow, but to be so lashed by the likes of George Bitterham was almost more than either of them could stand, and the squinted eyes and twisted faces they gave him back showed their anger at his statement.

It was at this moment that the bow of 'The Queen' struck

the end piling of the old dock, and everything aboard was shaken considerably. The table rocked up, but both Mo and the gambler quickly grabbed its top and righted it before anything was really disturbed.

Bitterham had intended to raise again, but now decided to call and take the stakes and thereby be rid of these river trash once and for all. He had failed, however, to consider his other opponents. When his two kings and three sixes were laid carefully on the table, the man to his left also dropped a full house showing the other kings and three eights. The gambler smiled and reached towards the center of the table.

Suddenly, Ralph Kirkpatrick shouted. "That can't be. I discarded that eight a' hearts!"

All eyes went to the table where the hand lay face up and then back to the man who had laid them down. "You're mistaken young man," he said sternly.

"I ain't."

"Then it's my pot," Bitterham said, and he too reached for the money tossed about on the green felt.

"It's none of yours," Mo said laying down a Jack-high flush of spades.

"You son-of-a-bitch," the gambler shouted and suddenly he was holding a cartridge model Smith & Wesson in his hand.

Mo raised his hands palm down over the cards before slowly easing out the Side Hammer from a shoulder holster and laying it on the table. "Easy now, Mister," he said.

A smile crossed the gambler's face, and he began gathering the money with his left hand, but Bitterham suddenly shouted, "Get the Captain!" and the man turned to him and slapped him on the cheek with his revolver.

He never saw the movement, but the flash of light reflecting off the silver blade did register, too late. The Arkansas Toothpick buried itself to the hilt in his throat, and he dropped the money and grabbed at the knife. He also fired off a shot that hit Bitterham in the leg. The overweight banker fell sideways and into the dying gambler.

Suddenly, both Kirkpatrick boys had Colt Navies out and stepping over the two bodies lying on the floor, aimed them at Mo's torso.

"I believe this round is really ours. The rest of you have been bilking. That's obvious," Rodney said.

"That's obvious," Ralph repeated as he began scraping the money into his floppy hat.

Mo's revolver was still on the table, and with both of them having the drop on him at such close range, he knew that there was no way he would survive the play. Suddenly, a large man who had been playing at the table behind them stood quietly and removing his Colt, put a ball into Rodney's right kidney.

Ralph turned to see where the shot had come from and never turned back. It was all Mo needed as a distraction, and he grabbed his revolver and sent a .31 caliber ball into Ralph's left temple.

The two brothers lay dead touching one another. Bitterham was cussing loudly as he struggled to get back into a chair and away from the man who was still striking out at some enemy with his left arm, but whose eyes were staring blankly at the coal oil lamp overhead.

Mo reached over and withdrew his knife from the dead man's throat and wiped it free of blood on the gambler's coat sleeve. He then turned to the man who had made the play that had saved his day or night as it was. Extending his hand he said, "I'm Morgan Crowe. I do believe I am in your debt."

"Ed Sholtz," the man replied, and then taking the handshake he added, "I've heard of you, Mr. Crowe."

Phil Sholtz was not at all happy with his father's decision to bring Crowe here. He was positive that he, with Chip Roper's backing, could take care of the stupid Copperhead and anybody else that tried to interfere with the Monia.

Chip now really had his hands full. Phil was determined to gun down Reb at his next encounter with the man, and Ed Sholtz had been quite clear when he instructed Chip to keep Phil out of trouble. He realized this whole affair working for Ed Sholtz was just too sweet a set-up to let the kid ruin, but he wasn't sure how he could keep the lid on Phil. *'At least the weather has turned bad again and it is well below zero every night. That should keep him out a' South Pass City for a while anyway,'* Chip thought.

At sunup the next day he found Phil gone from his room, and an hour of searching turned up nothing.

Chip was crossing the frozen street headed for the livery when he saw Morgan Crowe ride out on a chestnut mare, a horse he knew

Mr. Sholtz admired. The gunman turned towards the main street and headed out of town. Chip had no doubt where he was going.

This was one of those days when the sky was a beautiful blue and the wind so calm one would never dream they were on the high plains. The temperature was hovering around zero by the time Chip had saddled up, but he had no time to feel the cold. He knew somehow Phil had learned that this day Crowe would be out looking for Brown and had slipped out before dawn on his own quest. Chip also knew Phil was no match for Reb Brown in a fair fight, and he had better somehow find him before he found Brown.

Cliff left the hotel early and had taken breakfast at 'The Hitching Post.' He then wanted to see Judge Morris. Walking east on South Pass Avenue, he saw the lean man on the pretty chestnut stop in front of Kidder's Hotel and tie the horse there. There was something about his determined mannerisms that caused Cliff to continue watching the man, especially when he turned his direction and started walking towards him.

Suddenly, from his quartering left, he heard the cocking of a lever on a repeating rifle. Before he could turn, Phil Sholtz spoke. "I told him that Bodie and Bones were not the ones to take care of you. If I had been there you would be dead now, Copperhead."

"Boy, you're mighty young to be hung for shooting a man in the back," Cliff said trying to figure a way to either jump clear or get to his Colt and get off a shot before young Sholtz fired. In reality, he knew he had no chance of accomplishing either.

"Ain't nobody dumb enough in this dump to hang a Sholtz," Phil replied.

The rider of the chestnut had stopped walking and just stood there some fifty yards in front of him. *'Strange,'* Cliff thought, *'he should get out of the way.'*

Suddenly, there was the sound of gunfire, and Cliff instantly went for his revolver. He wondered if he had been hit. He didn't feel anything, but that is the way sometimes. During the war he had been hit and never knew it until the fighting was over and suddenly he felt weak from the loss of blood.

Turning, he saw blue smoke behind him, and then Phil Sholtz fell forward from it.

Cliff looked at the boy lying on the ice-covered street with the Winchester in his hands, red blood now slowly covering the yellow gun. Then he looked on the boardwalk as the smoke dissipated, and he saw several people standing there. The one holding a smoking revolver was Big Bruce. Beside him was Ash, and next to her was John Morris.

When Cliff turned and looked back towards the street in front of him, he saw the man was mounting the chestnut.

"I heard what he said," John Morris spoke loudly. "He vindicated you in the Bodie killing, and I will testify to that."

"We all heard him," Pebbles Stone added.

"And you, Mr. Whittacur," Morris added. "You were fully justified in saving this man's life from a sure murder."

"Thank you," Bruce replied. "I hope Ed Sholtz agrees with you."

The crowd was still milling around Phil's body, awaiting the undertaker's arrival, when Chip Roper rode onto the scene. He had met Crowe half a mile out of town, but strangely all the man did was touch the brim of his hat as Chip passed him.

Seeing who it was on the street, Chip immediately dismounted beside the crowd.

"The undertaker will be here any minute," someone said, but he didn't look to see who had said it.

"No, Mr. Sholtz would want me to take him back to Monia," Chip cried out and began looking around for Phil's horse. *'Damn! Why did you try him alone, Phil?'*

The .44 caliber ball had gone through Phil's back and exited his chest. Chip didn't realize he had been shot in the back until he lifted him onto his saddle. Suddenly, he turned and shouted. "Reb Brown done shot another one of our men in the back."

Chip was a little confused when no one picked up on his claim, rather they began shaking their heads and walking away. He was back at Monia when he learned what had actually happened, and suddenly the carefully thought out lie he had planned to tell Ed Sholtz went sour in his throat.

"Damn you, Phil," Chip said just above a whisper.

Immediately upon entering the office, Ed Sholtz looked his way but gave him no recognition. He was busy in conversation with Morgan Crowe, and Chip felt the intended cold shoulder.

"I had no time to get in any position to have a go at Brown. He and the boy were in the street, and frankly the boy had the drop on him. He would be dead now had not this big fellow with a beard shot him in the back," Mo said.

"You don't know the big man, then?"

"No. Never saw him before."

"Well, it's not your fault. It was not your instructions to keep my son out of trouble," Sholtz said to him still not looking at Chip. "Your job is not over, simply delayed a little while."

"The only large man with a beard there was Bruce Whittacur," Chip said, trying to enter the conversation.

"I don't think it would be good for anything to happen to anybody for a while after this. If any one of them should turn up dead right now, it would look bad on all of us, and until we finish with the shaft, we don't need no law snooping around," Sholtz added, and then he finished his thought with, "Little Phil sure put us in a bad spot."

"I still would like to get in some gambling. No need on getting rusty," Mo replied.

"Yes, sure, whatever you need," Sholtz muttered not really paying much attention to what Crowe had said.

Ed Sholtz looked over at Chip finally, with the coldest eyes Chip had ever seen, he left the room without saying a word.

"Damn," Chip Roper said to himself.

While he was slowly walking to his cabin with his head bent low and his mind on his only child, a dead child, Sholtz said to himself, *"Oh little Phillip, what would your mother say if she only knew."*

Sundown found Ed Sholtz sitting in a hard wooden chair in a room that was only saved from darkness by the flickering of a small flame in the fireplace. He was there in body but not in mind; his mind was in New York City during the summer of 1850, which was a joyful time to the young man. Jonah had indeed stayed there because of his love of Vashti Jude and in time had married her, but in the nine years since she became Mrs. Sholtz, she had lost the youthful charm that had so captured young Jonah's heart. Now she was over thirty and quite fat, having given birth to three little Sholtzes. Jonah was spending more nights in the bed of Elizabeth Hancock than that of Vashti.

Elizabeth enjoyed a good job as a cleaning woman with the New York Immigration Service at the port of New York, and it was her working companion and good friend Reata Nylen that soon became the interest of Titus Sholtz, Jonah's younger brother.

The brothers now enjoyed the comforts of leading a gang of less-intelligent ruffians in their neighborhood, positions which acquired for them sizeable weekly earnings from the petty theft and strong arm robberies committed on the weaker residents who lived nearby, or the unfortunate outsiders that mistakenly ventured into their claimed territory.

The cleaning women worked at night after the day workers had finished and this offered an opportunity of entertainment for the brothers while they waited for their girls to finish their jobs. They entertained themselves at the expense of newly arriving emigrants, by changing their names on the official documents that were often found lying about on the various desks.

It was here one night Jonah found the papers of a family named Salzman from Salzburg. "Hey, Titus, look at this!" he called to his younger brother.

"What is it?"

"Look, these people are from Salzburg, I wonder if they know Papa?"

"I don't remember any one named Peter Salzman."

"Augh, you don't remember. Hell, you were too young to remember Austria."

"Not so, I remember."

"Here, let's change their names," Jonah said removing the papers from the stack that the immigration officer had left on his desk.

"No, they are from our home, maybe kin."

"Maybe they are the ones who drove us away," his brother said as he began to write on the application.

"Look this girl is named Mona Lisa," he said laughing loudly. "I wonder does her father think she is so beautiful for a sissy to paint her face on linen," he said as he changed the spelling to Monia Lissi.

Titus Sholtz had a bad feeling about the whole affair this night, and he seemed to develop a cloud of depression as the evening wore on.

'*Somehow I must return and correct that paper,*' he thought.

When the others began to enjoy the wine Liz had found while cleaning, she and Reata soon became merry and full of mischief, teasing the boys. This was very much to the liking of Jonah, but not so to his younger sibling.

Titus became even more depressed as he drank the dry liquid, and finally he left the others and walked off into the dark streets by himself.

Jonah started to go after him, but suddenly the thought of perhaps the three of them enjoying the evening together without his pouting brother, stopped him. The idea of having two women in the same bed had always aroused a tremendous passion in him, and tonight he might just get to fulfill his dream.

Titus tried to return to the port office, but found the way guarded by a very large Irishman who Titus knew had a lust for bashing in the heads of Germans. He would wait until daylight, and looking about, he found a place behind some heavy barrels to sit while he waited for the morning light.

Unfortunately, this did not work out either, and it was several days before he located the family they had wronged.

They were now being called Saltsman, and the daughter had her official papers under the spelling Monia Lissia Saltsman.

He thought better of explaining why he sought them out, rather guided Peter Saltsman and his family to a home recently vacated by an Italian family the gang had run out.

Titus soon became totally infatuated with the lovely Monia and worked hard trying to please her.

Peter Saltsman did not find the young Sholtz boy the perfect suitor for his only daughter and made his feelings known to the whole family.

Saltsman was a hard-working man who found employment unloading freight on the docks and had little use for anyone who had so much free time on their hands. "He is up to no good. He has no work but always has money. This is not good, and no daughter of mine will occupy her time with such a man."

Forbidding Monia to see Titus only increased her desire to do so, and finally after several months of sneaking out at night for their secret rendezvous, her mother recognized the telltale swelling in Monia's belly while she was bathing one day. She then decided it would be better to have a daughter married to an unapproved of young man than being known as the mother of a bastard child, and she arranged for the wedding behind Peter's back.

Little Phil was born bright-eyed and full of screaming energy and the pride of the Saltsman grandparents.

After the arrival of the baby, Peter Saltsman lowered his hostilities towards his new son-in-law outwardly, but he still had a strong dislike hidden deep in his soul for the young man.

Phillip was nearly three years old when "The Adal Wulf," as the gang was now called, made a daring raid on the docks where several new Irish immigrants were disembarking. There had been a long-standing war between the mainland European people and the Scotch-Irish element in this area of New York, and this day several of the new arrivals were injured and two killed.

Peter Saltsman was not far away when the affray broke out and with the arrival of the law, the gang members fled past where he and his fellow workers were unloading a Dutch freighter.

Peter saw, without question, his son-in-law dash past him with a pistol held high in the air.

When he learned an Irish woman had been shot in the disturbance, his old hate for Titus Sholtz burst forth, and he took his daughter and grandson and placed them where they could not be found.

Titus was furious, and before his anger cooled he had fired a ball from the same pistol that had accidentally killed the redheaded woman the day before into the stomach of his father-in-law.

That night he waited in the darkness within feet of the body of Peter Saltsman, hoping his wife would return.

Just before dawn, he heard the soft steps approaching on the staircase and the gentle whimpering of a child being lead.

When the door opened, he struck the Lucifer only to see Anna Saltsman holding little Phil by the hand.

Seeing her husband lying in a pool of blood, she fainted, and Titus grabbed his son and fled before she could give alarm.

Try as he may, he never found his wife or ever saw his mother-in-law again. It was obvious she had seen him in the faint light of the match that night, for within less than a day, the police were looking for him on murder charges in the death of Peter Saltsman.

Soon after, with the encouragement of his brother, Titus left New York with Reata Nylen, on a boat bound for Virginia.

No one questioned the Edward Sholtz family when he boarded, and no one ever again heard him being called Titus.

He never loved Reata, especially after he had heard his brother bragging about having her and Liz in the same bed, but he needed her as camouflage and as a caretaker of little Phil.

When Phil was ten years old, Ed came home one night after a bout with a jug to find little Phil had been beaten with a leather strap by his stepmother, and he went into a rage and strangled Reata to death, while his son watched with satisfaction.

He and Phil loaded her in the back of a wagon and left Gibson, Tennessee, where they had settled after crossing the Cumberland's from Norfolk.

Sholtz never liked Tennessee anyway. They had only come to the state because Reata had family there. Now they were headed west again, and he felt good about their future.

Reata had been a thorn in his side for some time, often threatening to turn him in to the law on the New York murder charge. He was glad to be rid of her, although he realized that her death had truly been murder. The killing of Peter Saltsman had been in self-defense and the Irish woman an accident. He never gave the deaths of the Mullier brothers a thought. Those killings were justified in his mind because they had fooled him and stolen his money.

Ed and Phil traveled west to Cairo, Illinois, and then finally were able to cross the river and work their way up to Cape Girardeau where he had heard Monia and her mother were living, but when he found Anna Saltsman, she was not his mother-in-law, and she had no daughter.

For the remainder of his life, Edward Titus Sholtz would mourn the loss of his wife and although he had many women, would never love again.

That night sitting by the fire in the lonely cabin some twenty three hundred miles from where he last saw her, he cried out her name over and over with no one to hear.

Mo had been in 'The Monia Saloon' for almost two hours playing poker when she came down the stairs. He looked up over the hand of three sixes, a queen, and a ten, at the raven-haired beauty and suddenly became spellbound. It was his time to stay or throw down and take more cards, but he simply stared at her as she moved across the floor towards the bar. Her breasts were heavy and moved with a graceful rhythm as she walked. A white leg was seen with every other step when the thigh high slit in her ruby gown opened. When she began talking to the barkeep, he saw her smile and, he thought, '*That is the icing on the cake.*'

Mo neither folded nor spoke to the other players, he simply stood and gathered his winnings and then took a trail as straight as a Sioux arrow to where she stood.

"Are you real or am I dreaming?" Mo whispered into Nadine's ear.

"Oh, I'm real enough, but are you?" she replied.

"Try me, Lady, and you won't be disappointed with what you find," Mo fenced back.

She looked him straight in the eye and allowed a big smile to come across her face before replying, "You can try me if you are of a mind to, but it will cost you forty of those bills you have there."

"Forty!" Mo said back. "The going rate of a whore on the Mississippi is two."

"Well then, maybe you had better go east and get yourself a two dollar piece of ass 'cause you ain't gon'a see anymore of this one until I have your two twenties in my cookie jar upstairs," Nadine replied licking her lips with just the tip of her tongue, and still smiling she turned away from him and started talking to the man standing on the other side of her.

Mo swallowed hard and pealed out two twenty dollar bills from the roll he still held in his left hand and slipped them over her shoulder and dropped them into the cleavage below.

Nadine retrieved the bills, looked at them, and then turned and headed for the stairs without saying a word.

Mo followed two steps behind her.

During the next week, the weather was again at its "Wyoming's Worst," and no one ventured out unless it was absolutely necessary. Nadine had learned of the death of Little Phil, as she had always referred to him, and everyone around was feeling the cruelness that a bad mood brought out in Ed Sholtz. She was getting a case of cabin fever, or maybe whorehouse fever would better describe it. Morgan Crowe had taken a keenness to her, and several nights had paid her price of $100.00 for the whole night.

She didn't like him, but was not sure she really could put a finger on why. He had never mistreated her in any way, in fact, just the opposite. He would be at his favorite table early and have won several hands before it was time for her to come out and sing her numbers, then he would stop playing and gaze at her.

Sholtz required her to sing 'The Monia' as her first and last song every night, and she usually sang two or three other popular tunes during the two hours she was required to perform.

Sholtz had three women singers working there. Betty and Lois also had set times every night they were to be on the floor entertaining. This type entertainment began at eight sharp and lasted until two in the morning.

When it was their time to be the singer, the girls were not to leave the floor. At all other times they could work their trade as the customers demanded. Each girl was required to charge twenty dollars, half of which went back to the house. They were also encouraged not to entertain too many overnighters, unless the night was slow.

Nadine expected Sholtz to call her hand on Crowe at any time about this rule, and she told him so one night after they had finished their poke.

"He won't say nothing," Mo said to her swinging his legs off the side of the spring bed.

"Oh, you don't know him," she answered. "He can be a real bastard."

"He won't."

"I'm not so sure," she disagreed. "He's been a sure 'nuff horned toad ever since Little Phil got himself killed."

"That fool kid," Mo said. "If he'd just waited another half hour he'd had no one to be a-calling out."

"What do you mean?" she suddenly questioned.

"Oh, nothing. Just the kid was messing where a man should've been," Crowe added and then got up and relieved himself in the pot.

Nadine had always felt disgusted when a man peed in her pot. There were just some things that were private, and she usually informed them that their twenty dollars had covered the poke, to use her pot was an additional ten, but this time she said nothing.

The next day she did a little snooping about among the employees there and learned that Morgan Crowe was a gunslinger that owed Ed Sholtz. "He's on the prowl for sure, the story is he wus sent fur to take care of somebody Sholtz wants out of the way," Charlie Wilson the barkeep at 'The Monia', told her.

"That so?" Nadine replied nodding her head.

"Yep. I reckon he wanted this hombre kilt without Johnny Law being able to say it wus done by one of his men."

"I think you may be right, Charlie," she said and walked over to the front and looked out the window.

"Still snowing?"

"No," she replied. "Looks like it's stopped for today anyway, sky's blue."

"That's a blessing," the barkeep said rubbing the counter with his polishing rag.

She didn't know just what to do. She had little doubt the man Morgan Crowe had been summoned to kill was Reb Brown, but she didn't know how to get word to him. He seldom came to Monia after he and Whittacur had gotten into the scrape over Big Bruce's knapsack, and the weather was just too bad for her to go out riding around. She didn't even know if he was still in The Sweetwater Region any longer. It had been months since she had heard of him, but she felt he was. She had not heard anything about the trial over Bodie Johnson's killing and was sure had it taken place she would have heard; still she was both relieved and frightened to learn he was still there. *'Had it not been for Little Phil getting himself killed, I would not have known anything about him at all,'* she thought.

Nadine didn't understand why she found it so important to get word to this man. Even though she had taken a liking to him, she was convinced he had no use for whores. Besides, she had been told he had taken over Ernie Teachman's bedroom duties. She had to admit, it did cause a streak of anger to run through her veins when she heard it, nonetheless, she felt good at the same time. Ernie was such a bastard.

While looking out the window pondering these things, suddenly a Cotter & Houghton freight wagon came out from the alley beside the saloon and turned onto the street.

*'If you ever need to get word to me, you can always let Art Houghton know,'* his words rang out from her memory.

She was out the door in a flash.

"Hey, Miss Tipper, your coat," Charlie yelled after her.

"Mr. Houghton," she called in the cold morning air.

"Whoa, hold up there boys," he yelled to his mules.

"My, my, you're gon'a catch your death, being out here without proper wrap."

"Mr. Houghton, please step down," she asked almost in a plea.

"Why sure," he said setting the brake and twisting the ribbons around the long handle.

It was a long way from the spring-seat on a Murphy Freight Wagon to the ground, but he made it and setting his boot on the frozen clay he slipped on the ice and almost fell. She reached out and helped him get his balance and then said. "Mr. Houghton, you got to help me."

"Why sure little lady, what can I do?"

She turned and looked both directions before she spoke. "I got to be careful nobody sees me telling you this, but you are a friend of Reb Brown's, ain't you?"

"I shore am."

"He told me once that I could get word to him through you," she said the cold now taking its hold on her bare shoulders.

"Why shore, I'll tell him you want to see him."

"No, no," shivering she continued, "He's not to come here. You tell him that Ed Sholtz has brought a gun slick here just to kill him. A man by the name of Morgan Crowe, he's a real Curly Wolf[12]," she said, then added, "Reb needs to be a high-tailing it out a' these hills first chance he gets."

"I'll tell him, but if you know Reb Brown_____," he let the sentence drop.

"No, he's got to go. This man is a real killer, and he was brought here just to murder Reb, nothing else."

"How do you know this?" Art asked, seeing her frantic mood.

"That's not important. A whore knows a lot most men don't give her credit for knowing, now go and tell him before someone sees me talking to you."

"Alright," Art agreed.

When she stepped back inside, Charlie came over to her and placed his coat around her shoulders and began rubbing her arms. "What on earth got into you, a-running out there like that?" he scolded her.

"Oh, I saw that teamster slip and fall from his wagon, and I thought he was gon'a be run over."

Charlie looked out at the big wagon as it moved off down the street, then took her by the shoulders and pointed her towards the potbelly. "Well, you had better come over to the stove and get warmed up. I'll go fetch you a hot toddy."

Returning, he handed her the steaming drink, and she looked at the overweight man and smiled at his kindness. "Thank you, Charlie. You're an angel in disguise."

"Shucks, Miss Tipper, just seeing your smile makes my day."

She patted his hand with the palm of hers.

---

[12] Curly Wolf: Dangerous man

Cliff had not failed to recognize the voice of the man who had confirmed Mr. Morris' statement about their play being self-defense in the Phil Sholtz shooting. When a body is that far from home and suddenly he hears the accent, bells and chimes sound in his ears. Before Stone had gotten away, Cliff hailed him and thanked him.

"I can't help but ask, what part of Georgia are you from?"

"I'm not from Georgia."

"You sure do sound like homefolk," Cliff replied slowly shaking his head.

"What part of Georgia are you from?" the stranger asked.

"Valdosta," Cliff answered, immediately wishing he hadn't when the murder charge shot forward from the depths of his mind.

"Then I would say you are a Yankee."

"That'll be the day," Cliff shot back at the insult.

"Well, from Madison, we figure anyone north of the Withlacoochee is a Yankee."

"The Withlacoochee____, shucks I ain't heard nobody say that in years."

The stranger extended his hand, "Stone is my name. My friends call me Pebbles."

Cliff nodded his head slowly and accepted the handshake. "Brown, my friends call me Reb."

"Glad to meet you, Reb."

The next few hours were spent over a bottle as the two old neighbors got to know one another.

"In these times, it's hard to talk without bringing up the war," Cliff said.

"Yes, I know," Pebbles replied looking down at his glass for a few moments.

"If you had rather not talk about it, I'll understand," Cliff said seeing the quietness suddenly befall his new friend.

"No, it will come out sooner or later, better get my cards on the table outright," he thoughtfully replied.

Cliff was sure this man was about to tell him he had sided with the Union during the conflict, and he was not sure how he would take it, a man from the Deep South turning on his own kind.

"I was with The Ninth Florida Cavalry but was wounded by a shell that killed my horse at Sharpsburg, Maryland, in '62 and was captured and sent to a Yankee hospital in Baltimore. As soon as I could, I escaped and was working my way back south, when I was captured again, and this time, I was posted not eligible for exchange because I had escaped," Pebbles said looking off now at the other side of the room, but Cliff could tell he was not seeing the others there in the saloon, rather a distant land in another time, and he did not want to disturb the man.

"They sent me to The Bull Pen at Rock Island, Illinois and there I stayed for two years. Of the sixty-eight men I first bunked with there, I was the only man still alive in Barracks 12, at least that is what they called that tent we lived in.

"Then one day an orderly came there and offered us a chance to serve in the Army out west. They promised we would never have to fight other Confederates, only Indians," he stopped and took a deep breath. "At first I spit at their offer, but that night, two more of them in the tent died, and I knew I was down with the squirts and would not last long if I didn't get some medical attention and some decent food, so I asked to join up. Became a corporal in the 3rd U.S. Volunteers sent out here." He stopped, and looking around, he wet his lips before he continued, "They called us Galvanized Yankees and we were looked down on by the regular soldiers, but I didn't care. I was assigned to the Granger Telegraph Station and was there when we received a wire about the war being over. I was so glad I had survived, so many of my friends didn't. Not too long after that, we were replaced by the 11th Ohio Volunteer Cavalry, and they sent us home, but it just weren't the same. Too many bad memories, I guess. I wandered up to North Carolina and finally found a job there in a mill. Then this chance came to return to Wyoming Territory, and I took it," he said, laying his hands on the table and waiting for Reb to say his piece.

Cliff remembered when they had come by and asked the same of the men who he was serving with at Point Look Out Prison and how they all turned down the offer, but as bad as it was there, he had heard it was far worse at Elmira and Rock Island. He, too, was silent for a long moment, and then he said, "You did say your friends called you Pebbles, didn't you?"

"Yes."

"Well, Pebbles, I am shor' glad you lived though that damn war," Cliff said looking straight into the eyes of his new friend.

Art had to stop at the other mines to see if they had anything for him to take down to the railroad on his trip back to Green River City. This delay had caused him to pull up in front of Teachman's barn just shy of dark. He would feed and house his mules there for the night and head out for home come first light.

Next, Art took the bit to his teeth and began the long walk through town to the hill to *The Sisters'* for his supper. He cursed himself softly as he walked for his lack of courage. When he thought he might not live any longer he cursed himself for not making his feelings known to her, but now that he had the chance again he found he simply could not muster the courage to speak his mind to her. Just when he thought he was going to speak up, he would see her yellow hair flowing softly across her shoulders, and he would go all weak inside and begin stumbling on his own words. He never had trouble talking at other times, not even to her, only when he wanted to speak his mind. '*After all, I'm maybe seventeen, eighteen years older than her.*'

As Art rounded the front of Teachman's store, two men stepped from inside onto the front porch, and he was startled until one struck a match and lit the coal oil lantern Mrs. Teachman always kept near the door. Actually, it had been Ernie who used to leave the lantern burning at night, mostly so he could easily find his way home after he had spent the evening out at Morris' Saloon. Now that Ernie was gone, Marlene had continued the practice just because it gave her a sense of security should she need to come out of her room into the store area during the night.

Cliff lowered the globe on the lamp and saw him there just off the boardwalk. "Art," he said. "I didn't see you there in the dark."

"Oh, Reb, you're just the man I needed to talk to."

"Hello, Mr. Houghton."

"Why, is that Mr. Stone there with you, Reb?" Art questioned.

"Yes, Pebbles and I were just assisting Mrs. Teachman with a problem she had with her wood box."

"Problem with her wood box?" Art questioned.

"Yes," Pebbles replied, "You see it was empty."

All three laughed at the little joke before Cliff questioned, "Art, why were you looking for me?"

"Reb, I have something I must confide in you."

"It's all right. Pebbles can hear, I trust him," Cliff replied.

Art rubbed his chin and then asked, "Have you gentlemen had your evening meal?"

"Why no, we haven't."

"Then if you will endure the walk to 'The Sisters', I will treat."

Cliff seldom ate there anymore, not wanting to give Connie too much opportunity to flirt with him and surely not wanting Carol to launch into him, but he really didn't want these men knowing of such private business so he agreed. "I would love to sup with you Art, especially at your expense."

"Good, then let's walk. It's too damn cold to stand still."

Some one hundred yards up the street Art asked, "Reb, do you know the whore, Miss Tipper?"

"Yes. Why do you ask?"

"Well, she told me to get this message to you," Art said and then told him of what had happened in Monia earlier that day. He ended by saying, "I tell you, Reb, the woman showed genuine fear. I'd not take this warning lightly."

"I guess I should have expected this after what happened to Phil; he probably put a reward on my head."

"I don't think that is right," Art said. "I know this Morgan Crowe came here from Green River City before young Mr. Sholtz got hisself killed. I brought him on my wagon," he coughed and then cleared his throat and spit before continuing, "If the woman is right, and this man is a hired gun sent for just to kill you, then he was sent for quite some time before the Sholtz kid was killed."

"I see," Cliff replied. "I think we should warn Big Bruce."

"Oh, I agree, but the whore was most positive it's you they are after, and I tend to agree with her," Art said as a final statement of his thinking.

"Gentleman," Pebbles interjected. "Does not this whore work for this Sholtz?"

"Yes, she does," Cliff admitted.

"Well, all of this may just be a conspiracy to trick you into killing the man Crowe, and thereby adding another scrape between you and the local law, which, if I remember correctly, you told me the sheriff don't shine to you anyway."

"Well, that's certainly the truth, but no, I believe she would not be mixed up in anything that would do me or anybody else wrong," Cliff replied. Then he added, "She wouldn't be working for 'The Monia' had not she had problems and not of her own doings, right here." Cliff thought a moment and then added, "In fact, she would not be working her trade at all if she had another decent choice, I believe."

They arrived at *The Sisters'* as he spoke and then entered, letting the conversation lay outside.

After eating, Cliff took his leave and left his two friends behind with the sisters. He went straight to 'The South Pass Hotel' and up to Bruce Whittacur's room. Finding no one there, he knocked on Ash's door. She opened it only enough to peer out, hiding herself mostly behind the door. "What is it?" she inquired.

"I need to talk to Big Bruce. Do you know where I can find him?" Then he added, "It's powerful important."

She looked up at him and bit her lower lip and then slowly opened the door. Bruce was lying in the bed with a cover over him from the waist down. It was obvious to Cliff he had arrived at a most inopportune time. He gritted his teeth and shook his head one twist and then stepped in. "Gee, I'm sorry to barge in on you like this, but I do need to talk to you."

"Come in, it's high time we share our hearts with our best friend," he said.

Ashley stepped aside showing a slight shade of pink to her otherwise perfect complexion.

"Ash and me, we plan to marry as soon as we can," he said. "We should have already. Intended to tell you the day of the shooting. In fact, that was why I went down there looking for you. You know when I came up behind the Sholtz kid?" he said, shaking his head and dropping his bare legs off the side of the bed.

"Ash, fetch me my pants," he instructed in a kindly manner.

"It was just after the shooting, well, we weren't in no mood for it right then, and besides we didn't think it proper to be announcing a romance right after I done up and kilt a body."

"No need to explain, you said we was friends when I came in, and that says it all. I'm happy for you, but I do have something important to talk to you about. I guess both of you now," Cliff said and began explaining what Houghton had told him.

"You trust this whore?" Ash questioned, almost condemningly.

"Yes, Ash, I do," he replied. "She is a whore, but not until after her husband was killed, and she had nowhere else to turn, or way to make a living," Cliff said.

"Gee, I never thought of something like that," she confessed. "That could have happened to me I suppose, might still, if we have not found my brother's mine by the time my money runs out."

"No, Darlin', you won't have to worry about that none," Bruce told her and then looked closely at Cliff. "You think this man is maybe after me, too, don't you?"

"I do think we would be foolish to ignore that possibility," Cliff replied.

"I think you are right," Bruce said. "I also think it's time we started sticking together again, amigo."

"That would be good. If he's as good with a gun as Nadine thinks he is, then two of us would be more of a deterrent to starting a fight than a man alone."

"I think it is a good idea," Bruce said grinning at his brilliance.

"There is a new man in town. A man from Madison, Florida, not far from where I came from. His name is Pebbles Stone. I think we can count on him, also. I don't know his ability with a revolver, but three's a crowd and just that much more of a deterrent."

"Four is even better," Ash said, "If you think I'm just going to sit up here and let you two big lugs go out as walking targets you're crazy.

"No," Bruce said. "It is too dangerous for a woman."

"I'm going with you."

"No. I forbid it," he said strongly.

Cliff got up and headed for the door. Turning just before he opened it he said, "Yeah, y'all a' make a good husband and wife." Then he left.

The next morning while Cliff was having breakfast at 'The Hitching Post,' he saw the two of them walk in.

"You should have waited on us," Bruce said. Ash held his arm just in front of his elbow with her left hand and smiling, she winked quickly at Cliff.

Mo had, during a game in Natchez in the summer past, plunged his Arkansas Toothpick deep into the gamblers heart over a dispute of the deal. They found on the dead man's hips, two hand carved rigs, each containing a .44 caliber Freeman Army Revolver. Mo hefted the brace and fell immediately in love with how they seemed to become an extension of his hand. Thereafter, he had taken to wearing one on his left hip at all times. He seldom wore both rigs as he had never been able to shoot with any degree of accuracy with his right hand, and he considered two big revolvers simply too heavy for one to carry, besides, even when carrying the Freeman, he was never without his dagger and the Side Hammer Colt in the shoulder rig.

It was these three weapons Mo had secured under his frock coat as he rode from Monia City to South Pass City on the tenth day of February. Chip Roper and Bones Harvey rode with him.

They decided to take the long way past Hamilton and Atlantic City avoiding any chance of being witnessed by soldiers coming or going to Camp Stambaugh. The weather again was deep cold without a whisper of wind and a cloudless sky. The shoes of the three horses slapped loudly on the ice-covered road as they moved on at a pace barely above a walk. The pines here in the high country were almost covered in total white from the heavy snowstorm two days before, and the white-barked aspen looked to be ghost-like pencils dotted with smudges of black here and there. There were no birds flying about to sing to the riders. The only other living creature they saw, before reaching Hamilton, was a black wolf that sat on a large rock high above the road.

**44 Freeman Army Revolver**

Passing through the other two towns caused little attention as most of the residents were in the mines working or staying close to a heating stove.

On they rode with the only sound being that of the iron shoes striking the ice. There was no need for talk. They had spent a long hour the night before going over the duty each would carry out. Now, they simply rode on to accomplish the job they had been sent to do, nothing more, and nothing less.

Coming down the hill on the toll road they halted while Chip took from his saddlebags the telescoping glass he had wrapped carefully in the wool shirt. Extending it, he looked into the town first from one store to the next, until he stopped and focused the spyglass.

"There he is," Roper said dipping his black derby slightly as if it would do the pointing for him. "There, by the corner of South Pass and Dakota."

"I don't see him," Bones said.

"He's there," Chip assured them. "He's there by the Law Offices wearing butternut britches and a coat."

Crowe did not say anything; rather heeled the chestnut mare, and soon the others were following.

Klu was sweeping the snow off the boardwalk in front of Morris' saloon when they rode by, and he looked strongly at the three men. They never once looked in his direction, but each had seen him and decided he was no threat and then simply dismissed the man. Reaching the law offices, they pulled up, and Concho stepped out in front of them.

"He 'es there, in the cantina," the Mexican said pointing towards 'The Hitching Post.' "He eets his last desayuno, no."

"Is he alone?"

"No, he ees weeth the big hombre who balazo' leetle Phil. There ees a ingleasa with them too. Ingleasa linda, small tetas," he explained.

"That could work for us," Mo said looking around at his group. "Roper, you come with me. Concho, you and Bones go around and come in through the kitchen." Mo took the Freeman from its holster and added a percussion cap to the nipple under the hammer. Satisfied with it, he then did the same to his Colt. "Everyone had better load with all six, just in case."

Each man did the same, adding caps to the sixth shot of their revolvers, all except Bones that is. He still carried the new Remington Rolling Block that shot a fifty caliber rim-fire brass cartridge. It was always loaded or not, as it was a single shot, a single shot with great knock-down power.

Pebbles Stone was approaching 'The Hitching Post' at the time and saw the men loading up and then splitting. He had no idea as to what was their plan, but he had told Reb Brown that he would meet him there for breakfast and figured his friend was surely in danger, no matter who these gents were or who they were after.

*'It will be easy for those inside to see the pair coming in through the front door, but it is the two that entered from the rear that poses the surprise,'* he thought.

Reb was sitting with his back to a corner, Bruce sat to his left and Ash across from her man so she could look at him, a small pleasure often shared among new lovers.

Cliff saw the tall man in black step in even before he noticed Chip Roper was following him. Suddenly, he knew the time Nadine had warned him of, was there. Before alerting his companions, he slowly lifted the Colt from its holster and held it under the table. Feeling sure his movement had not been seen, as Mei Ling, the small Chinese woman who was bringing out a fresh pot of coffee, had passed between him and the pair of killers precisely at the moment he drew the revolver, he then spoke to his friends.

"Trouble coming."

Bruce looked up, and immediately his hand fell below the table into his lap.

Ash turned to look over her right shoulder at the pair. She recognized Chip and then focused on the other man. "Do you think it's him?"

"I do," Cliff answered.

"What should we do?" she asked, still looking at Mo.

"Putting your fork down would be a good start," Bruce replied.

Then she realized she had removed the tool from her mouth but no further. She was holding it two inches in front of her lips as if she were a statue. Feeling embarrassed she quickly sat it on the wooden bowl that contained the remainder of her scrambled eggs.

"Well, look at the trio. Don't they look family-like?" Chip said.

"I'm surprised someone hasn't shot you for a skunk by now," Cliff replied.

"Well, what really stinks around here is two fellows laying up with one whore," Chip replied.

At this time the three other people who were having breakfast there, pushed back their chairs and scrambled past the gunmen for the front door.

Ash gasped at the words Roper had used to describe their friendship, but Cliff moved his left hand over toward Bruce before saying. "He's just trying to buffalo us into a fight while we're here at a disadvantage." Pausing a second, he continued, "It's the way of cowards to pick a fight while there are womenfolk close by. They know we would be worried about Ash being hurt."

"Who are you calling a coward? You Rebel Scum," Mo spoke looking directly at his target.

"Ash, move away from the table," Cliff said.

"I will not," she responded.

"Move, now!" Bruce said almost in a shout.

Slowly she lifted the chair and slid it backward and then stepped back a couple of feet.

As soon as she was clear, or at least as clear as either of them expected her to go, Bruce spoke staring straight at Chip, "That woman will soon be my wife. You speak poorly of her again, and I will kill you with my bare hands."

"You are a big man, Whittacur, and I suppose you could do that very thing if it were not for the truth in the saying, 'God made man, but it was Colonel Colt who made them equal,' and I think he made me a little more equal than he did you," Chip said back.

Neither Mo nor Cliff had looked at anything except each other's eyes since Ash had moved. Cliff sensed his friend's building tension and now slowly let his eyes drop to Crowe's hands. He saw Mo had slipped the bottom of his heavy coat around so it no longer hid the revolver poised on his left hip.

A split second later, a flashing movement to his left, had to mean Bruce was starting it.

The hand he had been staring at moved, and Cliff shot from where he sat only a hundredth of a second after the table turned over from Bruce's huge left arm. He, too, had a revolver in his hand firing. The noise was suddenly terrific as the large wooden table crashed over, and then the six shots exploded almost as one huge roar.

Morgan's .44 ball hit the edge of the overturned table and ricocheted up and put a hole in Cliff's Stetson, where it hung on the hook behind him. Bruce's revolver spit lead into Chip's left arm causing him to spin around firing into the floor. Cliff's shots were one behind the other, both striking Morgan Crowe in the upper torso. The first entering over his right breast and the second passing though his hand into his stomach.

Crowe slowly dropped his Freeman and then with a surprised look, reached for his dagger. He pulled it and started to throw, but his strength was spent, and the knife dropped from his hand and stuck in the wooden floor at his feet. His legs slowly began to bend outward at the knees and then his soul departed for its eternal reward.

Ash had screamed sometime during the two seconds all of this had taken place, but it was the sound of other shots that surprised them all.

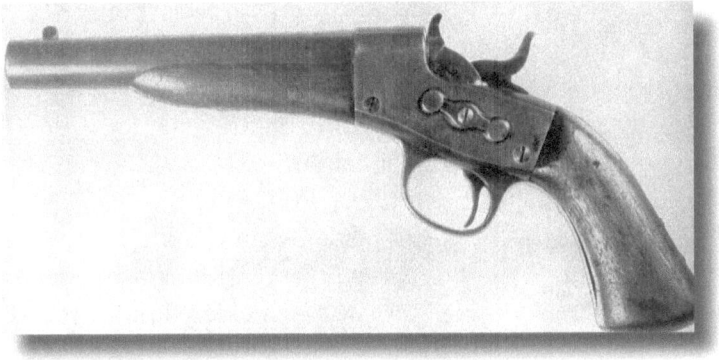

50 Caliber Remington Rolling Block Navy Pistol

Pebbles had entered the kitchen just after the Chinese cook had departed and had watched the two men closely. When Bones aimed his big pistol, Pebbles shot him in the back. The last shot had come from the Remington 50, when Bones squeezed the trigger as he was falling through the kitchen door into the outer room.

Pebbles then motioned for the surprised Concho to drop his weapon and walk out towards the others.

Even when the smoke had cleared, the smell of sulfur was strong, and everyone slowly began to catch their breath.

Ash hurried to Bruce and threw her arms around him. Cliff motioned for Chip to drop his gun, which he did and pressed his hand tightly to his bloody arm.

Pebbles turned to the people who were still in the back and said, "Someone go get the law and maybe a Doc."

Hurriedly, Mei Ling ran out the backdoor on the errand.

Doc Barnes arrived first, having been on his way to *The Sisters'* when he heard the gunfire.

Sheriff Boyd came some ten minutes later.

"Well, I see you two are killing people again," he said looking at the scene.

"No. They started it," Ash shouted. "He drew first," she said pointing at the bloody body that had housed the Carpetbagger Morgan Crowe.

"Yeah, he shot first, and he's dead," the Sheriff replied sarcastically.

"It's true," she said.

"It is true, Sheriff," Pebbles agreed.

"Just who are you?"

"Stone is the name. I saw these four men come to the front of the restaurant and then split-up after fully loading their revolvers. Two entered from the front and two from the rear."

"Wei, that is true," Mei Ling confirmed.

"They came here looking for a fight," Ash added, "That one there is a hired killer sent for to murder Reb."

"That so?" Boyd said, "And just how do you know that?"

"Word is out. We heard it yesterday," Cliff said before she said something that would let the wrong person know it had been Nadine who had warned them.

"I heard nothing of it," the sheriff said.

"It's all a lie," Chip injected, "Me and my friends just came in here for something to eat, and these bastards started shooting."

"Well, I'm glad you finally admitted Concho is your friend," Cliff said. "He's still wanted here for the Boeing break-in and the hanging that followed, as well as a bank robbery and killing down to Green River City."

The Sheriff turned to the Mexican bandit and raised his eyebrows before saying. "You are wanted here, I don't know about Green River City. Raise your hands, Concho."

"But, Señor Sheriff eet ees all a grande' mistake."

"Well, that's not my job. The courts can decide that. My job is to put you in the hoosegow."

"Hijo de pera'," Concho said as the lawman put iron cuffs on his wrists.

"I don't know anything else I can hold the rest a' you fur, so clear out a here 'afore I get over being so generous."

"What do you mean you can't hold him?" Ash questioned looking at Chip Roper. "He tried to shoot Bruce Whittacur. He's the one who really started it all."

"A minute ago you said it was the dead man, anyway it's your word against his. You can come down and swear out a complaint if you want, but fur' now he's free to go."

"Not before he pays me my $20, he ain't," demanded Doc Barnes.

Chip looked at the man with disgust in his eyes and flipped a gold coin in the air. The Doctor snatched it on its upward run and gave him an obvious fake smile.

Roper then reached down for his revolver before turning and starting out the door. Making sure the Sheriff was far enough away not to hear, he stopped and turned back looking at Cliff and mouthed, "This ain't over." Then he walked out and mounted the gray stallion that was among four horses tied to the hitching post in front and rode north, worrying all the way back to Monia about having to tell Ed Sholtz about their failure.

Walking back to the hotel, Bruce retrieved from his pocket the Colt Side Hammer revolver and placed it in Ash's hand.

"What's this?" she asked.

"Just a little present."

"Where did you get it?"

"Oh, it just kind a' jumped into my pocket, right out a' that gunman's shoulder holster," he said back with a sheepish grin.

She slapped his arm playfully and replied, "You are a devil, stealing from the dead."

"He didn't need it no more. Besides no man should have a pearl handle Colt. It's a woman's gun, ain't it, Reb?"

"Sure looks like it to me," Cliff agreed.

She then took each by the arm and walked between them, feeling great for a change.

# Chapter Ten
# Pacific Springs

In early April, the tops of the fence posts that surrounded the little two acre field across Grant Avenue from Esther's Millinery Store,[13] where she and John kept their riding horses in the summer, began to poke their little bald tops up through the white blanket that had hidden them for so many months.

"It's the first sign of spring, up this high," John said to Cliff as they were looking across the street at the progress that had been made on the new log jail. "Down lower, they have had flowers and green things for nigh on two months, but when you get this high, spring is a long time coming." A chill ran over Cliff's arm as the man spoke, and he thought how true his old enemy's statements were.

He had come to the store to see if 'The Judge' had heard any news of Mr. Snow. Although she was not there, her husband had told him, "No news."

The man then began to question Cliff, in a friendly way, about the shooting at 'The Hitching Post' some weeks before.

"Do you really think this man Crowe was summoned here to kill you?"

"That is what I had heard," Cliff admitted.

"But just who would do that?"

"Someone who has much to lose if I stay around. Mee'be he thinks I know more about his illegal operation than I do."

His attention was interrupted by the pounding of hammers as

---

[13] Millinery Store: A place where women's hats were made or sold.

the crew of men, who had been employed to construct the jail, began their work for the day.

"Who, who do you suspect, Mr. Brown."

"Suspicions often start rumors that turn out later not to be so," Cliff replied, and then seeing his statement had been taken wrong by John Morris, he added, "Not that you would start rumors, but I find it best just to keep such thoughts to myself until I can say for sure. You understand?"

Relieved he was not being accused as a gossip, he smiled and said, "You are a wise man, Reb Brown, and I am glad to call you friend."

"Well I tell ya, John Morris, I am sure glad we ran into one another again, myself. I do hold you and your wife way up high on my totem pole," Cliff replied looking at the shorter man, and he meant it, too. Had it not been for these two, he very likely would not have lived out this long year.

True, it had not been a full year since he had come to the Sweetwater Region, but he felt as though it had been ten years.

While they were talking, Art Houghton came by on one of his massive wagons and waved to the two men standing there; Cliff didn't recognize his shotgun.

"Now there goes a fine man," Morris said returning the wave.

"You got that right," Cliff agreed, remembering all the man had done to help honest folks since he had known him. This thought made him think of the Steele sisters. They would surely be out of business had it not been for Art Houghton, and that made him realize he was hungry, and it seemed like a good day to go back there and see if he could patch up some of the hurt he knew was felt by Carol. It had never been his intention to cause any hurt to her or anybody, but neither had it been his intention to take on a wife, although it was plain she had such ideas in her mind.

"Well, John, I must be getting on," he said. "Should the judge hear anything about when Mr. Snow might be arriving, will you let me know?" he asked stepping from the dry boards into the slushy snow covered street.

"You can bet on that," the older man assured Cliff before turning and reentering the store.

Walking towards the far end of town, Cliff let his thoughts return to Carol and Connie. It had been a good time back when he was living with them. Even had he not had the late night visits, it

The New Jail built at South Pass City

would have been a good time. Then he frowned. *'It was these late night visits that caused me to have to move,'* he remembered. *'Still, they had not been without pleasure.'* All of this brought on more detailed thoughts, and he began comparing the two sisters, and soon he had a throbbing in his groin.

"Hey, Reb!"

Cliff turned and saw Pebbles coming down Price Street.

"Where you headed?"

"Breakfast at 'The Sisters,' " he replied, pointing down the street.

"Me too, hang on I'll; walk with you," Stone said hurrying through the wet snow.

The streets were now a combination of ice, mud and slush. The steady travel of men, animals and vehicles had kept them from building drifts in town, and now with the warmer weather, the thaw had begun.

By the time the two men arrived at the restaurant, both were covered from the knees down with icy mud. Stopping long enough to stomp their boots on the wooden step, they tried to clear some of the clinging mess off before entering the building. Actually, it was more than a wooden step, yet it truly was just that. Some of the woodcutters, who furnished most of the town people with fuel for the winter, had found a large ponderosa pine and had split and hewn it into the step. It was perfect, and both sisters were very proud these men would think of them in such a way.

The building interior was quite warm compared to the air rushing down from the hills, and both men immediately removed their coats. Stone, a heavy woolen plaid garment he had bought from Mrs. Teachman and Cliff, a thick buckskin made from an old bull elk he had shot the past fall.

Connie was serving a table and had her back to them, but Carol had just come from the kitchen, and both of her hands were filled with plates. When she saw him, the old look of hate shot to her face, but Cliff smiled at her, and despite herself, she smiled back. She didn't know why she had done it, but she had, and she felt better after doing it. Cliff had long realized that a smile begets a smile, most of the time. Connie, looking up at her sister's expression, turned, and she naturally smiled, too.

"Well, now there's a fine looking brace of Johnny Rebs, I must say," she cheerfully sang out.

"And, so grand a pair of ladies," Pebbles replied. "We are simply charmed."

"You guys are a couple of flannel-mouths," Connie retorted.

"That they are," agreed her sister. "What can we do for you?"

"Food____wonderful food____as only your perfect hands can prepare," Pebbles continued.

"Yes, you are full of it this morning," Connie said again.

"Nothing new," Carol added before asking, "So what can we get for you?"

"Steak and eggs," Cliff ventured.

"How about hash and eggs," she countered.

"Hash and eggs was my second choice," Cliff said, pleased with her attitude. Not that she was warm, but at least she was not hostile. It was definitely an improvement.

By the time they had finished their meal and their second cup of Arbuckles, most of the miners had left the building, and Connie found time to come over to the table for some small talk.

Cliff could not look at her tiny waist without remembering how she had looked lying naked on the black bearskin there in the trapper's cabin. '*So small and so delicious.*' He felt the stirring in his groin begin. He was confident with a little encouragement he could have her again, but he dared not. It was then that Carol came out, and seeing her sister flirting with the men, she came over. Her intention had been to squelch it, but again when Cliff smiled at her, the anger melted away.

"What are you two up to this spring morning?" she asked, for nothing better to say.

"Just enjoying the brightness you ladies bring to these hills," Pebbles replied.

Looking directly at Cliff she said, "It's good to see you in such a pleasant mood, Mr. Brown."

Cliff was horny, and she knew it. She was there for the taking, and he knew it. She was truly a very pretty woman and could be a tiger in the sack, but he wasn't sure he could afford her price. Instead of making such a move, he countered with, "I must go over to 'The King Solomon Mine' and then on to Atlantic City, or I would love to show you just how pleasant a mood I am in."

"Really?" Pebbles questioned, "I, too, need to go there. Do you think the road will be passable?"

"I think so," Cliff answered. He needed to see George Owens, but there was no need to go today. However, he had used this excuse to keep from becoming involved again with Carol, and now he had set his own trap.

"Well, you boys go have a good time together," Carol said in a disappointed tone but not, Cliff noticed, a hostile one.

When they returned from Atlantic City, Cliff headed for 'The Hitching Post' where he planned to take his supper. Afterward, he intended to go by and see if Marlene Teachman needed to fit his shirt anymore, but as he left the restaurant he saw Pebbles enter Teachman's front door.

Still feeling the need of a woman, Cliff turned back and headed for the 'White Swan Saloon.' Immediately upon entering, he heard 'The Wildwood Flower' being struck, and turning, he waved to Jim Duncan.

"I see you hae' survived the warst of the lang winter," Cliff said to the man, mocking his acccent.

"Aye, kind a' surprised me, too, but I took your advice and stayed in town rather than trying to dig up some color in the frozen earth. Ain't done bad neither, if I do say so me'self."

"That so? That's great."

"Aye, I found me knowledge of dealing faro was as good as any and better than most. Been a good winter."

"Tell me, Jim, they got any good women working here?"

"Aye, if you ain't too canny, there's Rosy," Jim answered. "She's a mite hefty, but the lass gives a fair hurl, givin' it laldy, makes ye feel like she's glad you're bringing her the business, enjoy life no for you're a long time deid." He turned around, and spying Rosy, he nodded with his short brimmed black hat. "There she be, over to the faro table."

Cliff looked in the direction he had indicated. There were two girls there, both with dark brown hair. One short and slim and cute as a whistle, the other short and heavy. Her small breasts seemed to simply be an extension of her stomach, and when she turned, he thought of a big wooden whiskey barrel. Her fat lips were painted a bright red, and she laughed with gusto. Somehow Cliff just couldn't picture himself wrapped up in those legs.

"Who's the little one?"

"Yon be Sue, but dinnae fash yersel, ye'll no' be wanting 'er."

"Why is that?" Cliff asked watching the cute petite girl move around among the men playing cards.

"I feart ye be getting more pleasure out a' loping yir mule," Jim replied. "Tis better to take Rosy."

"That's hard to swallow," Cliff said back and moved away, in the direction of the far tables.

Twenty minutes later, he came back down the stairs and walked back to the bar where Jim was still standing.

"What did I sae to ya?"

"Damn, I don't think she ever moved a muscle the whole time," Cliff replied shaking his head before he turned and motioned for the barkeep to bring him a drink.

"Aye, she puts me in mind of me first ex-wife," the Scotsman added.

"You know, I think that was the worst piece of ass I ever had."

"Tis one thing I learned a long time back, my friend," Jim said smiling.

"I don't know that I want to hear this," Cliff replied just before he downed his rye.

"Colt revolvers and ugly women, that's where it's at," his friend said before he returned to the piano.

Cliff shook his head and reached into his vest pocket for another dollar only to find none there. *'I better find some way to make some more money,'* he thought. *'This long winter just about cleaned me out of the cash Ol' Puckett's dust brought.'* Actually this was not true, and he knew it. He had allotted himself so much to live on and left a small amount in the bank in Green River City. A stake, although quite small, that he did not intend to dig into unless an emergency arose.

Sitting his empty glass down, he turned and started for the front doors. *'I should a' stayed with the sisters,'* he thought, although he knew better.

Art Houghton had a hundred pound sack of good grade ore he had picked up at the 'King Solomon Mine.' They wanted it taken to Granger to be stored. It had been the practice of 'The King Solomon' to wait until they had at least five thousand dollars worth before they sent it back to the bank in Chicago. Not having a stamp mill of sufficient size, they had been sending most of their diggings as ore to Granger, where it could be riffled out.

The wagon was weighted down with a half load of broken parts from the stamp mill at Monia. The huge battery had cracked in late January, but with the ingenuity of Captain Nickerson, they had been able to patch it together until now. Without the stamp mill running, 'The Monia' was now slowed to that of 'The King Solomon', and Ed Sholtz didn't like it one bit.

The work had to almost be stopped entirely on the shaft Nickerson had been supervising, while he was overseeing the cracked battery. All of this became a huge thorn in Sholtz' side.

"At least now you can get back to work on the south shaft," he said to Captain.

"As you say, Mr. Sholtz, but we've not turned a' speck a color in all the drilling we've done, and I plain don't see the wisdom in running this shaft."

"Nickerson, I'll do the thinking, and you do the engineering. Now get them men back to work on that shaft," Sholtz shouted at the tall man before turning and walking away. Captain just shook his head before he motioned his crew back into the new shaft.

Art had stopped at *The Sisters'* for breakfast before he headed out southward with the load of broken parts. Cliff and Pebbles, accompanied by Ash and Bruce, arrived ten minutes later.

"Those axles sure seem to have a bend in them, Art. What you carrying that's so heavy?" Bruce asked his friend.

"Oh, that iron battery done up and broke over to 'The Monia,' and Sholtz thinks he can get it fixed in Salt Lake. I told him he'd be better off just ordering a new one, but he don't seem to want to wait that long. Plum foolish, if you was to ask me."

"What's Sholtz so rushed about?" Cliff asked.

"He's been like a crazy man ever since his boy was kilt," Art replied forgetting who had killed him.

"Well, the dumb kid shouldna' tried to bushwhack Reb here," Bruce replied a little defensively.

"Oh, I'm sorry, Big Bruce. I meant no bad words towards you. That kid was bound to end up shot dead sooner or later. Hellfire, he always pranced around acting like rules applied to everyone else but him."

"When you coming back?" Connie asked as she set down a wooden plate on which was a large rare elk steak and two runny eggs.

"Hey, that looks good," Bruce said looking at Art's breakfast. "I'll have the same."

"That wus the last steak we had," Connie replied. "Sorry."

"You got hash then?" Bruce asked, knowing the answer.

"Sure, we got hash," the pretty girl said with a big smile.

"Reckon we'll all have hash," Bruce replied eyeing Art's steak.

"Say Art, you don't need a shotgun to ride with you do you?" Cliff asked.

"No, these days I never haul anything light enough fur the bandits to carry off, and it appears the Indian trouble was just a big scare, but with spring coming, the Sanderson Company Stage will be running soon, and they might need a guard. Why, you looking fur a job?" Art questioned as he cut his meat with the thin bladed knife he always carried in the stovepipe of his right boot.

"Yeah, I need a little working cash," Cliff admitted.

"I'll let Wes Campton know you're a good honest man when I get back," Art said, "If there is a job, I'd bet he sends fur you," finishing the last bite of elk as he spoke, he then stood and reached for his hat. "Better be getting on the road or I'll never get to Green River City."

Connie arrived with the others' meals just as he was about to leave. "Oh, Mr. Houghton," she said stopping him.

"Yes, Connie?" Art answered with a big smile on his face as he looked at her. "Don't forget Carol wants you to stop by and see her on your next trip. She needs a list of supplies filled for her."

"I can take it now," he said quickly.

"No, goodness no," Connie replied. "She hasn't even finished it yet, just when you come back later in the week."

He touched the brim of his hat before replying, "You know, I wouldn't come to South Pass City without checking with Miss Carol and you of course."

She reached for Art's empty plate, but Bruce's huge hand overshadowed hers, and he spoke softly. "There's all that good egg yolk and meat juices there, and you'd just dump 'em in the trash." Reaching with his other hand, he tilted his plate of hash so the mush would slid off into the one just vacated by Art. "I'll just let you take this one back with you," he said, passing his now empty plate to her.

"Why Bruce!" Ash said looking startled at the big man.

"I wanted a taste of that steak, and them juices is all that's left," he said, and they all laughed.

Saturday following, a stage from Green River arrived. It was the first to make the trip in five months. The driver left a message for Reb Brown at 'The South Pass Hotel'. Cliff was handed the folded brown paper when he entered for the night.

He read the note just under his breath: "Mr. Campton said I should call on you, on account of you ridin' shotgun back to the RR."

"Is the man who give you this staying here?" he asked the clerk.

"No, sir," the man shot back defensively. "I believe you'll find him asleep in the barn, with his animals."

"Thanks," Cliff replied and turned and walked back outside. Seeing an empty coach in front of the barn behind 'The South Pass Hotel,' he looked inside the barn and found Jack Murdock there with his bedroll laid out in one of the stalls.

"You the stage driver?"

"I am, leastwise back to Pacific Springs Station," the man said leaning up on one elbow. "We change drivers there. You be Brown, I reckon."

"Yeah, most call me Reb though," Cliff said dropping to one knee and extending his hand.

"I wus in the Colorado Volunteers, First Regiment, infantry," he said looking hard at Cliff. "Got me a rebel ball in my thigh. Had ta walk with a limp ever since."

"You get hit in Tennessee?" Cliff asked.

"Naw, at Glorieta Pass."

"Weren't my ball then," Cliff said. "I don't even know where this Gloria Pass is."

"Glorieta Pass," Murdock corrected.

"Glorieta Pass," Cliff replied standing corrected.

The man slowly extended his hand until he clasped the other. "I wus with Major Chivington's infantry."

"I was with Nathan Bedford Forrest's cavalry," Cliff countered.

"I heard a' him," Murdock said.

"Yeah, I heard a Chivington too," Cliff replied, remembering the stories of the Chivington Massacre at Sand Creek. "Well then, you reckon we can lay down our arms and ride the same seat?" he asked.

"I reckon," the driver replied, swinging around so he was sitting on his backside.

"Good. Then what time you want me here?" Cliff asked.

"Be here come six, and bring your own scatter-gun."

"I ain't got no scatter-gun, but I got a repeating carbine."

"Guess it'll have ta do," Murdock replied reaching around into a croaker sack and pulling out a bottle of clear liquid. He lifted the jar and in a short swallow emptied the last from it. The strong drink took his breath, and he gasped for a moment then said, "Don't be late."

Cliff nodded his head before turning and walking away.

At that very hour, at a back table in 'The Monia Saloon', Chip was explaining to the other four men, "I have information the stage will be leaving here tomorrow with a large shipment of gold, both dust and nugget bound fur a bank in Green River City. Now we already hit that last summer and lost a couple a' men, so the boss wants us to take it off the stage before it ever gets to the bank."

"I saw the stage come in today, and there were no shotgun," Yuel said.

"That's good, but no mind," Chip replied. "We'll stop em' as they are headed up the long pull before they get to Pacific Springs. They change the team at Pacific Springs Station, and them horses will be good and tired trying to pull that hill, probably will only be a-crawling along up that long grade."

Turning to the half-breed he continued, "Squatty Devil, I want you up on that big bunch a' rocks. You know the ones I mean?"

"Si'," the breed replied. "I know 'dem."

"Good, let the coach pass you, and be ready." Turning to Carlos he said, "Mad Dog, you will be in the ravine in front of them. When the stage is abreast the rocks, you step out into the road and throw down on the Jehu[14]." Chip stopped and waited to make sure the Mexican understood. When the man nodded his head, Chip continued. "Yuel, Piggett, and me will then come up fast with the horses. Shouldn't be no passengers, I reckon."

Chip looked at each of them then asked, "Anybody got questions?" There was no reply, and he then poured each a drink. After finishing the whiskey, he left them with one last statement. "We'll leave here seven sharp and cutting across country, that should put us there half an hour or more ahead of the coach."

Cliff was at the Wells & Fargo station next door to the bank before the sun had crept over the little hills to the east. Murdock had the horses latched to the double tree when he rounded the corner.

"Whar' you been?" Murdock growled. "I wus thinking, I'd have to leave without ya."

"You said six, and it's only five-forty now," his new messenger said back sharply.

Cliff never was in a mood to put up with much in the early morning. The war had taught him that the morning was the time everything that needed to be done should be done. It was always up before first light for a forced march or an attack while the enemy was tending to their breakfast fires. He had always enjoyed the early morning just for itself and never liked having to do chores at that time, even though they had become his habit most mornings; still it definitely was not the time of day to rile him.

Putting his Winchester up in the driver's boot, he walked around and checked the team. '*They are a mixed six if I ever saw any,*' he thought, observing two duns were used for leaders, followed by a black on the right and a chestnut beside him as swings; and the wheelers were a pair of big roans; one blue and the other strawberry, but he figured, '*If they pulled together, that is all that is necessary.*'

---

[14] Jehu: a stagecoach driver, taken from the name of a Biblical character who drove fast and furiously

"You checking on my job?" Murdock questioned.

"I'll check you, and you can check me," Cliff answered otherwise ignoring the teamster. Satisfied with what he found, he then climbed up onto the left side of the boot and looked over at Murdock as the whip appeared to be taking forever to get going.

They left South Pass City northbound on the toll road and headed for 'The King Solomon Mine' where they took on a bag of rock Cliff judged to weigh forty pounds. Being tied with a strong horsehair cord, Cliff did not know if it contained ore or was lode, it really didn't matter.

The next stop was at Atlantic City where they took on a strongbox marked 'The Caribou' that weighed some fifty pounds. Cliff guessed it to contain pure lode. And then they took the road that led to 'The Miners Delight' and Hamilton City, where they took on another strongbox. This one was even heavier than the first. Pulling out, Cliff was relieved they did not turn towards Monia. Instead, they headed out on the stage road towards the Sweetwater River crossing.

The day was no better for the road agents, worse in fact. Squatty Devil had gotten full as a tick on rotgut whiskey and beaten the Ute squaw everyone called Candy. She worked her trade from a one-room log shack with a mud roof that gave shelter when frozen, but this time of year mostly rained mud during the daylight hours. She waited until he had passed out then she cut him deeply on his left bicep before she fled into the darkness. His shirtsleeve was a dirty mass of mud and dried blood; anyone could see, because of the obvious pain, he now favored this arm. Yuel had stayed too long at 'The Monia Saloon' and was dragging that morning with a huge hangover. When Mad Dog awoke, he discovered Candy had stolen his horse when she fled from Squatty Devil. It had been his charge to watch the stage and see how many pickups it made before leaving the Sweetwater gold fields. Without his horse, he had not seen the stage at all, and he was now mounted on a borrowed bay that obviously didn't like him or the saddle.

Chip Roper rode out of Monia with a bad feeling. They had not gone ten miles when the big bay found just the right situation he had been looking for and reared on his hind legs and dumped Mad Dog off and down a long slope that was spotted with lodge pole pine. There was a loud crack when one stopped his roll.

Chip was sure he had broken an arm and maybe several ribs from the sound of the crack, but it turned out to be the short scattergun he had in his right hand that had made the sound. Standing, Mad Dog raised the double barrel for all to see. The stock was broken just behind the pistol grip and now hung loosely by a small toothpick like strip of wood. Shaking the gun, the stock broke on off, and he climbed back up the slope where he used the busted gun to strike the bay across the side of his head. The blow staggered the animal, but the results were his mount seemed to realize he had met his match. There were no more mishaps as they rode southwest towards the stage road that along here followed the old Oregon Trail.

It was a little past noon when the team started up the long pull to where the ambush was waiting. It had been thirteen miles since they hit the Green River Road, and Murdock had not spared the horses on this leg of the route. Waiting a couple of miles ahead at the next stop, was his relief and a much-desired meal prepared by the only single woman on his run.

June DeWolf was Bill Crane's niece. Bill had operated the station stop there for several years. She had come from New York State to stay with her uncle the year before and was known to serve a fine meal for the passengers and teamsters alike. It was this meal, he was sure was awaiting him, that had occupied Jack's thoughts for the last hour, and it was these same thoughts that caused him to miss the flash of light as the sun reflected off of something metallic ahead. It was only there for a split second, but Cliff Brown had not failed to see the momentary flash, and instantly he was out of the seat and off the side of the coach.

"Whar' you going?" Murdock suddenly asked.

"I'll ride back here for a while," Cliff replied. "I saw something flash ahead, maybe off a gun barrel."

"I didn't see nothing."

"Good. Then you won't worry about riding into something, will ya?" Cliff called back as he slipped inside the coach.

"Damn fool Copperhead," Murdock said just above a whisper. He felt sure if there had been something, he would have seen it. "Hell, I been running this route nigh on three years and ain't missed a trick yet," he continued talking aloud with no one to hear. "Might a' been the top of Crane's windmill."

They were some two hundred yards away when Cliff had seen

the flash, and it took long dragging minutes for the tired horses to cover the distance.

Suddenly Mad Dog jumped from the deep ditch with the shotgun in hand. He was hoping he wouldn't have to shoot it without a shoulder stock, but still he had one of the hammers cocked just in case. "Hold up, Gringo!" he shouted and Murdock seeing the scattergun, did as he was told.

The stage stopped just a little too far forward, and Squatty Devil had to leap instead of jump for the top. He barely reached it, landing with his legs trailing down on the canvas trunk cover. This caused him to drop his revolver and use his gun hand to pull himself up on the coach.

Chip could see the blood running from Squatty Devil's left arm, where the jump had now started his wound leaking again, and he watched the breed struggling. Shaking his head at the bad luck that had already fallen upon them, knowing Ed Sholtz would be furious should something go wrong this time, finally Chip saw Squatty Devil make it on to the top of the coach.

The breed laid there for a second or two catching his breath from the struggle he had just experienced. Just as he was reaching for the Remington that lay only a foot ahead of him on the stage roof, three shots roared out, and then in the blink of an eye Squatty Devil jerked up, grabbed his chest, and screamed before he rolled off the top of the coach and out of sight. Chip looked about for the source of the shots, but saw no one.

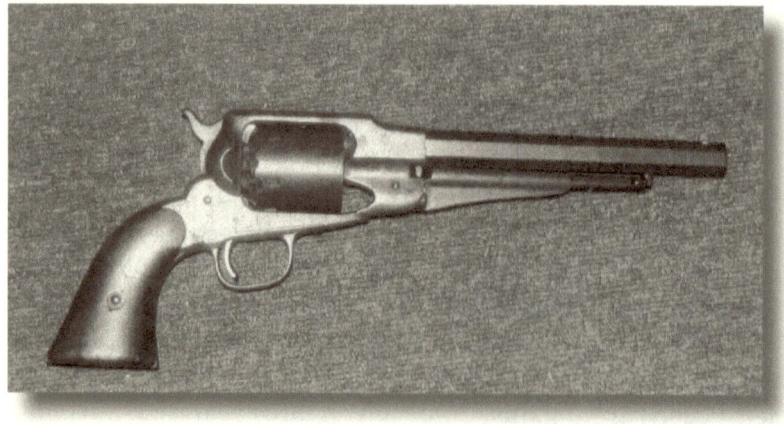

**Squatty Devil's 1858 44 Remington Captain & Ball**

The shots and scream startled both Murdock and Mad Dog. The Mexican unintentionally fired off the shotgun. His aim was high, and only two of the .31 caliber balls hit the driver, one in the right forearm and the other four inches to the left. This one entered his chest just below the breast. Murdock screamed and dropped the reins. The horses spooked and began to run. Mad Dog was struggling to cock the second barrel with his now numb hand he had received from the shock of firing the stock-less gun, when the stage passed him.

Chip saw the barrel of the repeater sticking out of the window, but before he could do anything the gunman fired from inside, and the rifle slug struck the old Mexican bandit in his Adam's apple causing a great gush of blood to exit the rear of his neck, and he dropped the shotgun.

Roper began shooting at the coach as it came towards them, but the rifleman inside was giving better than he got. Yuel screamed when one of the Henry slugs punctured his heavy stomach.

The stage rushed past them then and he fired the last of his six into it, but the return fire continued. Piggett was holding onto Yuel's reins trying to keep the wounded man's horse from throwing him off.

Finally, a hundred and fifty yards west the tired team just stopped, and it was then Chip saw the shooter emerge from the stage.

"Brown!" he gritted out, recognizing the man dressed in buckskin. "You son-of-a-bitch!"

Cliff saw the three men on horseback and took a fine bead on the nearest one and then lowered the rear sight until he judged he had the range and squeezed the trigger.

The slow moving bullet seemed to take forever to reach them, but suddenly a horse screamed and began jumping.

Piggett released the reins of Yuel's horse and grabbed his saddle horn. In doing so, he also dropped his Colt. The horse bucked three or four times before stopping, and then he began to dance around and Piggett still had to hang on.

The hot lead had passed through the man's leg muscle just behind and below the knee and through the stiff leather, to come to rest trapped between the saddle fender and the skin of the horse, burning the animal.

Chip made a quick decision, spurred his gray and was off the road and out of sight around a small rise before Cliff could get a bead on him. Safely over the hill, he quickly began reloading his revolver with his spare cylinder, but while doing so he heard the carbine bark twice again, and someone cried out.

Suddenly Piggett was coming at full gallop around the hill, and the two of them looked into each others' face, seeing the fear displayed there.

"Let's get out a' here," Piggett said. "That jasper is a shooter."

"Where's Yuel?"

Piggett raised his thumb and pointed it back over his shoulder before saying. "He was hit again. I reckon he's done for."

"Damn. I knew this was starting out to be a bad day," Chip sneered thinking of having to tell Ed Sholtz about another failure.

Cliff causally moved back along the road until he found the three outlaws. The one he had shot though the roof of the stage was dead in the west ditch. The man with the big sombrero lay in a bloody pool on his back in the east ditch, with open eyes staring at the sun. When he turned the third man over he recognized Yuel, and saw he was still breathing.

Cliff stopped the bleeding where he had been hit in the right leg just above the knee and patched the stomach wound as best he could and then with great difficulty loaded him into the rear of the stage. Next, he helped Murdock down and into the back also, giving him a revolver he had removed from one of the outlaws.

"Here, take this, and keep an eye on him until I get us to the next station."

"You know how to handle a six-up?" Murdock asked almost in a plea.

"Sure," Cliff lied.

Normally, he would have never tried to drive this many horses, but desperate times call for extraordinary acts. Besides, the team was so exhausted after their short run, they simply moved on off to where they knew there would be rest, water, and feed.

The Pacific Springs Station was little more than a few log buildings and a corral for the stock. One of the buildings was used as a tack house and also served as a blacksmith's and wheelwright's shop. The flat roof on it had taken on too much snow during the winter months and had mostly caved in. The smallest was nothing more than an entrance to the root cellar, and near it, was the largest building that had been used by the Express. After they had been disbanded, it was only used as a barn. The last building was also the nearest to the creek and carried the double duty of both dining room and living quarters. It was a fair-sized structure, twenty by forty, with a small room added where the backdoor used to be. Two chimneys told the observer there was a cooking stove and a fireplace for heating during the long cold months.

Bill had added the backroom for June when she came to live there a year or so back. He slept in the larger room on a cot. He had also made a corduroy road for a considerable distance on either side of the creek because of the mud becoming so bad during the thaw.

**Typical Wyoming Stage Station**

Bill Crane had come west when he was a mere lad of thirteen. Born in Sherman, New York, he had learned to love the devil's brew his grand-pappy, on his mother's side, made for trade. Bill had been one of the goats who drove a wagon around the county delivering the strong clear drink to the stores, bars, and tiger dens that were scattered about western New York. He was making just such a delivery to Seth Fox's place when one of the older boys there began teasing him about his manner of speech.

Bill had the practice of slipping out one of the quart jars each week for his own pleasure, and on this day had found there was not enough for two drinks left in the jar, but there was a little more than his usual swallow. Still, he had downed the burning liquid a few minutes before he reached The Fox Den. '*The thing any man would do,*' by his reasoning. In the time it took him to unload and carry the six cases into Fox's storeroom, the strong drink was rushing through his veins and filling his forehead with what felt like lead. His speech was obviously slurred and his judgment mostly shot. It was this manner of speech the taller fifteen-year-old boy was making fun of, when Bill cold-cocked him with a hefty piece of lighter he found near the wood stack.

It wasn't the blow of the lighter that killed Evans Fox, but rather the splitting of his skull when his head struck the potbellied stove.

Everyone around agreed Evans Fox was a bully who always used his father's standing in the county to sweep his ways on the less fortunate and especially on those who were younger or smaller than he, and most thought publicly or privately that Bill Crane had done the area a good deed. Still, he had been instrumental in the boy's death, and Seth Fox was a mighty influential man from Buffalo to Erie, and it just seemed the right thing for young Bill to become scarce around Chautauqua County. He was quickly sent to live with his aunt and uncle in Pennsylvania.

And it was there Bill saw the poster of a young man on horseback. Being without schooling, he asked Mr. Peter Rooks to read the colorful poster to him.

"Well Bill, it says here," as he began to read:

# Wanted
# Young Skinny Wiry
# Fellows
# Not over 18 years
# Must be expert riders
# Willing to risk death
# daily
# Orphans preferred
# Must not weigh over
# 120 pounds
# Pay $100

Looking up at the boy he added, "Sounds scary to me."

"Wow! Sounds great to me," young Bill exclaimed, "That's a heap a' money. How do a fellow go about getting such a job?"

"Well, let's see," Pete said looking closer at the poster. "It says here to apply at Saint Joseph."

"Whar' would Saint Joseph be, Mr. Rooks?"

"I do believe they mean St. Jo., Missouri, son."

"Whar' is that?"

"Well Billy, it's about 900 miles to the southwest a' here, I reckon."

"900 miles?"

"There abouts."

"Whew!" the boy replied and started out, but stopped at the door and turned around. "Mr. Pete," he called out.

"Billy?"

"Which way would a body go from here?"

"Go whar'?

"You know, to that thar' St. Jo."

"I reckon it would be best if he would go south till he came to the Ohio River and then follow it west."

"Naw," Waldo Kensly said, "it would be better fur a body to hop a freight and head west to Chocogee. The Mississippi River runs slap through the middle of Chocogee. From there you just float down river to St. Jo. Nothing to it."

"Hellfire, Waldo! St. Jo ain't on the Mississippi."

"'Tis too."

Bill remembered for the rest of his life that the last people he ever heard talking in Pennsylvania were arguing, and they both were wrong.

Three days into his journey, he did hop a westbound near Wheeling, Virginia, but a few hours later had to jump when a railroad bull started checking the cars.

Cyclone Thompson was riding the same car and being two years older and road wise, told Bill about the bulls and how they would beat a body near to death if they caught you riding for free. In return, he told Cyclone about the big paying job he was headed for, and the two made a pact to travel together.

Bill really liked Cyclone, but he being a Virginian, made it mighty hard to understand his way of talking.

They finally made it to the Miami River and there got work on a keelboat that was headed south to Cincinnati. There they worked for a month loading cotton bales on the big paddle-wheelers headed east until finally, they found that 'The Creole Queen', a stern-wheeler bound for Saint Louis, was taking on hands.

Bill shoveled coal while Cyclone chopped wood. Neither was sorry to get to Saint Louis and to be watching that big ol' boat head on south.

Captain Longcoy had offered them work to last out the summer, but they wanted no part of any more steamboats.

The two started out west across Missouri, walking. After several rides, a few jobs, and other typical adventures that make up everyday life, the two tired and very broke teenagers arrived in Saint Joseph, Missouri, the second week of April, 1861.

Both found immediate jobs as replacement riders. Cyclone Thompson was assigned to fill-in for a boy named Johnny Fry who rode from St. Jo. to Seneca, Kansas. However, the war had broken out, and there was much turmoil in Missouri and Kansas in those days. One month later, the southern born Cyclone headed back to Virginia, enlisting in the Confederate States infantry and fought for his home state until the war ended.

Bill Crane was assigned to Red Buttes Station overlooking the North Platte River and in sight of the location where old man Bessemer had built the first permanent structure in Wyoming some years before. Bill's route was westbound over the alkali desert, changing horses at Willow Springs, Horse Creek, Independence Rock, Devil's Gate, and Split Rock, then returning with the eastbound mail for the trip back to Red Buttes.

Bill rode this route for several months, then Slade, the Division commander, transferred him to Three Crossing Station where he rode west along the Sweetwater River to Pacific Springs. He was at the Dry Creek Station a little more than half way in his trip on November 12, 1861, when he was told the Pony Express was shut down, and they were to suspend all operations. Bill rode on down to The Pacific Springs Station and hung out there a few months until it was rented by the Overland Stage Company as a swing station on the route from South Pass City to the U.P.R.R. tracks at Green River City.

The station operator saw the stage coming long before his niece did. He immediately realized something was wrong, the teamster was not using his bullwhip, nor had he blown his horn; gestures Jack Murdock never failed to do. Murdock was never much of a horn blower, but he always gave it a feeble try to satisfy the rules, however it was the bullwhip he had mastered, and he seemed to enjoy the pain he could cause when he swung that nasty thing. It had become his signal he was approaching the station, and Bill was sure he did it just to impress June. Something that was not too hard to do to a sixteen year old girl in the middle of the desert.

When the vehicle was closer, he realized the man sitting in the box was not Jack at all, rather a stranger, and he was not driving the horses, they were just walking on their own to where they knew there would be relief.

"You have the look of trouble," Bill Crane said when the team stopped in front of the corral.

"Yep," Cliff said, wrapping the leads around the brake pole. "Murdock is inside; he'll need help."

"June Ann," Bill called out when he opened the door of the coach. "Get a pot a water a-bilein' and be quick about it."

"What's the trouble?" she questioned when she saw them lifting the man from the coach.

"Just do your job, and let us do ar'n,'" he spit back.

They carried Jack into the main house and laid him out on the long table, and then they went back for Yuel.

"Who's this dead man, a passenger?"

"One of the robbers, and he ain't dead, leastwise not yet."

"You shoot 'im?" Bill asked.

"I did," Cliff answered. "Him and two or three more. I ain't sure."

They removed Jack's shirt and blood-soaked bandages. "This arm is ruin't," Bill offered, then he looked at the hole in the man's lower stomach. "He's gut shot."

"I don't know," Cliff said. "That was a blast from a scatter-gun that went wide. Only them two balls hit him. I don't think it went in all that much."

"June!" Crane called out loudly.

"Yeah?" she replied. "I'm getting the fire a-going."

"I need my whiskey."

"It's probably where you left it last night," she spat back.

"Damn smart-ass kid," Bill mumbled just above a whisper.

Cliff thought surely they were married the way they went at each other all the time. *'A body that couldn't read faces would have thought them ready to fight and scratch at any minute, but I can see they each have deep affection for one another,'* Cliff thought proudly to himself.

Yuel began moaning suddenly.

"I reckon you're right about him being alive," Bill said without looking at the outlaw.

*'Hell, the blood he is looing is sign enough to see that,'* Cliff thought but said nothing.

Crane found his jug and lifted it up to Murdock's mouth and told him to drink. The man tried, but coughed badly when he swallowed. Crane then simply poured the firewater on his stomach wound, and the Jehu screamed loudly before suddenly passing out.

"There that ought to keep him down while I probe around fur that ball," Crane said, showing satisfaction with his last deed.

When the .31 caliber lead ball was dropped into the pewter plate it made a ringing sound, not unlike a small bell might make.

After looking closely at Crane's work, Cliff felt sure Murdock would live if they could keep the fever down. He then said to the station keeper, "Will you see what we can do for this jasper over here?"

"Hell! You shot 'im, you save 'im," Crane replied reaching for the jug and taking a long snort. "What you want a save 'im for anyway?"

"A witness," Cliff said as he removed the bloody shirt Yuel was wearing.

"You think he'll talk? Shit, he's as good as dead right now, and asides, he won't do no talking on his compadres."

"Maybe he will when he realizes they run off and left him there to die."

"Huh!" Bill Crane replied in disagreement.

Later they moved Jack into the little room where June slept, and it was then Cliff noticed the two sleeping cots, one in the front and one in the back, both narrow. He raised his eyebrows and shook his head, but said nothing.

When he had seen to it Murdock was alright, Bill came over and inspected the work Cliff had done on the outlaw. "That ain't bad fur a greenhorn," he said approving of the wound's condition. "He might just make it at that." Then turning towards Cliff he added, "We'd better take care of the stock before it gets too dark."

"And the gold," Cliff added.

"Gold, eh? That's what this wus all about, wus it?"

"Yep, we're carrying several hundred pounds," Cliff replied.

After feeding the horses, Bill placed a plate of stew in the floorboard of the Concord and then motioned for the yellow-haired cur dog to jump in. The dog made the leap towards the food without the slightest effort. "Joe'll stay here fur the night, and that will keep us from having to move the gold into the house," Bill said as he closed the coach door and picked up his jug. "He'll let out a bay should any fool try and get to it. Now this time of an evening, I favor a nip or two outside where I can watch the sun hide behind them hills yonder," he said nodding towards the west.

"Bring you a chair, and tell me your name, Mister," he said picking up one of the straight back chairs with his free hand.

Cliff had to admit, even though he missed the green of the east and the towering oaks and sweet gum that grew wild all over South Georgia, he did see a beauty in the early evening out on the open plains, a time when the sun was coloring the sage a deep purple, and the meadowlarks were singing to one another.

Sitting his chair on the hard clay under the short roof overhang, he leaned back until he rested against the side of the cabin.

"I'm called Reb Brown," he finally said.

"You headed to Green River City or sum'ers else?"

"I'm headed to the Sanderson Company Stage office in Green River City and then back. I'm the shotgun on this line."

"Huh. Would a figured you fur a dude," Bill said back, mostly seeing if he could get a reaction from the man.

"I understand how a man, living way out here in the middle a' nowhere, could be so foolish in his way a' thinking," Cliff said back.

Bill Crane almost choked on his swallow when he heard the stranger call him a fool, even if it was done in a round about way.

"You got sand, Reb Brown," he said wiping his mouth with a shirtsleeve and then handing the jug over to Cliff.

Cliff knew whiskey enough not to take a big drink until he had tested its pure content, and he just took a small sip even though he held it to his lips as long as he could stand the burn, making Crane think he had taken a long swallow.

"Damn!" Bill said. "I ain't give you that to finish off."

"Sorry," Cliff replied handing him back the jug.

They sat there close to an hour swapping one tale and then

another when Bill asked, "You answering to Reb like that, I spec you wus a rebel soldier?"

Cliff had detected the sharp northern accent of both he and the girl and was not surprised at the question finally coming.

"Yeah, I was at that."

"My best friend went back and fit with the rebels. I thought he wus crazy," he said, shaking his head as if it had occurred a day or two before. Then he asked, "You ever knowed a Reb soldier that went by Cyclone Thompson?" Bill asked.

"No, can't say I did," Cliff replied surprised at the question, as if one rebel would know all the others.

"Well, I guess that's the size of it. I just wus hoping someun' would tell me he wus still alive. He were from Virginnie, as I recollect."

"I was from Georgia."

"That near Virginnie?"

"Not really. I did most of my fighting in Tennessee."

"That's near Virginnie," Crane said with some confidence. "I see'd a map once, and Tennessee and Virginnie were right close to one another."

"Most of my fighting was from Nashville south, into Alabama and north Georgia," Cliff replied, trying to make the man see how far away battles could be from one another.

"I reckon I'll never know if Cyclone made it a' not."

"We lost a lot a' men in Virginia," Cliff said, then added, "But I knew of some fellows from Florida that fought in Virginia, they came home after the war."

"That so?" Crane said excitedly. "I do hope ol' Cyclone made it. Him and me bummed our way all the way out here." then he added almost affectionately, "Took the oath to ride fur 'The Express' together, but that wus the last I ever see'd a' him. Went back to Virginnie right soon after that."

Just as the last light began to fade into darkness, June came out with a coal oil lantern. "You men going to stay out here all night, or you coming in fur a bite to eat?"

"You planning on taking the stage on back to South Pass City tomorrow?" Bill said ignoring her as if she wasn't even there.

"Well, I'll tell ya, I ain't much of a teamster when it comes to a six-up," Cliff admitted.

"I could see that," Bill agreed.

"I asked you a question," she said harshly.

"Men's talking now girl. Go away until we need you," Crane ordered a moment before she dropped the lantern in his lap and slammed the door behind her as she entered the cabin.

"What the tarnation'?" Bill yelled as he jumped up trying to get a hold on the lamp so it wouldn't burn him.

Cliff laughed quietly at the scene.

Finally, Bill found the long wire handle and lifted the old Dietz & Company coal oil burner off his legs. "That damn girl will get us all charred to a crisp someday."

Cliff made no comment.

Crane rose and looked around at the stars that were starting to blink in the eastern sky and said, "I reckon I'll have to drive the stage on to Green River City fur you. We can take that bushwhacker with us. We'll leave Jack." Nodding his head approving of his decision, he then added, "Still, you better come with me. Never know when them owl hoots might try fur that gold again."

Cliff thought a moment then suggested, "We could all go. There's plenty of room. That way your wife wouldn't have to stay here practically alone."

"Wife! Hellfire, that there child is my niece," he said. "What you think a' me, a cradle robber?"

Cliff thought, *'She looks to be sixteen or seventeen, and there ain't no way he's more than seven or eight years older than her,'* but he kept his thoughts to himself and finally said, "I just thought you were hitched."

"No, hell no!" Crane said almost in a shout as he reached for the door latch, then turning to Cliff he added, "but if we leave them alone she might catch that fellow Jack Murdock, and I'd be good 'n rid a' her."

*'If he was to be her husband, a man of perhaps twenty-two or maybe twenty-three and be considered a cradle robber, what in tarnation would Jack Murdock be, him a man of at least twice her age?'* Cliff wondered as he followed Crane into the stage stop.

The man stopped at the table and looked at Yuel and then said, "We need to get him out to the tack house fur the night."

Yuel was still unconscious, but Cliff wanted him to live if possible and then suggested, "We can move him over there in the corner. There, he will be close to the fire should the fever come and chills take him."

"Then you watch him. I'd throw the bastard in the tack house, were it me," Bill said lifting Yuel's feet while Cliff took his shoulders. The man moaned loudly when they moved him but never woke up.

"June Ann, we'll be taking our vittles now," Bill said in a rough voice.

"Maybe you will and maybe you won't," was the reply he got back, but Cliff could see she was taking up two bowls of some sort of stew as she spoke.

"Jack said something about having a relief driver here for him?" Cliff said almost in a question.

"Yeah, that damn Happy Tom. Tom Ranahan was supposed to be here yesterdee but he ain't always too dependable when the weather is cold," Bill responded, but he had barely gotten the words out when the sound of horse hooves were heard. "Quiet," Bill said to all.

As the sound drew louder they recognized it was a lone rider approaching.

"Just one," Cliff said.

"Yeah," Bill agreed as he took the Spencer Carbine from over the fireplace where it hung on two antelope horns.

"Hal-loo the house," a voice soon called out.

"That's Happy Tom," June said smiling as she called out, "Come in, Tom."

"Another prospect," Bill said looking at Cliff.

Happy Tom Ranahan was another man a few years younger than Cliff. He was short and lean in a wiry sort of way. He wore a big brimmed Stetson felt that had started life a light tan color, but now was mostly dark brown from the trail dust, at least that portion not stained with sweat. He carried a revolving pistol on his left hip with the butt forward, and Cliff judged it to be a Navy Colt. His shirt was faded red, and he wore dark trousers with what had been at one time light pin stripes running vertical. His boots were of the Yankee Cavalry style, and they flared at the knee. "You still got some grub heating up in there?"

"Come over here, Tom," June said as he removed his hat. "I just got Uncle Bill and Reb here a bowl a' antelope stew. I'll get you some right away." It was obvious she was pleased to have so many young men around all at once.

"Antelope stew, alright," the lad replied. "I never knowed a white woman who could make antelope taste worth eating until I meet you, Miss June," swinging a leg over the back of a chair, he sat down before he continued. "But I got 'a tell ya, this here June Ann, well she's got the touch of an angel when it comes to cooking. A man would ride all the way out here from Green River City just to et at her table."

"If you admired her cooking so much, why weren't you here yesterdee like you wus suppose to be?" Bill said, not impressed with the young man's spiel.

"I got tied up working at the home office. Couldn't get away 'til 'smorning," the man replied not taking his eyes off the young girl.

"Phooey, you ain't worked a day in your life, Tom Ranahan, and both a' us know it," Bill said between gulps of stew.

Cliff agreed this was the best antelope he had ever eaten. Antelope reminded him of the taste of goat and he never favored goat. However, he had to admit this girl set a good bowl a' stewed antelope.

She was perhaps 5'4" and a little on the heavy side. Not enough to be called fat, but still no one would say she was slim. Her breasts were full and bounced around when she moved, and she seemed to enjoy the looks the men would give them when she felt them dancing. Cliff noticed she made them bounce as often as she could without being too obvious about it. She was not a beauty, but still not ugly and was pleasant to look at when he took the time from the conversation to do so. Besides, it was plain she was trying to attract Happy Tom more than him.

Suddenly, Jack awoke and cried out in pain.

Happy Tom jumped as if a snake had just run up his pants-leg. Turning around as he stood and going for his cross-draw, he shouted, "What the hell?"

"Easy boy," Bill said as June ran into the backroom to see about her patient. It was only then Bill Crane took the time to tell the relief driver what had happened to the stage earlier that day.

"Damn, Sam," Tom replied. "That could be me all shot up in there."

"Shoulda' been you," Crane said. "Jack's a more stable man than you."

"The hell you say, Bill Crane, you old crank," Tom spat back, losing the smile he usually expressed, "You been a crank ever since

I knowed you." Sitting back down, he continued, "You been mad at me ever since the days we rode fur 'The Express'. Just couldn't stand it when I got stationed in Green River, and you wus way out here on the Sweet Water."

"Hell, you don't know of what you're a-saying," Crane replied, but Cliff could tell the boy had hit on something that cut deep.

Taking a breath, Tom looked at the stranger, and the usual smile returned to his face. "You must be something else to get three of them with a six-gun."

"Truth is, I have a Winchester repeater. I think I hit another one, too, but it was just not in the cards to get a bead on the one I really wanted."

"You know who it wus then?" Bill questioned.

"Well, not enough to get the law on him. He had his neckerchief up over his nose, but I know who owns the horse he was riding and I'd bet a month's pay it were him riding it."

"Who be that?" Happy Tom asked.

"The horse that hombre was riding belongs to a jasper that calls himself Roper," Cliff said then added, "I don't make a rule a' accusing a fellow without proof, but seeing as you gents might need to know this information, I am telling ya."

"Whoo-we' that's Chip Roper I assume," Tom said.

"The same," Cliff agreed.

"I heard that name 'afor," Bill said.

"He's top gun fur Ed Sholtz up to Monia," Tom added.

"Yeah, that's the one," Cliff agreed again, and then he told them about the other run-ins he'd had with Roper since he had come to the region. However, he purposely neglected to mention the Scogins incident.

"I do think maybe he's running a gang of his own," Bill said, thinking hard on what he had heard.

"No," Cliff disagreed shaking his head, "Roper's smart enough, but he would have never sent for Morgan Crowe. He'd a made the play himself."

"Probably been a-back-shooting, then," Tom added.

"Well, I can't say for sure, but someone tried to back-shoot me when I had to kill Bodie Johnson. It could a' been Roper," Cliff admitted, then added, "Though the word I got was it was little Phil and Bones Harvey," Cliff said nothing of Ernie Teachman.

"They're both dead now?" Tom asked trying to remember all the names he had heard while Cliff was telling his tale.

"Yeah, Pebbles killed Bones in 'The Hitching Post', and Big Bruce took out Phil Sholtz."

"Boy-o-boy," Tom said. "Ol' man Ed must a' been mad as hell when that happened."

"Yeah, I reckon he was," Cliff agreed as he leaned back in the hard chair.

While they were talking, Cliff began cleaning his weapons; all present gave admiring glances as he was working on the Winchester. Not that they hadn't seen the brass framed rifles before, several men had acquired them after the war but mostly those were the Henrys. Here was the new Model 1866, sporting Mr. King's loading gate which was quite unique. Bill even asked how Cliff liked it.

"Well, truthfully, it's a mite light on anything larger than a man. I sure wouldn't want to try a bear with it, but it works good close up on a man, and it's real fast," Cliff replied handing it to Crane for his inspection.

"I also have a Henry rifle that I use sometimes. It shoots a mite farther cause a' the longer barrel, but it's a lot harder to keep dirt out a'."

Bill Crane was rubbing his thumb over the loading gate and gently pushing it in.

Tom had now moved closer hoping he would also get the opportunity to hold the gun. "I had me a Spencer once," Tom said. "I liked it, but it, too, wus no good fur more'n hundred steps or so."

"I never liked the Spencer because you had to cock it every time," Cliff replied, and then he told them about the first time he had seen the Henry in action back in Tennessee.

Tom was nodding his head in agreement when Cliff added, "Of course, the best reason for carrying the Winchester is it fires the same round as my Colt."

"What?" Tom asked surprised.

Crane looked off as if he had no more interest in the conversation after Brown had bad-mouthed his rifle.

"Here," Cliff replied lifting his Richard's Conversion from his holster. "I sent it back to the factory and had it converted."

"No shit?" Tom exclaimed then quickly turned around to see if June had heard his vulgarity. "Pardon," he added.

Anxiously, he scooted up beside where Cliff was seated, and with big eyes, he said, "I seen a Smith & Wesson that shot a brass shell once, but it was just a little thing, a .22, I think."

"Yeah, I seen one of them, too," Bill added trying once again to enter the conversation as the cartridge revolver was quite interesting. He had never heard of such.

"This is a gun I got during the war, and then a year or so back I sent it in to Colt. They cut off the back of the cylinder where the nipples were," he said pointing to the rear of the cylinder, "and fitted a new back on it. Then they added this here gate to keep the shells in when you are riding."

"And you say it shoots the same shell as the Henry?"

"That's right. I asked for that specifically, cost me a' extra dollar."

"What it cost you, altogether?" Tom asked still showing much interest, then added a little embarrassed, "I mean if that ain't being too nosey?"

"Cost me four dollars, three with it in Henry and another to have it posted," Cliff replied, now removing the five rim-fire cartridges from the revolver; he handed it to Tom.

The boy rubbed his palm lightly over the cylinder much like a man would do when he was trying to impress a woman by touching her arm. Then he opened the loading gate and closed it. "Carries five, huh?"

"Well, it will hold six, but I got in the habit a' keeping the hammer down on a bare nipple and still carry it that way just in case I was to drop it or something," Cliff replied.

"Remington's air' better," Bill Crane interjected, "they got notches in the cylinder fur the hammer to rest in so you can carry them with all six capped."

"You're right," Cliff agreed, "I shor' wish Colt had done that."

"I wonder, would they convert my Navy?" Tom said still with eyes big as a longhorn dogie that had been separated from its mom.

"I reckon they could, but I don't know if they could make it shoot the .44 or not," Cliff replied taking his Winchester from the outstretched arm of Bill Crane who was now more interested in the Colt.

"Yeah, I see what ya mean," Tom replied, a little disappointed. "Must be something carrying just one round fur both."

"Yes, I sure like it," Cliff agreed realizing he had better load his carbine just in case he needed a firearm quickly because he could tell he was not going to get his revolver back for some time.

"I'd admire to take a gander at it," Bill said reaching for the Colt. Tom reluctantly gave up the pistol to his friend. June came closer and saw what they were doing and said loudly for all to hear, "Grown men, acting like boys in a peppermint candy store over some fool gun." The tone in her voice showed she was trying to act tough, but she made a poor attempt at it, and Cliff easily realized she was simply jealous that they were paying attention to the guns, rather than giving her their admiration. He smiled at the young girl who now leaned over Tom as if she was trying to see what he was doing. Her heavy breast mashed against his shoulder. Tom quickly lost much of his interest in the Colt.

"Son-of-a-bitch!" Ed Sholtz exclaimed when Chip told him of what had happened in the attempted holdup. "You sure all three of them are goners?"

"Yeah," Chip replied. "I saw them all go down. Squatty Devil was shot in the chest right through the roof of the coach, and he blew Mad Dog's head nearly off."

"Yuel?" Sholtz inquired as he spit a large piece of tobacco that he had bitten from the cigar he now held in his hand.

"I saw Yuel hit, and Piggett said he took another one that kil't him. Piggett wus hit too, but he'll be alright if the infection don't get in him," Chip explained.

"We don't want Yuel to be captured again like what happened to Concho."

"Concho won't talk before we get him out."

"I know Concho won't talk. I'm not so sure about Yuel," Sholtz said turning quickly, as if he intended to hit something only there was nothing there for him to hit.

"Yuel's gone up the flume, no question about it," Chip repeated.

"He'd better be," Sholtz said and then stomped the heel of his right boot on the heavy planked floor. Turning around he looked at Chip and added, "I'm beginning to think this here Copperhead is a better man than you, Roper." Sholtz stared hard into the blue eyes of the smaller man adding this to his statement. "Maybe I ought a' hire him to kill you 'stead a' the other way around."

Chip took a deep breath and let it most of the way out. He started to say he would not let it happen again, then changed his mind and thought it best to just say he was sorry, and then he decided not to say anything at all. Reaching into his black leather vest, he removed his makins' and started to roll a smoke.

Two days later, he was again in Sholtz' office, this time having been summoned.

"Yeah, Boss?" he inquired.

Sholtz was wearing the tall lace-up boots that he only wore when he was going down into the mine, which he seldom did anymore.

"Captain tells me, he thinks they should have the shaft finished in two or three days. When they do, we will seal off the Scogins' hole altogether from the outside. I reckon it's good the old codger took sick; I don't trust his loyalties none too much." Turning and walking over to the glass window he looked out at the small bunches of snow that were still piled up on the stack of timber they had used to cover the original entrance to Rob Scogins' claim. "I plan to move Emit Barney's crew in there and begin bringing that color out and stacking it in tunnel # 3 until we get the battery for the stamp mill back. I got nigh on a hundred pounds a' pure here, we cleaned before the battery busted. Plan to send some of it down to the bank in Granger by stage next week." The man paused and took a deep breath before continuing, "We will send it a little at a time, maybe a thousand dollars or so each week, and then as soon as we get the stamp mill up and running again I will send twenty-five thousand at one time." Turning now, he looked straight at Roper, "You sure that damn Copperhead didn't recognize you the last time you failed a stage robbery, ain't you?"

"How could he, we all had masks on?" Chip replied defensively.

"Well, he sure as hell got to see three a' your faces, didn't he?"

"Yeah, I guess he saw them what we left behind, but he never saw me or Piggett."

"Still he knows Yuel and you have been seen together."

"So, Yuel's been seen with a lot a' fellows around here. Besides, Yuel has been out a' sight since the Boeing thing."

"Maybe," Sholtz replied not sure he agreed. "Anyhow, I don't want you to leave Monia again until I tell you. When we send the twenty-five thousand, you and the boys will hit it again, only this time, you'll take the stage station first and be waiting there for them."

"You aim to steal your own money?"

"That's right. I got me an insurance policy from 'The Saints Container Corporation,' big company down to Ogden and we'll clean up on both. Besides, it won't look bad if I get robbed a time or two."

"I didn't know you was a Mormon," Chip said.

"Hell, Roper, you ought a' know I ain't no damn Mormon."

"I didn't think Mormons would work with a body that wasn't one a' them," Chip said questioning the statement.

"I didn't say I told them I wasn't no Mormon," Sholtz replied. "Besides were a man to steal from his own church, it would be a sin." Sholtz looked at him as if the boy was crazy.

"You want us to hit them at Pacific Springs Station again?"

"Yeah, they change drivers there, don't they?"

"Yeah, I think so."

"Well, find out fur sure. I want them hit where you can get the relief driver too. That way, it will be longer before anybody finds out what's happened. I don't want nobody chasing you while you're loaded down with all that color. Some fool might drop his load to get away."

"All right," Chip answered.

"You questioning my thinking?" Sholtz shot back at his drawn-out reply.

"No, it's just we'll have to kill them all, and there's a woman at Pacific Springs."

"You a-feared a' shooting a woman?"

"Not a' shooting her, but town folks won't take to that at all."

"You're right," Ed Sholtz agreed. He knew people would let most things go without getting too riled up, if they weren't somehow involved, but when a body harms a woman, even a whoring woman, men just get their feathers up.

He went over to the old black trunk that had many rolls of paper maps stacked on it and pushing them aside, lifted the lid.

Chip could see him rummaging around until he stood with a bow and three arrows. Turning, he handed them to Roper. "Philip had saved this, he traded fur it to a Sioux squaw when we crossed the Platte back at Fort Caspar on our way here," Sholtz said in a tender voice and then added, "He was just a pup then."

**Fort Caspar**
**Near Platte River Crossing**

# Chapter Eleven
# The Anniversary

On the fifth of May, 1870, U.S. Assessor E. P. Snow was waiting at the Green River City Stage Station when they pulled in. He was a slight man in his late forties, and his dress was quite proper, and had it not been for his command of the local jargon, one would have taken him for an immigrant newly arrived, from the states.

"Mr. Snow!" Tom called out when he wrapped the long leather leads around the brake handle. "I ain't seen you since last October."

"Mr. Ranahan, I see they haven't run you off yet," the older man replied.

"Noo. I got me a home up here on this old seat," Tom said smiling as he climbed down. Shaking Snow's hand, he added, "Leastwise until they run the railroad up to the Sweetwater."

"I'd say then you will be employed for quite a spell," Snow shot back.

"No, I don't think so. I heard from a good source they's gon'a start it anytime."

"I'm a good source myself, Tom, and I say it'll never happen. The Sweetwater Region's about played out. Take my word for it."

"You got'a be wrong Mr. Snow. 'The Monia' is really cranking out some heavy metal now that they's got the stamp mill rolling again."

"Yes, well that is precisely why I'll be riding back with you," Snow said as he handed his heavy carpetbag to Tom.

Cliff caught the name and was sure this was the man Ash and he had been waiting on for so long. He started to say something to him, but just then a man with a horse pistol strapped to his side approached and stepped inside the coach ahead of Snow.

Cliff didn't like the looks of this man. There was nothing directly he could place his suspicions on; rather it was his mannerism that had rubbed him wrong. Soon, another man dressed in a plain cotton shirt and striped trousers approached and handed Tom his ticket. A woman about Cliff's age walked up also and handed Cliff a small leather bag to place on top of the coach, not unlike one a doctor might have, only slightly fuller in the body. The man in the striped pants then stepped back while Snow assisted the lady in mounting the stage. The two men then followed her. She was dressed in a prairie dress with a white bonnet tied tightly around her neck. She carried a small black book that Cliff took to be a Bible.

As they were getting the last of the six-up hitched, a fifth man approached the coach also. He was a man some ten years older than Cliff with a long fuzzy beard. He was dressed as a cowhand, a dirty outfitted cowhand. He too carried a large revolver on his hip and a Remington revolving carbine in his right hand. His other hand held the horn of a saddle that was swung over his left shoulder.

"I got me a ticket to go to Monia," he said and tossed the saddle and blanket onto the top of the coach.

"Seats are full," Tom said back, "you'll have to sit on the floor."

"I'll ride on top," replied the man, and without waiting for a reply he climbed up and began straightening up the saddle where he could use it as a makeshift backrest.

Cliff didn't like the idea of a stranger riding behind him, but had little choice at this point. Suddenly he was glad he had not spoken to Mr. Snow.

Pulling out of Green River City a little after ten in the morning, Cliff figured they should be getting to the Pacific Springs Station just about dark. It was there they would have to stay the night and take an early morning departure on to South Pass City. He was glad for the location also. The man behind him, and the other inside which he didn't cater to, were on his mind as they approached the station at McCullenn Bluff, and it was here he aimed to correct the situation.

Everyone got out and stretched their legs. The lady hurried to the little house out back. The only other building was little more than a log hut with a mud roof.

Cliff called to the man in the striped pants. "Mr. can you pitch-in a hand with the changing of the team?"

The others looked questioningly at him, including Happy Tom and Slick Rowan, the attendant at 'The Bluff,' as this stop was often called. The man in the striped pants, too, looked surprised, but he came over and replied, "Sure, if you need me."

Cliff nodded his head and handed him one of the long leads that was just being unhitched from the tired team. Cliff turned and said to the other passengers, "Slick usually has a big pot a' coffee on, there inside," and quickly he turned back to his work before anyone, especially Slick, could question his actions. When the others were out of sight he asked, "What's your name, Mister?"

"I'm called Cinch DeMoss," the man said with a strong drawl.

"Texican," Tom said.

"Tennessean," the man shot back quickly and then smiled and stretched forth his hand, "but I've been in Texas mostly, since the war."

"I thought I recognized that accent. I spent a big part of the war in Tennessee," Cliff replied feeling he had found an ally. "I'm called Reb Brown," he said shaking the man's hand. He then told him of his uneasy feelings.

"I'll help if I can," Cinch offered. "What do you want me to do?"

"Do you have a gun?"

"Yeah, in my bag," DeMoss said.

"Well get it, and while you're up there, stay there. I'll tell 'Black Beard' to ride inside."

"Alright," Cinch agreed as he climbed up to the top of the coach.

Soon the men returned from inside the shack, and Cliff said quickly to Cinch, "Lay back and make out like you are asleep."

When the passengers had walked almost to the coach, Cliff saw that right behind his man, was the woman. He spoke out before Black Beard could say anything. "You will have to ride inside."

"What?" the man asked sharply. "I don't like riding inside."

"Well, that's too bad, he said he didn't like riding inside either, and he's already asleep, so he rides up here."

"Well, we'll just wake him up," the bearded one said and reached up for the hand-hold but as he did, Tom dropped the long bullwhip gently on his hand. When the man shot a look at him Tom said, "He paid the same money as you. You had your choice the first half of the ride, now he gets his choice."

Black Beard dropped his hand and stared first at Tom and then Cliff.

"You can ride back up here tomorrow, if you still of a mind to," Tom assured him.

He turned and grumbled something that neither understood before he entered the coach ahead of the others. Behind him the other unknown man pushed ahead and got in, but Snow allowed the lady to enter ahead of him.

As soon as they were rolling again, Cliff nudged Cinch's boot sole with the butt-plate of his Winchester and the man raised up.

"I just didn't feel right with that jasper behind me," Cliff said.

"Yeah, I got the same feeling," Tom agreed.

"I'm glad to be up here," Cinch said. "That blowhard in the brown hat smelled to high heaven. I believe he had been rolling in tar water.

"Yeah, Ol' Black Beard, too," Cliff said back, then asked, "Say where in Tennessee you from?"

"Davidson County."

"That's Nashville, ain't it?" Cliff asked.

"Yep, my pappy had a little farm on Otter Creek."

"I remember that little creek well, out west past Granny White's old tavern."

"You got it," Cinch said back smiling. A warm feeling suddenly swept over him, realizing he had found someone that knew of his home, so far away.

"You did your fighting in Davidson County?"

"Some," Cliff answered. Then he went on to tell, "I was with Forrest from Lebanon all the way to Alabama and back to Nashville. That's where I wus captured, at Otter Creek." Then Cliff asked, "You?"

"The Otter Grays, Captain Winston's Battery. I enlisted there with my brothers and cousins, and we kept a-moving for four years."

"I remember those moves," Cliff said deeply, not fond of the memories.

"Yeah," Cinch agreed then turned and shouted to Tom. "How 'bout you driver?"

"Me?" Tom replied. "Shucks, I wuz right here riding fur the Pony Express during the war."

"No shit?" Cinch quickly replied. "I remember that outfit. There was something in "The Nashville Democrat" about it, 'afore the war."

"Yeah, several o' the station attendants around the Territory today come here as 'Express Riders'," Tom added.

"I knew Bill Crane had been an 'Express Rider,' but I didn't know of others," Cliff admitted.

"Sure," Tom said, "why, there's John Burnett who runs the Wells & Fargo Station over to Salt Lake. Some call him Smiley, but I never seen him smile in my life, and there is Bill Cody who works fur the U.P. and Billy Jones who drives between Red Buttes and Split Rock, and several others still around these parts."

"Say, Cinch," Cliff said, turning so he could look right into the young man's face. "I feel the need to tell you something," he paused and gathered his thoughts before he continued, "we've been having a mite a' trouble around these parts lately, and I got the feeling these two jaspers riding back there might be some more."

"What kind a' trouble?" Cinch asked.

"Owl Hoot trouble," Tom added.

"What's the call?"

"Well," Cliff started, "this is gold country, and that in itself is apple pie for jaspers, but there's more, we have had bank robberies and stage holdups and men shot over their claims and imported gun hawks and on and on."

"Why you telling me this?" Cinch asked as he swung around so he was lying on his stomach and looking forward at Cliff.

"'Cause, I think you are a man o' tall cotton, and I ain't sure, but I might a' got you into something by, ah, asking you to ride up here."

"That so?" Cinch replied and then reached under his sloppy homespun shirt and from the small of his back retrieved a Starr 44 double action. "I might be a-needing this then."

"I'm glad you feel that way, and I might be barking up the wrong tree, but I got me this feeling."

"I left a fair job in Texas, on account a' some damn carpetbagger who the Federal Judge appointed Land Overseer of Randal County, and we didn't see eye-to-eye on a certain subject. I reckon I can jump into a little more hitting a lick as long as it's for the right side."

"We are the right side, but that don't stop lead balls," Cliff replied.

"I know that to be true, I got me a fair size scar in my left thigh by stopping one of them lead balls at Murfreesboro."

"Alright, just so you know what you might be jumping into. By the way, I was at Murfreesboro myself."

Two hours later as they approached the creek, Cliff told Tom to stop in the little stream and let the team get a drink. It was still a long mile to the Stage Station, and when one of the passengers called out questioning what the stop was about, Tom just yelled back, "This here bunch of horses need a drink or you will be walking the last couple a' miles." Then he blew his horn.

The man inside grumbled back something, but it was lost in the wind.

When the reply came, Tom shook his head slightly and said, "Bill must be taken sick, he usually gives a lot better blow than that."

Cliff nodded his head, feeling his hunch was right, and he slipped out of the boot and stepping on the tongue nodded for Tom to go on. When they pulled up the east bank he dropped down and laid flat while the Concord passed over him. Then quickly jumping up he ran after them until he was able to grab hold and pull himself up and onto the leather covered trunk. There he rode as the stage made its way along the road towards the Pacific Springs Station.

The road made a straight run towards the fenced compound, but as it neared the creek bed, where Bill had made a corduroy road of lodge-pole on either side of the little bridge that crossed the stream, it turned sharply and then entered through an open gate into the wide yard. This had been fenced to keep any horses contained during the changing of the team. It was at this sharp turn Cliff dropped from the rear boot. He quickly concealed himself behind a large greasewood and waited.

Looking over the station he knew his feelings had been right, for no one came out to meet the stage. The girl always came out and greeted the passengers and helped with any bags they might need for the over night stay. Bill Crane should be out to help Tom with the unhitching and caring of the team.

There was a small trail of smoke coming from the chimney of the main building that was quickly lost in the evening breeze. He could see no other movement as the Concord came to a stop. Tom, too, was obviously suspicious, and he capped the sixth nipple on his Navy before climbing down.

"Whar's the shotgun?" the man in the dark brown hat asked as soon as he was out of the coach and saw only two men still there.

"He went around back to the outhouse," Tom said back trying not to seem concerned, however, he saw Mr. Brown Hat nod his head at the black-bearded man who then turned and started walking around the log building.

Immediately after the woman and Mr. Snow disappeared inside, the man with the brown hat pulled his horse pistol and pointed it at Tom.

"You two drop your shootin' irons whar' you stand."

Cinch immediately raised his hands and said, "I ain't got no firearms."

Tom slowly moved square to the outlaw and said, "Look Mister, I don't know what your play is here, but this stage line carries the U. S. Mail, and it's a Federal Offense to rob____."

He was unable to finish as the man interrupted, "I know you ain't carrying no mail on this run, so do as I told you and drop your hardware, or I'll drop you."

Carefully, Tom lifted his Colt, and bending slowly, he gently dropped it onto the hard dirt yard from about a foot off the ground, then he quickly stood.

"You in love with that thing or something?" the man said and then motioned with the barrel of his pistol for them to move towards the building.

Finding the outhouse empty, the accomplice returned to the front of the building just as his friend was pushing Tom through the door.

"He weren't there."

"He's got to be here somewhere. I was watching, and he didn't get off no whar' 'afore we got here. Look around, he might have seen me pull down on these two," the man instructed and then followed his prisoners inside.

By then, Cliff had worked his way into the barn through its backdoor.

The view from the front of the barn gave a good command of both the house and the gate, and it was there he hid his Winchester.

Watching as Black Beard carefully moved from building to building, he was obviously looking for someone or something, and Cliff had no doubt as to what he was looking for and moved deeper inside the dark building. There in the middle of the lane between the stalls, he rolled a large barrel, and standing on it, he reached up and pulled a few strands of straw and dropped them on and about the barrel. Then he quickly slipped back to the right of the front door where he hid behind a toolbox on which Bill Crane had piled a broken harness to be repaired at some later date. It was good cover there in the increasing darkness.

After several minutes someone called out, "Hey, Palmer. You need help?"

"Naugh, the barn is the last place he could be hiding. I'll flush him," the man with the black beard replied.

Hearing this, Cliff cocked his Colt and waited.

The door was partly open, and the sun cast a long golden ray into the barn that seemed to set on the bait barrel. The man's shadow was clearly seen as he cautiously took a quick peek inside, before jerking his head back. From where he was hid, Cliff could not see the hunter directly, but his shadow painted a perfect picture on the dirt floor. Slowly it began to grow larger, and then in a flash it moved in and disappeared to the opposite side of the door from where Cliff was concealed.

Palmer looked carefully throughout the barn. His eyes rested on the harness topped toolbox for but a second before they continued on their journey around the interior of the building. They moved slowly studying every foot of space, but finally the draw of the barrel was just too interesting and there they stopped.

'What is that barrel doing there?' Palmer wondered before he noticed the straw laying about, then slowly lifting his eyes to the loft and smiling he thought, 'Here is the answer.' Just above the barrel was the rail of the upper floor where it crossed the rear of the barn. 'It would be easy for a man to stand on the barrel and reach the rail, then pull himself up.' Now his eyes moved to the upper level.

The barn was not tall enough to have a full second story, but there was about four feet between the wood floor and the roof, enough for the stacking of some hay between the rafters. It was there he was now certain his quarry hid, and Palmer moved slowly out to where he could better see the top loft.

He was standing in good light about halfway between the door and the barrel when Cliff spoke, "Drop it or I'll drill ya where ya stand."

A cold chill ran up Palmer's back, and he tried to turn his head to see where his adversary was but he was not given the chance.

"I said 'fork it over. Do it now or you'll die in the middle of this miserable barn."

*'There are just too many places in this ol' dark barn to get to, and once out of the light I will have the same chance as the other fellow,'* Palmer thought. *'Even more, for the boys will come a-running when they hear the shooting.'* Suddenly Palmer moved to his left.

Cliff had been expecting this very move, and since the jasper had tried to spot him by looking to his left, Cliff figured he would move that direction and had already eased the muzzle of his revolver so it would send its bullet two feet to the man's left.

There is time to think, when you are expecting something very important to happen in your life, if you remain calm. It is only a split second difference in time from a jerked trigger and one squeezed quickly. The difference is in the mind of the man, a man who spent four years of hard fighting, mostly from horseback, who had learned to take that split second or he would have been where many thousand other gray backs were now, fertilizing the yellow clay of Tennessee. Cliff took the time, and 216 grains of hot lead entered Palmer's left side passing through his lung and stopping in the big muscle just ahead, a second later, when its container hit the floor, it stopped beating.

"You get him, Palmer?" a voice from the house asked.

Cliff raised his hand and held it in front of his mouth where it would act as somewhat of a muffler and yelled back, "Yeah!" Then slowly moved forward and checked the body that lay just into the darkness. He found, other than a big purple spot on the left side, there was no other blood, but the man was as limp as a sleeping tomcat in a warm bed. Cliff dragged him over to the side of the barn and threw a little hay over the body. He then slipped out the front door just as the big orange ball sank behind the tall hills a few miles to the west. The moon had been visible in the eastern sky for an hour before sundown, and it began casting some light on the yard soon after the sun had given up its command of the cause.

Inside the Pacific Springs Station, Tom had experienced a rush of sickening gall come charging into his stomach as soon as he focused on the scene. Bill Crane stood in the corner not far from June Ann. Behind her was a skinny man dressed in dirty array of a vaquero. His large sombrero was on his back hanging from his neck by a long piece of rawhide. His dark greasy hair was unkempt, and his long black mustache covered most of what was left of his front teeth. He held the thin blade of a stiletto under June's throat with the point pressing her skin into a dimple. There was a tiny run of blood that strolled down from this depression and disappeared into the collar of her blouse. True fear was clear in Crane's face, but what Tom saw in the girl's eyes was a combination of terror mingled with anger. She had obviously defied the Mexican in some manner, and the prick in her neck was the reward for her action. A sickening smile crossed the lips of the man with the knife, and he spoke softly to the girl. "Per'ap you weesh to warn 'em now, Señorita, eeh?"

Turning slightly, Tom saw the woman and the man who had been on the stage with him. The woman was sitting at a long, crudely built wooden table beside Snow, and the man with the dirty brown hat stood behind her. "The others are not here yet?" he asked another man Tom had not seen before.

"Chip, Harrison, and a couple a' others I don't know have gone up the trail to keep a look out for travelers," the man replied before adding, "He said the stage from South Pass City would not be here until around 9:00 o'clock or so. It got a late start because of a last minute pick-up at 'The Monia Mine'."

"Alright, what about them?"

"Chip said to wait until he got back," the same man replied.

Cinch noticed he walked with a limp when he moved over to the window and looked out, "I don't much like the idea. Quicker this kind a' stuff is attended to the better."

The man in the brown hat moved closer to him and then spoke softy. Cinch could only hear a couple words, "Woman and bodies," but it was plain what he was asking.

The man with the limp just raised his shoulders and then turned back to the window.

After several minutes he called out, "Hey, Palmer, you need help?"

There was a reply from outside, but Cinch couldn't understand it.

Tom and he were ordered to sit at the table across from the other passengers. There they waited each sizing up the situation and neither liking the results of their surmises.

It had been ten minutes after the man had called out through the window when they heard the shot.

Again, the man at the window yelled, "You get him, Palmer?" This time Tom heard a reply, and it sounded like a "Yeah." Suddenly that sickening feeling rushed into his gut again, and he swallowed, trying to keep a lid on it. Turning his head, he saw the same concern in Cinch's eyes.

Another several minutes passed, and finally the man with the limp spoke, "What's keeping Palmer?"

"I don't know, maybe he's hiding 'im," the man said rolling his shoulders as if he needed to work the long stage ride out of his body. Then he asked, "You want I should go see?"

"Yeah, I reckon so. We need to all be inside when that southbound gets here."

The man took a drink of water from the barrel before retrieving his dirty brown hat from where he had dropped it on the table. "Alright, I'll get him in," he said placing the hat on his head, he left by the front door and turned towards the barn.

He had walked only a few paces when he stopped suddenly; turning, he looked back and began searching the ground between the stage and the cabin, but he saw nothing. Slowly, he continued searching with his eyes, no longer looking for the gun, rather for who had removed the Navy Colt the teamster had so carefully laid on the ground. When he was fully turned and looking for any movement near the coach, he heard it. There are some sounds a man has to hear only once in his life, and forever after he will never forget them. One such sound is that made by a big diamondback, another is the burning of a fuse, and then there's the one Cody Orel had just heard, the clicking emitted from a Colt revolver when the hammer notches drop one after another on the trigger sear. Three distinctive clicks and you know it is fully cocked.

"Who are you?"

"I'm the man who is gon'a introduce you to Beelzebub[15], if you move."

Orel was not a bright man, but neither was he a fool. The sound of that Colt was too damn close for anyone worth his salt to mess with, and he made this Shotgun out to be top rail. "It's your call, Mister," he said as loud as he thought he could get away with.

"You speak that loud again and your friends inside will hear all right, but what they will hear is the sound of this here revolver having its say," Cliff said back, then added, "You compendia?"

---

[15] Beelzebub: Satan's Chief Angel, the Prince of the Devil, the opposite of Gabriel.

He could see in the moonlight Orel nod his head.

"Alright, then fork over that horse pistol where you stand, and then move around the house."

The man did as he was told, still not exactly sure where his enemy was.

Picking up the old Dragoon, Cliff closed the distance between him and the man and pushed him forward.

Once around back of the house he used the butt of the man's gun to buffalo him just behind his right ear. This brought forth a cracking sound a split second before he groaned, and then he simply collapsed.

'Must 'ave hit him too hard,' Cliff thought.

Moving on past the body he looked in the window of June's bedroom. From there he could see little of the main room, except Tom and Cinch sitting at the table and the rear of a woman's shoulder, but no more. He had seen enough to confirm they were alive and in a bad situation. Remembering the woman had a small bag that he had placed on top of the stage, he slipped back around to see if it was still there. He was pleased when he spotted it, and passing in front of the team, he went around to the far side of the coach before he climbed up and grabbed the handbag. Dropping to the ground, he raced back to the rear of the cabin before he looked in it. Rummaging around in the dark insides of the little bag he felt several items that he had no idea of their use, but finally he found what he was looking for. Pulling it free, he sat the bag on the ground and moved quickly back to the rear window.

His first look was just a quick peek, to make sure everything was as before. Satisfied, he took the hand mirror and carefully twisted it around until he saw the small spot move. He had not been sure if there was enough light given off by the coal oil lantern that hung on a roof pole above the end of the table where his friends sat. He slowly twisted the mirror just enough to allow its dull reflection to cross Tom's eyes only once, and then he turned it down quickly. It had been enough. Tom moved his right elbow slightly and touched Cinch's ribs.

Cinch looked at him, but Tom did not look back, he was staring straight at the dim face in the back window. Cinch let his eyes follow Tom's stare until he too saw Cliff. So as not to alert anyone who might also have seen Tom's elbow move, he immediately moved his head completely to his right and stared straight at the man who was by the south window. Piggett turned from the window, and looking around the room he questioned, "What the hell's keeping them two?"

"Desconocido," Concho replied lifting his shoulders. "You want I should go see, or 'me'bee I should take dis' puta in the backroom and see she no like the Mexican blood?"

Now that he had removed the knife from her neck he lowered his head and licked the blood from her neck with his long pointed tongue causing June to twist about, but his left arm still held her and at that time, he raised it a little and squeezed her breast with his hand. "Ah, granda teta. Muy' firma. Make bueno bolsa para tobacco, no?"

"Later, maybe," Piggett said, "Right now I am only interested in what's keeping Palmer and Orel."

"Dey come back."

"Hey Concho, I thought they hung you," Tom said smiling.

"Dey try. Concho no like calaboose of stone," he said, and dropping his arm from around June he stepped aside and raised his shoulders and then added, "Concho despedirse."

"Concho disappeared? Right. Concho left with the help of several others," Piggett corrected. He had never cared much for the Mexican, who he considered a little too blood thirsty for his liking. Not that Piggett would hesitate to kill in a heartbeat, but he preferred a clean gunshot to the knife. A blade usually took too long to kill and left everything so bloody and messy. Piggett had the inner feeling: to kill with a knife was an unclean sin. He also detested the pleasure Concho seemed to get from torturing his victims. He had little doubt, but the man truly had plans of making tobacco pouches from the dried breasts June DeWolf seemed so proud of. He just wondered if Concho would cut them from her body before or after she was dead.

Raising his head and turning his good ear towards the sound, Piggett said, "Riders coming," just before he rushed over and opened the door, peering out into the night towards the distant sound of several horses' hooves pounding on hard ground. "Must be them," he said. "Many horses coming."

"Just step on out and away from the door," Piggett heard the voice whisper from the dark corner of the house. Followed by, "I got a 44 aimed at your middle, and I wouldn't mind ventilating you one bit."

Carl Piggett knew several of his compadres would soon be on the scene. *'All I have to do is stall this man, but how in the hell can I go about it?'*

Cliff knew the importance of time as well, and when the man didn't move, he again said, "If I'm going to have to take on that bunch a' riders coming yonder, I had rather do it without worrying about you, so if you don't move and soon, they are gon'a be alerted by your death scream."

Piggett looked towards the voice and then tried to get a glance over his shoulder hoping Concho was becoming suspicious, but what he saw was the Mexican again looking down at June's breasts as he squeezed one.

He had few choices, and he took the one he thought best, by diving ahead drawing his revolver as he did. His shot went straight and true, but was two feet over Cliff's head. Cliff took the time to aim, and Piggett never got his revolver cocked a second time.

When he saw Piggett dive forward, Concho dropped his hand from the girl and reached for his own pistol, but June stomped the high heel of her shoe on the top of his foot, and pain shot through him like a white lighting bolt. "CHOcho, maleton, madama puta," Concho screamed in obvious pain and quickly dropped the revolver back to its holster. June, no longer held by him, backed away until she felt the hard wooden logs pressing against her back. Concho now turned towards her and jerked the knife once again from his right boot and moved slowly for June with a wildness in his eyes.

However, the fury left him instantly when the .44 ball from Cinch's Starr struck him square in the back, severing his spine.

There was a huge cloud of blue-gray, smelly smoke filling the air around the table, and when it began to clear, they saw Concho on the dirt floor staring at the ceiling.

The woman, who had sat so quietly until now, suddenly had a four barrel derringer in her hands and pointing it at Cinch as she cocked it. Bill Crane reached for the Colt in Concho's holster, but before he could get to it, Snow jerked the woman's wrist upward, and her shot buried itself in the lodge-pole overhead.

Tom was quickly over the table and twisted the small Sharps from her hand before she could cock it again.

"She____she had it in her diary!" Snow exclaimed.

They all looked at the opened book lying on the table. The pages had been carefully cut just enough to allow the little gun a spot of concealment.

"Why did you try to shoot Cinch?" Tom yelled to the woman, but she dropped her head and said nothing.

"Get her over there in the back and get ready. They no doubt heard the shooting," then turning to June he added, "That was great work. You'll have to tell me how you did it later."

Stepping to the doorway Cliff looked quickly inside, and seeing Cinch nearby he said, "Come on and help me, we need to get this body out of sight," just before he left, he pitched Tom his Navy. The boy grabbed it and immediately blew the dust from around its cylinder and then checked to make sure all the priming caps were still in place.

They had just pulled Piggett's body to the barn when four riders came through the gate and tied their horses to the top rail of the fence, but the coach was between them and the barn, and Cliff couldn't see them clearly until they came around the stage.

Chip looked at the Concord and then said to Bridwell. "Put a couple of arrows in that thing, and make sure the team doesn't get too nervous."

"Hell, them nags are all tuckered out," Bridwell replied as he got the old bow from behind Chip's saddle.

Cliff retrieved his Winchester from where he had left it, and squatting in the darkness took aim high in the moon lit sky until he got a good sight alignment, and then carefully he lowered the rifle at the men approaching the house.

He and Cinch could hear them talking, but could not make out what they were saying.

Suddenly one held up his hand and called out, "Piggett, Orel," he then paused and waited for an answer before he added, "Darla, you in there?"

At that moment a shrill voice screamed from inside, "Chip, run!"

"That's Darla!" Chip yelled and reached for his revolver.

Cliff immediately recognized the New England accent and drew his keen bead on him, but just as he squeezed the trigger, one of the others stepped between him and Roper; it was a fatal move for the short horn.

Instantly upon hearing the report, Chip dropped low and close to the station house looking for its source. Seeing the gunsmoke as another 44 Henry dropped a second man, he shouted, "They're in the barn!" and began firing towards the big log structure, but they were just too far apart for anyone to be hitting anything with pistols. It didn't take Chip long to realize their predicament. "Get inside, quick!" he shouted to Bridwell.

The tall lanky man had shot one arrow into the leather covering of the stage's boot and was nocking a second when the shooting began. Immediately he dropped the primitive weapons and followed Chip.

They both pushed on the door of the Stage Station, but found it barred.

"Darla, open the door!" Chip called out, but got no response. "Concho, Piggett, it's me Chip. This hombre has us pinned down."

Suddenly the door opened, and Bob Bridwell was the first inside only to meet a blast from Bill Crane's 54 Spencer full in the chest. The weight of the heavy slug knocked him backwards out the door into Chip, who lost his balance and almost fell.

As soon as the smoke had cleared inside enough for them to see a figure, Tom fired his pistol at the man he saw standing there.

Chip yelled out in pain when the .36 caliber ball struck him high in the chest breaking his left collarbone. He dropped his revolver and staggered back and out of view of the door.

Tom started out, but Bill cautioned him. "Careful Tom, we don't know how many of them jaspers are still out there."

Tom stopped and peered out into the night, the moon was now higher lighting the yard fairly well, but he could see no one, save the dead man lying just outside.

Slowly he moved to the open door, and then when he heard the sound of hoof beats, he went on out with his Colt cocked and ready, but all he saw of the outlaws was a single rider, laying low in the saddle, on a gray horse as it jumped the fence behind the cabin. Tom fired, but knew when he'd jerked the trigger his shot was off its mark.

Turning to go back to the house, he suddenly realized Cliff and Cinch were there beside him.

"Did you see who that was?" Cliff asked.

"I didn't see him good. He was sure lighting a shuck out a' here, but she called out to Chip."

"She?"

"Yeah, the woman from the stage," Cinch answered. "She wus one a' them. She damn near shot me."

"You can't never figure," Cliff said slowly shaking his head, "She looked to be the youngest wife of a Mormon preacher," he added, knocking the dust from his hat by slapping it against his leg and still staring out into the sagebrush covered prairie where his old adversary was once again escaping him.

"She might just be. That wus one of them Mormon diaries she had that little pistol hid in," Cinch offered.

"Well, let's go talk to her," Cliff suggested.

"Look here," Tom said pointing to the ground, "here's blood."

It was true, if you were to get at just the right angle, several spots of wet blood were visible in the moonlight.

"See, they lead to where the other horses were tied."

"Them's outlaw horses," Cinch said.

"Yeah, I think you hit 'im Tom," Cliff added, realizing where the blood trail led.

"That I did," Tom replied with his big smile returning.

The woman would not speak a word when they tried to question her.

"You know, this whole thing just don't make sense," Tom said. "We weren't carrying nothing worth stealing, and this wus well-planned."

"You're right," Cinch agreed. "Shucks, it took some planning to put these three on that stage down to Green River City."

"Mr. Snow, you ain't carrying something a' great value 'air ya?" Tom questioned.

"Why no, besides, no one knew I was to be on the stage. I just made up my mind an hour before I bought my ticket."

"You're both right," Cliff agreed. "It was well-planned, but it weren't us they were after."

"How ya figure that?" Tom asked. "They went to a mighty lot a' trouble to waylay us."

"Yeah, they did, and it was part of the plan all right, but what they was after, ain't got here yet," Cliff offered.

"The southbound stage will be carrying gold," Bill said.

"Yeah, I heard one a' them say something about it being late," Tom remembered.

"I saw one of them doing something strange, around the back of the coach," Cliff said, and he got up and walked out of the door. Returning, he held the bow and two arrows.

"Them 'air Sioux," Bill Crane said, looking at what Cliff had in his hand.

"Yep, they had already shot one into the stage and I'm sure planned to sink a couple in one or two of us," Cliff added.

"Make the whole thing look like a raid by the Indians," Tom injected.

"That means they could leave no witnesses," Bill added.

Suddenly, June leaped across the table and grabbed the woman by the hair and threw her backward. "You bitch! You were a part of them murdering bastards. What were you gon'a do while that stinking Mex there cut off my tits?" She screamed at the smaller woman who was now bonnet-less and lying on her back on the floor.

Darla Hickman Kimball was indeed twenty-five pounds lighter than June, but she was no city woman. On the contrary, her father was Colonel Bill Hickman known as Brigham's Destroying Angel, who had been largely responsible for many of the so-called Mormon Raids around the country. Darla had been raised well in the faith and was a true believer. She had lived most of her twenty-two years on a small farm on the American Fork River a few miles south of Salt Lake City.

She and her twelve sisters and eight brothers were obedient to the faith, as were her four mothers. Unfortunately, her father, being a Colonel in the defenses of faith, was seldom home during her teen years. Darla had been married to James Kimball when she was sixteen, and they had gone with a train of Saints to California shortly after. But two years past, her husband was hung by a party of raiders who had been sent by the local priest to cleanse the territory of polygamists.

Being James' first wife and after four years, having borne him no children, she was not taken by another man as wife. Her striking good looks had not endeared her to the other women of the community either. So Darla had decided to return to her father's farm where she was sure she would be welcome. It was on this journey home she had met and fell in love with the handsome tall blond man who was on his way to the Sweetwater Region of the newly formed Wyoming Territory.

They had enjoyed a long stopover at Cove Fort awaiting the stage from the north to arrive. Cove Fort was a transfer station where the passengers changed coaches. The stage they had been riding took on new passengers and returned south. The one they awaited came south to Cove Fort and then returned north, just as Pacific Springs was on the route in western Wyoming. However, Cove Fort was also a settlement with a good hotel, a fine restaurant, and other things of interest to young lovers.

After three days of no stage from the north, a cavalry company was sent in search of it. Their return several days later brought grim news that they had found the coach a hundred miles north. Everyone aboard had been massacred by Paiutes, who had stolen the team and left their bodies to the buzzards and the coyotes.

"A horrible sight," one of the returning soldiers had said.

It took another week before the stage was retrieved and made ready for the journey north. When they did leave, an escort of troopers went with them.

Darla was torn when she arrived home. She had great faith in God and their cause here, but she also knew she was very much in love with Chip Roper who was not LDS. For her to marry outside the church would surely mean excommunication, which she could never endure.

They parted, he continuing to The Sweetwater Region, and she stayed on the American Fork River, but they never stopped their love affair in their hearts. The stage seldom went north without a letter from her, and finally a month before, he had written he would convert to the faith so they could be married. She immediately agreed to meet him at Granger, but when she arrived, a letter was waiting there instead explaining he would be detained, but would meet her at The Pacific Springs Station.

From his numerous letters, Darla was well aware Chip made his living as a bodyguard for the wealthiest man in the Region and that he often had to use his gun performing his duties. That bothered her only in fear for his safety. Her father had, from her first memories, been required to use his guns in service of the church, and it all seemed to simply be a part of the times, so long as he did not harm any of the Saints. For these reasons, she was more than prepared for June's assault.

Darla slapped the surprised June in the face hard enough to send her backward. She then rose to her hands and knees and shouted, "It would serve all of you gentiles right."

Everyone could now see the hate in her eyes. Hate that had been bred there by endless nights of overhearing the others talk of the atrocities done to the Saints back in the United States, hate that was confirmed by the murder of her own husband on the orders of a Catholic Priest, here in the west. Hate that she could draw within herself as the need be and bring it forth with sureness, when the time was right, and at this moment she knew the time was right, to put these gentiles in their rightful places. The only thing she did not realize was Bill Crane and June Ann De Wolf were believers of the same faith.

"You come here stealing land from the Saints. Stripping Deseret[16] of her gold and bringin' on the Devil's work. I wish you all had been killed."

Bill Crane reached around the small waist of Darla Kimball and easily lifted her and shoved her back into the rear wall, then pointing his finger at her he shouted, "You twisted bitch, you stay there or I'll let June Ann have ya fur dinner."

The young woman sat down on the dirt floor and looked away from the others but kept a keen ear tuned to their conversation, seeking any information that might help in their destruction. She had heard them say her lover's name, but the name only. She longed to hear of his fate and if they were worrying of his return. She had faith that God would send him with an army of Saints to destroy these gentiles. She only had to be ready when he arrived.

Chip Roper had less faith in God's blessing on him. It was true he had fallen in love with Darla and would join her religion in order to obtain her hand in marriage, but he had little faith in anything he could not put his hands on. At this moment in Atlantic City he mostly had faith in Doc Irwin who was cleaning his wound.

"The ball passed on through so you're lucky, but it did break your collarbone, and that will put you down for a while. You bled enough so I doubt there will be any infection, but with the loss of all that blood you better stay here tonight."

"Thanks Doc, but I got 'a get to Monia."

---

[16] Deseret: The land the Mormons claimed for themselves as their own country including all of present day Utah, part of Wyoming, Colorado, New Mexico, Nevada, California, Oregon, and Idaho. About the same size as The United States at the time.

"I would be surprised you make it that far, without you passing out."

"I'll make it," Chip said as he stood on unsure legs.

"Well, if you aim on trying it, you better pay me now. Hard to collect from a man found dead on the road."

Chip struggled to get a coin from his vest pocket. Finally he flipped the gold eagle to the doctor and staggered outside. His saddle was covered with blood and very slippery, but he managed with great effort to climb aboard and start out, but in his condition he turned the wrong way and ended up in South Pass City. Realizing his mistake, he turned for the stage road and then gave his horse his head, and the faithful stallion moved steadily towards home.

Pebbles Stone and Marlene Teachman were just leaving *The Sisters'* when he rode past leaning forward over his horse.

"I do believe that is that gunman who works for Sholtz," Pebbles said as he watched Chip ride down the hill.

"Yes, his name is Chip Roper, and I think he's hurt," she answered.

"I agree with you. He is hurt," Pebbles said. "We should tell Reb about this. I'm sure he will be pleased with the news."

Chip passed out before they got to the cutoff that led to Camp Stambaugh, but Thunder knew the way home and slowly walked on until he was in front of the bunkhouse next to the mine, there he stopped and waited. Chip was lying forward over his neck when a miner, coming from the saloon, found him.

It was two hours later before they could revive him. Immediately, as instructed, Ed Sholtz was summoned.

"It's about time," he said entering the bunkhouse. Looking around he then said to the men gathered there, "You all leave. I want to talk to him alone."

Seeing the last miner exit and the door close behind him, he turned to the young man and demanded, "What the hell happened this time?"

Chip told him what had happened when they arrived.

"Was it that damn Copperhead again?"

"I don't know. They wus ready fur us. They cut down on us from the barn and the house both. They got Harrison and Logan before we even cleared leather."

"The arrows? They didn't get them did they?" Sholtz asked angrily.

"I don't know. Bridwell had them. I guess so, Bridwell is dead, too."

"Son-of-a-bitch," Sholtz screamed, slamming his fist down on a small table, almost over turning the lamp that was sitting there. "You know what that means? If they got any of our people alive or if they recognized you, they can put the law on us for staging an Indian massacre."

Chip started to tell him about Darla, but decided to keep quiet about her. Sholtz didn't like him marrying her anyway, saying it would cut into his loyalties.

# Chapter Twelve
# The Southbound

The southbound arrived an hour later empty of people except for Jack Murdock, who had just started driving again, and a messenger,[17] who went by Monroe Jones. Happy Tom explained what had happened, and they both shook their heads realizing what had almost been their fate.

"What ja carrying that wus so all-fired important?" Bill asked.

"Ten thousand or so from 'The Mary Ellen', another couple hundred pounds o' ore from 'The Buckeye' that's headed fur the mill in Granger, and a last minute pick up from 'The Monia', twenty-five thousand pure. That damn Ed Sholtz made me sign a receipt fur it, and I made 'im count and weigh it all too, that's what made us so late," Jack said then added, "That and Monroe here had to stop at John Mean's store in Hamilton fur some chawing tobackee"

"Good thing we wus, too." Monroe added just after he spit.

"I think it was you they were after," Cliff said. "The last time they tried to hit this stage, we shot 'em up pretty good, didn't we, Jack?"

The teamster knew he had done nothing to help in the last holdup, but he was grateful to Reb for including him in front of the others, and he nodded his head in agreement.

"This time they took over the station, and planned to make it look like the Sioux were to blame."

"Would have, too, had not Reb suspected something and slipped off the top back at the crossing a' the creek yonder," Tom added.

"What made ya suspicious, Reb?" Monroe asked.

---

[17] Messenger: Man who rode shotgun for a stage line.

"I just didn't like the looks of them two jaspers that got on back in Green River City, and then when Bill and June didn't come out to meet us, I knew my hunch was right."

"We're all damn lucky you had a hunch," Bill Crane added while they were changing the horses.

"Jack, I aim to ask you a favor," Cliff said.

"Sure, Reb, what can I do fur you?" Cliff noted the change in attitude Murdock displayed since the last time they were together. "I think this whole bunch needs to go on to South Pass City, it being the county seat and all. It's powerful important we make our statements to the Sheriff and see if Judge Morris will issue a warrant for Chip Roper."

"I can't leave here," Bill said.

"Well, mee'be not you, at least not tonight, but the rest of us, and we need to take these bodies with us as proof."

"I also have something to say on that," Mr. Snow injected.

"Yas, Sur?" Cliff offered.

"Mrs. Morris is no longer the judge there."

"What?"

"No, Governor Campbell has appointed a man to replace her. He will be coming from Cheyenne in a few weeks. I have the letter with me to deliver to her."

"Do you have any news for Ashley Scogins?" Cliff asked him.

Snow looked straight at him and then asked, "What business is it of yours, sir?"

"Don't get your dander up, Mr. Snow. I'm Cliff Brown. I'm the one who sent for her to come to Wyoming to see about her brother's mine."

Snow looked at him silently for a few moments and then said, "I do have some information for Miss Scogins."

"That's great. I know she will be happy to see you here at last." Cliff let it drop there, still not wanting too much of her business to be public knowledge.

An hour before sunup the stages pulled out, Jack and Monroe Jones driving the southbound on to Green River City and inside the northbound were Cinch DeMoss and E. P. Snow in one seat and across facing them sat June DeWolf and Darla Kimball. Cliff had tightly secured a thin horsehair rope around Darla's ankle and had given the other end to June with a smile. He also gave her Darla's derringer. On top, Happy Tom Ranahan drove the team while Cliff rode shotgun. Behind them tied to the top rails, were the seven corpses, Bill Harrison, Tom Piggett, Robert Bridwell, Cody Orel, Bob Palmer, Pete Logan, and the Mexican known only as Concho.

It was just after one in the afternoon when they pulled across from 'The South Pass Hotel'. The sight of a stage arriving with seven dead bodies was not to go unnoticed by anyone, and before they could get everyone unloaded from inside the coach a crowd had gathered. Soon afterward Sheriff Boyd arrived asking, "What is the meaning of this?"

"Another robbery attempt," Cliff answered walking around the coach to face him.

"I might have known. Why is it every time a dead body shows up, Reb Brown has something to do with it?"

"Wait just a minute here, Sheriff. I'll have you to know were it not for Mr. Brown here, we all would surely be dead, instead of these desperadoes."

Boyd looked at the small-framed man in the dark blue pin-striped suit and asked, "And, just who might you be, dude?"

"I, sir, happen to be E. P. Snow, District Assayer of Mines for the Territories of Dakota and Wyoming. I represent the United States Government. I also resent your attitude and can see very quickly that Governor Campbell finds a good replacement to your office."

Boyd raised his eyebrows at the man and quickly cleared his throat before replying. "Gee, Mr. Snow. I've heard a' ya, but never met choo before."

"Well, now you have, and if you will be so kind as to lead me to your office, I have a complaint to file."

Boyd nodded his head and turned to start for the jail when June spoke. "Hey Sheriff, this one's a prisoner," and with that, she handed the Sheriff her end of the rope.

"What?" Boyd exclaimed looking at the petite Darla Kimball. "I got no place to hold a woman."

"Well, you better find one, Sheriff. She tried to shoot me in the back," Cinch said.

Boyd released two men from the newly completed jail on their word they would return and serve out the remainder of their three-day sentence when called, and in one of the back cells he put Mrs. Kimball.

"I think it best if we talked somewhere where she can't hear," Cliff suggested, and with all agreeing, they walked over to Morris' Saloon.

There, Snow gave the letter to Esther, and she smiled upon reading it. "Whew, that takes a load off my shoulders," she said.

Mr. Snow spoke then, "You know, you are still judge until your replacement arrives."

"I suppose so," she agreed. "I just hope nothing happens until he does."

"Well, there are a couple of things that need immediate attention," Snow continued.

"What's that, E. P.?" she asked.

"Come sit with us while we give the Sheriff the details of what happened at The Pacific Springs Station, and then you will know, too," he said.

**Esther Morris**

Sitting at the big round table near the back of the saloon, Snow and Cliff told what had happened with additions from Cinch, Happy Tom, and June.

"I can't believe Ed Sholtz would have anything to do with robbery and murder," Boyd said.

"You never have," Cliff said disgruntled. "Perhaps, if you had done your job with an open mind some of this would never have happened."

"I never did anything, but my job," Boyd shouted back.

"Alright, Sheriff," Esther said, "don't get all het up. I too, remember you wanting to blame everything that went wrong around these parts on Mr. Brown here."

The sheriff sat back with a big huff.

"Now that we know Chip Roper is definitely mixed up in these killings, I suppose you want me to issue a warrant?" she said, looking at Snow.

"That is precisely what I want. That and a hearing to have that woman bound over as an accomplice."

"I see," she said. Leaning back she thought a moment and then answered, "I don't see I can do anything else." Turning, she called out to the barkeep, "Klu, fetch me a clean sheet of paper, a pen and some ink."

She thought a few seconds and then began to write. When finished, she handed it to Boyd. "Here, Sheriff, is the warrant for Chip Roper charged with attempted robbery. Do your duty."

"Yes, Ma'am," Boyd replied and got up and left.

"Well, if there is nothing else____?" she asked rising, but Snow spoke before she could complete her statement.

"There just may be one more thing," he said.

"Oh?"

By now, all the men were standing, and feeling out of place, June rose, too.

"Yes, but I'll let you know that tomorrow, Esther."

"I'm sure you will, E. P." Then she turned and went into the backroom.

After she was gone, Cliff turned to Snow and asked, "Where will you be staying, sir?"

"Next door at 'The Idaho House'."

"Good. Then as soon as I can find Miss Scogins, we will be around to see you."

"That will be fine, Mr. Brown," Snow replied, and then he left by the front door.

Cliff went to 'The South Pass Hotel', but did not find Ash or Bruce; finally he located Bruce in the barber's chair in The Grecian Bend Saloon.

"Where is Ash?" Cliff questioned.

"Hey, ol' buddy. That's some greeting for a close friend who you ain't seen for nigh on two days," Bruce replied.

"Snow's here," was all Cliff said back.

In a flash he was out of the chair and jerking the sheet from his neck.

"Hey!" the barber exclaimed.

"I'll be back," Bruce replied and pressed a gold coin in his open hand. The chubby man looked at it and nodded his balding head.

"Where is he?"

"Over to 'The Idaho House'," Cliff replied, then asked, "Where's Ash?"

"Gone doing woman stuff, shopping I reckon."

"Where?" Cliff asked disturbed.

"I think at Teachman's."

"If Sholtz gets wind he's here ___," Cliff said.

"How is he gon'a do that?" Bruce shot back.

"Sheriff Boyd knows, and he's on his way right now to arrest Chip Roper."

"Holy shit!" Bruce said and started taking longer strides. Cliff had to increase his speed to keep up.

Ash was indeed at Teachman's, and soon the trio was headed for 'The Idaho House'.


"Your brother filed a claim May 12, 1869 on a plot two hundred feet due south of 'The Monia Mine'. It's registered here and in Cheyenne," he said.

"There is no record of it here," Cliff offered.

"There must be. It was this office that sent the notice to Cheyenne," Snow replied.

"It's not there," Ash told him. "I had the local assayer look when I arrived."

"Then someone has removed it," Snow replied before adding, "But how? These things are written on large ledgers in a book."

"I don't know, but it's not there."

"Wait a minute," Bruce said, rising to his feet. "You say her claim is two hundred feet south of 'The Monia'?"

"Yes. Why?"

"Because that explains the shaft Sholtz started last June."

"I don't understand," Snow said, shaking his head.

Cliff started the story with how he had met Rob Scogins on the trail near Independence Rock the first of June the year before and with Bruce's help, by explaining about the sudden change in policy in the diggings at 'The Monia' beginning about the same time. Snow stood and exclaimed, "We must see Judge Morris again immediately," and quickly put on his coat.

"Esther, I need another order from you."

"What now, E. P.?"

"I want you to summon Captain Nickerson here for a hearing immediately."

"What?"

Snow ensured the urgency to her, and she called for another sheet of clean paper. "As soon as Boyd returns I'll have him serve this," she said.

"Ma'am if you will permit me, I will take it to him," Cliff suggested.

"Maybe, if you were to make him your Constable," Snow suggested.

She looked up at her old friend and then at the tall Georgian with narrowing eyes and a tight lip before she said, "Hold up your right hand and repeat after me." Esther took a deep breath, and after exhaling she added. "Maybe I should have done this a year ago. You know E.P., I've worked harder after I have been removed than before."

"You aren't removed until your replacement arrives," Snow reminded her.

"Well, I do wish he would hurry up," she said and then recited the oath to Cliff.

# Chapter Thirteen
# The Constable

Big Bruce, Pebbles, and Cinch rode towards Monia City with Cliff late that afternoon. Each had a reason of their own to see justice done in the region, and Reb knew each of his companions would back him with their life if it came to that.

They took the lower road, it being a little shorter, and where it crossed Beaver Creek they met Sheriff Boyd returning. The Sheriff was alone.

"Where is your prisoner, Sheriff?" Bruce asked.

"Couldn't find him," Boyd said then added, "Everyone there swore he left the territory a week ago for Salt Lake."

"That's a bunch of lies," Pebbles said back with a loud strong voice. "I seen him last night."

"Where?" Boyd asked showing some concern.

"He rode right past Mrs. Teachman and myself as we were coming out of 'The Sisters'.' He looked to be hurt quite badly," Pebbles told him and added. "If you don't believe me go ask Marlene."

"I will," Boyd said, "and if what you say is true, and I 'spect it is, there will be hell to pay fur lying to 'The Law'."

"Go do your job, and we will do ours," Bruce told him.

"Just what do you think your job might be?"

Cliff then moved up beside him and handed him the paper he was carrying.

June 6, 1870

Know Ye by these Presents:

This is an order to Constable Clifford Brown to bring before this bench one known in these parts as Capt. Nickerson for the purpose of answering any questions the court may have. Failure to appear will result in a warrant for arrest of said Capt. Nickerson.

Further: Any interference with my Constable in performing his duties will result in additional warrants for persons so interfering.

Esther H. Morris

Justice of The Peace

Sweetwater County

Territory of Wyoming

"This ain't right," Boyd said, "I'm the Sheriff here. Any papers to be served on people of this county will be served by me."

"You'll take too long," Bruce said. "And you never find your man, anyway."

"Yeah, you'll just come back with some cock and bull story about Nickerson being gone to San Francisco or some other place," Pebbles added.

"Remember, Boyd. It said anyone who interferes with Constable Brown, and that includes you," Cinch said adding his two cents worth.

"Sheriff, I'm sure she would have had you serve this if you had been there, but you were already gone, and when that bunch a' jaspers know we're closing in on them, they just might get rid of anyone who could talk them into a noose," Cliff said. "That's the reason she appointed me her Constable."

"Well, I'm going with you, and if I do find they lied about Roper being there, I'll bring more back than him."

Captain Nickerson was just coming out of the Monia's Office building when the riders arrived.

"There, that's Captain Nickerson," Bruce said pointing to the tall thin man of fifty.

"That's right," the man agreed. "What can I do fur you?"

Cliff leaned in his saddle and handed him the letter. He read it and nodded his head. "I'll get my coat and be right with you," he said and started for the bunkhouse then turned and added. "I'll need some transportation."

Boyd looked about and saw a big gray stallion there in front of the bunkhouse. "That gray dapple there. Ain't that Thunder?" he said.

"Why, yes, I believe it is," Captain replied. "Chip must be inside."

Boyd was off his mount like a lightning flash, and with pistol drawn he entered the bunkhouse. There was some shouting from more than one inside, but they couldn't make out just what was being said. Finally, the Sheriff came back out.

"Find him?" Pebbles asked knowing the obvious answer.

"Nope, he ain't in there, but he wus. There's blood on his bunk," he said, and walking to the gray he rubbed his palm across the saddle, "and there's blood here."

A man came out of the bunkhouse and headed for the office building at a fast pace. Shortly thereafter, Ed Sholtz came out and called out. "Boyd, what is the meaning of this? I already told you. Roper ain't here."

Sholtz looked at his men who were gathering in a semicircle around the four who were still mounted. "And what's this about you arresting Captain Nickerson?"

"We ain't arresting him," Cliff replied. "We're helping him get to see the judge. Kind a' like being his bodyguards," Cliff spat on the ground and then in more of a statement of fact than a question, he added, "You know about bodyguards, don't you Sholtz?"

"I don't understand, Sheriff," he said no longer recognizing Cliff. "If the judge wants to talk to Captain, I'll see that he gets there tomorrow."

"No," Cliff said back sternly. "He's going back with us. Right now."

"Surely, Sheriff, you haven't made these saddletramps your new deputies. Come in, and we'll talk this over like intelligent men."

"They're not my deputies, but he is the new Constable for this district, and he has the authority to take Nickerson," Boyd said, and then added, "Besides, you told me Roper ain't been here. That's his horse right there."

"Yes, and I told you the truth. He left here a week or more ago, headed to Salt Lake to get married. He did, too. I received a letter from him by stage a couple days ago. He and his bride are staying there with her family for the summer," Sholtz said. "I suppose someone must 'ave stole his horse, and it run off on 'em first chance he got, and he just came back home. Horses do that, you know."

"He must 'a went off to marry Darla Kimball?" Cliff injected.

"Why yes," Captain Nickerson replied. "Chip seems so in love with her."

"Yes. That is the woman he said he had married in his letter," Sholtz added.

"That don't hold no water. There's blood all over that saddle and more inside on his bunk. Besides, Roper never got married. I got his gal friend locked up in my jail," the Sheriff said back sternly.

It was obvious to all who cared to look, anger was building on Sholtz' face, "I said nobody's going to take Captain Nickerson nowhere, and I meant it," turning, he said, "Men?"

There was a rustle of men moving around mixed with the sounds of picks and shovels intermingled and at least one gun being cocked.

"Look here, Sholtz!" Boyd said, "I've given you the favor of doubt, several times when people made complaints about you mistreating them, but this here is interfering with the law. Now back your men off."

"In Monia, I'm the law, and nobody is taking Captain Nickerson anywhere."

Cliff looked about. There were maybe fifteen or more miners and other employees gathered there. Most of them were holding some kind of weapon. There would be no possibility they could come out without bloodshed and a lot of it would be their own. He then said very calmly, "Boys, we ain't got a chance in hell a' getting them all, so let's make sure the head of the snake is dead when we go down." He slowly pulled his Colt and aimed it right at Sholtz. "Every one of you shoot Sholtz if anything goes wrong, anything at all. Some of us might not get a hard hit on him in the scuffle, but a couple of us will for sure, and that will kill the bastard that caused all the pain to begin with."

The other mounted men also drew their revolvers and pointed them right at Sholtz, including the sheriff.

The large man suddenly became nervous. It was obvious to anyone he was going to die if anything started the fracas. There was just no winning this round, and he knew it. "Alright, men, back off! I don't know what they want with poor Ol' Captain here; we all know he ain't done nothing wrong. We'll get him out come morning."

"Since Sholtz swears Roper ain't in these parts, I guess he won't mind if Nickerson rides his horse."

The engineer, glad to see the storm clouds breaking up, quickly wiped the blood from the saddle and mounted the gray.

"Tell Roper he can pick him up at the jail in South Pass City, if you happen to see him, that is," Cliff said and pulled on his left rein.

It was nine o'clock when the group tied up in front of Morris' Saloon. They had worried some on the trail about an ambush, but none materialized.

"I'll see if she's inside," Cliff said, dismounting.

"Hell, we all need a drink," Boyd said, "we're coming with ya."

Even Nickerson seemed grateful for the whiskey.

"You know, Brown, I've had my doubts about you on several occasions, but you played it plenty cool back there."

"You know, Sheriff, I wouldn't a' given even money on you not being on Sholtz' payroll, until today," Cliff replied.

"Oh, I have taken favors from him, but he never before asked for me not to do my job," Boyd admitted. "He's a powerful rich man, the biggest man in the Region, ain't no disputing that. His say had to go a long way."

"He might not be so big after tonight," Bruce suggested.

"Augh, we didn't hurt him none," Boyd replied.

"It ain't us that's gon'a hurt him."

At that time Klu came over to the table and said, "Mr. Morris wants all of you to come into his office."

They followed the large man through the door in the rear of the big open room. There sat John and Esther Morris along with E. P. Snow. "Come in men," John said rising and offering his chair to Captain Nickerson.

"I don't understand why I have been brought here," Captain said.

"We just need to ask an honest man some questions about the operation at 'The Monia Mine,' and Mr. Whittacur tells us you are an honest man," the judge said to him.

"Thank you," he said. "I'll be truthful with what I know."

"Good," she said, "Mr. Whittacur says he used to work at 'The Monia Mine', do you know him?"

"I've seen him, but I didn't know his name. There are so many miners there."

"Yes, I'm sure there is," she continued. "What we are interested in here is the new shaft you were drilling to the south of the main tunnel."

"Yes, we started it about a year ago now. At first I thought Mr. Sholtz was simply out of his mind for going that way. You see the Monia was mostly played out. Just a little float rock here and there after March, last year, but Mr. Sholtz got this idea in his head that there would be a rich strike were we to drill straight south, he ordered that ten stamp mill and all. He built the town and put on more workers. I was sure he was headed for bankruptcy, but he was right, and I was wrong."

"What do you mean?" she asked.

"We dug hundreds a' feet straight south. Took us nearly six months, and then we busted into an old hole that had the richest reef I ever seen. Why, 'The Monia' produced more than a ton of pure gold since we hit that lode."

"My God," Bruce said "I'm going to get Ash," quickly turning for the door.

"Don't say anything outside this room," Cliff said. "hotel walls have ears."

The big man smiled and nodded his head just before he left.

"I have a map here of the 'Little Beaver Creek' area," Snow said unrolling a large sheet of brown paper. "Can you show us the precise location where the mother lode was found?"

"Let me see," Nickerson said looking at the map, now on the table. "Here, this small 'x' is right where we found it, just over the hill from the Monia's main shaft."

Snow looked up at Judge Morris. "That is precisely where Rob Scogins filed his claim in May of '69."

"Son-of-a-bitch," John Morris said.

"You don't have to be vulgar, John," Esther snapped, then turning to Boyd she asked, "Sheriff, how many men will you need to secure 'The Monia Mine' as evidence?"

"I don't know? Several."

"I believe Miss Scogins will be willing to pay the salaries for all you need Sheriff," Cliff offered.

"I'm ordering you to arrest Roper for the murder of Rob Scogins and Ed Sholtz for conspiracy to commit the same murder. Close down the Monia and seize all properties there. Place whatever number of guards you need to see that nothing is removed from the town that is not personal property of a miner or other employee."

"My, a ton of pure gold, why at $18.50 to the ounce that's nigh on $600,000," Snow figured aloud.

"You, you mean, Mr. Sholtz is a thief?" Captain Nickerson asked.

"A thief____and a murderer," Pebbles added.

"That's fur the court to decide," Esther reminded everyone while getting up from the table.

"I do believe it would be better if Captain were taken some place where he will be safe until he can testify," Cliff suggested.

"Oh, I'll be fine."

"Listen, I know these men. They have murdered before for this gold and tried to murder many more times; if they find out what you have just told us and that we plan to have you testify against them, your life won't be worth a plug nickel," Cliff said.

"I hate to say it, but you are right, Mr. Brown," the judge agreed. "See he is kept safe," she ordered and then left the room.

# Chapter Fourteen
# Haggai Magraw

The long winter and his job riding with the stage company had kept him pretty busy, and when he went to Teachman's barn, the big red horse gave him a disgusted look. "Come on, Red, let's shake a leg, and enjoy some of this pretty weather."

When he entered his stall, Red turned quickly and got several teeth into Cliff's britches, but he twisted before the horse could pinch his skin. "Hot damn!"

Getting the saddle on him was not as easy as normally it had been, and while leading him out of the barn, Cliff kept his eye twisted back watching out for another bite. Mounting him was no trouble, but when Cliff touched his heel to the side of the horse, Red began to buck like a green broke stallion. Cliff just barely was able to hang on, and finally after a minute of this, Red settled down; he had had his say.

It was an hour before sunup when he and the other rider headed south, leading a pack mule. They moved slowly so as not to attract interest, should anyone be up and about to see them.

When the sun finally slipped over the barren plain, Cliff turned straight into it and on they rode. Two hours later they came to the river. After crossing it, they turned to their left and keeping to the east bank, followed it another hour. Finally they saw a thin trail of smoke rising straight up.

Cliff stopped in a narrow ravine a couple hundred yards from the lone cabin and watched for a long time. When satisfied, he heeled Red and led off.

"Hal-loo in the cabin," he called out, just out of rifle range.

"Hal-loo back to ya," was the reply. "Who you be?"

"Reb Brown, I brought you some grub."

"Praise the Lord. We're nearly out. Come on in."

As they approached the small house, several children started coming out, first one and then another until there were seven in all; all seemed to be about the same age, between six and ten. Finally, a bent man with a short black beard came through the open door and lifted his arms high in the air. "Praise God, praise God," he repeated.

"Hello, Magraw," Cliff said dismounting. He had not ridden much lately, and his inner thighs were stiff with soreness, however his companion was a great deal worse off.

"This here is Captain Nickerson," Cliff said raising his hand to the thin man next to him. Then he asked, "You keep that ol' bandit alive for me?"

"He's alive, but there wus a time there," Magraw replied shaking his head.

"Hadn't a' been Bill Crane who ask this a' us, we'd allowed him to shake the hand a' ol' Lucifer[18] a week after you left him here."

"I'm obliged you didn't," Cliff said back. "I need him to testify."

"That's what you said," the shirtless man replied. "Yous' come on in and sup with us."

"That's kind of you," Captain said to the man.

Magraw raised his arm gesturing something between a praise and a welcome beckon, "Mr. Nickerson needs to meet the Misses anyway."

Entering the cabin, both Captain Nickerson and Cliff had to bend to clear the short doorframe. Inside, Captain was surprised to see everything seemed to have a place of its own and everything was in its place. The small cabin was very clean and gave the appearance of a home with servants to care for it. Standing in front of the fireplace that also served to heat the cabin and for all the cooking, were three women, one of whom was almost six feet tall and perhaps thirty-five years old. The other two were both shorter and looked to be less than twenty.

---

[18] Lucifer: In the old Bible in the book of Isaiah it is written, that Lucifer was 'The One' cast down from heaven. In other words, the Devil himself.

Captain Nickerson was somewhat taken aback, even though he should not have been, when they were introduced as Hannah, Ruth and Hope, Haggai Magraw's wives. Captain now knew why all the children were the same or near the same age.

To the right of the fireplace, sitting in a crude wooden chair, was another man. He was old and looked sick, his hair was long and stringy, and his beard was gray streaked with white. The corner of the room where he sat was darker than the rest of the house, but Captain could see his shirt was dirty, and what had once been white military suspenders were dark with filth.

*'They may keep the house spotless, but that hombre there is a pig,'* Captain thought.

Cliff walked over to where Yuel sat and asked, "How you feeling, Yuel?"

"What a' you care?"

"Well, I must care some or you would be dead along with your other friends back on the stage road."

"Might as well be," Yuel replied bitterly. "Them heathen bastards yonder done cut off my leg."

Cliff then saw he truly had only one leg. The right leg ended a foot above where his knee should have been.

"He got the gang'-green," Magraw said. "It got ta stinking so bad we had to whack it off, or he'd a' died fur sure."

"He's right," Cliff agreed. "If gangrene set in, it would a' kilt you sure, if he hadn't taken it off."

"Maybe. Who gives a rat's ass?" Yuel replied. "A man can't ride no horse without both legs. I might as well be dead. A' sides, they gon'a hang me anyways."

"Mee'be not," Cliff said. "All of your friends are dead except Roper and Sholtz. Sholtz is busted, and Roper is shot up," Cliff informed him.

"The hell you say!"

"It's true," Captain agreed.

"I know you," Yuel said, looking strongly at the thin man, "You work fur Mr. Sholtz at the mine."

"I used to, but no more. 'The Monia' is closed down," Captain told him.

"The hell you say?" this time the expression was truly a question.

"It is, and they are going to arrest Mr. Sholtz fur murder."

"I ain't been away that long," Yuel said, not being able to believe what he was hearing.

"It's true, Yuel," Cliff agreed. "Concho is dead, Piggett is dead. They're all dead, except the one who rode off and left you to die, Chip Roper."

"Yeah, he did do that," Yuel agreed. "The pretty little bastard."

"Well, you think on it. The next time I come, I will be taking you back for the trial. There you'll hang or___," Cliff paused a second or two before finishing, "If you testify against Roper and Sholtz, I can get you off with some jail time."

"I ain't telling nothing on Sholtz."

"Well, you think on it," Cliff suggested, and then he left and went outside. The other two men followed.

"Haggai, I need for you to allow Captain here to stay with you until the trial also. He can help you around the place, and you will be well paid for your trouble," Cliff assured him.

"How long you reckon?"

"I think not long."

"Alright, then he's welcome."

"Thank you," Cliff shook his hand, and then turning to Captain he said, "If you were to try and convince him to testify, he might just listen to you."

"I'll do what I can," Nickerson agreed.

It was at that time Hannah appeared in the door and called out, "Buttermilk and corn pone is on."

When Cliff arrived back in the mining region, he stopped first at Monia. The place was like a ghost town. The only living thing that could be seen were the two armed men who stood guard at the ends of the streets and three who rode horseback in a large circle around the town.

'Damn, they did this one right,' Cliff thought, and when he tried to get close he was facing several muzzles so he backed off and headed for South Pass City.

There he found Bruce who filled him in on what had happened in the two days he had been away.

"Sheriff Boyd went to work, and did he ever do a job. A brass monkey couldn't get in or out of Monia."

"Yeah, I stopped there on my way back."

"Well, that man Snow, he seized all the records from the Monia's office and has been going over them. He says Sholtz has been slipping gold out and putting it in banks down to Green River City and Granger. He had Boyd send a deputy down there to place a lien on both accounts," Bruce said and then continued, "He's a good man that Snow. Sholtz' men are all gone, the whole kit and caboodle."

"What about Chip and Sholtz?"

"Naw, didn't find either one a' them," Bruce said shaking his head.

"Damn!" Cliff said back, and he slapped his gloves on his forearm. "Can't let them bastards get away."

"They'll show up."

"We got 'a find them soon, or they will slip out and be long gone before we know it."

Bruce continued telling him about what had taken place and finally ended with, "You know, we might a' been wrong about Boyd. He's done a slap up job since he's found out Sholtz is the king crook around these parts."

"I hope you're right," Cliff admitted and then turned and left.

When he walked into 'The South Pass Saloon' an hour later, Jim was at a new piano, and Nadine was leaning against it singing about *Sweet Betsy From Pike.* A smile crossed her face when she saw him.

He ordered a large schooner of beer from Klu and then eased over to the piano. When she had finished her song, Jim ended it with a short run of *The Wildwood Flower.*

"When did you start here? I thought you were buying stock in 'The White Swan.'"

"'Tis a more fitting piàna mar seo pub," Jim replied, then seeing the opportunity to brag a little he offered, "The Morris' air a' bhith enticing me with this here grand music box, a da-rìribh Decker Brothers Piano Company straight from New York City, 'course this one is some eight years auld, but the brothers, David and J. J. must a' put den' heart in this auld lass, for after a wee bit a' tuning, she sings a sweet song. So it is obvious, me destiny is to be with her."

Cliff smiled at the Scotsman's story, but what he wanted most was to enjoy the sight of her, and he then turned his attention to the lady and spoke softly, "Hello, Purty Thing," and grinned.

"Hello, Georgia," she answered, "I hear you've been a busy man since I seen you last."

"Yeah, I've been busy. Had to take a job, almost ran out a' money."

"Almost ran out of lead, too, the way I hear it," she remarked with that teasing twinkle in her eyes.

"I've used some of that, too," he nodded his head and then motioned over to a table. "You want 'a sit for a spell?"

"Sure, Cowboy."

"Now, don't be a calling me something I can't live up to," Cliff said back as he followed her to a wall table.

"Oh, I think you can live up to it, one way or the other," she said looking deep into his face.

"Tell me, you still beddin' down with those blond sisters?" she asked.

"Me, naw; I haven't lived there in a long time. You gon'a be working here now, I guess."

"Yeah, since you put me out of the best paying job I ever had," she said back with a smile.

"Well, it was nothing personal," he replied looking around trying not to stare at her. "You had no business working for that bastard anyway."

"Sometimes a working girl must go where she has an offer."

"I suppose," he said still staring off across the room not really looking at anything.

It was then Pebbles came in and spotted him.

"Reb, I've been looking everywhere for you. They've found Roper; he was still in the mine shaft."

"Great," Cliff replied as he stood, then looking back at her he said, "I'm sorry. Miss Tipper, this is Mr. Stone. Pebbles Stone," he added.

"Pebbles?" she said almost in a laugh.

"Yas Ma'am, I was a mite small, till I grew up."

"I see," she said, and then with a big grin she added, "and you're from Georgia ,too."

"Why, no Ma'am, I'm from Florida. It's twenty miles from where I grew up to Georgia."

"Oh, that far," she said, still almost laughing.

"Yas Ma'am, ah fur piece."

"Purty Thing, I got 'a go. I'm glad you're back in South Pass."

"I am, too," she said and watched him as he walked away. Then she came to the piano and asked, "You know how to play Dixie on that thing?"

Jim replied on the keys.

Both Cliff and Pebbles were just mounting when they heard the piano begin.

"Kind a' brings tears to my eyes," Pebbles said.

"Yeah," was all Cliff said back, before he turned Red and led the others south out of town. Just as they were passing the cemetery, they noticed several horses tied in front of Doc Barnes house. "That big bay there belongs to Boyd," Pebbles pointed out.

Nodding in agreement, Cliff pulled up, and they went inside.

"We found him way back in the old shaft of the Monia. He would a' starved to death had not Jim Karnes come to me. He told me he had seen Sholtz take Roper there just after I was there looking for him, and then when we closed up the town, no one thought to get him. That shoulder wound had started bleeding again, and he has lost a lot of blood. The Doc doesn't give him much of a chance."

"Did you get to question him?"

"Naw, he was nearly unconscious when we found him, and he's been out ever since we got him in the spring wagon a fetchin' him here."

"I got an idea," Cliff said. "If the Doc says it's alright, take him down and lock him in the jail."

"But that woman is still there," Boyd said.

"Put him in the other cell, and let her see him. Mee'be loosen up her tongue."

"Might work," Boyd agreed.

"I think it would be worth a try."

When Happy Tom arrived late the next night, he had a message for the Sheriff. Sholtz had tried to withdraw money from his account at The Green River Bank. Snow's hold on the account had held up, and he was seen leaving shouting threats to everyone inside.

Boyd carried the note to Snow who nodded his head with satisfaction. "I have found evidence in his books that he also has accounts in Cheyenne, Denver, and Chicago. I will have the stage driver deliver a note to the telegrapher at Camp Stambaugh and have wires sent out freezing them also," he told Boyd.

"I aim to get Mrs. Morris to issue warrants, and then I can mail out posters on him, and maybe we can pick him up that way."

"That's a good idea," Snow confirmed. "My work is almost over here. When you have him back for trial I'll come again to present the Government's case against him for claim jumping. I have sufficient proof of that from his records and what Captain Nickerson can testify to. Of the murder charge, well, that's none of my affair."

Ed Sholtz was furious when he learned his bank accounts had been frozen in Granger and Green River City, but some of that anger had subsided when he was able to close his account in Cheyenne. He then took the train south to Denver with a little over three thousand in folding money. He arrived at the Cherry Creek Station at 8:00 o'clock in the evening on June 12 and took a room at 'The Palace Hotel,' just six doors from the 'Colorado Miners Bank and Investment Corporation' building on Silver Street.

Twelve hours later, he was there when the doors opened. Half past eight he was being escorted by a police sergeant to the city jail. Mr. Snow's wire had not arrived in Cheyenne in time, but it preceded Sholtz to Denver by one day.

"That's great," Bruce said, "but Denver is not in Wyoming Territory. How we gon'a get the bastard back here?"

"That should present no real problem," Snow replied to the question. "Your Mr. Scogins was wiser than most who strike a little color. He registered his claim with the Federal Assayer's Office as well as the local. The falsification of federally registered claims is a Federal Offense. I will send a wire to Denver and have the U. S. Marshal there deliver him back for trial."

# Chapter Fifteen
# The Trial

The trial was set for July 1, 1870 in the county courthouse on South Pass Avenue where it intersects Washington Street. It was a two-room structure, with the smaller room in the rear where a defendant could be held and only brought in the trial room as each was being accused.

The main room was situated so that the judge's table was in the corner facing the open room. To his right was placed a small table and two chairs, where a single defendant and one attorney could sit. To the left of the judge and about in the center of the north wall was another chair for the person doing the testifying to sit. This placed him or her facing the jury who were seated ahead on two benches of split Ponderosa. To the right of the jury were three chairs that no one sat in.

The first defendant was Ed Sholtz, charged with three offenses: Falsification of Federal Records, Conspiracy to Commit Armed Robbery and Conspiracy to Commit Murder. His attorney, Thomas Gallagher, entered a plea of not guilty on all charges, and the two of them occupied the chairs behind the second desk.

The plea was so accepted, and then Miss Darla Kimball was brought before the bench, and her charges were read to the court. "Attempted Murder and Conspiracy to Commit Armed Robbery". She also pled 'Not Guilty' and was led over and seated in the middle of the three chairs to the jury's right.

Last, Chip Roper was brought in, and he heard as he stood before the bench of Judge Kingman, "You, Mr. Roper are charged with the

Murder of Robert Scogins, Conspiracy to Commit Armed Robbery and Conspiracy to Falsify Federal Records, namely recorded gold claims."

Shocking the court room and especially Tom Gallagher and his client, Chip replied, "Guilty to all charges except the murder of Rob Scogins, Phil Sholtz did that."

"I protest!" yelled Gallagher.

"Nothing to protest yet, Tom," the judge said back.

Roper then took the chair on Darla's left.

The first witness called was Clifford Brown. It was the first time most there had heard him called anything but Reb.

Cliff told his story, from his being so close to the ambush and murder of Rob Scogins, the bushwhacking attempt with Bodie Johnson, the fight in Morris' saloon where Bruce Whittacur had helped him against Phil Sholtz and Chip Roper, his witnessing the planting of gold coin in Bruce's saddlebags, and the fight that occurred when they went to pick up Whittacur's poke at the bunkhouse in Monia.

Gallagher was constantly objecting, but the judge kept overruling him.

Cliff continued and told of being informed of Crowe being brought in to kill him.

On this, when Gallagher objected as it was pure hearsay, the judge had to agree with him.

Charles Black, who was acting as the prosecuting attorney for the territory, at that point made an unusual move and addressed the judge with, "Your Honor, I do think it necessary when a conspiracy is being proven that the story be presented in the correct order of events and time, a proper chronology, if it pleases the Court. Therefore, I request this witness be excused for a few moments while we hear from another of our witnesses."

"Your honor, I object on the grounds of____"

"Objection overruled," the judge cut him short. "A chronological recitation of the facts is easiest to follow in such a complex and clearly convoluted matter such as this."

Tom Gallagher cleared his throat and sat back down.

"The prosecution now calls Mrs. Tipper."

There was a stirring throughout the small room as the woman was brought to the witness chair. She, too, was dressed in a plain cotton dress, but unlike the other women in the room, her jet-black hair was not parted down the middle.

"I object," Gallagher called out. "This woman is a known harlot, often seen with this Reb Brown. Her testimony will surely be as tainted as is her reputation."

"Your Honor, Mrs. Tipper was employed by, until only a few weeks ago, the defendant Mr. Sholtz," argued Charlie Black. "Is it a greater sin to be a prostitute or to make one's living by selling the services of prostitutes?"

"We will certainly give credence to whatever credible and relevant testimony this witness has to offer," the judge ruled.

"Now, Mrs. Tipper, what is your occupation?"

The young woman stirred a little in the old wooden chair and looked out at the forty or so people there in the small room. Most were standing, but a few women were seated behind the jury. Everyone was looking at her. She suddenly seemed very ashamed, and a streak of hate went out to her husband. *'Damn you Brady. Why did you have to go and get yourself killed?'* she thought. Her eyes had descended down to her hands, but when she looked up again, she could see the faces of many who had paid a handsome fee for her services during the past three years, men who also feared her testimony. Suddenly, all her strengths returned.

"One never knows what secrets a whore might reveal when she is being questioned on the witness stand," Dick Goddard had said to Windy, not an hour before as he saw their wives approaching from C Street.

"Now, it's all right Mrs. Tipper, remember you have friends as well as customers here," Charlie Black said in a comforting tone.

"I'm a prostitute," she finally held up her head and said loudly as she looked into the faces of those who had stared at her so strongly.

"How long have you made a living as a prostitute, Mrs. Tipper?" Black asked.

"Ever since my husband was gunned down, right here in this town," she said.

Cliff remembered her telling him about her originally being ushered into the trade in Kansas City before she married Brady Tipper, he also approved of her not sharing her whole life with those who had no reason to know. He was confident she had been a good wife while married to Brady and had returned to this life only when she had no money and no other means of making any.

"I see," Black said, "and just who employed you as a prostitute?"

"I object," Gallagher said, "I object to anything this woman has to say. She is an admitted and known whore of the region, and we all know women of her kind will sell their word as quick as they sell their bodies."

"Mr. Gallagher, this court sees the whore to be no worse than the whoremonger, and I venture to say others who might testify here today would fit into that category," the judge emphasized, "Overruled."

"Now, Mrs. Tipper, who employed you as a prostitute?"

"I have been working for Mr. Ed Sholtz for the last several months," she said.

"During that time did Mr. Sholtz ever require your services?"

"I, err, it is required by him, before he puts you to work," she said staring hatefully at Sholtz. "He calls it his tasting of the wine,____to see it is not poison, before he serves it to his customers."

"I object."

"I said overruled, Mr. Gallagher."

"Now, Mrs. Tipper, while employed by Mr. Sholtz did you know Mr. Roper?"

"Yes, he is Sholtz' errand boy."

"I object."

"Sustained."

"Did you know a man by the name of Morgan Crowe?"

"Yes, very well."

"You say, very well, just what do you mean?"

"He paid fur me to stay only with him from the first night we met until he was killed."

"During that time did he tell you anything that would lead you to believe he wasn't here to dig for gold?"

"Yes, he____"

"I object, on the basis of hearsay," Gallagher said jumping to his feet.

"Your Honor, it's not hearsay for her to tell us what this man said to her for his statements do not go to proving or disproving any of the elements of anything in issue."

"Overruled."

Gallagher sat back down so hard his chair almost turned over.

Nadine continued, "Morgan said, Little Phil had gotten himself shot because he was just a boy, and it took a man to do a killing."

"Did he say anymore on this subject?"

"He told me once, not to worry about Ed Sholtz bothering me while he was around, and that he had been sent for to do a job for Sholtz."

"Did he say what that job was?"

"No, not directly, but he patted the butt of his revolver when he said it."

"You heard Mr. Brown testify that he had received word Crowe was gunning fur him."

"Yes, sir, I did."

"Do you know anything about that?"

"Yes, I sent word to him that I had been told Crowe had been sent for, by Sholtz, to gun him down."

"You sent word?"

"Yes, sir."

"How did you send word?"

"I told Mr. Arthur Houghton."

"Just what did you tell him?"

"I told him to get word to Reb, that Crowe was a gunman that Sholtz had brought in just to kill him," she said then added, "or something like that."

"Thank you, Mrs. Tipper. We all know how hard it was for you to come here and give your testimony."

"Your witness."

"Miss, Tipper did you hear Mr. Sholtz say anything, anything at all, about this Crowe fellow working for him?"

"No."

"Did you hear Mr. Sholtz say the name Morgan Crowe at any time?"

"No," she replied.

"No other questions."

Henry Black recalled Cliff to the stand to finish his story. Tom Gallagher continued to object, but was overruled almost every time by Judge Kingman. After Cliff finished, the next witness called was Ashley Scogins who testified about her brother and that she was the sole heir to his estate.

The next to be called was Bruce Whittacur, who confirmed he had worked at 'The Monia Mine,' and that in early summer of 1869, 'The Monia' appeared to be about played out, and then suddenly a new ten stamp mill was brought in, and a new shaft was started due south from the main one. He, too, testified about the shooting of Phillip Sholtz and the encounter with Morgan Crowe.

After Bruce, came the testimony of Jack Murdock about the stage robbery when he had been shot and the fact that the man who had gotten away was riding a gray dapple horse.

After Murdock, Bill Crane was called, followed by his niece June DeWolf. They each told of the siege at the stage station, and the ladies in the courtroom were especially distraught when June told of how Concho had threatened to cut off her breasts and make tobacco pouches out of them. She also was the one to point an accusing finger at Darla Kimball as one of the co-conspirators.

Then it was Tom Ranahan who told of the attack on the stage at Pacific Springs Station and how three of the passengers had been in on the taking over of the stage and the station, and that he had shot at a fleeing bandit who sped away on a gray dapple horse.

Cinch DeMoss completed the confirmation of what Cliff had told earlier.

Next was the real test of Sholtz' future.

"I now call as my next witness, Mrs. Darla Kimball."

"I object, she's a defendant."

"So what?" Kingman said back with a slight twist of his head.

Darla Kimball wore a light blue summer dress and a white bonnet tied behind her neck with a small silk ribbon. Around her neck and lying gently over her upper chest was a crocheted white lace bib. She was still wearing her riding boots that she had on when she was arrested, but no one saw them; her dress was simply too long. She walked up to the table where the judge sat and raised her right hand awaiting her oath.

Sheriff Boyd administered the oath and she affirmed before she was led by the elbow to a straight back wooden chair that appeared to be the only piece of furniture not made on the site.

When seated, she sat straight with her head upright and her pretty face quite stern.

"Mrs. Kimball, you have heard the testimony given here today. Do you have knowledge of any of it being true?"

"I have. I was one of the people who were sent to rob the southbound stage."

"I object."

"Overruled. Go ahead Mrs. Kimball and answer the question."

"A Mr. Piggett met me at the railroad station in Granger with a note from Chip," she said, and then looked at her lover. He nodded his head.

"What was in the note?"

"It said I was to accompany Mr. Piggett to a stage station where Chip would meet me. Also Chip told me to assist Mr. Piggett in anything he might ask of me, as all of this would lead to our getting the money for our marriage."

"When you say, 'He told you,' do you mean in person, or was it also in the note?"

"Oh, it was in the note."

"And how did you know it was truly from your intended, Chip Roper?"

"It was in his handwriting and I know it well. He has written me several letters while we were apart."

"Just who is this Mr. Piggett?"

"He was one of the men killed during the siege of the stage station," she said back, as if he should have already known that.

"And what did this Mr. Piggett tell you? What you were to do?"

"He said Chip would meet us at one of the stage stations, where they were going to rob a coach full of gold. He told me that I was to act like I didn't know any of them, to fool anyone else on the stage. Then he gave me a diary book that had been cut out to conceal a Derringer gun. He said, if I had to, I should shoot anyone who might be about to interfere or kill one of us."

"Were you willing to do that?"

"Yes. Chip had told me to do whatever Mr. Piggett said for me to do."

"Did you know what was to happen to the people at the stage station?"

"Yes, I overheard Mr. Piggett and the man they called Concho talking, and he told him they would have to kill everyone there. He said they were going to make it look like Indians had done it."

"Now who was it that said they were going to make it look like Indians attacked and killed everyone?"

"Mr. Piggett. He was the one who told the Mexican that."

"Did you actually hear Piggett say to Concho they were going to make it look like Indians had done it?"

"Well, perhaps not in those very words."

"How then did he say it?"

"Mr. Piggett asked the man Concho if he would mind scalping the woman there, and he said no, if he could have her first."

"Did you hear this man Concho say that he intended to cut off the breasts of Miss DeWolf and make tobacco pouches of them?"

"Yes, I heard him say that," she said looking down at the small handkerchief she kept rolling in her hands.

"Did you believe him, when he said it?"

"Oh, yes. He meant it all right."

"I object. That calls for a conclusion," Gallagher said as he rose.

"Sustained."

"Let me rephrase the question, Mrs. Kimball did you believe he meant it when Concho said he wanted to make tobacco pouches from Miss DeWolf's breasts?"

"I object. It still___."

"Oh, sit down, Mr. Gallagher," Judge Kingman said. "She can testify if she believed him or not."

"But Your Honor."

"Tom, I said sit down."

"Did you ever hear the name Sholtz before you were arrested?"

"Oh yes, many times," she said looking up.

"When did you first hear it?"

"Chip wrote me last year he worked for Mr. Sholtz."

"And while on this trip, did you hear the name Sholtz?"

"Yes."

"Who used it?"

"Well, Mr. Piggett said it several times and so did some of the others, too."

"Do you remember what Mr. Piggett said when he used the name Sholtz?"

"Yes," she said looking up at the ceiling as if she was thinking hard on the question, finally she continued, "He said, Sholtz was sending a bow and some arrows for them to shoot into some of the people there, so it would look like an Indian attack instead of a robbery."

"I object."

"Overruled."

"Any other time, Mrs. Kimball?"

Again she looked up before replying. "Well, like I said, I heard it several times, but I do remember the man called Palmer. He was talking with Mr. Piggett in Granger while we were waiting at the station there, and he asked about his cut. Mr. Piggett said Sholtz had promised they could have everything on the coach except what he himself was shipping."

"You heard the testimony of Miss DeWolf, did you not?"

"Yes."

"Did you try to shoot Mr. DeMoss?"

Again she lowered her head before answering, "Yes," she said in a low voice.

"Were you prepared to help in the killing of the other people at the Pacific Springs Stage Stop?"

"No, not if I didn't have to," she said looking up.

"But you were prepared to stand by and watch them get killed?"

"Well, they are all gentiles you know," she said very positively looking him straight in the eye.

There was a rush of whisper that ran among the listeners in the room at her answer.

Judge Kingman slapped his polished oak gavel down on the table twice before saying, "If the people in this room cannot remain quiet, they will be removed."

Black then looked at Darla's face and asked sternly, "Does that make murder all right in your eyes, Mrs. Kimball?"

"Not my eyes, sir, rather the eyes that approve of ridding Deseret of gentiles are the eyes of the Lord. We Saints are purely his instruments, sent to do his deeds."

"Your Honor, I object. Obviously the woman is insane. She admits to the condoning of murder of innocent citizens. Nothing she says should be taken with a grain of salt," Gallagher argued.

"I see no insanity in one's belief in God. The question that offends here is whether she has the teaching of Christ in her background or some other leader. Overruled."

"Your witness," Black said to his opponent.

"Mrs. Kimball, have you ever seen Mr. Sholtz before this day?"

"No, sir."

"Have you ever heard Mr. Sholtz say anything to anyone?"

"No, sir."

"Have you ever heard Mr. Sholtz say anything ever?"

"No, sir."

"No other questions," Gallagher said turning and looking at the jury, and then with a sigh he added, "Please remove the murderess from our sight."

"I now object," Black said. "It is true Mrs. Kimball is charged as a co-conspirator to Mr. Sholtz' murder plans, but she has not committed any murder to our knowledge."

"I object to his statement that Mr. Sholtz had murder plans."

"Oh, both of you sit down," Kingman ordered.

"I would, Your Honor, but as you see there is no chair for the prosecution," Black replied, and the people laughed loudly.

Again, Kingman was pounding on the table yelling for order.

Next called to the witness stand was Chip Roper. It was obvious to all he had been wounded. When he moved he appeared to be in great pain, but he managed to get to the stand and sit down.

"Your name, sir?"

"I'm Chip Roper."

"Is Chip your Christian name?"

"No, I guess not. My mother once told me my real name is Granville. I wus named after her father, but I've been called Chip, as far back as I can remember."

"Very well, Mr. Roper. Let the record show that Chip Roper and Granville Roper are one in the same," Black said loudly.

"Hell, Charlie, there ain't no ones keeping no record a' this," someone called out from behind the jury. Again there was laughter throughout the small building.

Rap, Rap went the judge's gavel.

"Mr. Roper," Black began. "Who do you work for?"

"Ed Sholtz there," he replied nodding to the man who was staring daggers at him.

"What is your job?"

"I, err, I. I guess you could say I wus his hired gun."

"I object."

"Overruled."

"Did you ever kill for him?"

"No, sir," Roper said back sternly.

"Did he ever tell you to kill for him?"

"Yes, sir," Chip said turning his head so he was avoiding having to look at Sholtz when he spoke.

"Did he tell you to kill Rob Scogins?"

"Yes, he did."

"Why did he want you to kill Scogins?"

"I object. That calls for a conclusion on the witness' part."

"Sustained," the judge ruled.

"Alright," Black said looking at Sholtz directly when he spoke. "Did he tell you why you were to kill Scogins?"

"Object."

"Overruled."

"He said Scogins had hit the mother lode just over the hill from 'The Monia' and only a few hundred feet if we drilled through, and he planned to take over Scogins' strike."

"Those were his own words?"

"Yes, I believe they were his very words," Chip replied still looking at Black rather than Sholtz.

"Did you shoot Rob Scogins?"

"No, Phil shot him," Chip said as he stirred around in the chair a little.

Cliff knew he was lying. He remembered well that night and what he had heard out there on the big open. The voice he heard say, "I know I hit him," was the same voice he now heard on the witness stand, but it mattered little. Chip Roper was headed for the Federal Prison in Laramie, and he just might be the one who would send Ed Sholtz to the hanging tree. Cliff was well satisfied with the trial so far.

"Did Ed Sholtz ever tell you to kill Cliff Brown?"

"Yes, more than once, but he wanted it to be done out of town and away from Phil. He was always wanting to keep Phil out of anything that people would find objectionable, he really loved that boy."

"That was hard to do though, wasn't it? Keeping Phillip Sholtz out of trouble that is."

"Yeah," Chip agreed nodding his head. "He was a real hell raiser. He always wanted to show his Pa he was as bad as he was."

"I object."

"Sustained."

"Do you know anything about the killing of Bodie Johnson?"

"Yeah, some."

"Were you there when he was killed?"

"No."

"What do you know then?"

"Well, Mr. Sholtz had give me orders to have Reb Brown killed, and I was setting it up with Bodie to get him out of town. Little Phil wus with me when I laid out the plan to Bodie and a Mexican vaquero called Mad Dog Carlos. Bones Harvey wus the third man who wus on this caper."

"Did Philip Sholtz go, too?" Black asked.

"Yeah, he wasn't supposed to, but he went anyway. It wus Little Phil who told me what happened."

"So, Bodie Johnson was in on the plot to kill Cliff Brown?"

"Yeah, he wus to lead Brown out there where they could get a shot at him, but Mad Dog shot too soon and then when Bodie tried to get at Brown. Brown shot him."

"I object, hearsay."

"Sustained."

Black walked away from the witness chair, and with his back to Roper he looked straight at the jury and said, "Tell the court what you know about this man Morgan Crowe."

"Oh, he wus a gun hawk Mr. Sholtz brung in to kill Brown."

"Object."

"Alright, Mr. Gallagher," Black said. "I'll ask a different question."

"When did you first hear of Crowe?"

"Mr. Sholtz told me Crowe owed him a favor and for me to send for him."

"Where did you send your message to, to find him?"

"Natchez, Mississippi."

"That far?" Black replied. "He must a' owed Mr. Sholtz quite a favor."

"Yeah, Mr. Sholtz saved his life once," Chip replied.

"I see."

"Did you ever hear Mr. Sholtz tell Morgan Crowe to kill Cliff Brown?"

"Yes, I did," Chip admitted. "Right after Crowe arrived, the three of us were in Mr. Sholtz' private office, and he told me to keep little Phil away from Brown, and then he turned to Crowe and said, killing Reb Brown is your job."

Sholtz was a large man, and he was now showing a lot of nervous motion, moving about often in his chair, a fact that did not go unnoticed by several members of the jury. Gallagher leaned over and whispered something to him, and he stopped moving, but only for a few minutes.

"You were with Morgan Crowe when he was killed, were you not?"

"Yeah," Chip agreed nodding his head. "Sholtz sent the four of us here to kill Reb Brown and Whittacur, too, if we could work it out."

"I object."

"On what grounds, Tom?" Judge Kingman asked.

"How does he know Mr. Sholtz sent them to kill anybody?"

The judge turned and looked straight at Roper and asked, "How do you know Sholtz sent you to kill anybody?"

Chip looked back bewildered and replied, "Well, he said to me and Crowe, go kill 'um."

"That satisfy you, Tom?" Kingman asked. Again there was laughter, but this time the judge did nothing to stop it.

Gallagher raised his arms and turned around and walked back to his chair and sat down.

"When Crowe was killed, there was a man named Concho who was arrested that day. Do you know how he escaped from custody?"

"Yeah, Mr. Sholtz told us to slip a gun and a pick in the window of his cell that night. We did, and he chipped away some of the clay mortar and removed a few of the stones so he could get out," Chip replied lifting his palms as final statement.

"When you say 'we did,' who were 'we'?"

"I gave the gun, an old horse pistol, to him while the sheriff was gone, and that fool deputy wus asleep."

"Is this the gun?" Black asked holding up a Remington .50 caliber single shot.

"Yeah, that's it. Where did you get that?" Chip replied.

"The sheriff was good enough to keep it for us."

The weapon was very large compared to the more common revolvers of the day. It had an 8 inch barrel and was stocked in a fine grade of what appeared to be red cherry or blood wood. It made a very impressive sight to the jury.

"Where did you get it in the first place?"

"Mr. Sholtz gave it to me to give to Concho," Chip replied, as if everyone should know that.

"Mr. Roper, I understand you have a beautiful horse," Black said.

"Yes, Thunder," Chip replied showing pride in his mount.

"What kind of horse is he?"

"I was told by the man I got him from he is pure Arabian."

"Arabian. They are very rare in these parts are they not?"

"He's the only one I've ever seen," Chip agreed.

"What color is he?"

"Gray, gray dapple," Chip said.

"Who was the man you got him from?"

"I don't know his name. He was a friend of Mr. Sholtz."

"Thank you for that," Black said back, fully intending on using these statements strongly in his closing argument.

"Mr. Roper, you heard earlier Mr. Murdock say a rider on a gray dapple horse was one of the men who attempted to rob the stage in June, did you not?"

"Yes," Chip replied.

"And you heard Mr. Ranahan say he shot at a robber on a gray horse during the siege at the Pacific Springs Stage Station?"

"Yes," Chip replied again.

"Could that have been you riding your Arabian Gray at each of those stage holdups?"

"Yes, it was me both times."

"Why did you attempt to rob the stage?"

"Mr. Sholtz told us to."

"Told us?"

"Well, he told me, and I planned the robberies, mostly."

"Did you plan the robberies or did you just arrange for the plans to be carried out?"

"Yeah, it wus more like that," Chip admitted.

"I object. He's leading the witness."

"Sustained, but I think you are too late, Tom," the judge said.

"Who really planned the robberies?"

"Mr. Sholtz did," Chip answered, still not looking at Sholtz, but aware of his boss' moving around in his chair.

"Didn't 'The Monia' mine ship gold on those stage coaches?" Black asked now standing right in front of the defense table and staring straight at Sholtz.

"Yeah, sure."

"Why would Mr. Sholtz want his own gold stolen?"

"He always took out insurance on any shipment he sent out," Chip said, then added, "besides we always gave him back all his money."

"You netted no monies on these two robbery attempts, so I take it there were others?"

"Yeah, three last year," Chip said.

"Was anyone killed during these?"

"One man on the Cannonball near Bessemer Bend, but it wus his fault. He should a' never tried to draw his gun. We had 'im cold."

"You shot him?"

"No, Concho stuck him with his throwing knife. He was deadly with that sticker."

"How much money was stolen in these robberies?"

"I really don't know. I always took the loot back and gave it to the boss. He paid us well every time."

"Who do you mean when you say 'The Boss'?"

"Why Mr. Sholtz, of course," Chip replied as if everyone should know that.

Chip continued with his story, explaining about the plans of the robberies that had been given to him by Sholtz and how he executed them. Finally, Black looked around at the jury and paused for a long time and then back at the twenty-four year old blond boy with the deep blue eyes and said, "Your witness."

Tom Gallagher was a man in his early fifties with thin graying hair. He stood about 5'-7" and weighed some 220 pounds, but he had an air about him that demanded respect. He had not really wanted this case, but Sholtz had offered him $100,000 if he could walk from the court room a free man, and Gallagher was one of the few who realized that the gold rush in 'The Sweetwater Region' was mostly a thing of the past. The one hundred thousand would be enough to live well on, until he was able to relocate to a new up and coming boomtown. He was not so foolish as to believe he was a great attorney, and that is why he had always gone to the new towns where he, though not great, would be in demand, as there would be none better at his trade. It was a strategy that had served him well for twenty years and in six different boomtowns.

There was another reason though, that had caused him to work for Sholtz. His partner, Charlie Black, had been appointed to prosecute the case by Judge Kingman, and he knew he was the better attorney of the partnership, although Black seemed not to realize it. When Sholtz walked a free man out onto the streets of South Pass City once again, everyone, including and especially Charlie Black, would also know.

Tom had a good defense, but he chucked it when Roper had entered his plea of guilty to almost every charge. He was sure Black had made a deal with the kid, and that would be his downfall. The people of this territory were not the kind to be siding with a turncoat, especially not one who traded his testimony for a light sentence; this is where he would crush Black.

"I must say, Mr. Roper," Gallagher began, "you sure tell a wonderful story. It is so interesting, that there for a while I was beginning to believe it myself, as I am sure the good men of the jury were, too," he paused and walked over and stood inches from the boot toes of the men on the jury's front row. Clearing his throat he continued, "But you see I know one little fact that these men don't know. Just one small detail that will taint your tale and show you up to be the liar you really are."

Turning now to Roper, he walked halfway between the witness and the jury, and there he stopped. "Do you know what that little detail is, Mr. Roper?"

Chip shook his head without saying a word.

"I want to hear you tell the jury about the deal you made with the prosecutor."

"What kind of deal?" Chip questioned.

"You know very well what kind of deal, Roper."

Chip thought hard and knew he had not discussed any money at all with Black, and Chip Roper always thought deals involved money. Finally he replied. "No sir, I don't know of no such deal."

This time when he began, Gallagher spoke quite loudly. "The deal Charles Black made with you not to prosecute you if you would tell lies about Mr. Sholtz. That's what deal I mean."

Chip had been Sholtz' top Lieutenant for several years now, he allowed Sholtz to raise his voice at him, but no one else had better do so, not if they wanted to live very long. He realized here he would not be able to reach for his trusty Colt and drop this sleazy attorney, at least not now, but neither did he have to take insults. With a voice as cold and as calm as anyone ever heard coupled with a stare that brought a chill rushing up the spine of the defense attorney, he replied, "My life has been full of wrong doings, especially since I went to work for Mr. Sholtz, but this day I have spoken no untruths and I speak none now when I say, nobody made any deal with me to tell lies to get me a lighter sentence. I ain't kil't nobody that weren't trying to kill me. I did try to, but it didn't come off, and I ain't done it. I know it is prison I'm bound, but don't get me riled, lawyer man, or maybe it will be to the gallows I'll go."

Gallagher looked weakly at the man and realized he had just almost lost his bladder, and then he looked to Charlie Black, finally he said, "No other questions."

Black slowly and quietly released the breath he had been holding. To make deals was common. This was known by all attorneys, but the common man did not go for this practice, and he felt sure it would have hurt his case had it come out that he did offer Roper a deal. Not a deal to lie in exchange for a lighter sentence, rather not to prosecute Darla Kimball in exchange for his truthful testimony. The truth was more damaging than a lie anyway.

The next witness Black called was Captain Nickerson who told of his employment as chief engineer at 'The Monia Mine,' and most damaging was his testimony of Ed Sholtz ordering him to stop drilling the cut that they had been working on for six months and to begin a new shaft directly south from 'The Monia's' main shaft.

"Why did that surprise you?" Black questioned.

"Well, I knew 'The Monia' was mostly played out. We were only getting small chips of ore and that from placer, more than drilling. There was a little granite in the cut shaft that could maybe bring a few thousand but little more, and I told him so."

"Who did you tell?"

"Why Mr. Sholtz, of course."

"Was that when he told you to begin the south shaft?"

"No, it was later. I told him in June I wus moving on. You see, I had a new job down in Boulder, but he offered me two years wages to oversee this new south shaft," Captain replied and then gave his head a slight twist. His long thin neck seemed to extend from his white stiff collar when he did.

"I thought he had gone mad, so I asked for it in advance."

"Did he pay you?"

"Yes, two years pay. He gave it to me the next week."

"Why did you not think it a good idea to drill the south shaft?"

"Well, he said he wanted it to run due south less than twenty feet underground and for perhaps three hundred feet."

"Is that so strange?"

"You bet it is. A fellow will get nothing from his diggings running like that."

"When did you start on this south shaft?"

"Let's see, I recollect it wus around June last year."

"Let me see now," he paused and let everyone begin thinking themselves, wondering what his next point might be, satisfied he had the jury's attention, he continued, "That would be just about the time Rob Scogins was murdered."

"I object," Gallagher said rising from his chair.

"Sustained, for once," Kingman said back.

"Did the new shaft ever turn out to hit anything worth the trouble?"

"Well, the shaft didn't, but right at where he had told me to dig to, we broke into an old hole that went some seventy or so feet, and there we found the richest vein I ever seen in my life. I wus sure surprised, I will tell you."

"Now, when you said an old hole, just what do you mean?"

"Well, I wasn't there the day they broke into it, but it looked like somebody had dug it there sometime in the past. Didn't make sense though to me, at the time. The old dig ran straight to that super vein, and nobody in his right mind would have abandoned that."

"Not if they were alive. I agree," Black added.

"I object."

"Sit down, Tom," the judge said overruling him.

"Let me see if I understood you correctly. You say the Monia Mine was all but played out last spring, and then suddenly you were told to stop drilling in the only shaft that still was producing any color and to start out in a due south direction and go for three hundred feet at precisely twenty feet below the surface on what to the best mining engineer in the region considered a work of folly?"

"That's pretty close to it, all right," Captain agreed nodding his head.

"Are you aware of 'The Monia' shipping any gold out, during the time after you began drilling the south shaft until you hit this rich vein?"

"Well, yes. I was surprised to hear they did find some good color in the old mine, but I don't know much about that, as Mr. Sholtz kept me busy overseeing the drilling of the new shaft."

"So, after you determined that there was little or nothing left in

'The Monia,' suddenly men with far less knowledge and experience than you, began bringing out good color."

"Yes, but I still don't understand it."

"I think I do," Black said, turning and looking at the jury. "Could you give an estimate of how much was shipped after you began working on the new south shaft?"

"I'm not sure, but many thousands of dollars worth."

"I object. This calls for speculation from the witness," Gallagher argued.

"Sustained."

"That's all right Captain we can find that out from persons who had direct knowledge of it."

"Let me ask you this, from your knowledge as an expert on mining, could that old hole you described before have been less that two years old?"

"No, I don't think so. I was told they replaced old rotten timbers with new ones. I wasn't there when they finally broke through. You see I had come down with a severe sore throat and was in bed for a week. Just ask Doc Barnes."

"Oh, I believe you Captain, but let me re-ask this question. You never saw the old rotten timbers that were replaced, so it is possible they were never replaced, and this old hole was not so old after all. Is that not so?"

"Well, yes. I guess that is so."

"Your witness," Black said to his adversary.

"How long did you work for Mr. Sholtz?"

"Two, almost three years. He hired me right after he won 'The Monia'."

"Did 'The Monia' pay good?"

"Oh yes, for a year and a half it was a very good strike, but all veins run out sooner or later," he said lifting both shoulders.

"During the years you worked for Mr. Sholtz, did you ever hear him tell anyone to kill someone?"

"Oh, heavens, no! If I had, I would have left him right then."

"Did you ever know of him doing anything that would be considered cruel or harmful to anyone?"

"No," the thin man said and then added, "Not unless you were to consider his trying to stop Sheriff Boyd from bringing me in to give a statement."

Gallagher cleared his throat concluding, "No more questions."

Next, Charlie Black called Arthur Houghton who confirmed Nadine's testimony about the Crowe incident, and then he gave accurate reports of the amount of goods he hauled to Sholtz and the amount of gold he hauled away.

"Mr. Houghton," Black asked, "how do you know all this so precisely?"

"We at Cotter and Houghton keep exact records of all our business. I can tell you how much the law books weighed you had me bring in fur you, Charlie," Art said back, and the whole room suddenly was in laughter.

"Well, that's reassuring, Art, but it won't be necessary. We are interested in what business you did for 'The Monia' and Ed Sholtz though."

When Art had finished, it was plain to all that 'The Monia' had produced well for about a year and four months and then began to decline, and when it was shipping its least, suddenly Ed Sholtz had contracted Houghton to ship for him almost singularly and had built a whole town during the next few months. He had freighted in the largest stamp mill in the region for Sholtz and just as suddenly began moving out huge amounts of gold, the weight of which was given to the court, to the ounce.

When Gallagher got to him, his questions were few.

"Did you ever hear this Morgan Crowe say he was going to kill Reb Brown?"

"No."

"Did you ever hear Mr. Sholtz tell him to kill this Rebel Brown?"

"No."

"Did you ever hear Mr. Sholtz tell anyone to kill anything?"

"No."

"Did you ever hear of Mr. Sholtz harming anyone whatsoever?"

"Well, now seeing as you put it that way, I____"

"Withdraw the question. Witness is dismissed," Gallagher said cutting him short.

Charlie Black then walked over to where Chip Roper and Darla Kimball sat, then slowly walked behind the empty third chair, and placing his hands on the back of it, he took a deep breath before he spoke. "I now call to the stand, Vernon Yuel."

As if a storm had suddenly come rushing into the small room, a dull roar moved quickly over the lips of those seated there.

"Yuel's dead," Gallagher said to the judge.

"He was, or so we thought, but he was brought to us just this morning by a good Mormon family who has nursed him back from the gates of hell," Black said with a sneer.

"I object. I knew nothing of this witness."

"He's not here as a witness, he's here as an accused co-conspirator," Black argued back.

"I haven't had time to prepare for his defense."

"You aren't his attorney, Tom."

The room was still buzzing with activity as the Sheriff began assisting the one-legged Yuel in from the front door and past the benches where the jury was seated. When they passed the table where Gallagher was standing, suddenly Ed Sholtz shot forward and grabbed the Smith & Wesson the lawman carried in a cross-draw holster, and shot him in the stomach. There now was screaming from the women near the rear of the room and blue smoke filling the air along with the pounding of Judge Kingman's gavel. Boyd fell backward and sat against the wall with a surprised look on his face.

When Yuel saw his old boss turning the top break revolver toward him, he struggled forward trying to get away. This time when Sholtz fired, the 32 rimfire shell sounded loud in the confines of the room, but the bullet went over the one-legged man's head. Yuel was now diving ahead trying to get away. Sholtz cocked the pistol again and fired once more at Yuel, and this time his shot was deadly. The ninety grain lead projectile struck Darla Kimball just above her left eye, and she simply jerked her head back, and then it fell forward until her chin rested on her upper chest.

Silence suddenly descended upon the courtroom as if it were a heavy blanket falling from the ceiling.

Sholtz, realizing what he had done, turned the gun towards Judge Kingman before he spoke. Stuttering he said, "Hold it! Hold, ho-hold it right there!"

Before he uttered another word, a huge man who had sat quietly immediately behind the jury during most of the trial lunged forward, and with the speed no one would have believed so large a man could achieve, he grabbed Sholtz' throat with a mighty right hand and held his chin up to where the dangling man could see nothing but the ceiling.

Sholtz tried to twist free, but it was to no avail, so he brought the revolver around towards where he judged the man's chest should be and cocked the hammer.

From where Cliff sat he could see the trigger on the small silver revolver moving back, but suddenly the huge blade of the bowie knife blocked the gun from his sight.

There was another report from the Smith & Wesson, but the round struck the overturned table.

Sholtz' head had been twisted back to the point he made no audible sound when the knife was buried to the hilt under his fifth rib, and blood gushed from his black coat.

The big man held him there for several seconds until he heard the sound of the revolver falling to the wooden floor, then he slowly released the hand that had Sholtz' head in a vise like grip, and as Sholtz began to collapse, he swiftly withdrew the bowie with his other hand and wiped the blade, first one side then the other on Sholtz' clothing and then returned it to a crude leather scabbard that was protruding on his left hip.

There was a strange expression on Ed Sholtz' face and no one else there knew why, but he was remembering the time he had watched his father slip a dagger into a man's chest the very day they had fled Reinarburg. Gorman's blood had flowed the same as his was now doing. He thought that queer and then a little funny, and he wanted to laugh, but he couldn't. Try as he may he couldn't, he had forgotten how.

# Chapter Sixteen
# The Telegram

Two weeks after the courtroom killings found South Pass City experiencing its first double wedding. Arthur Houghton was standing beside his bride, the former Miss Steele and Paul Bunyan Stone beside his. The event had brought new lives to four people and an end to a historical event. The weddings she performed that day were to be the last official acts of Judge Esther Morris, the first woman judge in North America.

That day also brought other happenings to other people who at that time called 'The Sweetwater Region' home. Ashley Scogins received title of the mine her brother had filed on more than a year before and with it came the judgment. The court had seized all known accounts of Ed Sholtz and 'The Monia Mine.' Based on the figures that had been kept by Captain Nickerson and The Cotter & Houghton Freight Company, a settlement of what was believed to be as near as possible the monies taken from the Scogins property was delivered to her: a sum of two hundred and seventy-three thousand dollars in monies and all the equipment and real property of the town of Monia.

Ashley would become Mrs. Bruce Whittacur within a month.

The southbound stage, driven by Jack Murdock, had two passengers: Chip Roper and a United States Marshal who was escorting his prisoner to the territorial prison in Laramie.

When it stopped at Pacific Springs to change drivers and teams, Chip was surprised to find no hostility towards him from Bill Crane or June DeWolf. They had not let the sinful deeds of a few place a dent in their faith and devotion to the saints or the church.

The northbound stage into South Pass City had brought a telegram from the telegrapher in Green River City, and Reb now sat on the old wooden bench in front of 'The South Pass Hotel' and read the note over and over.

```
To Clifford Brown
Sweetwater Region
   Wyoming Territory
August 17 1870


   Clifford your brother Sammy
has been killed by the Federals
for murdering a nigger
               STOP
   But he never done such
               STOP
   Your little brother Johnny
Boy is suspected for same crime
and is fearful and hiding out
               STOP
   They said they was arresting
your Pa if he did not produce him
               STOP
   We have lost everything
but the old shack
               STOP
   Need you desperately
son please come home
               END
       Signed Your Mother
```

He had gone through all his belongings and had come up with a total of $163.13, only a little over a hundred dollars above what he had when he arrived in the region more than a year before.

*'This gold prospecting ain't what it were made up to be, I guess. I got 'a go back, and I don't even know that this will get me there.'*

Cliff rubbed his chin with the palm of his hand as he thought, *'I ain't sure Ol' Red will make the trip or even if he will let me ride him, if he is able.'*

He knew he had to tell her he was leaving, but he desperately wished somehow this chore could be lifted from him, and after half an hour of watching Morris' Saloon and not seeing Nadine, he left and headed towards Teachman's Store. Approaching by way of the back porch he felt guilty, but time was short, and he went on and knocked. There was no answer at first, but after the second knock he heard heavy boots approaching.

The thin white curtain was pulled back, and then he heard, "Darlin', it's Reb."

The door opened and Pebbles grabbed his arm and pulled him inside. "Come in, come in."

Cliff still felt out of place and was very unsure of himself as he walked into the familiar kitchen.

Marlene Stone came in from the bedroom still dressed in her wedding gown with an inquisitive expression. "Hello, Reb," she said.

"Come in, Reb, come in. Do you want some coffeecake?" her new husband asked.

"No, no. I do got 'a ask a favor," Cliff said, embarrassed at being there.

"Sure, you know anything we can do."

Marlene saw the trouble on his face and lost her earlier fear. "Reb, tell us what's the matter."

Cliff slowly handed Pebbles the yellow paper. Reading it, he looked up before speaking. "My Lord, that's terrible."

He handed the telegram to Marlene, and when she had read it she asked, "When are you leaving?"

"I guess today. I have to get my horse and a few supplies."

"Reb," she said earnestly. "You take everything you need, anything we have here in the store you can use. Don't give it a second thought."

"That's why I came here and bothered you," Cliff said. "I hate to do this, but right now, after I paid off the people I owed, with the trial and all, I'm nearly broke."

"You need some money? We'll loan it to you, won't we, Marlene. Why if it weren't for you, we may never have met."

"If it weren't for you," she added, "I would still be married to that low down miserable Ernie Teachman."

"You just tell us how much you need," Pebbles said placing his hand on Cliff's shoulder.

"I ain't gon'a accept no money, but I do need trail supplies and if you will let me, I'll take them now and send you the money from Georgia."

"Take anything you need, Reb. You don't have to send back no money."

"No Pebbles, I won't take it if I ain't gon'a send the money back," he said and then felt like he needed to explain something.

"I would sell you the Henry, but it sounds like I might need all the good guns I can get my hands on for back home."

"No need to think about such. You just take whatever you need, and I will send you a bill when we get back from our honeymoon. Did I tell you we are going to Denver?"

"Yeah, you told me," Cliff replied as he slipped the brim of his Stetson around and around with the fingers of each hand.

"Well, just go on into the store, and take whatever you need. If you want, you can leave a list along with your address back in Valdosta; just leave it there on the counter, and we will send you a bill when we get back," Pebbles offered. Then he turned to his new wife and said, "Honey, we had better be packing."

Cliff could tell it was not packing he had on his mind, and he said softly. "Thank you, I am much obliged." He then walked into the closed mercantile and began gathering the supplies he figured he would need for the long ride back to Dixie.

He had found a croaker sack and filled it with as much of Teachman's stock as he needed, but knew he would have to get some of the other items from John McGlinchey's, or maybe over at Means' Store in Hamilton.

He left through the same door he had entered and walked back to the barn some fifty feet behind the porch.

Red was as unfriendly as he had been the last time he had been there, and Cliff felt guilty for not spending more time with him during the last few weeks.

While saddling his horse he looked across at the pretty little pinto in the stall next to Jim Carpenter's roan and swallowed a bitter pill. There was no question he was headed back to Georgia, but somehow he hated to leave Nadine. She was the prettiest woman he had ever known, and he had always felt she was the truest friend he had in Wyoming Territory. *'Oh sure, Pebbles and Art, as well as Bruce and Happy Tom are my friends, but they are man friends, Nadine is a woman friend, and that is something special. Truly, she will be the one I miss the most.'*

Leading Red from the barn, he thought of the little cottage where he had spent so many nights right after coming to town. *'Funny, most anyone who looked at the two would have thought it was Carol that had Art Houghton spending so much time at 'The Sister's,' but we all wus surprised when Art and Connie announced their wedding intentions.'*

Cliff mounted Red who immediately began to dance about in sure protest, and then he started moving off.

*'Poor Carol'*, he thought, *'she won't know how to manage without the need to protect her sister.'*

Suddenly, he stopped and looked back at the barn; he then dismounted and returned inside.

Twenty minutes later, when he once more entered The South Pass Saloon, he was grateful to hear Jim stop what he was playing and begin the sweet sound of *The Wildwood Flower* as only an old fiddle can whine.

Almost immediately, he spied Nadine across the room talking to some men who were seated around a table playing cards. She was dressed in a pretty red and black silk dress with black leather lace-up shoes. Hearing the tune attracted her attention and she turned. The usual smile crossed her face that always seemed to control her expression when she would first see him. He smiled back, touching his hat as he did.

Cliff noticed his friend had laid the old fiddle across the top of the piano and was seating himself on the little cushioned chair where he could rest his elbow on the piano, and as he approached, he spoke, "Howdy, Jim."

"Fit like you," his friend replied and then asked, "What dae' ye' think thay be doing to Wild Bill Hickman?"[19] It was the thing to ask; everyone in South Pass City was asking it of everyone else when they had chance to bring up idle conversation.

---

[19] Wild Bill Hickman was the admitted henchman for Brigham Young and known to history as "The Destroying Angel" of the nineteenth century Mormon Church.

"Oh, I don't see them doing anything to him. He had just witnessed Ed Sholtz kill his daughter, mistakenly perhaps, but still it was him that kil't her, and he shot the sheriff," Cliff replied lifting both shoulders, then continued, "My guess is he will be a model citizen of this here metropolis for the rest of his life," Cliff sighed, and then he added, "Which I won't be."

"Oh, now Reb, I see you biding here for lang a year."

"No, you're wrong. Fur two reasons, you're wrong." Cliff replied pushing his Stetson back revealing most of his forehead. "First, I don't think this here city will be here that much longer."

"Nae," Jim disagreed, "thaim hills out there got too much color in them."

"Don't you believe it. The region is nearly played out. Mr. Snow told me that."

"Well, I sae he's wrang. So what be ye other reason?"

"My other reason is that I'm leaving today."

"In the name of the wee man, is-nae possible!"

"Just came in to say goodbye and ask Miss Tipper something. I'll be seeing you, friend," Cliff said extending his hand.

"A-nis does sound a wee bit like a fareweel," the man in the striped shirt said.

"I'm afraid it is. Got bad news from home, and it's there I'm bound."

"'Tis too bad. We'll miss ye around here," his skinny friend replied, "So here's tae the heath, the hill and the heather," Jim said raising his own mug as a toast.

"Who are we gon 'a miss?" Nadine asked as she walked up to where they were talking.

"Reb here, saes he's dol back to Alabama."

"Georgia," both Cliff and Nadine corrected at the same time.

Feeling she suddenly had a large hollow ball stuck in the middle of her chest, she turned to face him and asked, "You are leaving, for real?"

"That's right," Cliff said looking into her green eyes.

"But why? Everything's alright now."

"My oldest brother has been murdered, and my Pa and little brother, my last living brother, are in trouble. Ma sent word; they need me."

"But, but what about the trouble waiting fur you down there, the trouble that caused you to leave to begin with? You can't go back, they'll hang you," she said searching desperately for something to cause him to change his mind.

"I'll have to deal with that when it comes up, I guess," Cliff replied lowering his head so as he was not looking directly into her eyes.

"So then, it's goodbye. Just like that?" she said feeling the water building in her eyes.

"Well, not exactly," he replied.

"What else?" she asked turning so he would not see the tears begin their long run over her cheeks.

"Come over here, Purty Thing, I want to show you something," he said reaching for her right arm and gently, but forcefully, guiding her across the plank floor towards the front of the saloon. When they reached the bat wing doors he stopped and said, "See there."

She looked out and saw Treasure saddled and tied to the hitching post beside Red.

"What?" she questioned shaking her head, not understanding.

"Well, I was just thinking, if we could convince Judge Morris to do just one more marriage, we might make it to a little picnic spot I know of before dark, down on the Sweetwater."

"What? Are you saying what I think you're saying?" she asked with a strange expression.

"Only if you wash your face, and get your fanny in gear. You got thirty minutes to get packed."

"Thirty minutes! I'll be ready in half that time," she screamed and threw her arms around his neck and kissed him hard on the lips.

Jim was just laying his fiddle on the top of the piano as she shot past him towards the staircase, "Where ye be gangin' in such a hast?" he asked.

"Dixie!" was her only reply.

Don't Miss Book Two
of
The Owl Hoot Trail
*The Withlacoochee Renegades*

Ride with Cliff and Nadine back to Georgia where they organize a vigilante group to protect innocent home-folk from an occupational government gone wild with power, led by corrupt officials more horrible than the war itself; more thrilling than the battlefield.

# The Withlacoochee Renegades
## by T.H.Bear

Book Two of T.H. Bear's Trilogy, *The Hoot Owl Trail*, *The Withlacoochee Renegades*, is the story of Reb and Nadine's return to Georgia during times many considered more horrible than the war itself, "The Unholy Reconstruction Period," where Corruption outnumbered Christianity in the Occupational Government.

Clifford received a telegram telling of the murder of one of his brothers and the threat of the same to his other brother and father. Clifford Brown and his bride arrive to find the worst, and not only to this family, but to almost all of the home folk. He then forms and leads a vigilante group, that the local newspaper names, "The Withlacoochee Renegades," until most of the corruption is cleaned from the area and many of those responsible for their cruel deeds are either dead, arrested, or have fled the state.

----------------------------------------

You may order online at www.bluewaterpress.com/renegades or by mail:

Bluewaterpress LLC
52 Tuscan Way Ste 202-309
Saint Augustine FL 32092

Name: _____

Address: _____

City, State, Zip: _____

Phone number: _____

Email Address: _____
(All information kept in the strictest confidence)

Please send me T.H. Bear's *The Withlacoochee Renegades*. Cost is $25.95 per copy. Shipping & handling is $3.95 per book for one copy, $6.95 for up to seven of any titles, and $1.15 per book for any combination of more than seven.

Number of books _____ x $25.95 = _____

Shipping and handling = _____

FL residents, please add sales tax for county of residence = _____

Total remitted = _____

We gladly accept payment of your choice: check, money order, or credit card.

## *Bad Times* by Denny Williams

Jack O'Mally is a decent kind of man. One who has lived his life with integrity, a man who always strived to do the right thing.

In the twilight of his years, he finds himself going west to find a way to live out the rest of his life. He encounters, just as he did when he was a youngster, that life is hard and filled with bad times.

This is not a somber story however. Jack laughs in the face of bad times. Denny Williams brings a richness and wonderful humor to the characters of his western novel, Bad Times.

This is a cowboy tale, a rich, funny, cowboy tale written in a fresh new style that will doubtless leave you laughing out loud for a while. Readers are sure to enjoy each twist and turn in the adventure that is Jack O'Mally's life.

-----------------------------------------

You may order online at www.bluewaterpress.com/badtimes or by mail:

BluewaterPress LLC
52 Tuscan Way Ste 202-309
Saint Augustine FL 32092

Name: _____

Address: _____

City, State, Zip: _____

Phone number: _____

Email Address: _____
(All information kept in the strictest confidence)

Please send me Denny Williams's *Bad Times*. Cost is $15.95 per copy. Shipping & handling is $3.95 per book for one copy, $6.95 for up to seven of any titles, and $1.15 per book for any combination of more than seven.

Number of books _____ x $15.95 = _____

Shipping and handling = _____

FL residents, please add sales tax for county of residence = _____

Total remitted = _____

We gladly accept payment of your choice: check, money order, or credit card.

## The Last Sunrise
By Shane Barker

The Last Sunrise is the story of General George Custer's historic fight along the Little Bighorn River, as seen through the eyes of Marcus Reno, Black Elk, and some of the other officers and warriors who were there. It is not the simple rehearsal of a familiar story. With careful attention to historical fact and detail, the author puts the sights, the noise, and smell and terror of the battle to pages for the readers. Shane Barker wrote this historical novel to allow readers to experience the fight, to know what it was like to really be there. This story puts the readers right in the saddle alongside Mitch Boyer and Crazy Horse, bringing them face-to-face with Sitting Bull, Frederick Benteen, and George Armstrong Custer himself.

-------------------------------------------

You may order online at www.bluewaterpress.com/sunrise or by mail:

Bluewaterpress LLC
52 Tuscan Way Ste 202-309
Saint Augustine FL 32092

Name: _____

Address: _____

City, State, Zip: _____

Phone number: _____

Email Address: _____
(All information kept in the strictest confidence)

Please send me Shane Barker's *The Last Sunrise*. Cost is $15.95 per copy. Shipping & handling is $3.95 per book for one copy, $6.95 for up to seven of any titles, and $1.15 per book for any combination of more than seven.

Number of books _____ x $15.95 = _____

Shipping and handling = _____

FL residents, please add sales tax for county of residence = _____

Total remitted = _____

We gladly accept payment of your choice: check, money order, or credit card.

*Honeymoon Vengeance*
by Roger Scott

Scott Mckendree is all cowboy. The real thing. Nothing about the man is false or fake; he is strong, he is a survivor, and he lives by doing the right thing. He does not like it when people take advantage of the weak and his gentle manner always compels him to help those in need when he crosses their path.

One spring day, his path crosses with those of Larin and Lynn Willbright, a young couple from back east, newly married and trying to make their way in the new frontier. Unfortunately, their life together is cut short by men with no conscience and it is up to McKendree to help the young bride.

-------------------------------------------

You may order online at www.bluewaterpress.com/honeymoon or by mail:

BluewaterPress LLC
52 Tuscan Way Ste 202-309
Saint Augustine FL 32092

Name: _____

Address: _____

City, State, Zip: _____

Phone number: _____

Email Address: _____
(All information kept in the strictest confidence)

Please send me Roger Scott's *Honeymoon Vengeance*. Cost is $13.95 per copy. Shipping & handling is $3.95 per book for one copy, $6.95 for up to seven of any titles, and $1.15 per book for any combination of more than seven.

Number of books _____ x $13.95 = _____

Shipping and handling = _____

FL residents, please add sales tax for county of residence = _____

Total remitted = _____

We gladly accept payment of your choice: check, money order, or credit card.